DEATH

&

OTHER LIES

DEATH &OTHER LIES

CAROL L. OCHADLEUS

Hope you enjoy it !

Carol Ochadleus

DEATH

&

OTHER LIES

CAROL L. OCHADLEUS

ZIMBELL HOUSE
PUBLISHING
UNION LAKE MICHIGAN

For permission requests, write to the publisher
"Attention: Permissions Coordinator"
Zimbell House Publishing
PO Box 1172
Union Lake, Michigan 48387
mail to: info@zimbellhousepublishing.com

© 2014, 2019 Carol L. Ochadleus, Author
© 2019 Brian Kotulis, Cover Design

Published in the United States by Zimbell House Publishing
Http://www.ZimbellHousePublishing.com
All Rights Reserved

Hardcover ISBN: 978-1-64390-062-9
Trade Paper ISBN: 978-1-64390-063-6
.mobi ISBN: 978-1-64390-064-3
Epub ISBN: 978-1-64390-065-0
Large Print ISBN: 978-1-64390-066-7
Library of Congress Control Number: 2019942528

Second Edition: July 2019
10 9 8 7 6 5 4 3 2

ZIMBELL HOUSE PUBLISHING
UNION LAKE

DEDICATION

In Memory of
Dorothy and Charles Genetti
May their loving and generous souls continue to guide
my footsteps.

ACKNOWLEDGMENTS

First and foremost, I must thank my husband, Don, for his support and unwavering encouragement. He is a guiding light who draws sunshine out of the gloom and offers the steadfast rock I cling to in the dark. I do not thank him often enough for the joy he brings to my life. All that I can do is because of him and his delusional optimism.

I also must thank my children: Brian and Elizabeth Kotulis, Lauren and Brent Baginski, Nichole and Joe Szyszkiewicz, Kathryn and Brandon Davis, and Don and Stacey Ochadleus. I love each of you and am fortunate to call you my friends as well as my children. You and your children generously share with me your spirit, wisdom, laughter, and just the right amount of chaos to keep my life deliciously unbalanced.

Brian Kotulis deserves a sincere thank you for designing the cover of this book. I am in constant awe of his amazing artistic talent.

A sincere thank you, as well, to Holly G. Miller, of the Saturday Evening Post. Early on, she reviewed my synopsis and encouraged me to publish. Without her pushing, this book would not have been possible.

Chapter One

Phil Forester would have rudely ignored the young man who approached him as he left work, but the large wad of bills Rashid Zand held, caught his attention.

Minutes later the two men sat facing a rotating platform as a stripper named Luscious Lana caressed a pole.

"How much money are we talking about?" Phil asked Rashid, his eyes straying to the dancing girl.

Lana's legs worked seductively, while her pendulous breasts, coated in glitter, bounced with the beat of the loud music. Two dozen men, regulars of the Rumpass Room in the shady end of Philadelphia, whistled and waved fists of cash in the air.

"Enough to pay off your gambling debts and give you a good deal extra," Zand answered.

Phil's head snapped around. "How do you know what I owe? You bugging my phone?"

"You sit every night in the Landing Zone. The more you drink, the more you complain about your money troubles. Do you not wish to be free of such debt?"

"Maybe. But I'm sure you're not going to give me money for nothing, what do you want?"

"You work at Marsh Laboratories, run by your government."

"Yeah, you saw me walk out fifteen minutes ago." Phil's face darkened. "Now you're following me too?"

"I have friends who work in the casinos you frequent, the expensive stores you shop, even the restaurant where you eat. We are everywhere. I know a lot about you. But it is not necessary to follow your footsteps, Mr. Forester. You are quite vocal about your job as well."

"What of it? It's a free country."

The two men shared a small table in the darkest corner. Zand's face was in the shadows. "You sound like a brilliant scientist, Mr. Forester. A genius maybe. You talk about the power of your knowledge, how it can build or destroy businesses, even governments. I know as a biological chemist, you work with viruses and diseases which make you powerful," Zand's voice dropped to a whisper. "But that power is wasted on a simple paycheck when it could be worth so much more. I decided to approach you because you may have what I want, and I can provide what you need. Are you interested?"

Keeping his eyes off the stage was hard. Phil shifted uncomfortably in his seat. "Keep talking. I might be interested but get to the point. What the hell do you want?"

"Let me tell you a story, Mr. Forester." Zand paused while another patron was seated near them by the hostess. He lowered his voice and continued. "I have been in your country for over two years and must return home soon to my village near Tehran. I have learned many things here. Americans live in a different world than my people do. We must constantly defend ourselves from those who wish us harm." Zand waved off the approaching waitress. "Last summer, my family was attacked while going about their business. Several people were killed, including my mother and two sisters. We have no protection from our government or the police. We must protect ourselves. The attacks are frequent throughout our village, and hundreds are killed each year. They must be stopped. With your help, we can give my people some security. We wish to build a weapon that will scare our enemies into leaving us alone."

"Scare them … or wipe them out?"

Rashid spread his arms wide, palms up. "Mr. Forester, do I look like a murderer? I simply seek a way to protect my family's home. You have freedom; we do not. A weapon, a deterrent, will buy us freedom."

Zand was a good-looking young man, with a slight build and neat dark hair, dressed in jeans and a cotton shirt. His serious but youthful face seemed sincere as he leaned forward folding his arms on the sticky tabletop. "Not all middle-eastern people are terrorists, Mr. Forester. Some of us only want to protect our way of life. Balance the power, so to speak. Surely you can understand the pain of losing one's family and our wish to prevent further bloodshed."

Phil sipped his beer and digested the story that was probably fictitious. His attention was distracted yet again by the bouncing breasts. It didn't matter to him why the guy wanted a weapon. The whole middle-east was a hotbed of shitheads ready to blow each other away for century's old feuds. He knew what they did to the U.S. on 9/11. Not that he was particularly patriotic, but it galled him that he had been near ground zero only the week before the attack and could have died along with the thousands of others who did. He didn't care if they wanted a weapon to scare, or even to kill off a few hundred of their neighbors. He briefly wondered if he should turn the guy over to the Feds. Phil took a long drink. *No, better nix that idea. The guy knows way too much about me and would probably go down swinging.* Phil's fingers drummed the table top matching the beat of the music. *The guy is right about one thing, I can use the money, and I'm smart enough to know they'll just get what they want from someone else.*

"There is something that might work," he said. "We have a special project, one that uses an old virus."

"What does it do?"

"If it is prepared right, it can cause immediate paralysis and eventually death. A guy at Marsh has worked on it for a couple of years."

"Could it be released in an air born manner?"

"Probably, if it's added to some type of aerosol component, you could turn it into a spray."

Zand's eyes grew darker with interest, and for the first time, he smiled. "We will need a sample."

"That could be difficult. That shit is crazy dangerous and usually locked up."

"Of course, but I am sure you can get it. We will need all of the research, as well. I assume there is an antidote."

"Yeah, that was the point of the project. It's unstable. It's not finished, but it may be close."

"How long will it take for you to get everything?"

Phil clenched the arms of the chair and shifted in his seat. "Hold your camels; I didn't say I would … or even could, get it. Errington is extremely protective of his work. I can't exactly ask him for it, can I? And what am I supposed to do with a dangerous virus? Just walk out with it in my pocket?"

"Let me help you figure it out." Zand ignored the perceived insult and put a friendly hand on Phil's arm. "Please. Hear me out." He removed a fat envelope from his pocket and laid it on the table. "For a sample of this virus and the research that goes with it, you will be well rewarded. I am prepared to offer you ten-thousand American dollars right now if you agree to help. If you are not interested, you are free to walk away, and this conversation never happened. Must I find someone else who wants our money?"

"That's not nearly enough. I want at least a hundred grand; no … make that a hundred and fifty grand."

"You ask a great deal, but it is not unreasonable. It can be arranged. You will get the balance when I have what I asked for. Are we agreed?"

Phil downed the rest of his beer. "I can probably figure out a way, but it will take some time … a few months. Errington's still working on it. You guys want it complete, right? Won't do you much good until I can get it all."

"We do not have endless patience, Mr. Forester. We must have it as soon as possible. Perhaps I should talk to this Errington."

"That's a laugh. I thought you knew everything. No one else there will help you, especially Matt. He'd run right to the authorities if you even hint at what you want."

"And what assurances do we have, Mr. Forester, that you won't run as well?"

"I'd say the ten big ones you have here says I won't." Phil picked up the envelope and wrestled it into his jacket pocket. "What you guys do to your fellow countrymen is your business. I gotta take care of my own problems."

"I like to know who we are dealing with, what can you tell me about this Errington?"

"Matthew Errington. He calls this virus his *Project Hope*. You know the type. Wants to save the world. He's got his head stuck in a test tube all day … no idea what goes on outside his lab. I can get into his computers and copy his work. He's a workaholic, probably takes his work home as well … so if I can't get to it at Marsh, I might have to make a house call."

"Is that wise? What about his family?"

"Doesn't have any. Single. Lives alone. I know where, and I know when he won't be there. Let me worry about Errington. Just don't get too antsy, it will take time like I said. But, yeah, I think I can get it for you."

Triumph flared briefly in Zand's eyes. The torment of living in the bowels of these American cities was finally paying off. His master had been correct. The disgusting Americans were stupid and easily manipulated. To Phil, he meekly nodded. "That is good. I get what I need, and you will be happy."

Luscious Lana finished her routine and was making the rounds of the room looking for private business. As she approached their table, Rashid Zand stood to leave.

"These lovely women are most entertaining," he smiled at the stage where three new dancers demonstrated their skills, "unfortunately I have another appointment. Here is a phone for you to reach me. It is untraceable to either of us. I will contact you soon to learn of your progress. Until then, please be aware Mr. Forester, I would hate to see anything happen to you, but if you betray me …"

Phil hoisted his empty glass in Zand's direction. "I got it. I am a genius, you know."

Zand pulled out the wad of large bills and handed Lana several. "Take good care of this man." To Phil, he added, "Please stay and enjoy yourself. Consider this a taste of how we treat our friends."

"Suits me. I was surprised when you wanted to meet here. Didn't think you guys like this kind of joint … loud music and naked girls."

"We are all men, Mr. Forester. And I find the setting to be most conducive to business. If questioned, no one here will remember seeing either of us. In here, no one looks at faces."

Chapter Two

September 15th

"Kate, I'm home! Kate?" Matt Errington was barely inside the door of his apartment in suburban Philadelphia before the load in his arms spilled over. "Damn," he cursed as an avalanche of bills and junk mail hit the floor. His irritation was immediate but short-lived. He even forgave the key which was stuck in the lock and threatened to break as he wiggled it free.

He hoped Kate was ready. It had been a long day in the lab, and there wouldn't be much time to get to the arena before the Flyer's game started. If they were late, it would mean a smelly shuttle ride from an overflow lot. But none of it actually mattered. Nothing was going to ruin his good mood or the evening he planned. He patted his pocket for the small velvet box, and a boyish grin split his face as he pictured their romantic dinner after the game. He only feared that she would think it was too soon.

Carefully balancing his briefcase and laptop, he nudged the door shut with his shoulder and dumped everything on a small table. As he stooped to retrieve the mess, he yelled again for Kate, but still, no sweet voice echoed back.

Matt knew Kate should have been home hours before, yet the apartment was dark, cold, and uneasy. It wasn't like her to be late. An inner alarm poked him, but he shook it off and in his logical fashion listed several possible reasons for her delay. She could have lost track of time, had car trouble, or sometimes her appointments did run late.

Regardless, he was a bit piqued she hadn't called. She should know he would worry. He reached to turn on the lamp.

Nothing in his logical life prepared him for what he saw. Like a punch to the gut, it nearly doubled him over. The difference to his home was dramatic. White slits of light poured through the mini-blinds and settled on the pale walls. Immediately his pallor blanched to match them. A quick sweep of the room forced the breath from his lungs. The fear he kept in check for months that the dream would end, had come true. All of Kate's things were gone. She had left him.

Her laptop, her soft rug, her knick-knacks, all gone. So were her pretty water-colored prints of graceful old homes of the Eastern Shoreline gone off the walls and his old posters, lifeless and immature, were back again. The blue sweater usually flung over the chair, her raincoat on the hook, and the slippers she left by the door, every sign of her was gone.

Matt's eyes clenched shut, and he fought to breathe. He knew he shouldn't jump to extreme conclusions, but what other answer was there? Would she leave him like this? Without warning? Without an explanation?

Slowly he studied the room again, stark, and functional. *How did I live like this before Kate? No color or warmth.* In just a few weeks, she had filled it with energy, brought it to life. She made it home.

On a Sunday afternoon, after she moved in, they found an art festival in the park. In a small tent, a young man was selling offerings made from metal, wood, and clay. "A typical starving artist," Matt had laughingly called him. A ragamuffin in ill-fitting clothes, the man's long hair blew wild about his thin face. Kate must have seen something in the indefinable objects that escaped Matt. There was a true concern on her face when she asked him, "What do you think?" Matt thought they were ugly but surprised them both when he let her pick two. She was genuinely pleased. The twisted forms which took up residence on an end table were now gone as well. In their place lay several old issues of a scientific journal, spread out, each with a slight coating of dust.

Pain sharp as a saber pierced him as he swung around to face an empty window. Kate collected small glass vases and had several in a rainbow of colors. Her favorite was cobalt blue. Matt felt terrible the day he chipped its top by accident. He had turned it around so she wouldn't notice. She kept them all on the windowsill where they caught the early afternoon sun. As through a prism, the carnival colors danced upon the walls. Bile rose in his throat. Life without Kate would again be as bleak and bare as the dusty ledge in front of him.

His apartment's décor had always been functional but simple. The one piece of furniture with any character was a desk from the 1800s. It had nooks and crannies, a great workspace, and a secret panel in a false-bottomed drawer. When he purchased it from the antique shop down on the boulevard, he knew it would make a perfect place for the work he brought home nightly. When Kate moved in, he pushed everything off to the side and cleared the surface for her laptop. Impossible, but once again the top overflowed with an unsightly stack of papers all waiting to be sorted. *How?* With painful clarity, he remembered the day Kate tackled the mess and filed his papers methodically. The pigeonholes she filled were empty, and her computer was gone.

In the middle of the floor were three red drops that looked like blood. *Maybe Kate hurt herself and left to get care? It could be an answer, but then where are her things? Or did someone else hurt her? Take her away?*

That didn't seem plausible. No, as much as he wanted to deny it, the answer was obvious. Fear as unstoppable as an incoming tide yanked him back to the apparent truth. He always knew he didn't deserve her. *Maybe she finally discovered it too.*

Each room contributed more to his loss. Memories of the past flashed like lightning during a storm.

Kate curled like a cat reading a book.

Kate seductively smiling over a glass of wine.

Kate dancing to the music from her laptop. Each memory pushed the hurt deeper.

Three days earlier, he had jogged three blocks to a small market and brought her a huge bunch of sunflowers. They no longer adorned the table, instead only his cold cup of coffee sat just as he left it before he headed out the door that morning. He frantically searched for any remaining sign, but there was nothing left. There was no visible evidence left of Kate.

A wisp of her fragrance lingered somewhere on his clothes, and as he turned his head, he caught it again. Its sweet feminine essence had tantalized him all day. Just thinking about the past morning made his knees feel weak, and he clutched a chair for support.

That morning, he tried to leave for work and headed for the door, but a backward glance at the soft shape buried in the bedclothes drew him back to her. She was still asleep in their bed. A curl lay gently on her cheek, and a shapely leg poked out from the covers. Just one small kiss to her forehead was all he wanted, and he planted one as softly as he could, breathing in her scent. But as he straightened again to go, Kate stirred, grabbed the front of his jacket and pulled his body back down to hers. The look on her face told him he was going to be late for work. It was unusual for them to make love in the morning, and while he fleetingly wondered why this day was different, he didn't dwell on the question as the unexpectedness made it even sweeter and all the more exciting. Within minutes the warm bed and her soft limbs ensnared him, and he completely forgot about the time. They made love quickly, urgently. Two souls fused in a timeless dance, their combined breaths held the promise of everything and forever. The air around them was electrically charged, expectant, and the room was aglow with the early morning light.

He kissed her eyes and was surprised to find them wet. He hated to leave, to let her go. Her scent kept him spellbound. Eternity could have come and gone, and Matt was content to let it pass them by if he could stay forever by her side. Kate was everything he would ever want or need, and it took all of his will power to climb back out of bed. It was several minutes before he could get his head acclimated to the real world, the one outside the door and away from her, before he could leave for work a second time. As he finally made his exit that morning, she softly called goodbye. He blew her one more kiss and quietly closed the door behind him.

It was now ten hours later, and Matt was dreading the final blow. He tried to stop his feet, but they moved of their own accord. The bedroom was only a few steps away, yet his heart pounded, and he was out of breath. Little was changed except when he last walked out the door she was still there, half asleep, waving good-bye.

The bed was unmade, but there was not a single wrinkle in the smooth pillow to prove it ever cradled her sweet blond head. With each discovery, the magnitude of his loss mounted and made him physically ill. Forced to sit down until his nausea passed, he perched tentatively on the end of the bed, afraid to get too close to her side, as if it would invade her space and invalidate her ownership.

He hadn't deserved her, he knew it all along, and now he would pay for his folly. Irrational as it was, he continued the search for his shattered dreams. If only he could find the missing piece to the madness that had become his home, perhaps he could save himself from the agony that was tightening around his heart. There was no need to continue to search, he knew it was useless, but he couldn't stop. Room by room, drawer by drawer. Hoping in some deep inner place, some sense would be found. Some logic to make it all right again. But no such salvation was forthcoming.

Inspection of the closets was anticlimactic. Like everything else, like Kate's other possessions, her clothes were gone and only his remained, spaced out like the pickets of a fence in measured cadence. Drawers too were fully occupied as if they never shared their home at all. On closer inspection, he was stunned to discover his worn, gray sweatshirt, folded neatly near the bottom. It was Kate who convinced him to throw it away, and he laughingly agreed. *So how can it be here?* Secure in its place as it always was, even though he remembered the day she took it to the trash. Only his toothbrush and toiletries remained just as he left them. Even the towel she usually chose, the deep blue one which matched her eyes, mocked him as it hung clean and neat with no sign of use. Words like a refrain from a song repeated over and over in his head, *It's as if she was never here. Logic is on my side,* he argued, *there has been no clue she was unhappy. Didn't she make sweet love to me this morning?*

But the doubts he buried for years; that he didn't deserve to be happy, snickered at him, climbed up out of his past and played havoc with his heart. *How did I fail her?*

He wanted answers. He needed answers. Repeatedly he called Kate's cell phone and listened to it ring and ring and then finally go dead. No message came on in Kate's melodic voice instructing callers to leave a name and number. Unable to reach her, he looked up the number where she worked.

"Atlas Medical, how may I direct your call?"

"Hi. I've been trying to reach my girlfriend, Kate Champion. Her cell phone isn't working, and I hope you can help me reach her."

"I'm sorry sir, I don't have a listing for anyone by that name."

"Kate Champion. Maybe she's listed under Kathryn. She's in sales and handles the Philadelphia area."

"No, I'm sorry. We don't have anyone like that. Perhaps you have the wrong company. There are several medical sales offices in this area."

"No, I am not wrong! I need to talk to her, please, just transfer me to your supervisor."

"Okay, if you wish, but it won't help." Matt's long fingers drummed a tattoo on the desktop.

"This is Tom Barrett. How can I help you?"

"Mr. Barrett I'm trying to reach one of your employees, Kate Champion. Your operator can't even find her name."

"Look, I'm sorry, but she doesn't work for Atlas. The operator, my wife actually, is correct. We're a small business with only twenty-two people. Maybe you have the wrong company."

"I know that can't be it. I'm sure I don't. Is there another company with a similar name?"

"I don't think so. Sorry."

Matt's head pounded, and his stomach roiled. He knew he wasn't mistaken. He was sure she had told him Atlas Medical. *Is it possible I got the name wrong? Why would she lie?*

Minutes went by, maybe hours. Agony clouded time. *Perhaps the police should be notified.* A shudder went through him that Kate could be hurt or in trouble. *Is it selfish to hope there is another explanation? That she hasn't left me? Could any answer be better, make her disappearance hurt less?* Shaking his head to clear such forbidden thoughts, he reached for the phone. He needed someone to help him make sense of what he had found. Reality made him hesitate. *What am I going to tell them? The cops can't do anything if she left on her own, but what if she didn't, what if someone took her? But then who would have put my old things back ... or why?* Again, the questions and doubts came back full circle. *What about the blood? It's only three drops, but what does it mean? If she loves me, why would she leave me, and even if she doesn't, couldn't she leave a note? It's not like her to be cruel.* So many why's, but no answers. He didn't know if talking to the police would help, but at least it was action, and he needed to do something besides stare at the four walls which chose to keep their silence.

"Is this an emergency?" a woman asked when Matt dialed the local police department.

"I don't know, yes it could be. When I got home, I discovered my girlfriend was gone. She just disappeared, and all of her things are gone too."

The voice answered routinely, "Was there any sign of violence or foul play?"

"Well yeah, sort of. I found some blood. Kate could be hurt, and I don't know why she would leave on her own."

"What's your name?"

"Matt Errington."

"Okay, Mr. Errington, hold on."

The strain of the past hour ate at his nerves, and it was difficult to be patient. "Yeah, fine, of course," he said under his breath. His long fingers clenched and relaxed repeatedly. As he ticked off the minutes, his fears grew.

"Mr. Errington, I'm transferring you to Sergeant Brian York."

"Thanks," was all Matt could say before he was put on hold again. Minutes went by before someone finally picked up the phone.

"Sergeant York. How can I help you?"

"Yes, Sergeant, as I told the lady … when I got home from work, my apartment was stripped of all of my girlfriend's things. She's gone, there's no explanation, and I'm worried about her. I can't figure out why she would leave so I think something might have happened."

"Sorry to hear that, you said there was blood. How much are we talking about?"

"Yes, just a few drops, but I'm sure it's blood."

"Okay, but are you also reporting there was a theft? Did she empty your apartment, you said everything is gone?"

"No, no, I don't think anything of mine is missing, just her things."

"Uh, huh. Listen, Mr. Errington, we're pretty short-staffed right now, why don't you come down to the station and we can talk."

Like a shot of brandy, heated blood pulsed through Matt's veins. The relief was overwhelming. They would help him. The police would know how to find her.

On the road, Matt attempted to put together a report in his head, trying to make some sense where there was none. He couldn't explain what happened, and he didn't want to sound like an idiot. The clock on the dash showed seven-thirty, about the time the hockey game was to start. *What a waste of money those tickets were*, he decided, closely followed by self-castrating remorse. *Geez, what a horrible thought to have right now.* He couldn't believe something like that even entered his head. Kate was gone, he had no idea what happened to her, and he was worried about losing money on tickets. *What a shmuck.* Still berating himself, Matt pulled into the parking lot of the police substation, and immediately the old terrors washed over him.

Terrors, he buried for many years after his mother died.

He had forcefully kept the horrific memories of the dark days of his past in the back of his mind, imprisoned in the shadows. Like paper cuts on the soul which never quite healed, they were occasionally snagged by life and ripped back open. Patrol cars filled the lot. The sight of their blue and red lights tested the dam that kept the horrors at bay. He saw police cars every day with no great relapse, but tonight, stunned by what he had found, their presence threatened to undo more than a decade of pills and therapy.

It was hard to control the trembling that made his hands shake as he put the car in park. He had come so far from that time. His heart pounded, and he could feel the muscles in his chest painfully contract.

"Control it," he ordered aloud, and remembered the voices of the doctors and their calming advice, *"Focus on better thoughts, good memories."* He took a deep, ragged breath, held it for ten seconds, and let it out. His pulse slowed, and the attack lessened its grip. It was especially hard this time to focus on better thoughts and good memories when those things all centered on Kate.

The one thing the years taught him was to face forward with logic. Logic and facts had rescued him in the difficult times and armed him well as he carved out a scientific career. They were the bedrock upon which he built his life, his guide to the future. That's what was needed now. *Calm, rational, logic.*

But calm, he was not. After the accident and his mother's death, his history with police was knotted with pain and loss. There was so much he fought to keep buried. The thought of opening up all the old feelings again nearly made him turn the car toward home.

Panic almost won. Then Kate's face floated before him. Her blue eyes sparkled, and her smile dazzled. He just knew the love was there, and this time he could help. "Keep going," he said out loud. "She is worth whatever it takes to find her."

Matt stepped out of the car while the chimes reminded him to take his forgotten keys. A chill wind blew up his back, and a light rain began to fall. He hugged his jacket tighter and somewhere in the distance an ambulance raced through the streets, its siren clearing the way. A shiver went through him, worried it could have something to do with Kate, and he prayed it did not. He headed toward the heavy glass doors etched with POLICE in bold block letters. If he must, he would surrender his soul to find her, or at least, to find out why she left.

Chapter Three

The station was well lit, and a half dozen people could be seen through the thick glass window of the lobby, still working despite the late hour. A uniformed young woman looked down at him from a raised platform. She had a small frame, round face with doe-brown eyes and dark hair pulled into a loose knot at the back of her head.

"I'm Matt Errington. I called a little while ago and spoke to Sergeant York."

"Yes sir, I remember talking to you. I'm Officer Pettingway. Follow me," she said, as she buzzed him through the door.

They headed toward the back of the building, passing through a large room broken into personal workstations. Desks overflowed with stacks of papers, photos of employee's families, and coffee cups. Each desk had a waterfall of computer wires and cords which snaked down the back of monitors, phones, and lamps. A basketball hoop was mounted prominently on the back wall over an overflowing wastebasket of papers and discarded lunch containers. Stacks of files were piled on chairs, and nearly-dead plants completed the décor. The few people in the room barely gave him a quick look, but still, he was uneasy. *Deep breath.*

Surprisingly, as he followed the young woman down the hall, his prior anxiety abated. It reminded him of the time he was nine and was escorted to the principal's office for passing notes to his friend Sam. It was an innocent note about a ball game they planned for that afternoon; he wasn't cheating or doing anything wrong, but his teacher made a big deal of it.

Officer Pettingway stopped at the last door on the right and motioned for Matt to go in. An older man behind the desk half rose from his seat and extended his hand to Matt.

"I'm Sergeant York," he said, "C'mon in," a thick mustache dusted his wide smile. "Thanks for coming. I prefer face to face, you know. I get a better sense of what's going on that way."

Matt nodded. "It's no problem if it helps me get some answers and find Kate."

"Kate is your girlfriend?"

"Yes, as I said before on the phone, she's disappeared, and I'm concerned. Something terrible could have happened, and I'm hoping you can help me find her."

Sergeant York motioned for him to sit. Two mismatched, straight-backed chairs were pulled up close to his desk, and Matt chose the closest one and dropped heavily onto the seat. Stacey Pettingway popped her head in the door. "Either of you want a cup of coffee? There's a new pot." Taking his lead from the Sergeant, Matt nodded.

"Yeah, maybe that would help clear my head."

"How do you want it?"

"Black is fine, don't go to any trouble for me."

"Same for me, Stacey," the Sergeant added as she disappeared out the door.

Less than a minute later, Officer Pettingway walked back in holding two steaming cups out before her. Her walk was stilted, halting, with a stiff-legged gait. Matt hadn't paid much attention to her earlier as he took in the station house, but now he openly watched her entrance.

Noting his eyes on her as she set the cups down on the edge of Sergeant York's desk, Stacey turned to Matt. "Sorry if some coffee sloshed out of the cup. I took a bullet in my leg in my first month on active duty, and it doesn't always work as smoothly as I want it to."

"I'm sorry, Miss, I mean, Officer." He flushed; embarrassed she caught him staring. "I usually have better manners, but I'm not myself tonight."

"It's okay; I hope you get some answers about your girlfriend." Matt noticed she had dimples in both cheeks as she smiled and was pretty in spite of the severe hair and drab uniform.

"Thanks for the coffee," added Sergeant York as Stacey left them and made her way back to the front desk.

Sergeant York took his time, taking out a clean yellow pad, moving a stack of papers and files off to the side and getting himself comfortable. The surface of the green metal desk, worn shiny in spots from age and use, was cluttered with photos. The good sergeant had a full house at home. Several smiling shots of children of various ages, arrayed in Easter finery and sports attire, stared back at Matt. Judging by his age and appearance; the gray hair, mustache, and deep-set wrinkles which hugged his mouth and crisscrossed his forehead, Matt figured he had been on the force for many years. *Probably not too many things would surprise him,* Matt thought as he watched the man clear a space to write. *I know I'm going to sound strange, but I'm sure he's heard just about every kind of weird tale there is.*

"So," Sergeant York said, finally taking note of the good-looking young man in front of him, hunched over, head hung dejectedly, "how about if we start at the beginning." With a practiced eye that immediately sized people up, the detective studied the man before him. Neat and well dressed, late twenties maybe, clean nails. Tall and trimly built. A lean body that reminded the sergeant of a runner, with short dark hair that framed his strong face with its straight nose and dark hazel eyes. Not chiseled looks, but a handsome young man. Only Matt's dark beard, which was becoming thicker as the evening wore on, marred his youthful face, that and the pain that swam in the man's eyes when he looked up.

"Okay, spell your name and give me your address." Matt's hand shook as he took a quick sip of the hot coffee and answered the Sergeant's questions—age; occupation; where he worked; how long he had known Kate; etc. They spent about ten minutes going over what Matt thought was trivial information. They were wasting time filling up page after page of the yellow pad.

"Why is it so important to know all about me? She is the one that's missing."

The Sergeant nodded, ignoring the question. "When was the last time you saw Kate?"

"This morning before I left for work," Matt was getting more impatient. "As I said before, she sells supplies and equipment for Atlas Medical, but she didn't have to get up early this morning, no appointments until eleven o'clock. She was still in bed when I left about eight-thirty."

"What time do you normally start work, Mr. Errington?"

"Please call me Matt. I don't see what difference that makes, but I am usually there early, around seven-thirty, but I was delayed this morning." He immediately regretted the remark.

"Delayed by what?"

Matt was getting red and felt the heat rising from his collar just thinking about the morning's session, and he would rather not have to explain it to a total stranger. "We, I, ah got up late this morning that's all," stammering as the lie tangled up his tongue. Matt was beginning to ramble and knew the Sergeant watched him struggle. Feeling like he was disloyal to Kate talking about their private life, Matt said, "I was late because we had sex this morning." Sergeant York looked bored.

"Look, Matt, you're the one reporting something is wrong. I want to be sure I can fill in the details about the last time you saw Kate. Gaps throw up red flags. You know what I mean?"

They went over and over again all the facts he knew about her, how they met, where she worked, filling in all of the details Matt could provide. After what seemed like an eternity to Matt, Sergeant York leaned back in his chair and folded his hands across his rather rounded girth.

"Matt, from what you have told me, there doesn't seem to be any sign of foul play. It sounds like Kate just wasn't as much in love with you as you thought. You know it does happen … people change their minds, find someone else, get scared, or they don't know how to say goodbye, so they move on. I don't know what you want the police to do."

"No," frustration launched Matt out of the chair. He slapped the desk so hard the empty coffee cup nearly bounced off.

"I know she loves me, I'm sure of it. I can't explain what happened to her, but don't you think you should send someone over and at least check out the apartment. Check out the blood. Do some fingerprinting or whatever the police do. Look for evidence?"

"Evidence of what, Matt?" Sergeant York said quietly. "Evidence of what? From everything you told me it sounds like she packed up and left and maybe cut herself on her way out."

Matt was tired. It had been a long day in the lab, and the discovery of Kate's disappearance drained him. Slumping back in his chair, his head throbbed. The slow dawning of her apparent rejection of him was nearly as painful as the tragedy of his youth and the horror that shredded his life. Taut muscles and nerves twitched and cried out for relief. The ache in his chest grew stronger and more insistent. His mind raced, and he desperately sought something that would make them take her disappearance seriously, but he could find nothing to add to his story.

Sergeant York was sympathetic, but without more to go on, there wasn't much the police could do. "You shouldn't give up hope. This could be some sort of misunderstanding between you two. Kate may have needed some space and felt like getting away for a while. You said there was an uncle in the area. Are you sure you don't know his name or where he works, anything that would help find him?"

"No," Matt barely mumbled through tight lips. "She only mentioned him once, and only called him Uncle Ben. I never knew any more about him than that. Because she was so vague about him, I felt maybe he wasn't an uncle. You know? Maybe a former boyfriend she didn't want to discuss. It was just a feeling I had; I didn't want to pry."

"I see," Sergeant York looked down at his folded hands and made mental notes. "Well, I can't do much about a missing person's report for the first twenty-four hours anyway unless we suspect foul play, criminal activity or believe the person is in danger. None of which apply here. A few drops of blood hardly indicate foul play and not enough for me to go to my Lieutenant and request an investigation. Most missing people show up within that timeframe, you know. Matt, people do come back, and there is no sign of any crime here. That's good news. A kidnapper wouldn't stop to put things back on the walls or restock your cupboards. It sounds to me like she was getting scared about your relationship and didn't know how to tell you. Maybe she just needed some distance. Go home and try not to worry too much. If you don't hear from her in the next day or two, give me a call. I have a friend who does some investigative work, maybe he could ask around and see where it goes. Okay?"

"Yeah, fine."

The Sergeant handed him a business card. "She may have gone to stay with her uncle. You said she stayed there before."

The drive home was a blur, and he never saw or felt the dark eyes watching him from the lot outside his door. Matt was so tired he could barely think, and his head pounded. Walking up the steps he was prepared to wrestle with the key again, but instead, he found the door unlocked and it swung open easily at his touch. Matt could have sworn he pulled it shut and tried the lock as was his habit, but in his state of mind, anything was possible. As he pushed open the door, an arrow of light from the streetlamp outside raced across the floor ahead of him into the cold dark apartment. Once inside the inky chill moved up his legs and a tremor ran over him head to toe. He passed through the rooms in blackness, not wanting to turn on a single light which would only reinforce the emptiness and his loss.

In spite of his grief, he saw the irony. Only yesterday his home, their home, was a sanctuary from the world. Warm, welcoming, and safe. But, now, barely twenty-four hours later, the real world went on as before on the other side of the door, and he had re-entered a barren place devoid of life.

Night found him edgy and restless, and the weight of his loss pressed him deeper into the bed, nearly suffocating him. Lying alone in the space they shared was lonely and forbidding. Unmanly or not, he couldn't hold back the sobs of his tormented heart. He missed her warmth and how their nights together banished the anguish of his past and offered his future healing he hadn't even known he sought.

Sleep was elusive, and his mind played tricks as he could almost hear her gentle breathing next to him in the dark. With closed eyes, he tried to find her scent among the sheets. The fragrance was a part of her, and he'd been branded by it. She told him it was called Beautiful. And it suited her. Kate was beautiful, petite and slim, with soft, strawberry blond hair that cascaded like silk over her shoulders when she pushed it back behind her ears. Her smooth skin glowed with health and was perfect as the rest of her. But the feature that touched him more than the deep blue eyes that held him captive was her warm and constant smile. Disappointment racked his body when no trace of her perfume could be found.

When sleep finally claimed him, bizarre scenes played out in the muted landscapes that are dreams. Kate was there, holding his hand, and then running behind huge boulders the size of houses.

She blew him a kiss as she disappeared and gigantic waves crashed over the rocks dragging her away. "Kate!" he yelled, as her golden hair floated effortlessly on blue-green water caressing her lovely face. He watched helplessly as the waters closed to him and she sank beneath the surface. Gnarled, disembodied hands motioned to him; waving a small bunch of dried flowers and a thousand different voices hissed what sounded like his name. Walking away, he was startled by the sound of his feet crunching on a path littered with bones, and he awoke in a cold sweat, breathing hard, his alarm clock grating in his ears. He was tired and thoroughly drained, but the memory of his nightmare drove him out of bed. He needed daylight and reality to exorcize the fear and dread it evoked.

It was going to be another long day he knew. His project was nearing completion, and under normal circumstances, he would have been excited to get to the lab and share his results with his boss, Dr. Jeff Nowak, but how could he possibly concentrate on anything with his mind still on Kate? His body ached with his loss as he headed to the shower and he tripped over his clothes uncharacteristically discarded on the floor. The memory of life with Kate continued to play over and over in his head, like a video stuck on replay.

Heated blood moved faster through his veins as the hot water beat away some of the strain and a new vigor overtook him. He didn't care what the police would do he decided; he couldn't just let Kate go, not like this with no explanation. He would find her somehow. But, again, exactly where he was going to start was the definitive problem. None of the facts added up, round and round and back again his mind churned.

Why would she leave without a note? The question taunted him. *I could have handled her decision to go; she should have known that. And, of course, it would have hurt, but I would have taken it like a man and respected her choice.*

As he stepped out of the shower, he started to grab his rumpled towel, then stopped and deliberately took Kate's. He couldn't stand to see it mocking him, looking fresh and unused next to his. Denial was dying a slow death; reality was going to win. He knew what the answer was in spite of what his heart refused to admit. Besides, nothing else made any sense. What would be the point of anyone wanting to hurt her? Take her away? Briefly, he thought of the broken door lock and the odd chill he experienced from time to time, or the feeling he was being watched. *Paranoia,* he decided and tamped down any idea of sharing such nonsense with the police. His story already sounded strange. *No sense making them believe I'm a total fruitcake.*

As he pulled out of his parking space, he spotted two of his neighbors and only hesitated a second before deciding to ask them if they'd seen Kate leave. Although in the past they had nodded politely to each other in passing, he didn't know them, so the conversation was a bit awkward. It took a minute of small talk to get to the point. They were polite, of course, at his new friendliness, and they seemed genuinely interested, but they could not help him. They were astonished to hear anyone except Matt lived there. They blankly looked at each other and then at him, shaking their heads. They never saw her leave. They never saw her at all.

Chapter Four

Matt paid no heed to the light overhead as it turned green, he was focused inward. The shock of Kate's disappearance overshadowed everything else in his life. The not so patient driver behind him honked angrily at the delay. With a sheepish wave in the rear-view mirror, Matt hit the gas and hurried to catch up with the line of cars now far ahead of him.

The day was unseasonably cold, but the sun streaming through the car window warmed him as he sped along the boulevard with its neat row of trees. Fall was definitely in the air. Green leaves, their edges trimmed in gold and red showed traces of the glory to come, but Matt was blind to their beauty as he passed beneath their colorful branches. He slowed as he passed the shops on the outskirts of the city, searching for the small jewelry store, its windows decorated with fake pumpkins and twinkling orange lights. Wrenching pain seared his insides as he spotted the little building near the row of restaurants, a few doors down from the antique shop. His future had looked so different just a few days before.

"Good morning Doc, you oversleep again today?" Hank, the security guard, grinned as he waved Matt through the rolling gates. "Two days in a row getting in past eight o'clock."

"Yeah, had a bad night." Matt grimaced as he pulled into the private lot. He hoped no one else would notice his late entrance. Matt was not in a sociable mood. If he were lucky, his co-workers would be too busy to see him walk in.

The heavily protected facility had security scan stations at both doors, and it took Matt a few extra minutes to empty his pockets, swipe his badge through the reader and slide his briefcase and backpack through the grill. There were elevators off the main lobby, but they often ran slow, so Matt chose the stairs. His long legs dragged heavily as he climbed the steps to his floor. The labs were locked behind double doors, and once again, he swiped his

I.D. card and spread his fingers to allow the scanner to read his handprint. Matt was in luck; his colleagues were bent over their work-stations and never noticed his late entrance. *Good,* as only their backs greeted him; already dressed in their blue bio-suits they were oblivious as he hurried past. The last door on the right was his lab, and with one more swipe, he was in.

Usually, Matt was eager to dive into his work. Two years of research were wrapping up a truly fascinating project, and by this time of the morning, his computer would be humming as he entered data. But today it would be difficult to keep his mind on the work.

Kate brought magic to his days. It was hard to describe how being with her changed the fabric of his life. As if when they were together, they stepped out of time, or perhaps into another dimension. Whatever powers she possessed, she somehow transformed his mediocre existence and filled a void that had been growing for years. Her presence muddied his head, but her warmth clarified his life. He reveled in being alive. No other woman ever affected him like Kate. He was rough stone, flawed with a tormented past, but she was a jeweler's cloth who healed him, rounded out his edges, and made him whole. But now, she was gone.

Could I have been so mistaken about her? If she didn't love me, how had she deceived me so well? Maybe not love, he corrected, wanting to be completely honest, since she never actually said the word. He had never suspected she was unhappy. The fact that Kate had fallen so unexpectedly into his life was something he often wondered about but didn't examine too closely lest the dream should end as quickly as it began. Although it was useless, Matt continued to call her cell phone, hoping just once she would answer.

The hours crept slowly, and a glance at the oversized lab clock showed it finally to be five-thirty, and most of his co-workers were headed to the doors. He was in a hurry to put the day behind him, but because of the confidential nature of his work, he preferred to do clean up himself, adding another half-hour to his work day.

Perhaps if she left town on business, she might have taken her clothes, but what of the rest of her things? And a note? Why couldn't she have left me a damned note, even if it was to say goodbye? Cold as that would have been, at least it would have explained her actions. He still couldn't believe she would leave him without a word. He had spent the entire day wrestling with the problem, which only made his head hurt more. By the time he headed home, he was exhausted mentally and physically, but no closer to an answer than before.

The following day, Detective Don Orliss called to see if there was any news about Kate. Matt painfully informed him Kate had not returned, there was no message from her or anyone else about her, and he was more confused than ever. The Detective told him he received the report from Sergeant York, and although they didn't believe it was a police matter, he would conduct a pre-liminary investigation for their records. Matt sincerely thanked the man and hung up. Once again, a flicker of hope shot through him knowing he was not alone, at least the police were going to look into Kate's disappearance.

A long and frustrating week went by before he heard from the detective again. There was still no word from Kate. Intently focused on his work, Matt finally realized the phone was ringing in the lab. He put down the tubes he was holding, turned down the flame on the burner, and grabbed the phone on the sixth ring. "This is Matt Errington,"

"Matt, it's Detective Orliss. I didn't think you were there."

"Sorry, I can get pretty involved, and the noise from our equipment drowns out the phone. Did you find Kate? Are you calling with good news?"

"I'd like to talk about my findings in person. Could we meet sometime today, say around four?"

"Yeah, of course, although I can get away earlier if you wish, but if you think …"

The Detective cut him off. "Four is good. I'll take a run up there. I need to get out of the office this afternoon."

"I guess that's okay," Matt answered; frustrated, he would have to wait to get any news about Kate. "The labs are off limits to visitors, but we have a conference room down on the second floor we can use, it's usually empty later in the day."

"Great, I'll see you then." As Matt hung up the phone, an eerie feeling gripped him that he couldn't shake for the remainder of the day. He wasn't expecting miracles or anything, and he might not be able to get her to come back, but at least if he could find her, talk to her, he would deal with the rejection. He only wanted to know the reason.

Matt was washing up as the security guard at the gate announced over the intercom a Detective Orliss was there and would be waiting for him in the front lobby.

"Thanks, Hank, tell him I will be right there." Matt groaned wishing the guard hadn't been told the visitor was a detective. Hank Brooks loved to gossip and speculation about the purpose of Matt's guest would be the break room topic tomorrow. He had worked straight through lunch, pushing hard all day to finish his reports so he could get out of the lab earlier than usual, but now hurrying down the hall, his stomach growled loudly reminding him of his neglect.

The Detective met him at the elevator, and together they rode back up to the second floor to which visitors were allowed. "Pretty tight place you guys have here, there isn't this much security at Fort Knox." Matt again swiped his I.D. to allow them access and held the door open for the Detective.

"We are a government funded research lab, and what we do is pretty confidential. We work with sensitive materials and nasty products. I'm sure the U.S. Government would be unhappy if the research they pay for were lost to some Wall Street pharmaceutical spy trying to cash in on our discoveries. Unfortunately, in today's world, there is a real need to prevent any kind of theft."

The conference room was empty with only the remains of a cold coffee pot, an overflowing wastebasket, and a bulletin board badly in need of cleaning. Although Matt was extremely eager to get some answers about Kate, he did offer to make a new pot of coffee for the detective, hoping he would refuse.

"Thanks, but I've had enough for today. My wife is probably right; she's always trying to get me to drink tea, thinks I get too much coffee. That's the English for you."

"Okay then," Matt said, eager to get started as he shut the door behind him. "I want to hear everything you have found."

What is it about cops, Matt wondered, *they all look alike? Short cropped hair, mustache, loose and casual sports coat, dark shirt, jeans. This guy could never work undercover,* Matt noted immediately as he pulled out a chair. Even to Matt's untrained eye, the guy shouted police.

Detective Orliss picked a seat facing the door and folded his hands on the table in front of him. "Matt," he began unceremoniously, "just how long did you say you have known Kate?"

"Probably about three months. We met in late June or early July I think, why?"

"Well, I'm sorry to tell you I can't find any news about her."

"You mean, where she went or why?"

"No, I mean anything about her at all. Not where she came from; not where she worked; not a birth date; nothing."

"But I told you guys those things," Matt responded. "Her birthday is August seventh, and she said she worked for Atlas Medical, all that was in the report I gave Sergeant York."

"Yep, that's what the report says, but I can't find a single fact to corroborate anything you said. Not one single fact." Matt's head pounded harder. "You seem like a nice guy, intelligent, and you have a responsible position here, and we believe your story, but we can't find any proof that Kate even exists or if that's her real name. I have checked records throughout the state and made contacts with departments in Illinois, particularly around Chicago where you say she is from. So far, we have turned up empty. There is nothing else to go on. Your story sounds plausible, but that's where we're at."

The late afternoon sun smothered the room and turned it hazy and unbearably warm. The detective took off his jacket, and draped it around the back of the chair, exposing his badge on his belt and the gun under his arm. Even with his years of experience, the pain in the young man's face made him uncomfortable.

"I don't understand what has happened," Matt stammered, shaking his head to clear the fog away. He was surprised the search had not found her. He never expected the detective to fail. *How could there be no trace of her?*

"I mean," the detective continued, "I can find no record of one Kate, or Kathryn or anything similar, last name Champion, no school records, no past address, no condo in Chicago, no work record, hell, Atlas says they don't even have a female salesperson."

"I know. I checked with them, too. I don't know how I got the name wrong."

"I see. Well, at any rate, there is no driver's license, no charge cards, no phone records. The cell number you gave us is a non-working number, nothing. The surprising thing is when I asked around where you live, talked to some of your neighbors; they have no recollection of seeing her. Ever. Didn't know she even existed. Seems pretty bizarre to me."

The detective sat quietly, feeling a bit guilty about the obvious pain he was inflicting, but watching Matt closely for his reaction. Stunned, Matt was unable to speak; he just shook his head in disbelief. *What the hell is going on, why is this happening?* The near constant headache since her disappearance was making him nauseous. How stupid he felt. *What proof can I offer?* He couldn't even provide a photo of her to back up his story. That was her choice. She said cameras made her look fat and as farfetched as that could be, he complied with her wishes. So, there was no proof to aid their search or even prove her existence.

Detective Orliss was not surprised by Matt's refusal to accept the truth but tried to help him work through the facts. It wasn't often he couldn't find a target, and he was amazed at the lack of results. When he did a little digging into Matt's past, a lot of things jumped out, including the accident, his head injury, and length of recovery. It was possible, he confided to his friend Sergeant York, that the Errington guy imagined the entire story. He could be just another loony who created the whole thing in his subconscious to make his boring life more bearable. In his twenty-four years on the force, he had seen odd people like that all the time. Mental illness was as familiar in police work as were crimes and criminals. The information eased any doubts they may have about a woman's disappearance.

After kicking it around with Sergeant York, they knew they were wasting their time. The guy could be suffering some kind of mental trauma. At least there did not appear to be a missing woman to investigate.

"I'm afraid we are baffled as well," the detective told the shaken man before him, as he started to rise. The detective, however, was not completely convinced it was all in Matt's head, there was a slim possibility a con had pulled a scam on him. Although that was only a hunch since there didn't seem to be any motive or any apparent crime.

"You know Matt, to be safe, I'd keep a close eye on my bank accounts and charge cards. It's possible you've been the victim of a con."

"No. Not possible. Kate would never do anything to hurt me." Matt winced at the irony of his words.

"Well suit yourself; I'm just passing on some advice." It was possible the guy was a lonely heart who was duped by a pro, but the detective couldn't prove it, and for now, there was nothing more he could do. After the meeting with Matt, he filed a report with his Lieutenant and suggested the case be left open, but not active.

More than a week had passed since Kate's disappearance. Matt's mind reeled with the conflict and the disappointing report. Strange had just gotten stranger. *None of it makes any sense. How could someone as vibrant as Kate disappear? Is she in some kind of trouble? In hiding? From whom?* The whole idea was insane or someone's idea of a bad joke. As the day passed, the questions grew. *Why is there no logical answer to anything?*

A little before seven o'clock, Matt pulled into the lot of his apartment complex and was surprised to see Fred Lafferty, the skinny superintendent, coming out of Matt's door as he pulled up in front. "What's going on Fred?"

"You reported the lock was broken, just checking it out. Nothing much wrong with it." Seeing the surprise and doubt on Matt's face, Fred hurried on, "but I took it apart and greased it a little just in case." He held up his dirty fingers for Matt's inspection as proof of his words. Fred started to limp away, his dirty mullet of curly gray hair sticking straight out behind his head, muttering to himself about white-collar type guys who can't figure out a simple doorknob.

"Well, okay, thanks," Matt said, then turned and called him back with a question. "Hey Fred, hold on a sec. Have you been in my place in the last couple of months, I mean before today?"

Fred immediately chafed at the question and wondered why Matt would ask him that. Taking his time to spit a wad of tobacco juice at the curb, he finally said, "Well sir, can't rightly say I have, I'd have to go back and check the books. I keep the work orders for a while, might have come by to check on things, why?"

"I thought you might have seen my girlfriend in the last few weeks, pretty little blond." Fred uncomfortably danced from foot to foot.

"Nope can't say I have. Why, did you lose her?" Fred's sideways grin showed several twisted or missing teeth.

"Just wondering." Matt had missed the joke. "But if you had gone in, would you remember what my place looked like, you know, decorations, knick-knacks, that sort of thing?"

The questioning was getting Fred spooked. In spite of the cool day, he felt the sweat running down his neck with the third degree. He hadn't taken anything from this guy, at least not that he remembered. He didn't mess with folks who were sharp enough to know something was missing. Not like the old guy in 219 who wouldn't miss a few old coins and some civil war trinkets, but Fred hadn't touched anything lately and wondered what Matt was getting at. Careful not to look suspicious, Fred drawled, "Well mister I have a hundred-twenty units on this side of Benning Road and eighty on the other. They are all about the same size and layout. They all look pretty much the same to me. Can't possibly remember who did what to their place, you know. Unless it was something obvious like the nutso sisters in 103, who painted their entire apartment bright purple and slapped big yellow stars all over the ceiling. Yeah, that one I remember. But, as for the average place, no way." Getting more and more distrustful of the questioning, Fred wanted to be done with the conversation and again started to turn away.

Fred considered himself crafty as a coyote and didn't miss much in his little part of the woods but decided to be more careful around this guy. With his background, it was best not to say too much about life in general. The less people knew about him, the better. The rape charge when he was younger could have been a hard bullet to dodge, but the stupid bitch finally came around. If she had pressed charges, he would have spent years in the slammer. Sweet talking her had been easy, and so what if he'd had to marry her, it didn't last long. He just dumped her when he found something better. She was pissed, but it was too late to go back and make a complaint, especially after she convinced her parents she was the one that seduced him.

Fred knew how to handle women. Over the years he'd had the pleasure of consoling lots of neglected wives after their husbands left for work. Not that he'd ever had the pleasure of meeting the little blond this guy was talking about and thought it weird he'd never seen her. Fred prided himself on knowing everything about everybody.

"Thanks anyway," Matt said and headed toward his front door when Fred called him back.

"Hey, Mr. ... uh, sorry, don't know everyone's name."

"Matt."

"Um, yeah, well Matt, do you mind if I come by during the day and take a look at your dishwasher?"

Matt shook his head. "No, I guess not, why?"

"Some folks have been complaining they make too much noise. I got some insulation for it. I can pull yours out and see what I can do for it."

That was true enough, Matt nodded, thinking about how loud the machine was. He and Kate laughed about it and usually washed their dishes by hand just to avoid the clatter. Fresh pain ripped through him again with the recollection. "Yeah, that's fine." It hadn't been worth complaining about, but since the guy was offering.

Whistling through his teeth, Fred smiled as he threw his tools into the back of his beat-up grey truck. It sounded to him like they had a fight and she might be looking for some sympathy. He'd keep an eye on this place. Maybe he should tell the guy there was a piece of metal stuck in the lock. Looked like the tip of one of those professional picks the cops use broke off and got jammed in there. But that was probably offering too much information. Guys on the streets had picks too. Or kids. There was always some fooling around in the area. If he mentioned it to this guy, word would get around and pretty soon the residents would expect him to patrol their neighborhood. Wasn't his job. Let sleeping dogs lie. He wasn't a damn cop.

Chapter Five

In the weeks before Kate's disappearance, the pressure at work had mounted, and the stress was pretty intense. Matt's boss, Dr. Nowak, and the corporate heads were pushing him hard, although everyone knew their government funding was always an issue, and the threat of losing it was constant. Money allocated for his project could be suspended at any time, and he and Dr. Nowak wanted to get as much done as possible to show progress and ensure continued support.

Before he met Kate, his work would have kept him in the lab for days and nights on end, but when Kate moved in, Matt found it was easier at the end of the day to put away his vials, jot down his daily notes and turn out the lights of the lab. He tried to work regular hours to spend more time with her. She was always interested in what Matt was doing, how his work was progressing, and what stage of the project he was at. Although she claimed to have no head for science, she was a logical thinker and encouraged him to try new approaches to the problems he laid out before her.

They often discussed his day over the dinners they prepared together, and he made her laugh with stories about his co-workers. Kate was never bored, which amazed him. She wanted to know everything about his job and the work he was doing with a nasty virus, how it could paralyze people and how he was so close to finishing a cure. His research was promising but untested. Science took a great deal of time and patience. Matt always thought he had both.

Fresh out of school, Matt was offered the job in Philadelphia to work for Marsh Research Laboratories, a private company, and he jumped at the opportunity. It was a government-supported pharmaceutical lab with ties to the Centers for Disease Control in Atlanta, researching various known diseases and their causes. Financed by grants he was free to spend his time experimenting with a variety of bacteria and viruses, and not worry about producing a product, like some of his buddies from school did when they found similar employment in companies who answered to Wall Street. He lived for his work, and before he met Kate, it gave him the only pleasure and satisfaction his limited life held.

In Matt's three years at Marsh, he made some rather dramatic progress. Nothing earth-shattering yet, but his results had the potential to influence medicines in the future. He liked that part of his work the most and hoped the good he did for people to change their lives would help compensate for his horrific past and the role he played in his mother's death.

On the steamy summer afternoon when he met Kate, and she told him she worked for a small medical equipment firm, it seemed to be fate that they had something in common. They met accidentally in town in front of the antique shop where he purchased his old desk. Alone on the street, she stopped him to ask directions. She was so friendly, and her laugh was bewitching. She said she was from out of town and looking for a good place to eat. Matt was pleased to give her his best suggestion and more than surprised when she asked him to join her. Entranced by the sparkle in her eyes, he was quick to jump at the offer.

After dinner and the heat of the day faded, they walked a short block to the park and spent the rest of the evening talking, and then his life took a dramatic turn. For Matt, it was love at first sight and although he tried to hold back, go slowly and use caution, as their relationship grew, he knew he was a drowning man with no desire to be saved.

One evening after dinner, it was Kate who asked if she could spend the night. As Matt walked her out to her car, she reached inside and pulled out a small travel bag. He knew he would never hear sweeter words. Kate usually stayed with an uncle during her brief visits to town.-Although Matt was curious about 'Uncle Ben' and asked a lot of questions, he; never got much information, then eventually quit pursuing the topic. After that evening, she stayed with Matt on all her trips to town, and to make her more comfortable, he quickly cleaned out half his closet and half the dresser drawers, giving her plenty of space.

Even more unbelievable, within a few weeks, Kate informed Matt she had been offered a permanent position in town, and if she accepted, she would not be traveling so much anymore. Without hesitation, Matt insisted she move in with him, and their life took on a more permanent feel. He had never known such happiness and didn't want to question why he deserved it. He only knew she transformed him and made it his daily resolve never to give her a reason to leave.

Matt didn't consider himself handsome, certainly not the movie star hunk he felt someone like Kate deserved, so he couldn't imagine what Kate saw in him. Sharing his life with someone like her was like winning a lottery without a ticket. He was willing to do anything to make her happy and keep her in his life, and he made every attempt to come out of his introspective, workaholic shell for her. Life was so much better with her in it.

Although she shared little of her life, she was always extremely interested in his. On a cool summer evening, as a mock fireplace snapped and crackled on her laptop, Matt and Kate shared a bottle of wine, and he finally felt he was ready to share the torment of his past. It was uncomfortable at first; the pain had deep roots, but as he noted the soft encouragement on her face, his anxiety lessened. Always a private person, Matt was reluctant, and he hesitated to share his story afraid of what she would think of him. Afraid the spark would die in her eyes. But her gentle prodding opened the floodgate, and the years of pain and agony he tried to bury gushed out in a cathartic flood.

"As a teenager, when I was learning to drive, a terrible car crash killed my passenger." He paused a moment to take a deep breath. "It was my mother. I relentlessly begged her to let me drive. She didn't think it was a good idea, I hadn't had much practice, but I was in a hurry to feel grown up. A lot of my friends were driving, and I wanted to prove I was ready. I probably gave her a pretty hard time about it."

Matt hesitated and looked to Kate, who only nodded gently for him to go on. "I didn't cause the accident, a guy in a pickup ran a red light and hit us broadside, but a more experienced driver might have watched for it, seen the truck coming. I only thought about how cool I was. She was killed instantly. I had a serious head injury … what the doctors labeled severe brain trauma. I was in a coma for nearly a month. When I woke up, I learned about my mom's death. It was more than I could handle, and I was pretty messed up for months. She was gone … and in spite of what people said … I knew it was all my fault. I didn't care if I lived or died. Which didn't help my recovery. The docs at St. Anne's Hospital worked hard to heal my brain, which was the easy part. Healing my mind was another. I went through personality changes, headaches, and blackouts. For months I was on some different meds which turned me into a walking zombie." Matt flinched at the memory, but Kate merely took a firmer grip on his hand and nodded again for him to go on.

"My mom was all I had in my life. She never married my dad, and I never met the man. My entire family consisted of Mom, a distant aunt and uncle, and my elderly grandparents.

"My mom's name was Sara, and she was only twenty-two when I was born. My dad was in the army stationed at Fort Stewart, not too far from her home in Richmond Hill, a little town on the Atlantic coast, south of Savannah. The summer they met was a scorching one. She told me how they would sneak away in the evening to catch the cool breezes coming in over the marshes. There was a wooden boardwalk jutting out over the swampy mire, with a thatched hut at the end. The hut had a wooden floor with a bench that hugged the circular walls. Mom would tell me that they'd bring a radio and dance or watch the white egrets go by. She loved to see them float silently, their feathers barely skimming the water as they scooped up a fish mid-flight. When the cooler air blew in from the sea, the fronds of the hut's roof would sway in 'golden unison.' Those were the exact words my mom used, 'golden unison.'"

"From the time I was little, Mom would tell me the stories of their one summer together. I think she wanted me to at least know something of Gil. It was all she had to give me about him. Out on the beach, sitting in the sand with the waves tugging at their feet they talked of the future and Gil proposed. When Mom told him she was pregnant with me, he took it hard, but she thought he eventually made peace with the idea of becoming a father. Early in the fall, Gil said he was to be transferred to Fort Bliss, Texas with his unit and was scheduled to leave two months before I was due.

"My grandparents thought they should have a quick wedding, and Mom didn't hesitate to make plans. All seemed to be going well until a month before the wedding. She said he changed. He became distant. She was scared, but she finally asked him what was going on. I guess he was pretty embarrassed because she said he was red-faced and couldn't look her in the eye, but he told her, "I just don't love you enough." Mom canceled the wedding and Gil left a few weeks later for Texas without her. As far as I know, she never heard from him again. I was born on a cold, drizzly morning in early January, the third ... right after New Years. We didn't have much, but we had each other."

Matt's eyes clouded at the memory of his early life, alone with his mom in the small apartment they shared. Wiping away the moisture that threatened, he went on with his story. "Money was pretty tight, but she was a good mom and did whatever she could to make up for me not having a father. I was about six when she married Mickey, a hardworking man several years older than her. He was a foreman on the shipping docks in Savannah. Mickey didn't have much formal education, but he had a passion for learning, and the three of us spent evenings together pouring over library books on subjects from amoebas to dinosaurs. It was his love of nature and science which set me on a lifelong career in science, something I've never stopped being grateful for.

"Life was good for all of us, but then our little family fell apart once more. Mickey was only forty-three when a winch broke on the dock. He was killed instantly as a pallet crashed down on him. Mom was inconsolable and never recovered from fate's second blow. Although she was a loving mother, her youth melted away before its time. I knew it was because of me that she lost Gil. And indirectly even Mickey. He worked a lot of overtime to give us a better life. I grew up feeling it was my responsibility to keep her happy."

Kate wiped away a tear and squeezed his hand again. "I made up stories on my way home from school to cheer her up at the end of her workday. Stories about dragons and kings, damsels in distress and their knights in shining armor. Anything that might make her smile and be happy again. By the time I was in high school, Mom had left the boat company where she had worked and went to work for a law group in town. Financially, we were doing better, and we even talked about taking a vacation in the summer and going west. Then Mom died ... and I spent nearly two years wishing I had. It seemed like all of my life ... I just caused her pain."

The story left him spent and unsure what Kate would think now that she knew his background. Knew how damaged he was. In her usual tender way, she took his face between her hands and kissed him softly. Matt finally knew he would be able to heal.

Growing up, it always seemed to him love was a train wreck waiting to happen, and getting on board was not the wisest thing you could do. Then he met Kate, and the magical healing she offered changed all that he had ever known. After she disappeared, Matt couldn't help wondering if sharing his past with Kate had been the wrong thing to do. *I probably told her too much.*

Of the little Kate shared of her life, she told him she was from Chicago where she owned a small condo near the shores of Lake Michigan. They talked about taking a weekend trip there in the coming summer to retrieve some of her things and maybe put the place up for sale. When Matt questioned her about her mail or when she would change her address, she gave him one of her dazzling smiles and said she would take care of it. After she moved in, she seemed happy, and he didn't push her to talk about her past. He was certain when she was more comfortable, she would tell him all he needed to know. He could wait.

After she left, although it was useless, he couldn't stop calling her phone, hoping just once she would answer. But the phone only rang and rang. Days passed, then weeks, and Matt went through a dozen levels of hell. He was worried, scared, and then bounced back and forth between anger and frustration. He had no idea how he could prove she had ever been there. His neighbors, who should have seen Kate, had no recollection. Of course, she came and went at odd times. It was possible, he assured himself over and over, they had missed each other as a matter of timing, besides no one in his apartment complex paid much attention to anyone else. To Matt, they seemed pretty cold and detached. But in all fairness, it was hard to criticize them; he didn't pay much attention to them either.

The details of their brief time together tormented him over and over, as he tried to remember the life they shared. They shopped at a local mall and ate out a few times, but upon questioning people in some of the more familiar spots, he could find no one with any memory of her. He was especially disappointed by the local pizzeria. But the changing string of kids who worked there could barely remember him, let alone Kate, and he was a frequent customer for years. No matter where or how hard he looked, he could find no trace of Kate or anyone else who remembered her.

Lonely, weeks passed, and Matt was forced to accept she was truly gone and wasn't coming back. Long before, and as gentle as they could be, the police informed him there was no further search for Kate. They concluded amongst themselves she did not exist. At Matt's pleading, Detective Orliss finally sent a technician to test Matt's apartment for fingerprints, only to have the same negative results. Except for Matt's and the super's, there were no others to be found.

In the weeks around her strange disappearance, there were other unexplained events. Dangerous things which made him question his sanity again. Pages of his lab notes disappeared and reappeared days later, exactly where they should be. There were changes he didn't remember making, in handwriting that didn't look like his. He would turn his machines off at the end of the day only to find his computers and equipment humming again when he returned in the morning. A thought that terrified Matt for some reason was the possibility that he was losing touch with reality. Neither Marsh nor Dr. Nowak would be too pleased to learn Matt was having mental difficulties. They couldn't have a crazy scientist on their staff.

Considering the stress with Kate's disappearance and the pressures of his job, he quietly checked in with his doctor and submitted himself to a whole series of tests. Matt's physician concluded he was suffering residual damage from his past closed head trauma and the emotional problems which plagued him after his mother's death. Symptoms which could show up after all these years. He issued new medications, and after a few days, the effects were startling. In spite of the overwhelming memories he hated to part with, the drugs worked their magic. Even Matt began to question Kate's existence.

In retrospect, it was a good decision Matt had made, not to talk to his friends or colleagues about Kate. They were a bunch of nosy gossips, and his life with Kate was personal and private. Perhaps it was some inner fear early in their relationship that if it didn't work out, he would be talked about or worse, pitied. Matt found it easier to let them all think he remained alone by choice, married to his work. After Kate left, he knew it had been the right decision. How would he ever explain her disappearance to them now? He couldn't even explain it to himself.

Eventually, Matt accepted what the police believed all along. It was an emotional breakdown due to the stress of the job and past head injury. He must have invented Kate and their life together. As unbelievable as it was, he could find no proof she was ever a part of his life. He was a scientist, after all. His life was rooted in facts which he trusted, and the facts could not prove anyone wrong but him.

Chapter Six

Saucy Abernathy opened his shop door and peered out down the street. "Goddamn what a beautiful day," he said out loud, to no one in particular. "Finally, we got some sunshine." His bones were becoming more brittle each year, and all his joints ached in the autumn dampness. "I need to move farther south, that's for sure. I've stayed too long in this place." But he always got stuck on the same problem. Saucy didn't have any money to move unless he sold the store and with all the stupid building codes, he knew it would cost too much money to fix things up before he could sell the damn place. "Damn government, always sticking their noses into simple folk's business," he often fumed. Shaking his gray head, the owner and manager of House of Antiques and Oddities, walked back inside, flipping the sign on the door from Closed to Open.

Walter Abernathy, or Saucy as he'd been called since childhood, had taken over the place from his father, who got it from his father. Built in the mid-eighteen hundreds, the little shop morphed from one business into another. The story went it was originally a brothel, which would explain the dozen or so small rooms upstairs he used for storage.

His grandpa got the place by winning it at cards, hell, according to some people, his grandpa won his grandma at cards too, but no one ever proved that. His grandma just laughed when she heard it told. Grandpa turned it into a pawnshop, made himself a nice living until World War II broke out.

In 1959, Saucy's grandpa died, and the place fell to Saucy's dad who changed the name to Abernathy's Emporium and had a thriving business selling a mishmash of items from hammers to curtains, plumbing supplies to toothpaste. By the time Saucy took it over, antiques were the name of the game. Folks came from cities all around to shop in his cramped, dingy little building, and they came in a steady stream. Saucy didn't have to get on the confusing

Internet people were always talking about to sell his goods. Nope, didn't have to. His store was always busy, mostly tourists bringing their money from upstate.

Yeah, he knew the place was run down and needed a lot of work, but that meant putting money into it. Besides, he thought age and decay added to the charm of the place. Nope, he was stuck there, he thought again, as he closed the door, shaking the wall of the old store and making the little bell tinkle over his head.

He turned as he did each morning glancing at the shelf running across the front window. That's where he had placed a row of tiny, brightly colored glass vases. He enjoyed the dancing lights they made on the ceiling on the few days the sun came through. "Pretty little things," he mumbled. "Even the cracked one." He was glad the little blond brought them in. It was funny; she didn't want money for them. Just handed him a plain card with a phone number before she walked back out. Abernathy was glad he could keep them if he wanted to, even though they would have fetched a nice profit if he chose to sell them. They brightened up the front of the store with their rainbow of fractured lights. Just like the little lady said they would.

February 10th

Matt was feeling better. He'd been a little crazy, but he was much better. His head didn't hurt as much anymore, and he could conduct his work without the aching sense of loss that had invaded his life for months. The holidays had come and gone, and the few decorations he still had from his mom remained at the bottom of the closet. It didn't matter to him if they ever saw the light of day again. *What was the point after all?*

The new reality, the one where Kate didn't exist, was getting stronger each day and he almost looked forward to the new position he had been offered in Washington. If Matt accepted it, the job would be a huge leap for his career, and he'd be the envy of his friends and colleagues. However, it was a position that would take him far away from the small apartment where he still felt the remnants of a life complete with love and the treasured but dimming memories. As unreal as it was, Kate in whatever form she had been, left an indelible mark on his soul and he didn't want to surrender to the bleakness of life devoid of love, even though he knew deep in his bones he must move on.

Whatever the answer to the mystery was, whether she was real and left of her own accord, was spirited away by some inexplicable force or was only a figment of his imagination and vanished with a giant *poof*, the end was the same, she was gone. Just like after the death of his mother and his struggles to survive, he needed to close the door again, put his shattered past behind him and move forward.

However, that firm resolution made it more difficult to ponder the thing he found in his apartment one evening. The thing which sent him back to square one. Something he had overlooked, something unexplainable, which would once again prove him wrong.

Stuck in a dog-eared paperback, Matt found an unmailed post-card from a beautiful old hotel in London. He knew it wasn't his book. Not wanting to jump to any conclusions, and perhaps with some concern, his medications were failing him, he fingered the edges of the stiff paper and gingerly danced around the idea the book and the postcard could have something to do with Kate, and if not, then how were they there? Although there was no address on the card, no date, nor signature, it was addressed, "To my darling daughter." The short message read:

Hope all is well with you. Your aunt and I have had a wonderful trip. I should be coming home on schedule. Will tell you all about it when I see you. Love M.

That was it. Nothing more. Even though it created more mystery, Matt burned the picture of the hotel into his mind. In spite of all that he had endured and begun to accept as truth, he wanted to believe it was a postcard to Kate. *Does the 'M' stand for Mom?*

Matt had no idea who it belonged to or why it was there. He didn't remember ever seeing the strange book before. Indeed, it was not something he would have picked out—a lengthy work called, *InSight*. He lived in that apartment for several years with few visitors. *If Kate doesn't exist, then where did these items come from? Who is the card from, and who is it to? And why does my gut tell me it belongs to Kate?* Once again, hope roared through his veins. An invitation, flimsy though it was, for a chance to resurrect his other self, the happy one, waggled a finger in his direction. If his suspicions were right, she lived and so again could he.

For most of his life, Matt was a logical man. He lived in reality. Facts anchored him. Bending reality as best he could to accommodate what could be his salvation, he concluded he must have picked it up unknowingly from her things and stuck it on the shelf. Maybe if he could talk to someone in the hotel of the postcard, he may be able to ask about Kate or a relative, assuming they stayed there. *But of course, they did,* he reasoned, *why else would they choose that particular card to send?* The more he thought about the possibilities, the more his hope roared up and through the roof.

Perhaps he could get a forwarding address or something else that would turn the world upside down. Just finding Kate's mother would prove Kate was real, and not as the police tried to make him believe, a figment of a lonely mind. But running off to London would take time, and time was something he didn't have.

The new position in Washington loomed on the horizon, and Matt knew his boss already noted the bags under Matt's eyes, even teasing him about his disheveled appearance of late and quite openly questioned Matt's hesitancy about accepting the new position. To refuse the promotion and stay in Philadelphia to search for Kate would probably be a big mistake in his career, but to go to Washington would take him away from the only place he shared with her and leave him forever wondering about his mind and his sanity. So many questions from such a small card.

What if this was indeed addressed to Kate and what if he was able to track the sender, presumably her mother, from the hotel, could she or better yet, would she, tell him where Kate was? And of course, there was always the bigger question that had toyed with his heart for months. Should he even try to find her? That was a moot point at the moment which he quickly pushed aside. Just proving she existed would be enough he argued. If he found her, the decision to make contact could be decided then.

If this was indeed proof, and he could use it to find her, he reasoned he would have to do it himself. It wasn't enough for the police to start a search again. The fanciful side of Matt took instant flight. Just like in his make-believe stories for his mother, he could picture himself winging over the ocean, hot on the trail. He'd knock on doors all over England if it meant he could find Kate. But playing detective wasn't so simple. Matt's head started to pound, and he ordered himself to get a grip on his emotions.

He had to deliberately tamp down the growing excitement in his belly as his logical mind refused to be ignored. *What the hell am I doing? Am I seriously thinking of running halfway around the world, to track down someone who may not exist? And if she does, I also know she deliberately disappeared with no trail and obviously doesn't want to be found.* Even if he miraculously found her, maybe he should pay more attention to the question of, should he? If she was real and she had chosen to leave, did he have the right to intrude in her life? Torn between his euphoria that she could be real and his doubts about the dilemma it would be if he found her, Matt didn't know whether to laugh or cry. Besides, running out on his career for what could be a ghost chase or worse could take weeks or months of searching. Just to be disappointed in the end, only to find her unwilling to see him, or she may even turn her back on him should he be fortunate enough to find her. *God what a mess,* he thought again for the thousandth time, lovingly stroking the small book with the precious postcard gently tucked inside.

In his memories of Kate were bits and pieces of conversations they may or may not have had. Perhaps his knowledge of Kate's life was severely limited because she was purely his imagination. Or, perhaps, the few things he seemed to remember about her childhood were only carryovers from his own stories for his mother. But somewhere in the elusive web of memories, he was positive Kate had mentioned Great Britain. *Was it England or Wales?* Unsure, he wracked his brain for any tidbit that could be found. Anything that could give him answers. But the discussion he remembered had been late one night when he was half asleep; she hadn't given him many details. For all he knew, he dreamt the whole thing, and of course, there was even more possibility the conversation never happened because she was never actually there. At any rate, he needed answers, and he needed them soon, or it would be too late.

Logic be damned, his mind screamed again. Here in this apartment, in this town was where he found Kate, loved her, and then lost her. How could he just go off to Washington pretending he didn't? In spite of what others believed, his memories were too real. But on the other hand, he couldn't just go traipsing off around the world on a whim. He hadn't flown much before and didn't enjoy it. He did have a passport, *but is it still good?* The arguments raged on. His mind was in turmoil and again his twin factions debated for his future.

What in the hell am I doing? Hours went by, and still, he clutched the book while staring at the walls trying to decipher what was best for his future. *What is best for me?* But no definite answer could be found.

He could lose a bright, promising position which brought him real satisfaction. At least he knew his work was real and he could hopefully make a difference, especially when he knew only too well others would like nothing better than to beat him out of a job. Like Phil Forester, for instance. Matt knew Phil wanted the job in Washington and could barely conceal his jealous hostility toward Matt. Matt thought it was just a career move for Phil, as it was to him, but neither he nor anyone else in the department had any way of knowing the other scientist's agenda was much, much different.

Chapter Seven

Phil was several years older than Matt and in a hurry. He knew the importance of convincing management he was dedicated to the cause, but his cause was much more personal. Phil wasn't looking to save the world with new cures, and if anyone in the department suspected he was less than altruistic, they kept their silence. Phil wanted money. Phil needed money. There were organizations that would help him get it. Phil discovered how lucrative the scientific world could be when he was approached by an individual from the shadier side of life.

He didn't care why he was approached. The guy was interested in the work that Marsh, and particularly, what Matt was doing. It didn't take him long to figure out his job could spin into a lucrative side game. When he was contacted several months before, he was promised a figure that would pay him well just for passing on a few pages of research. Phil secretly borrowed from Matt's test results, which helped him whet their appetites. The fact that what he was doing was highly illegal, probably treasonous and he was stealing from the U.S. Government, who owned their research, never entered the picture. Minor technicalities were not worth losing any sleep over.

The job in Washington would put a fortune in his grasp. The Federal lab would give him access to data he couldn't get in Philly, and there were a lot more potential buyers on the market than the guys from Iran. If one group would pay him dearly, others would probably pay him more. The type of research Marsh did was invaluable and could be offered to the highest bidder. Washington would be a gold mine.

At the end of the day when their colleagues left, Phil pored over Matt's work. It wasn't difficult to gain access in spite of the security systems in place. Phil and Matt worked side by side earlier in the project, so no one looked askance at his presence. He hacked

Matt's computer almost on their first day together anyway, planning even then on borrowing Matt's work to enhance his career. When he was approached from the outside and asked what was available, he knew instantly he was going to be a rich man.

The buyers wanted a formula to scare their enemies in the middle-east. Prove to all, who had the hand of Allah on their side. They would pay dearly for a product to make people sick and the powerful antidote to restore their health. Matt was working on both, but going too slowly.

Months went by, and back in the summer, Phil promised the work was nearly finished and chafed at the fact that if Matt left for Washington before it was completed, he would lose the deal. Even though he unscrupulously copied Matt's research and boldly made changes to speed the process along, the golden goose was not yet in hand. When Phil learned Matt was chosen for the position in Washington, he marched to Dr. Nowak's office, slamming the door behind him.

From the open disgust on his face when he walked out, the whole department was pretty sure he was unsuccessful in his attempt to convince Nowak he should be the one to get the job. Phil was a real pain, and Dr. Nowak wanted Matt to take the job. But if for some reason he turned it down, Phil was there in the wings just in case.

Matt and Phil hadn't been close, right from the first day they worked together, and Matt chafed at the idea of giving up a great opportunity. It only made it worse to think Phil would get his spot if he turned it down.

But, to find out what happened to Kate, and if she even existed at all, he would go anywhere, do anything, including giving up a future that without her seemed bleaker by comparison. Wouldn't he? Still, every doubt since her disappearance made the decision nearly insufferable. After months of stress and his crippling loss with all its questions, he had serious doubts about his sanity. He knew there needed to be a decision, and soon, but no matter which way it went, it was going to change his life.

Friday afternoon, Dr. Nowak sent Matt an email, asking him to stop by his office before he left for the day, and Matt knew there was no more time. It was pretty clear the Washington office wanted to know who was going to fill the position and they wanted the name by the following Monday. How could Matt explain Kate at this point and what she had meant to him? Or why it was so important to find her or at least prove she even existed. It was his sanity he was dealing with, after all. *That issue, however, is probably not a topic of discussion you want to have with your boss,* he mused. There was no room in his career or the company for a lonely nutcase.

Dr. Nowak was bewildered. He couldn't understand why the decision was so difficult to make. Matt had earned the promotion, and it would be a huge career move. As much as he hated to let Matt go, he could not understand why a young man with Matt's potential hesitated. He had no way of knowing Matt's tortured mind was at the breaking point. Matt begged to have the weekend to decide and would give Dr. Nowak his answer on Monday.

After days of mind-numbing doubts, he had finally decided he would take the job and go to Washington, but he just needed the weekend to let it sink in. In spite of the postcard, he was fairly confident the right choice was to get on with his life and try to forget everything that had happened. It was the only thing he could do anyway. There would always be doubts, but he knew there was only so much his head and his life could bear. Each night as he turned off the lights, the argument raged deep in his heart. *Why is it so hard to let go of her?* He still wanted to believe she existed. He wanted to believe she had loved him, and although he knew something happened that was weird and unexplainable, he also knew he wasn't crazy. He just knew it! He also knew if he didn't let it all go, let her go, it would drive him crazy.

Friday night was mild, and a dense fog billowed about the roads as Matt headed to a local restaurant for a quick dinner before going home. The night and the earthbound clouds harbored an unexpected surprise. As he got out of his car and approached the blue canvas windbreak by the front door, someone came around the side of the building and headed straight for him. The stranger, a short, rather slight man, was deep in his coat and never slowed his pace as he bumped into Matt and shoved something into his hands. Matt regained his balance and was ready to let a few choice words fly as he turned quickly to confront the stranger. The words froze on his lips, and an involuntary shiver went down his spine as he found himself alone in the mist.

In a mere fraction of a second, the man vanished, swallowed by the night and was nowhere to be seen. Bewildered and a bit annoyed, Matt started again for the door and remembered the piece of paper in his hands. Turning it over, he discovered it to be an envelope. He stared at the printing, mesmerized. It was addressed to him. Even in the dim light, he was sure it was Kate's handwriting. His hands shook, and dozens of questions raced through his mind as he fumbled to get the paper inside. Written in what he was sure was Kate's neat script, were the words, *Go to Washington.*

Stunned, first by the stranger, then reeling from the force of instant clarity, he fell backward into the taut canvas fabric. As if by some intervention of a magical, mystical 'Director of the Universe,' he instantly knew what he must do. His decision about his future was as clear as if it were blinking like the neon sign above his head.

February 13th

It wasn't easy to put a trip together so quickly and to work out the arrangements with Dr. Nowak about the job. Poised as he was to accept the move to Washington and finally move ahead with his life after Kate, he was handed the mysterious envelope, and everything changed.

Matt hadn't taken a day off from work during the three years he was with the company. In spite of the urging of his boss and his co-workers to take some time off, relax, live a little, he chose to work and his vacation time had built up to a considerable amount of days. He was entitled to use it whenever he wished, as long as it didn't jeopardize the department's schedule. Matt walked into the lab on Monday morning and headed straight down the hall to Dr. Nowak's office. He saw several heads turn as they watched his progress, but never stopped to even acknowledge their morning waves.

If the envelope was from Kate, why would she tell him to go to Washington? Maybe she sensed he would forfeit his career to stay and search for her. She seemed to be telling him to go and move on. By the same account, if it were from her, that was proof she existed, and she cared about him. He must follow that lead. *Shouldn't I? If it wasn't from her, who else would have sent it?* Only a handful of colleagues at Marsh knew about the job offer. Why would any of them question his acceptance of the offer or even try to influence his decision?

Certainly not Phil. Phil would be more inclined to bid him hurry off to old London town if he knew that was a choice, rather than encourage him to grab the plum job. No, it only made sense it was from Kate. Which meant his decision to look for her was the correct one. If she cared enough about him to worry about his future, maybe there was some hope for their relationship after all. It didn't explain why she left him, but he loved her enough to want to marry her. To be able to put her behind him, he needed an explanation. Meeting her was one of the most important things in his life, but losing her was one of the worst. At least he deserved an answer. He was willing to give her up if that is what she truly wanted, but he needed to hear it from her.

Dr. Nowak looked up when Matt tapped on the open door. "Hi Matt, come on in. I was going to catch up with you this morning. We need to talk." Matt had spent the weekend going round and round in his head between the job and Kate, the job and Kate. Somewhere an answer came to him slowly. Maybe if he played it right and with a little luck, he wouldn't have to surrender the job opportunity and could buy some time to look for Kate. He slowly outlined his proposition to Dr. Nowak. With his approval, Matt could take a few weeks of his built-up vacation, follow whatever leads he could find in London and put off reporting to his new job until he returned. They owed him the time, and there was nothing to lose by asking. He certainly had everything to gain if they agreed.

There would be no need to explain to Dr. Nowak about Kate or explain to anyone why he wanted time off. His story was simple. He'd been working without stop for years and could use a break to get his move in order, find a new place to live in Washington and spend some time with friends here before he left. The whole office knew he was under a lot of strain. Dr. Nowak sat still, hands clasped behind his head, listening to Matt's request.

"Yes, I know how much time you have," Dr. Nowak said, leaning back in his creaky old leather chair. "However, we do encourage our employees to use it regularly, keeps you guys from burning out. I'm not sure this is a good time to do it, you know. The Washington branch has had some early success with some of their projects, and there's been a lot of pressure from the government to keep the process moving. They need you there soon. I don't know how they will feel about a delay of several weeks. You know how funding works, Matt. I don't have to remind you we are always walking on thin ice."

"I know," Matt said, clasping his hands in front of him, looking like a man pleading for his life. He felt exhausted from the battle he fought all weekend yet more alive than he had in months. Dr. Nowak honestly liked Matt, and although he hated losing him to Washington, he wanted him to take the job, and the thought of Phil getting the nod if Matt turned it down made his stomach hurt.

"Look, Matt, against my better judgment I will check it out for you."

"Thanks, thanks a lot. I owe you one." A slight smile eased the grim line of his mouth. Matt was optimistic. Since he received the envelope, he just knew it down to his toes; maybe, just maybe, life was going his way for a change.

It didn't take long for Dr. Nowak to get an answer. As he guessed, the Washington office wasn't happy about the delay, but he fudged a little on the dates he could release Matt pending the conclusion of his current assignment. Not wanting to tell them Matt would be using several weeks for vacation, Jeff lied about his projects not being fully complete as of yet and stretched the truth that given a bit more time, the results would prove more valuable. What a waste of money it would be, he told them, if Matt was unable to finish or thoroughly document this exciting project and his results. The guys in Washington agreed to let Matt have one month before he must report to Washington instead of the expected one week.

Matt was finally free to look for Kate and not jeopardize the satisfying career he worked so hard to achieve. He knew he owed Dr. Nowak a great debt and he heartily promised he would put himself into the remaining week in the lab with great diligence and make sure his entire project was completed. The only thing left was to get a ticket to London. Matt's headaches had nearly disappeared.

Walking down the collapsible skyway off the plane, Matt could hear a din coming from up ahead. It was a long flight, and his legs were stiff from sitting in the cramped space. The tunnel ended in the vast canopy that was London's Heathrow Airport. The noise was nearly deafening, people were yelling, babies were crying, and voices on loudspeakers made continuous security announcements and warnings. Large screens flashed flight departures and delays.

He stood off to the side, trying to get his bearings. The line for customs went pretty fast, and he was finally free to move toward London. Where was he supposed to go from here? *At least the signs are in English,* he assured himself, relieved since he never did have a head for other languages. Amid the crowd, a young man off to Matt's right held up a sign. Matt turned to see his name on the card. *Sergeant York's cousin holds no family resemblance,* he decided immediately. As Sergeant York was rather portly, dark and of shorter stature, this sandy-haired young man was all arms and legs with no meat on his bones.

Striding in the direction of the sign, Matt held out his hand to the rather cold looking character. *Typical English mannerisms; stiff, formal.* He couldn't have been more wrong about Jeremy York.

Jeremy grabbed the extended hand with both of his and gave Matt a warm smile which split his ruddy face from ear to ear. "You must be Matt, how nice to meet you. Welcome to London."

"Yes, thanks, and it's great to be here." Matt smiled and tried to hide his surprise. "God, you sure don't look like your cousin, though. I would never have recognized you without the sign. Your cousin told me you were tall, but geez, what are you? About six-three?"

"Six-five to be exact," Jeremy's lopsided grin answered. "From my mother's side." The two men let the other arrivals jostle them about until a path cleared and they could head for the stairs. "Bring any other luggage with you," Jeremy asked.

"Yes, one larger bag. I couldn't fit all my stuff in the smaller carry-on. Wasn't sure what type of clothes I would need over here for this time of year."

Jeremy nodded. "Our weather can change by the minute, but as long as you brought a mackintosh, a jumper, and an umbrella, you'll get by."

"A Mackintosh, a jumper?" Matt raised an eyebrow at him.

Laughing, Jeremy said, "Yeah a raincoat and a sweater to you."

"Gotcha."

"Oh, and a taste for warm beer," Jeremy added.

"Your cousin said you were from the States, but you seem to have picked up some local color," Matt said.

"Well, yes, I guess after two years here, you do alter your vocabulary. You know the old saying, 'when in Rome.'"

"Right," Matt repeated. "'When in Rome.'"

As soon as his decision was made to go to London, Matt remembered Detective Orliss's comments about his English wife. He contacted him and asked if he could help him out. Detective Orliss was surprised to hear from Matt and explained his wife was born in the U.S., and as far as he knew there wasn't much family left in Great Britain. "However," he added, "You remember Sergeant York, don't you?"

"Of course."

"Well Brian's cousin lives in London, maybe he would be able to help." Hanging up the phone, Detective Orliss chuckled to himself, "well there goes my friendship with Brian. Wait until he finds out I dumped Errington back in his lap again." The Sergeant and the Detective had both come to the conclusion the guy was a little wacky. Although they did feel sorry for him, they knew there wasn't anything they could do for the guy.

Sergeant York, however, wasn't upset when Matt called him and explained his decision to look for Kate. He knew the guy was wasting his time but thought it was pretty sad the man needed to chase ghosts, and he offered to contact his cousin in London for him. The police had long since decided Matt wasn't dangerous, just lonely, so if Matt wanted to go running across the ocean on a wild goose chase, hey, more power to him. He knew Jeremy would take care of him. York called his cousin, briefly explained Matt needed a hand and thanked Jeremy for his trouble. "Poor guy," Sergeant York mumbled again as he looked at the pictures on his desk. He was glad he had a nice normal family to go home to. He and his wife had their share of problems, but at least she was real.

Riding down the escalator with Jeremy to the lower level, Matt was able to take in the size of the airport. "Wow, the place is old and enormous."

"It's the busiest airport in the world," Jeremy answered. "People from all over the world walk through here every day. It was bombed during the German's Blitzkrieg in World War II. The Germans bombed London for nearly eight months and devastated the area between St. Paul's Cathedral and the Guildhall. Several historic churches were damaged as well as Buckingham Palace and Westminster Abbey. But the British rebuilt their jewels, and since then, this airport has become the hub of Europe and has had several additions over the last sixty-six years."

It was a new experience for Matt, and he felt alive to be amid such chaos. He appreciated Jeremy's anecdotes and was impressed by the airport's history. People dressed in a myriad of styles representative of numerous countries and cultures teemed around the main mall. Even if nothing came of his search, he was glad he'd come. Life flowed through his veins once more.

The turntable creaked and groaned as luggage came bumping along its path. Matt's was a plain black suitcase, and more than once he leaped forward to claim a bag which didn't turn out to be his. He noted how several people tied bright ribbons or even silly stuffed toys to their bags. Matt thought the idea goofy, but eventually as one black bag after another went by, he saw the sense of it. It took longer than they thought, but as the number of bags eventually dwindled, he was finally able to spot his and grab it before it could make another journey around the loop, then they headed out toward the car park.

"I'm sorry if I'm taking up your day," Matt said, "I'm sure I can find my way around if you need to get back to work."

"Nope, not a problem. I have a pretty good boss who is flexible. I told him I was taking a late lunch and he won't mind if I'm a little late getting back."

"How far is it to the hotel?"

"Maybe twenty minutes or so. I don't mind Matt, honestly, gets me out of the office for a spell."

"Your cousin said you were with a car company."

"I do marketing for an auto company here in the London office. And you? Brian mentioned you have a big job in a lab doing secret government work. Creating super wonder drugs, are you?"

Matt laughed for the first time in months. "Not a big job, I'm just another small cog in a big company and my work is all for good, but I just finished something that has great potential. When I get back, I'm heading to a new position in Washington and hope to take it a lot further."

The drive from the airport was like a trip through his old geography book. The names of the places they passed spoke of history and culture, royalty and intrigue and the inevitable wars and transformations that centuries of civilization produced. The Tower of London; Big Ben; the Royal Gardens of Green Park; Piccadilly Center; places and landmarks he grew up reading about but never thought he would see. As they neared the hotel in west London, they passed the distinguished homes and shops of Hyde Parke. Matt was amazed to be there in one of the oldest cities in Europe, riding around on the wrong side of the street.

"How long did it take to get used to driving like this?" Matt asked.

"Not too long, if I wanted to live."

"No kidding, I find myself looking the wrong way each corner you come to. Probably would have been killed by now if you weren't driving."

"Yeah, lots of tourists get hurt that way. It does take some getting used to." Matt was enjoying the drive completely trusting Jeremy's maneuvering of the British roads, almost wishing the ride would go on and on when Jeremy pulled up in front of a stately old brick building. A large burgundy canopy extended right over the sidewalk out to the edge of the street. Two doormen in crisp blue uniforms framed the swinging glass doors.

"Will you need anything else?" Jeremy asked.

"No, this is great. I appreciate your time and getting me here safely. I'll be okay from here."

"Well, here is my business card in case you need me for anything. I don't live in London; I have a small place near Kent, Southend-on-the-Sea. Healthier for my family away from the city."

"Your cousin said you had kids."

"Yep, two with maybe a third one on the way, we're not sure yet."

"Well thanks again for the ride and the tour, I'll give you a call in a couple of days, let you know how I'm doing."

"Oh yeah, Brian told me a little about your search, your girlfriend went missing or some such thing, right?"

"Yeah, 'some such thing' is a good way to put it," Matt said. "I'll let you know what I find out."

"Right, well then here's your suitcase," Jeremy popped open the boot of his car, "I'll be off."

"Cheerio," Matt wanted to say but held it back. He didn't want to seem flippant to this nice young man. Jeremy folded his long frame back into the small car and headed out into the traffic. Matt nodded goodbye, then turned to let the doormen eagerly do their job. The hotel of the postcard stood before him in all of its brick and granite majesty.

Entering the Royal Arms Hotel was like entering another world. Class, that's the first word which came to mind. *Class and money.* The room gleamed. From the twenty-two glistening chandeliers overhead to the polished black and gray marble floor. Brass lamps with little black shades sat on dark mahogany tables scattered around the cavernous lobby adding focal points as they illuminated a wide selection of seating arrangements. High backed chairs in plush fabrics cuddled up to curved backed couches with deeply etched brocades. Small groups of people were seated in two's and three's, some sipping what appeared to be tea from white porcelain teacups. Three nuns dressed in their identical black habits, sat huddled together with their knees almost touching, giggling together like school girls. Remembering the nuns who had terrified him in his youth, Matt smiled at the sight. *Guess they are human, after all.*

The registration desk was at the far end, and Matt headed in that direction winding his way around the center of the room where an enormous vase of fresh flowers dominated the view. It sat regally on top of what could have been King Arthur's roundtable. It was massive, and he felt Lilliputian in its presence. This was the hotel on the postcard he found in his book at home. He hadn't known from the picture what it would be like inside, but he was awed, and in spite of the cost, he was glad of his decision to stay there.

At the registration desk, Matt waited behind a well-dressed elderly couple who were retrieving their mail and a suited businessman who was checking out. He approached the high, dark wood counter when it was his turn.

"Yes, may I help you, sir," was the brusque request from the little man just barely visible behind the gleaming marbled top.

"I am Matt Errington; I have a reservation." Matt fought the urge to peer over the top of the ledge to see the rest of the man.

"Very good sir, if you will just wait one moment."

"Thank you," responded Matt crisply as well. Conscious of his pronunciation of every syllable, he didn't want this guy to label him an unpolished American.

The little guy with rosy cheeks, like a beardless Santa, came out of the back room and with arms stretched nearly over his head, turned the registration book, which sat on a swiveling base, toward Matt. Handing him a gold pen, he said, "Would you please sign here. Your reservation is in order, and you should be in your room in no time, sir." When he turned the book back around, the clerk handed Matt a large brass key.

Matt was surprised by its size and weight. "In the states, they use plastic access cards instead of keys for hotel rooms," he remarked to the clerk.

"Yes sir, so I have heard," Santa's bushy eyebrow made an inverted check mark over his eye. It was clear from his tone; plastic would not be used in his hotel any time soon. "Do you have luggage, sir? I would be happy to call a bellhop for you."

"No, that's okay, I can manage these myself," Matt held up his suitcase in one hand and smaller bag in the other for confirmation.

"As you wish sir. The lifts are to your right. Your room is on the seventh floor, number 782. If there is anything further you require, please do not hesitate to contact this desk. We are here twenty-four hours a day to serve your needs. Will you require anything else at this time, sir?"

"No, thanks, ah, wait, on second thought …"

"Yes, sir?" Santa was practically standing at attention, stretching himself to his tallest height.

"I would like to find out some information about this hotel."

"Of course, sir," Santa beamed, seeming to grow another inch. "We are so proud of our fine establishment."

"Well, yes, I can see that, but I'm interested in locating someone who either lived here or stayed here for a time."

"I see," the clerk's eyes flickered with a barely perceptible twitch. "We have a strict policy of privacy, Mr. Errington. I am not sure how much information we will be able to provide to you."

Matt had been afraid of that but pushed on anyway. "Is there a possibility I can make an appointment with the hotel manager?"

Santa blinked and said, "We will have to wait until tomorrow to see. Mr. Gillian, our General Manager, is away this afternoon, but I will pass on your request when he returns. Will that be satisfactory, sir?"

"Yes, that's fine. Please let me know what he says. It's vital to me. It could be a matter of life and death." He didn't want to sound melodramatic, but if he didn't get some answers, his whole trip was in vain.

"Very good, sir. I will leave a note for you in the box. Good day sir."

"Good day," Matt nodded, heading toward the lifts and a possible short nap before dinner.

Tea time was nearly over by the time Matt arrived at the hotel, but a note on his bed said the kitchen was available for light meals twenty-four hours a day.

Famished, he looked around his room done up in various creams and shades of blue, with burgundy sashes at the windows. It was beautifully laid out, and he inwardly noted what a stark contrast it was to his rather drab apartment. The room was not large, but each piece of furniture was polished to its' mahogany finest. The water closet was downright tiny, he could hardly turn around in it, but Jeremy briefly told him how the hotel converted most of the rooms by carving out a space for private bathing for its guests. Originally, there were larger community washrooms on each floor. *That would have sucked having to run down the hall to use the john at night.* Small or not, he was happy for the privacy.

There was a menu tucked into a large black leather folder on the desk; the Royal Arms emblem pressed into its cover in gold. He called the main desk and was transferred to someone in the dining room who quickly took his order. He didn't care what they served as long as it was fast. He hadn't eaten much on the plane because his stomach felt queasy going over the ocean. There was some turbulence, and he didn't want to be sick even though he took the Dramamine that Sergeant York suggested. But now he was starved. The kitchen promised his order would be sent up within twenty minutes. Just enough time for a hot shower and to unpack his bags. He hoped to get a short nap after he ate then he wanted to take a stroll downtown, maybe find a nice restaurant for dinner. There was so much to see and do in London. No sense staying cooped up in a room. There was nothing he could do to find Kate's mother until tomorrow and his meeting with the manager, so he might as well enjoy himself tonight.

The water was hot even if the spray was weaker than he was used to. Matt laid his toiletries out on the narrow sink edge. He barely had enough time to finish shaving before a slight tap at the door announced his meal's arrival. Within minutes Matt finished the sandwich, a crisp salad, and a piece of cheesecake, all served on delicate china and delivered to his room on a heavy silver tray. He washed it down with bottled water and immediately felt better than he had all day. Matt's eyes were heavy, and finally, as he relaxed in his hotel room with a bit of food under his belt, he lay back on the big poster bed with its satin cover and fell instantly asleep.

Chapter Eight

Slamming doors, the sounds of running water, and water pipes that rattled, hissed, and moaned, heralded morning in the old building. Matt opened his eyes and couldn't believe he slept right through the evening and the entire night. He hadn't even undressed. *Lord, I must have been more tired than I thought, or maybe it's just the jet lag I've always heard of.*

Waking as he did in the strange hotel room with unusual noises coming at him from all the walls, Matt took a few minutes to clear his head and get his bearings. He'd had a great sleep and wonderful dreams, strange and compelling but welcoming. A gentle wind blew across a patchwork field of colored grasses, muted blue and maroon hills scampered over to the horizon and a voice, melodic, warm and beckoning left him calm and full of anticipation. He couldn't remember many of the details, but the feelings they left him with were peaceful, serene like he was in the right place at the right time, and all was as it should be. *Well damn, that sounds corny. But okay, my subconscious must be telling me it's okay to screw with my future, travel halfway around the world chasing a shadow of a shadow. So, it's good to know I have the full support of my mind.*

Matt jumped out of bed, hungry again, and couldn't wait to get downstairs. When the doors of the brass lined lift slid silently open, he nodded a curt good morning to the young couple holding hands who entered before him. Breakfast in the dining room just off the massive lobby was more relaxed than Matt expected, considering the hotel's reserved opulence. The white tablecloths he glimpsed the night before had been removed from all of the tables, and delectable aromas assailed him before he even reached the entrance. Several waitresses in crisp linen uniforms bustled about the well-stocked sideboards where the food was served.

The maître d escorted him to a table along the wall and left Matt with instructions to help himself to the buffet. By now, Matt was practically drooling with anticipation and quickly piled his plate high. Fried 'eggy bread' as they called French toast, muffins, different kinds of eggs, sausage, bacon, and toward the end of the table, he spotted an unfamiliar seafood, cockle fish. *Like something out of a nursery rhyme,* he thought. Well, like Jeremy said, '*when in Rome*', and he added some to his plate. He grabbed a large glass of orange juice and headed back to his table. The price of the hotel was going to take a bite out of his savings he knew, but breakfast was included, and he certainly couldn't complain about the food. A steaming pot of coffee was waiting for his return.

One plate left him completely satisfied, but there were sweets and fruits further down the line, and he didn't want to miss a thing. He was heading back in that direction when a stately, white-haired gentleman with his hands clasped behind his back, headed right toward him.

"Good morning sir," the man said, putting out his hand to Matt. "Our clerk pointed you out to me; you are Mr. Errington?"

"Yes, good morning," Matt took the man's hand in his. "But please, call me Matt."

"As you wish Matt, I am Roger Gillian, the house manager. I was informed you asked to see me."

"Oh, yes, great," Matt beamed his surprise. "I am so glad you have time to talk to me. I was going to finish eating and then go check at the desk to see if you had gotten my message."

"Of course, Mr. Errington, I am happy to speak to any of our guests. It only depends upon which topic you wish to discuss, to determine exactly how much service I may be to you."

Matt nodded in the direction of his table and asked Roger Gillian to join him.

"I have a few minutes," Roger bent imperceptibly, allowing Matt to precede him to the table.

When seated, Matt could hardly contain his questions and nearly burst out with the purpose of his visit to London. But taking the lead from the more reserved, proper Mr. Gillian he felt he should make some small talk before he got into the gist of his story.

"You have a stunning hotel, Mr. Gillian," Matt told him, glancing around for effect. "I am so impressed. Have you been with the Royal Arms for a long time?"

"Thank you for your kind words. I have been here nearly thirty years," Mr. Gillian proudly replied. "We at the Royal Arms are dedicated to maintaining a proper environment for our guests. Did you find your first night satisfactory?"

"Oh, absolutely. I intended to take a short nap yesterday afternoon and then stroll around the city a bit later in the evening, but I never woke up until this morning. The bed was great."

"Well, I'm certainly glad you had a restful sleep. These old buildings can be noisy with creaking and groaning going on all the time. Most of our guests like the ambiance and very few ever complain, but it is always nice to hear our talking walls did not disturb your sleep."

"No problem on that account," Matt reassured his host. Glancing at his pocket watch, Mr. Gillian remarked, "I apologize, Matt, but I am required to attend a meeting shortly. Perhaps we could move on to why you asked to see me. Mr. James, our clerk, informed me you hoped to obtain some information about former guests at the Royal Arms, is that correct?"

"Yes," Matt said. His mind was going a mile a minute. He wasn't sure how to get around the privacy issue, but he had to try.

Matt wanted to pull out the postcard from his pocket and give it to the man, explain the whole thing with Kate leaving, and this being his only chance to find a link to her, but he wasn't at all sure the proper Mr. Gillian would be sympathetic to his story and help him out. Instead, he asked innocently, "Do you keep records of past guests, going back several months, maybe even years."

"Yes, we do. They are kept in our vault. Is there someone, in particular, you are inquiring about?" On the flight over the Atlantic, Matt concocted a story he could use if he got to this point, something more plausible than just looking for the mother of a ghost of a girlfriend. He needed a convincing story to sway the privacy matter in his favor. "Yes, I work for a medical laboratory in the States. We do a great deal of research seeking cures for a variety of diseases."

"Ah," Roger said nodding, "a most noble endeavor to be sure."

"Well," Matt said going on, sensing encouragement, and tweaking his story a bit, "my company sent me here to track down some former test subjects. They were part of a research project with some new drugs for diabetes. We would like to do some follow up with them but have unfortunately lost a few addresses and have been unable to contact them."

"I see," said Roger, looking down at his hands. "And you think they may have been guests at the Royal Arms at some time in the past."

"Yes, yes I do," Matt said, pleased it was going so well.

Lying was not his forté, but he found it rolled off his tongue better than he hoped. All across the ocean, he practiced the few lines in his head, and it seemed to be paying off.

"Matt, our guest's privacy is of the utmost importance; however, if you give me the names of the individuals you wish to locate and the dates they were here, perhaps I may be able to help you since it is for science, and perhaps, even their health. There are no guarantees, however, but I will see what I can do."

"Um, yeah, I do have the name of one person who stayed at this hotel, but I have no idea when she was here," he answered.

"I see."

Unease ran through Matt's body, churning the breakfast he had just eaten.

"Hmmm. Without a timeframe, it may be a bit more difficult. Perhaps you can tell me why you believe this particular test subject was a guest here at the Royal Arms at all. Maybe we can begin with that."

Matt hesitated; maybe he should bring out the postcard and see what his host would make of it. But with no names for either the addressee or the sender, it would prove nothing.

Putting on his best poker face, he decided to go with another lie. Matt looked Roger in the eyes and said without a blink, "A member of our staff received a postcard from one of these subjects, from this hotel. The guest's name was Mrs. Champion."

For a split second, the placid demeanor on Roger Gillian's face drastically changed. With a barely noticeable shake of his head, he quickly regained his composure and stared at Matt as if he misheard him.

Matt caught what appeared to be a flash of recognition that verged on panic and was startled by the intense look he was receiving as if Roger was trying to peer right through him.

Roger Gillian opened his mouth to speak, thought better of it and closed it again with a little pop, then completely caught Matt off guard when he said, "Are you referring to Elizabeth Champion?"

SHE EXISTS! Lights exploded in Matt's head nearly springing him from his seat as that knowledge also confirmed that Kate, must indeed, also exist. "Yes, that's her." Up to this point, Matt could only hope Kate, and her mother had the same last name. "Elizabeth Champion. Do you remember her staying here?"

There was still something odd about the way Roger was looking at him, but Matt shook it off in his eagerness to learn more about Kate's mother.

Roger took a long, deep breath before letting it out slowly, still staring through Matt. Roger wondered what the young man was looking for. The police had already cleared the hotel of any wrongdoing. Was he only looking for some former clients? Nothing Roger knew or had heard about Elizabeth Champion suggested she was diabetic or suffered any other health ailments. In spite of his misgivings about discussing the matter, Roger realized there was nothing to hide. The death was ruled accidental, and although the gentleman from the U.S. attempted to eliminate all of the details, bits of information about the nasty accident did appear in the smaller local papers. He would not be breaching any hotel confidentiality rule by giving Matt information about her.

"I am sorry you have traveled all the way to London to find this woman," Roger began, "but I cannot give you any forwarding address which will be of any help to you." Disappointment raced through Matt's veins like cold water. Without her mother to help him, Matt would have no further clues to Kate's whereabouts.

"Are you absolutely certain, you remembered the name, are you sure there is no information you can provide to help me find her?"

"Mr. Errington, I can tell you where Mrs. Champion is, that is not the problem. But knowing her location will not help you with your study." At first excited the information was available then confused why it would not be useful, Matt could only stare at the man, his eyes begging an explanation.

"I am sorry to be the one to tell you, but Mrs. Champion was found drowned in the hotel pool several months ago. She is deceased, Mr. Errington."

The blood drained from Matt's head, and his vision wavered. "What? Are you certain we are talking about the same person?" His heart skipped several beats and threatened to stop altogether. He couldn't breathe. *All this way for nothing. How will I ever find Kate now? This is too cruel, one second, she exists, and in a blink of the eye she's gone.* Matt was at a loss of what to do now. His only shred of hope at finding Kate died with her mother.

Chapter Nine

Six months earlier.

Lilly finished taping up the last box and slid it with her foot across the floor to join the others by the wall. Her twin sister walked into the room with several photographs in her hand just as the door opened and Ben Madison popped his head in.

"You girls ready, we should have been out of here ten minutes ago. Don't want to drag this out. That nosy little super is always driving around. I haven't spotted anyone else, but let's get a move on. You checked everything out?"

The girls looked at each other. "Yes," Kate nodded, "it's all back to normal. I compared the whole place to the pictures we took before I moved in. We put it back correctly."

"Well, make sure," Ben, said, "Don't want you to leave anything personal behind."

"I've already wiped the place down," Lilly said, "it's clean of Kate's prints."

The sisters picked up the rest of the boxes and headed for the door. Taking a quick peek outside, Ben motioned them to follow and close up the place behind them. "I feel bad about doing this," Kate said, as she walked down the steps, quickly wiping away a rebellious tear threatening to blur her vision. "He is a great guy and doesn't deserve this."

"Yeah, yeah, I know," Lilly answered. "Don't go getting mopey again. You knew this was a difficult assignment, and you had to be out of here soon. It was necessary to cut it off with Matt one of these days anyway; we just needed to cut the job a little shorter than we expected. Ben wouldn't have pulled you out today, but since Matt got those hockey tickets, he didn't have a choice. You would have been seen by a lot of people at the game, and the dome is televised. We can't take the chance their cameras might pick you up in the crowd, or you could be seen on TV, there would be a record of you. It's much harder for you to disappear if there is evidence of you on tape. Just in case Matt goes looking for you. Police could check on seat tickets, people around you would swear you were there. They'd be able to describe you.

"It was different with the neighbors and people around here. No one has paid any attention to you, that's how people are, but the hockey game would have been a different story. You know that. Besides we've talked about this *many* times, it's just a job. National security and all that stuff … have to save the world you know."

"Yeah, right." Kate could barely answer. Her mind was on the past morning, and the feel of Matt's arms around her.

"Do you think he might look for me?" she asked, a bit of hope brightening her heart. "Just once I would like to hang onto some normalcy in my life. You know, be the person a man like Matt wanted to come home to and live a normal life."

"Yeah, you will someday. If it's meant to be, you will find someone like Matt again. I believe that." Lilly said, giving her sister a quick hug.

"It's hard to explain, but from the day I met him, I could tell Matt was perfect for me. He's been through a lot. I didn't have to pretend much. It was easy to try and make him happy. Make him believe he deserved to be happy. He has horrible baggage he carries with him. Pain he doesn't deserve. It's so sad I have to hurt him like this, and he'll never know why … or what happened."

"You know that's Ben's way. He doesn't like loose ends, and Matt knowing who you are would just cause problems, and—"

"Got it all?" Ben interrupted.

"Yes."

"Okay, then lock it up and let's move."

"Done," Lilly said, throwing a warning look at Kate. "You'll be okay, I promise." Ben started the van. They had learned all they could from Matt. It was time to end the assignment.

Kate Champion and her sister Lilly had worked with Ben Madison and the CIA for more than eight years. They were recruited right out of high school. Both girls were national honor students and graduated at the top of their class, earning their highest awards in science and math. When Ben first approached them with the prospect of working for the government, neither girl took him seriously, but eventually, they were convinced enough to sit down and listen to him with open minds.

Ben had been with the agency for nearly twenty-seven years and was one of their main recruiters. He drafted over eighty government employees. His job was to identify potential employees from every region of the country to work in over twenty-two different departments of the government. If he took a personal interest in the employees, as he did with Kate and Lilly, he often acted as their handler if they proved worthy. The girls caught Ben's attention as he reviewed student records from across the U.S. They had exceptional scholastic abilities and well-rounded backgrounds. Both girls were athletic and excelled in sports. They shared a love of the arts and were members of their school's drama group, even taking the lead roles in several stage presentations. Kate, with Lilly as her campaign manager, was elected class president. Lilly was class valedictorian.

Since childhood, the two were inseparable and often made a formidable team, whether it was in sports, politics or playing pranks on friends and family. The latter was always a great source of amusement to them due to their identical features. Only their mother could distinguish which one was which if they chose to deliberately confuse people.

Their father, however, was never sure which little blond angel was wrapping him around her tiny finger. As young as five or six years old, they learned what being identical could do for them. Parents, teachers, friends, and neighbors all became pawns in their games of fun. It didn't take them long to discover they could raise all sorts of havoc and no one was sure whom to blame. The poor parents realized the only way to control their exuberant offspring was to punish both regardless of the culprit.

When Ben approached the twins, he outlined for them successful careers with the U.S. Government if they were able to maintain their high academic standards throughout college, and achieve stringent goals within a curriculum, which would be directed by Ben himself.

The choice of the finest universities in the country was open to them, paid for of course, by government scholarships. The girls and their parents met several times with Ben before they were all comfortable with the concept. A contract was drawn up explained all expenses would be paid for their entire college experience. In exchange, upon graduation, they would work for the U.S. State Department, for not less than ten years, at assignments of the government's choosing, wherever they were needed.

Having a guaranteed job as soon as they graduated didn't seem to be a bad thing to the twins or their parents. However, the parents did have some concerns about where they may be posted, but Ben assured them the careers he had in mind for the girls would pose them no danger.

Ben's emphasis was on national security and the contribution the girls could make to their country's welfare. As he explained it, "the cold war was dead." He was not recruiting agents for cloak and dagger operations. To be selectively chosen and groomed as one of the best and brightest in the country, to help staff some of the highest departments of the nation's capital were honors not to be taken lightly. It was also good business for the country. By the time he was through with the sales pitch, they practically stood up and saluted him. The way he told it; the government was pleading for their support. The patriotic family could hardly refuse. Ben was a good salesman when he was inspired. And for the girls, he had intriguing ideas on how he could use identical twins in the field to his advantage.

The twins excitedly chose the University of Michigan and settled into college life, embarking on four years of a grueling test of their abilities. In spite of the unusually varied program, Ben designed for them, including science, psychology, languages, human cultures, law, and the arts, the girls did Ben and their parents proud. They lived up to every expectation. As graduation drew closer, Ben's visits grew to be more often.

"Checking up on your investments?" the girls chided him, although by this time the trio had bonded to a unique closeness.

Ben was like family to them. He guided, mentored, pushed, encouraged, threatened, and cajoled them. He celebrated their successes along the way and picked them up when they needed encouragement. In May, shortly before their graduation with honors, their father suffered a massive heart attack and was dead before he reached the floor.

Elizabeth Champion was pragmatic enough to realize, at least, the girl's futures were secure. However, their long-awaited graduation was diminished by their father's absence.

In the following weeks, Ben made more frequent visits to see them. They were allowed a brief vacation spent at home before the girls were asked to report to Langley Air Base in Virginia for a thorough training in government protocol and the more serious business of espionage.

Chapter Ten

Mr. Gillian was correct in his assumption. The police had indeed cleared the hotel of any wrongdoing in Elizabeth Champion's death. It was still a mystery why the CIA was involved, but Roger was deeply grateful for Ben Madison's intervention which prevented most of the information from reaching the press about the accident, much to the hotel's relief.

"As was her habit for several nights in a row," Roger Gilliam continued his story to Matt, "Mrs. Champion desired a late-night swim. Although the pool was officially closed, the doors were seldom locked, and she would not have difficulty accessing the area. Mrs. Champion appeared to be an excellent swimmer, and because she enjoyed her quiet time in a tranquil pool, the staff did not interrupt her."

Mr. Gillian was careful not to give away any personal information but saw no harm in sharing limited details of the accident with Matt.

"The exact method of how she drowned was never identified," he continued. "The police theorized she developed swimmer's cramps or hit her head on the diving board. Both events were possible, and there was a rather nasty red mark on the side of her head, which did match the end of the board. Perhaps she misjudged her position, came up under the board and was knocked out by the impact. Without someone to help her, she must have drowned immediately."

Halfway through his story, Roger halted, took out a fine linen handkerchief and wiped his eyes. "Her sister-in-law was staying here with her. It was she who discovered the poor woman. After a preliminary investigation by the local police, the sister-in-law made arrangements for Elizabeth to be sent back to the states for burial. That is all we know, and I am deeply sorry to complicate your study with such a sad tale, but there you have it."

Matt was reeling with the information about Elizabeth's death and the fear he had reached a dead end to his search when a new lead struck him. "I apologize, Mr. Gillian for reviving a bad memory for you, but if you don't mind just one more question. Do you have any information about Mrs. Champion's sister-in-law? She wasn't listed in Mrs. Champion's medical records, and perhaps she could provide some useful information."

"As far as I remember, the woman lived in a small rural village in western Wales and left for her home immediately. I can have the clerk look up her name for you if you wish, although I doubt there is any further information or forwarding address. I would suggest you check with the local police. They probably kept some records on her. Mrs. Champion's death is a blemish on the history and reputation of the Royal Arms Hotel, and although it was an accident, the fact it happened in this beloved establishment is still rather upsetting."

Matt nodded his understanding, and Mr. Gillian excused himself with apparent relief the discussion was over. The mere memory of the event and the thought of any investigation disturbing the atmosphere of his hotel or his other guests had nearly brought Roger Gillian to coughing spasms. Simply recalling the whole affair had given him heartburn, and Mr. Gillian could barely contain his impatience to end the conversation. He was thoroughly relieved when Matt finally ceased his questioning and accepted Roger's suggestion to take his interest to London's police department instead.

Without any further information from the hotel, Matt was facing certain defeat unless the aunt could be found. With no forwarding address, he would not be able to find out where she directed Elizabeth's body for burial. Perhaps since her body was returned to the States, the police might have the information he needed. It seemed his day's agenda was ordained.

The London streets were as busy as downtown New York City at midday. The air was misty, but not cold, as the crowds pushed and surged in both directions. The entire scene flowed with a surreal but electric quality. There was little space on the sidewalk to keep one's footing, and if a person found himself too close to an edge, it was difficult to keep his balance and could easily tumble into the street. Trams, bicycles, the famous red buses, and a variety of small vehicles—Matt thought resembled props from a Mr. Bean comedy—honked noisily and roared past. Once or twice, Matt discovered if he hesitated at all, he would almost be lifted off his feet and carried along with the crowd.

It was fortunate he was not more than five blocks from the police station, and Mr. Gillian's directions were quite precise. If he was a little less vigilant in watching for his exit from the crowded sidewalk, he would have been swept many blocks further and would have lost his way. It was somewhat intoxicating to be jostled along with the crowd in a strange city, more so because it was not a familiar experience or one he would have thought he would enjoy. *But I guess, 'when in Rome,'* he thought again, mimicking Jeremy York's cliché.

The London Police Station seemed ancient. The building appeared to have stood its ground for centuries with high granite steps that rose up the front with watchful lions standing guard on each side of the doors. Officers were coming and going, up and down the stairs, two and three at a time. *It must be the changing of the guard,* Matt mused, watching the pattern of activity. Inside, the building smelled old. The yellowed ceiling held ten or twelve little fans circling slowly like buzzards over their dying meal. A staircase went up one side of the entranceway, disappearing into the ten stories above his head. Locating the main desk, Matt started across the foyer toward his goal.

Three detectives were standing by the desk, their hats, coats, and umbrellas already in their hands, apparently, they were on their way out. One of the men, younger than the others, looked up and made eye contact with Matt as he made his way in their direction. His companions stopped their conversation only long enough to assess the visitor, determine he wasn't someone they needed to pay much attention to and started toward the door. The younger man, however, had the look of an eager youth. Anxious to be of service, he stepped around his departing colleagues and waited for Matt to approach. "May I help you, sir?"

"Thanks, I'd appreciate that," replied Matt. "I've come from the Royal Arms Hotel seeking information about a woman's death a few months ago. Can you point me in the right direction?"

"I'll try," the young man replied. "Do you know if there is an open investigation about her death?" he asked.

"No, I don't think so, her death was ruled an accident, I think."

"In that case, it should be easy to find what you are looking for. You can take the stairs if you wish, but if you head down the corridor on the left, toward the back of the building, there is a small lift that will take you to the second floor. Find the room down the way, on your right, marked Archives. It is easy to find. The clerk inside should be able to assist you."

"Thanks for the help." Matt shook the young man's hand and hurried on his way down the hall.

Terry Healy watched for a moment to make certain the man was following his directions, and then headed out the front door to catch up with his older companions. They were headed for the Flying Eagles Pub, and he hoped they would save him a seat.

Chapter Eleven

Over the years, not only were Kate and Lilly his protégés but also after the death of her husband, Elizabeth was receptive to occasionally helping Ben and the CIA. She assisted on brief assignments, which called for a more mature participant. While she had none of the specialized training her daughters did, she possessed an intuitiveness about people which Ben recognized. Elizabeth was an accomplished pianist and performed at numerous concerts. With her polished ease and quiet elegance, she was able to fill particular roles within certain settings Ben needed to fill. After word of the accident in London, Ben headed off to London to handle the affair. Ben knew the drowning was no accident.

It was pretty clear what happened. As at all the major hotels throughout the world, Iranian agents worked at the Royal Arms. Rather than use an agent from the London CIA office, who may be recognized, Ben sent Elizabeth to the Royal Arms on a rather benign assignment to listen for word of a growing cell operating in the British Isles. Internet chatter and intelligence reports of terrorist activity had been escalating for several months, and it was obvious something of great importance was buzzing in the air. Large numbers of CIA agents, as well as several other international security teams, flooded most major European cities, all attempting to sniff out the details and find the proverbial smoking gun.

Ben realized in spite of the CIA's precautions and Elizabeth's careful demeanor, something must have given her away and although she should not have been in any danger, for some reason she was targeted for elimination. Although Ben knew it would have the opposite effect, he speculated her death was meant to be a warning to the CIA, Interpol, and other agencies to back off their probing. Her nightly swims provided ample opportunity to take her out with little risk to her attacker. However, although Elizabeth was to be the intended victim, it was her sister-in-law Lauren that met the deadly fate.

On their last night before leaving London, Lauren decided to join Elizabeth in the pool. Elizabeth stepped out of the pool to use the restroom, leaving the pool and her sister-in-law alone. The Iranian waiter peeking through the pool's glass doors saw only one lone swimmer and assumed it to be Elizabeth. Lauren probably never heard the man who hit her broadly on the side of the head with the edge of a heavy silver tray. The injury resembled a blow which could have been caused by the diving board, and the investigation was determined to be an accident by the local coroner. Although Lauren was a fairly good swimmer, unconscious, she never had a chance.

Ben Madison was never one to leave loose ends and efficiently cleaned up all the details. He was able to stop most of the news reports about the accident and head off a police investigation. After a couple of phone calls from the U.S. State Department, the London police were agreeable to leaving the case in Ben's hands for cleanup. Ben and his superiors decided to let the operatives in London, the ones Elizabeth was investigating, believe they had successfully killed Elizabeth Champion, a fact backed up by the coroner's report, the police files and some local newspaper coverage.

It was Elizabeth's death that was reported and not Lauren's. They were similar in height, and general appearance and the hotel staff accepted the women's switched identities, and with no one to present a challenge, the ruse worked. It was a pointless tragedy that her sister-in-law was killed, but Ben and Elizabeth harbored no doubts the numbing blow to the side of Lauren's head had been intended for the girl's mother. Lauren's body was sent to her home in Wales by way of a route through the states.

Elizabeth wanted to help find the killer, but Ben knew it was best to get her out of London and out of danger. With Lauren's passing, her home in Wales would belong to Elizabeth and her daughters. It was a perfect spot to send her. Elizabeth slipped out of the hotel under cover of night, safe from further attacks.

It was no mystery to Ben or the State Department what group had committed this terrible act, but they were unable to pin down the actual perpetrator within the hotel staff. They knew the murderer eventually would be found, but this was one crime they would have to leave alone for the time being. Ben turned over the investigation to some of his allies in London. Their investigation would be conducted quietly and behind the scenes.

As he did with all his recruits, Ben used whatever circumstances he might have at his disposal to shape the individual's character to mesh with his. It was his way and his job. People's lives depended upon it. The twins had proved to be exceptional students, but their hearts were still too soft. Unfortunate as it was, the drowning in London was precisely the kind of tool he needed to strip away the twin's innocence and indoctrinate them further into the agency's philosophies.

Ben also worried if Elizabeth remained a target, he should be more vigilant with her daughters. His gut told him there was a connection between Kate's assignment with the Errington guy in Philadelphia and the attack on Elizabeth. Particularly because about the same time, another agent, Samir Ali Mansoor, had been exposed and killed while undercover in a suspected terrorist cell in Philadelphia. Before his death, Samir was able to send a brief message to Ben, but the meaning was difficult to decipher. *"Imminent air-born attack Errington."* Ben just knew the events were tied. He could feel it in his bones. He didn't know what it was yet, but he was determined to find out.

The CIA had limited information about the terrorist group operating in London, but they shared a similar footprint to a suspected group working with one of Matt Errington's co-workers. That alone set his radar twitching. Just to be safe, he decided to pull Kate out of the relationship and end the assignment.

Thanks to Kate's resourcefulness, the ugly artwork she and Matt purchased had been fitted with a transmitter that worked undetected for several weeks. Conversations Kate and Matt shared gave the department enough information to confirm their suspicions about Matt's colleague, Philip Forester. There was a situation to be investigated. The assignment was nearly ready to conclude, and Ben felt the love affair between Kate and Matt was becoming too real for both parties. He decided it was better to nip the whole thing in the bud. With the timing of the hockey game tickets, he gave the girls the order to evacuate the apartment and perform the standard procedure to wipe it clean.

Matt found the Archives room at the London police station jammed floor to ceiling with shelves holding boxes and folders with barely enough space inside to fully open the door. There was an overwhelming smell to it of old dust, old ink, and old air. *How many centuries are buried in here?* he wondered. After only five minutes in the building, he knew it would be a ghastly place to spend a workday. Two little lights, which hung from the ceiling, gave the dusty room a sepia look. Limited light, cast from two narrow windows, streamed down murky twin columns of golden dust. A single table amid the overloaded shelves was the only visible workspace.

Not spying anyone at first, Matt was about to walk back out when a raspy voice spoke to him from high up on the wall.

"May I help you?"

Turning in the direction of the voice, Matt spotted a slightly built man, who appeared to be about a hundred and ten years old, hanging sideways off a ladder. Without hesitation or small talk, Matt got right to the point. He wanted to get what he could and get out into the fresh air. I'm looking for some information about a death that occurred in the fall of last year at the Royal Arms Hotel." *No time for chitchat,* he thought. *Not in here.*

The surprisingly spry senior caretaker of the dust room quickly descended and limped his way over to Matt. "Just what date are you looking for?"

"I don't have an actual date. Do you need one to begin a search?" Matt asked.

"Well," the man answered, scratching the bald spot on the top of his head, "it certainly would help if you did. My files are organized very carefully. As you can see, it is important not to lose something in here, might take quite a while to find it again." He smiled a near-toothless grin.

"Yes, I can see that would be a problem," Matt answered, tilting his head back to take in the sheer volume of boxes.

"I like to file reports under the dates, but I do file things under certain categories too. You said it was a death. Was it murder, accident, natural causes, or suicide?"

"I believe it was an accidental drowning."

"Well then let me look for that. Last year, huh? Know what month?"

"October," Matt said. "I think it was October."

The curator of the archives limped back to the ladder and started pulling it toward the front of the room. He scratched his head again, thought for a moment, and then lined it up with one of the shelving units that reached clear to the ceiling.

"Hold on a moment, this may take a moment," the clerk said, climbing his way to the top.

"No problem," Matt answered, but wished the man would hurry. The clerk dug around for a few minutes, pulling one box forward after another. The cloud of dust that rose with each action dimmed the lights even more. "Nope," said the raspy voice in between hacking coughs. "There are no reports from last October about any drowning deaths at all. I have four stabbings, one suicide, a fall off a double-decker bus, and several traffic-related deaths but no drownings. Sorry. Are you sure this station handled the case?"

"I think so," Matt nodded.

"Well just in case you didn't know, there are two different police forces, the Metropolitan Police Force and the City of London Police. Besides, there are seventeen different station houses around London with two others much closer to the hotel than this one."

"I was directed here; I didn't know about the other stations. Is there some way to find out which one would have taken the report?"

"Well," drawled the clerk as he stopped to spit in his handkerchief, "not really." Trying to catch his breath, he wheezed in Matt's direction, "If I were you, I would try station Number Eight, on Arlington Road. They have better computers."

Great idea, Matt thought. *I can't wait.* "Thanks," he said out loud. "I'm sorry I made you climb up there for nothing."

The clerk just stared back at Matt. "No bother, that's my job, you know."

Practically running through the stationhouse, Matt couldn't get out the front doors fast enough. Filling his lungs with fresh air, Matt was not sure if Mr. Gillian had sent him there on a wild goose chase. He had clearly directed him to that station. *Why would Gillian mislead me? It's as if he didn't want me to find anything. Wouldn't he have known which police department worked on the case,* he thought. *I guess he could have been mistaken,* Matt chafed at the waste of time. Reluctant to go back to the main desk and ask directions for the Arlington Station, Matt wanted to stay outside but knew he would never find it on his own. Even as foggy and damp as it had become, at least he could breathe. *Lord,* as he walked back in through the doors, *I will never complain about where I work again.*

The Arlington Station was further away than he wanted to walk and the officer at the desk suggested he take the bus from the opposite corner. The ride was bumpy and cold. Matt stood near the door of the full bus and clung on for dear life as he watched London go by. Shops and little houses, big buildings and historical landmarks, all mingled together and tightly hugged the ribbons of road upon which they traveled. It took close to a half hour to reach his destination with all the stops the bus made. He jumped off and started his search all over again at Station Number Eight.

Although much brighter and less cluttered, this station house was of about the same age as the last one. Matt waited patiently while an officer made him a copy of the brief report. According to their records, Elizabeth Champion was listed as an accidental drowning victim. The event happened on the eighteenth of October of the prior year. Because it was not a threat to the public, a murder or other act requiring a police investigation, there was little to go on except that she was an American, with few details about her death. Nothing more that would help Matt find her or give him another lead. He would have to go back to the hotel and figure out his next move.

Disappointment fogged his mind. He was tired. He lost his direction several times and finally hailed a taxicab to get back to the hotel. Matt collapsed in his room, chilled to the bone from London's damp air, which soaked his clothes, and thoroughly drained by frustration. His last thought before sleep ensnared him was a mental note to have another chat with Roger Gillian. There must be something else he can get from him, even if that meant telling him the truth about Kate.

Somewhere in the night, as he thrashed about unable to sleep, Matt remembered a name from one of Kate's sparse disclosures about her life. Matt was telling her about the stories he made up for his mother about knights and dragons, and she briefly mentioned a place that his story brought to mind. *Such a funny name,* he thought at the time. *What was it? Ceridian, Currigean, something like that.* Without exactly knowing why, Matt's instinct told him it was essential and could have something to do with her aunt. On a hunch, he called the front desk about three-thirty in the morning and inquired of the clerk on duty if he'd ever heard of a place called something like Kerrigan. "Are you referring to Ceredigion?" was the response. "It's a county in western Wales along the coast of the Irish Sea."

Hanging up the phone, Matt lay back and took a deep breath. *I'd make a good detective.*

Instead of trying to locate every Elizabeth Champion in the United States and chasing down the right one, he might have better luck trying to find the aunt who accompanied Mrs. Champion to the hotel. There was little mention of her in the police report, but it did say something about Wales. His mind raced. Kate had talked of Ceredigion, and it was in Wales. *It shouldn't be too hard to find her. How big could a place with a name like that be anyway?* His decision made; he was finally able to settle down into a deep sleep. The next day he was going to Wales.

First thing in the morning, Matt headed down to the dining room and stopped briefly at the concierge desk. He made arrangements for a packet to be prepared with directions to get to Ceredigion and the city of Aberystwyth in particular. There was the National Library of Wales in the city, and that was where he could start his search. *I'm going to hunt this woman down,* he decided. *I'll go door to door if I have to,* he vowed, nodding his head for emphasis to his reflection in the polished brass elevator doors. *I'm not going home without an answer.*

After breakfast, he picked up the information from the clerk and went back up to his room to pack a bag. He stuffed his small travel bag with some overnight things and headed out to hail a taxi. The concierge had made a reservation for him on the First Great Western from the Paddington Station to Swansea with a connection to Carmarthen, a total of about two hundred-forty miles and nearly a four-hour ride. Not expecting to be back by evening, he thought it prudent to take along a change of clothes and a few toiletries. He grabbed some euros and his hotel key, shoving them deep in his pockets. As an afterthought, he grabbed his passport and slipped it into the fold of his wallet. Too big to fit in his back pocket he tucked the wallet in the side slit of his jacket, and he was off to Wales.

The journey through the countryside was delightful and ran along a beautiful stretch of land. The train sped past mountains in the far distance and followed rivers which wound themselves in and out of forests where they puddled every so often to form pristine lakes. On he sped on the Teifi Valley Railroad past cities and villages, the names of which Matt didn't even try to pronounce. They rode past the highway that would have taken him to Wiltshire and the mysterious Stonehenge boulders. *Another trip, another time*, he promised himself, he wanted to return someday when there was more time, and he wasn't on such a mission. There was so much to see.

Once they crossed the border into Wales, the signs became much larger, conveying both the English and the Welsh spelling for sites along the way. Here was the land of King Arthur that he used to dream about as a child. If only his mother could be here with him, for here was where the knights and damsels lived their storybook lives with dragons and castles as their props. *Ah yes*, he said to himself, *I could have made her smile with my stories today with such a backdrop as this.* They passed the charming border town of Monmouth, home of the twelfth Century Benedictine monk, Geoffrey of Monmouth, who wrote the original story of King Arthur and his Camelot. Had it been a different occasion, Matt would have enjoyed the trip more. The tapestry of the Welsh history was rich and fascinating, and he wanted to spend more time touring this ancient land from which notable people, such as kings and poets sprang.

As the miles raced by, Matt dredged up what he could recall from his old history classes about Wales and its people. Although most of what he once knew was as foggy as the mist coming down upon the train, he remembered bits and pieces of stories of the Romans, the Celts, the Normans, and the Welsh. He remembered stories about the battles that tore apart the land and the fierce pride that put it back together. U.S. Presidents descended from here, Thomas Jefferson, Abraham Lincoln, and Richard Nixon. Three of his favorite movie stars were from Wales, Richard Burton, Sir Anthony Hopkins, and his favorite Catherine Zeta-Jones. *Sure would be nice to see her skipping through the meadows on this trip,* he thought with a smile, yet immediately felt disloyal to Kate as he did so.

Thoughts of Kate brought him back to reality, and he worried how he would go about finding her aunt when he arrived in Aberystwyth, the biggest city of Ceredigion. But his heart was so much lighter. He was sure now that Kate was real, no matter what had occurred or what mystery took her away, she was real, and he was on his way to finding her. Nothing would stop him; he was surer of that than anything else in his life. "I will find you, Kate," he whispered to the passing landscape, his head resting on the cool glass. "You may be angry when I do, but I need to see you, touch you one more time. At least you will know how much I love you. Then if you still wish it, I will let you go."

The city was much larger than he anticipated. The concierge in London suggested he pick up a taxi at the train station and instruct them to take him to the Red Lion Hotel. The ride by taxi took him through picturesque towns on one lane roads, often blocked by herds of sheep. A tractor that was probably a hundred years old slowed their pace to a crawl just outside of town. Sinking back in the seat of the taxi, Matt tried to slow his mind and his heart to the pace of the land.

"No sense trying to hurry, ya knows," the driver threw over his shoulder to his passenger. "It never does ya no good."

When they finally arrived at the hotel, Matt found it small and eccentric, but he was pleased to see it looked well-kept and clean. *What a change from the Royal Arms,* he thought striding through the door, only to be greeted by two of the largest dogs he had ever seen. The Irish wolfhound's heads were bigger than his, and they probably weighed more than he did. Matt could have ridden them around the yard. Signed in, he was shown to his room, one of only six in the establishment. A colorful, clean, handmade quilt was upon the big four-poster bed, which looked to be as old as the building itself. There was no sign of a private washroom, but it did have a hand basin, a pitcher of fresh water and a pile of fluffy linens. An old wardrobe was painted with what he believed to be Celtic designs, and although he didn't have his own loo, he did have a telly.

Arriving late in the afternoon, he decided to find something to eat, and in the morning after breakfast, he would head out to the local library and begin his search for Kate's aunt. Matt probably could have found a restaurant with something more familiar, but he decided to join the other guests of the hotel for dinner downstairs, which promised to be unique, at least to him. The menu for the evening meal was Welsh rarebit, potatoes, and carrots with laver-bread made from seaweed. *Well, this will be a first.* Having washed up from the long trip, he started down the stairs and his first taste of Wales.

"Croeso gymru, Welcome to Wales," his host said to him as he signed in to the hotel earlier in the day, trying to keep his balance while the great hounds rubbed against his legs.

"Uh, thank you," Matt replied.

"Will ya be needing a room with us for more than a night?"

"No, I don't think so. I will probably be leaving tomorrow."

"That's alright ma boy; we are happy to have ya. Do come down and join us for supper," his host added. "My wife is a fair good cook; she will be pleased."

By the time he headed back up the stairs for the night, he patted his full stomach and applauded the landlord's wife. She was a fair good cook he agreed, and he wondered what other surprises Wales had in store for him.

Chapter Twelve

In the morning it was softly raining outside, gloomy and cold. The clerk told him it had not let up all night. The world was wet and slippery. Matt successfully sidestepped the two great hounds and stepped through the door pulling the collar of his jacket up around his ears. With directions to the local library in his hand, Matt traveled nearly two blocks in the cold, with the dampness chilling him through to the bone. In spite of the weather, he was sure it would be his lucky day.

As he approached the main street, he looked in both directions in an attempt to get his bearings. The mist was heavy and forced him to squint against the moisture blowing in his face. As he looked across the street, he could see an old church on the corner and stood rooted to the spot taking in the ancient decorative architecture. He was barely aware of a woman coming out of the door until something flickered in his subconscious, making him turn his full attention to her. What he saw caused his heart to stop. Strawberry blond hair escaped the hood she wore, which was pulled up around her face. Her frame was slim and petite. She was walking briskly in the other direction, but the little he could see, something about her seemed familiar. His heart thudded in his chest. He didn't want to appear crazed, but he needed to catch her, see her face. He practically leaped forward in his haste, looking briefly to the left before stepping into the street, yelling out as he did across the mist, "Kate!"

At the sound of the voice behind her, the woman turned to see who was shouting, just in time to see the motorcycle with two riders hit a dark-haired young man and send him flying to the curb. Matt never saw or heard the motorbike, which came from an unusual direction. His last thought before he passed out was of Jeremy York's affirmation that tourists were often hurt in Great Britain.

Elizabeth Champion heard the name Kate and turned to see a young man hurled to the curb by the force of the impact. Two other bodies went sliding past as the bike skidded by her, narrowly missing an oncoming car. The young couple was thoroughly shaken and badly bruised by the event, but they survived to enjoy the rest of their honeymoon. They were fortunate enough to walk away with limited injuries.

Matt was not so lucky. He landed unceremoniously with his head and one leg on the curb, and his body bent in half like a broken toothpick. Immediately Elizabeth ran to his side as the two bikers began to pick themselves up off the road. Matt, however, was a different matter. Unconscious, he was bleeding from a broken leg bone which jutted raggedly through the skin. His face was scraped along one side, and mud, stones, and a cigarette butt clung to his hair. A pool of blood was forming under his head as a result of the blow to the curb. Several passing cars stopped and offered assistance to the young bike riders, and someone called for an ambulance for Matt.

Elizabeth was drawn to the helpless young man without knowing why. She had no idea who he was or why he came after her, but he called her Kate and instinct told her it was something to do with her daughter. When the ambulance bundled him into the back, Elizabeth asked if she could ride along with him to the hospital. Matt had sustained a severe concussion and was bleeding from his ear. He was taken into surgery immediately, and the broken bone in his leg was set. After a series of x-rays, it was determined he also had three broken ribs, a sprained neck, and a depressed skull fracture. Although the doctors knew the head injury was serious, they were forced to wait until the swelling subsided to determine the extent of the damage. They could set his leg, wrap up his ribs, and put a brace around his neck, but surgery to repair his head injuries would have to wait.

Elizabeth was anxious to talk to the young man and find out why he stepped in front of the motorcycle calling Kate's name, but it was clear from the doctor's prognosis, and Matt's unconscious state, that might not be possible for several days. Without logic or reason, she felt a responsibility to this young man and became a frequent visitor to the hospital over the next couple of days, waiting for him to awaken. After the death of her sister-in-law, Elizabeth was more in tune with anything that seemed out of the ordinary. This was a mystery that needed an answer.

Two days later, with the swelling subsiding, the physicians decided they waited long enough, and Matt was wheeled into surgery the following morning. Matt slept for two more days before he finally opened his eyes. The nurses immediately called the doctor along with Mrs. Champion, who had asked to be notified as well.

Matt immediately panicked when his eyes eventually opened in a hospital room. He had no idea what happened but instantly knew it was not a good place to be. There were bandages on his head and his leg. Tubes were sticking out of his arm, which was strapped to a board. He had trouble breathing and felt like a vise was holding his chest. It was difficult to see anything, and he couldn't turn his head. Every inch of him hurt. He had no recollection of how he got there or even where that actually may be.

"Hello! Anyone?" he called out loud. The nurse on duty heard him, and happy to see him awake, rushed over to try and keep him calm.

"There, there, my fine lad, don't be going on quite yet."

"Where am I? What happened to me?" Matt asked, turning as best he could toward the strange woman who flew into the room.

"You are in Saint Hedgewick's Hospital," answered the white-smocked nurse. "You had a nasty spill. The doctor will be with you in just a short while."

"Where?" he asked again.

"Why, Aberystwyth," she answered with a perplexed tilt to her head. "Aberystwyth, Wales."

Noting his alarmed look, she lowered her voice and gently asked him, "And just what is your name, my fine lad?" her voice thick with a Welsh accent. "You had no identification with you when you decided to pay us a visit."

"I'm not sure," Matt searched his memory for a simple answer. His lips were cracked, and his mouth dry. His tongue felt thick. It was hard to talk. His name wouldn't come easily to him, and it made his head hurt to think about it. "I'm not sure," he said again.

"Well, no matter," the nurse said, patting his good leg, "it will come back to you shortly. You got a nasty bang to your head, and most likely it will just be a while before it all comes back to you. Try to rest now; the doctor will be here shortly to check up on you. Are you in any pain?" she asked before stepping out into the hall.

"God, yes, I hurt everywhere," Matt answered.

"Everywhere?" she questioned.

"Yes," he replied, expecting her immediate attention. "I hurt from my head to my toes."

"Good," she replied with a little shake of her head. "That is good. If you can feel all that pain, it means you will be alright." She left him lying there and walked out the door.

When the ambulance delivered Matt to the hospital, there was no information on him, so he was given a number, and they left the chart unnamed. The only thing found on him was some money in his pocket. No wallet, no I.D., nothing to help the hospital staff find his relatives if there were any in the area.

Upon impact with the motorcycle, his body went sailing into the curb, and his wallet and passport went skidding through the grime and mud on the side of the road right through the grate of the gutter. There it fell to the bottom of the sewer, slowly buried by the steady trickle of bloody water and mud. The rain cleaned the pavement and washed away the evidence of the accident, and with it, Matt's identity.

Chapter Thirteen

"Here it is, number fifteen," Lilly yelled, as she counted grave markers. It was the last one in the row, straight east of the huge black granite marker named Fleming, just where they had been told it would be. Kate headed in the direction of Lilly's voice. They had searched for nearly a week to find this gravesite, checking ten different cemeteries and coming up empty. She hoped they had finally found the right one. Nothing exactly fit the description the Intel department gave them.

"This has to be it," Kate cried as she joined her sister. The twins were getting tired of chasing ghostly headstones. "What a place to leave your legacy," Kate chuckled to Lilly.

"No kidding, way out in the middle of nowhere. This guy can keep a secret," Lilly quipped. Dirt and dead grass nearly covered the small plain marker, but when the girls brushed it aside, the name stood out clearly.

"Edwin G. Forester. Yep, it's the right one," Kate remarked. "At last! We thought we would never find you Eddy old boy."

Edwin Forester had died nearly two months before. He grew up in a dirt field on the outskirts of Litchfield, Illinois, but his remains ended up one-thousand miles away in a neglected and overgrown cemetery in Las Vegas.

An older model, tan car drove by slowly. The three occupants waved and nodded at Kate as she headed toward her car. *Guess I should have changed clothes before we headed here,* Kate thought, wiping the dirt from her slacks.

"As soon as we have the cemetery director dig this guy up," she yelled over her shoulder to Lilly, "I'm heading back to a nice cool shower." Kate was feeling pretty bedraggled in the afternoon heat.

Edward Forester, or Eddy as he was known, was a weird little gambler who haunted the casinos from Las Vegas to Reno for a few years. He was extraordinarily lucky. Too lucky, the casino owners thought, and decided to block him from their establishments. They never could catch him cheating, but the consensus was anyone with his uncanny luck was bad business anyway, so he was banned.

Eddy never finished grade school, and the taunts of 'dumb retard' and 'idiot' followed him all of his life, ironic as they were. Far from it, Eddy was a savant and possessed an uncanny ability at cards. Years of watching the games while he was growing up on the streets gave him almost instant recall of the placement of the cards in the deck. It wasn't perfect, but damn close. He could predict with nearly eighty to ninety percent accuracy what card would appear each turn—a talent not appreciated by casino management.

He spent weeks trying to teach his buddies on the street all the secrets of the cards, but without his specialized abilities, they couldn't get it. Time after time they failed, never even coming close to the skill Eddy showed. One particular street boss felt Eddy was making a fool of him and was annoyed. Eddy could do something he couldn't, and he decided to teach Eddy a lesson. He ordered his gang to bundle him up, toss him in a box, and send him to Mexico City in the back of a pickup truck. He arrived five days later, barely alive. Eddy stayed in Mexico for a few weeks keeping a low profile but eventually found his way back to Las Vegas.

Eddy's brother Phil was a hotshot scientist in the east. Phil didn't have much to do with Eddy, so it was a real surprise when Phil called him and hinted he had the key to making them both rich. He gave Phil his address, but all he got from Phil was a book. And it was a Bible of all things.

A couple of Eddy's buddies in Las Vegas were hatching a plot to borrow some of the casino's funds, and they allowed him to join their little band of miscreants. The plan was to dig a tunnel beneath the Frontier Casino on the old main strip. The misguided crew got their hands on some underground schematics, albeit a bit outdated, but clear enough to follow, so with Eddy in tow, they pried open a manhole cover and headed underground in the direction of the Frontier.

Chuckling at their good fortune as no major barriers stood in their way, they followed the plans to where they estimated the casino back offices and vault would be located. The noise from above would hide or diminish the sounds of digging and the small blasts they made with some homemade explosives. It took the crew a few weeks of work, but they finally believed they were within a few feet of the main floor.

One of Eddy's cronies spent most of his life in Sing Sing and was educated in the finer skills of cracking electronic locks. They were sure once they broke through the floor, they would come out just in front of the safe. They checked and double checked their equipment and set a larger charge to blow a hole in the floor of the casino. Eddy lit the fuse and jumped away ahead of the blast.

Unfortunately, while the floor above they were trying to breach was barely dented, the walls of their makeshift tunnel collapsed with the blast. The explosion was heard from the casino floor, and it didn't take long before armed guards were swarming the area looking for the way in. Within minutes they discovered the tunnel and the bodies of Eddy and the crew. When the tunnel collapsed, a new water main which was new and not on the old plans, exploded right behind the wall. It flooded the tunnel and nearly drowned them all. Two of the crew survived the blast and the water to spend the next several years in prison, but Eddy and his buddy from Sing Sing weren't so lucky.

The Bible Phil sent to Eddy a few weeks before had a short note attached. "Hey Bro, hold onto this book and don't let it out of your hands. It is one fucking lucky book and will make us rich." Phil knew perfectly well if he explained exactly what was so special about the book to Eddy, his stupid loser of a brother would blab it all over Las Vegas or try to sell it for a few bucks. But if Eddy thought it would bring him more luck at cards, he would defend the damn thing with his life. Apparently, he did just that. After Eddy drowned, the book was found in a plastic bag, in his shirt pocket, next to his heart.

With no known next of kin to claim the body, the county morgue laid Eddy to rest in an old cemetery near the outskirts of town. His only possessions were a couple of lucky coins and a small Bible. As strange as it might seem, him being such an irreverent little bastard, the Bible must have been important to Eddy, and according to the few friends who attended his funeral, was with him wherever he went. The morgue usually would disperse the deceased's belongings to family members if they were known, but in cases like Eddy's, they would dispose of them in the trash. A Bible, however, was something that could be buried with the body, and so it was with Eddy's. The mortician could not in good conscience throw it away, so he placed it in Eddy's hands before he shut the coffin lid and sealed it tight.

It was ironic there wasn't much luck in the book for Eddy even though it did hold the potential to make the brothers a lot of money. In the binding, Phil glued a microchip with Matt's research notes he copied from the lab and stole from Matt's computer. He didn't trust the Iranian group he was dealing with; they knew too much about him. He figured they would screw him if possible, and in a panic, sent the chip to Eddy to keep it out of reach of the Iranians.

One investigative department of the CIA was suspicious there was more to Eddy's good book than just scriptures. Agents assigned to watch Phil noted all of his phone calls to Eddy in the weeks before he died. The CIA suspected anything that left Phil's hands was worth following, and immediately began their search for Eddy. But he had disappeared into Mexico, and they lost the trail for weeks.

His death was not notable, and no one cared about the would-be robbers or their stories except for the U.S. Government, who with the news of his attempted heist hitting the police blotters, finally learned where Edwin G. Forester was. Ben sent the twins to find Eddy's remains and retrieve the Bible if it still existed. Not sure what the book contained, the CIA nonetheless was sure of one thing; intelligence noted there were several people following a trail to Eddy, and that alone was enough to know it was imperative they must find him first. Now the Bible and its secrets were hopefully in the girls reach.

"Come on Lilly," Kate said, "I want to get over to the cemetery office and get this guy dug up before it gets dark. I can't wait to get out of this heat." When Lilly didn't answer, Kate looked back again in Lilly's direction. Just as she did, a bag whipped down over her head. In one quick glimpse, Kate saw that the couple she had waved to moments before was now bending over her sister, hooded and lying on the ground. The woman was busy going through Lilly's pockets. Then the world exploded into tiny twinkling lights.

"Let's get them over to the vault," Muhammad Mushtari yelled to his wife, Lenora. "There is not much light left, and we need to dig fast before anyone else comes around." To the supine figures of the twins on the ground before him, he smiled. "Allah thanks you young ladies, for helping us in our search. It would have been most difficult to find your infidel book without your help."

Chapter Fourteen

Finally recovered enough to be discharged from the hospital, Matt was moved to a rehabilitation center outside of Cardigan. The semi-private room was on the first floor of the center with access to the veranda. Through the open door, Matt could smell the damp earth and hear voices from outside. Flowers were beginning to bud along a well-tended pathway that led to a circular stone patio, where there were benches that held the old and the young, patients and caregivers alike, absorbing as much of the warm healing sunlight as their bodies could retain.

Farther out, away from the protective buildings, toward the sea, there was a grove of small fruit trees, hunched over and gnarled, their twisted branches showed the swellings of spring, while their tenacious roots clawed sustenance from the rocky ground. Matt's nurse, Maya, bent his ear on more than one occasion about the stark beauty of the landscape around Cardigan Bay and the bluffs where she was born and raised. Although they were several miles from the ocean, Matt could see sea terns and kites slowly dip below his horizon, and at night he was sure he could hear the waves upon the rocky crags, which jutted out far below Maya's bluffs.

Matt's condition slowly improved, and Elizabeth's visits continued. They formed a friendship of sorts. He was often scared, but more often angry about everything around him. Only when Elizabeth was present did he make an effort to be calm, holding himself in check until she was gone.

Continuously frustrated without his identity or how he ended up in Wales, Matt paced the small room he was assigned, rarely giving any notice to the fragile old gentleman who shared the space. Severe headaches continued to plague him, and the drugs they prescribed gave him weird dreams, a lot of dreams. Dreams that seemed to involve this lovely woman, but she was different. Dreams that confused him and made him wake up in cold sweats.

He was sure he knew her in the past but chided himself over and over for the absurdness of it all. The doctors told him he showed signs of previous head injury and his nocturnal visions were only a result of the drugs and the current trauma, which perhaps inflamed an old injury site.

It was half-past ten in the morning, and sunlight poured in through the window like liquid gold, flooding the room in streaks of color, and yet he slept. Lost to the world around him, Matt was running, no, that wasn't quite right. He was moving, but not of his own accord. He was floating or being carried over the ground. He passed rows of white tombstones, and their names flashed before his eyes; Ensign, Reamer, Gilhardy, Johnson. Names as unfamiliar to him as were their faces which swept past his line of vision, gently bobbing like corks in the water. An old man, a young man, two women, a child. Somewhere in his dream state, he wondered who they were, and did he know them? He could almost reach out and touch their wispy clothes. Their eyes were on him, urging him to remember. Charging him with a duty. "Remember," they whispered, "Remember."

The subtlety of the dream changed and what filled his head was hot, black, and terrifying. He was suffocating; he couldn't breathe. The room was so dark, only a crack of light shone high above his head. His head, oh how it throbbed. Not like his usual headache, with pain from the inside, this was different, painful from the outside, too sore to even touch the scalp above his ear. He wasn't alone, but he couldn't see who was with him. He wanted to yell out, but fear held him back. Tossing in his bed, Matt awoke with a start when a hand in the dark reached over and touched his leg. A voice next to him in the blackness said, "Kate is that you? Are you alright?"

The local police tried, but they too were unable to find an identity for the young man involved in the accident. There were no missing person reports or any way of knowing if he had relatives in the area. No one recognized him, and although he could be a resident, they assumed he was probably a visitor and slowly began to check the hotels. The area was a frequent spot for Britons to spend their holiday, and the marketplace in town drew people from all over Wales. He could have come from anywhere. It was a busy time of year.

Days went by before they eventually hit on the right place. The Red Lion Hotel on High Street reported a young man named Matt Errington had stayed with them the week before. The man was to check out the next day, but after breakfast, he left the hotel and was not seen again. They assumed he conducted his business and returned from whence he came. They thought it was unusual he did not return for his few belongings, but since the bill was paid when he arrived, they packed up his things and forgot all about him. The police were given his small bundle and a heavy brass key. A railroad stub indicated he arrived from London. But London was a big place, and the key could have come from anywhere, and it would be difficult to match to a lock. Spring was a busy time in their city, and the small police force was limited to tracking down the stranger's past in their spare time. Weeks went by before they were able to trace him and the brass key back to the Royal Arms.

Mr. Gillian was not surprised when the police from Aberystwyth contacted them about Matt Errington. He had been informed from the day manager, who was told by the chamber-maids, the gentleman in room 782 had not slept in his room for several nights. When Matt's reservation was up, they boxed up his things and stored them in the hotel vault. Although he wished he could be of more help, Mr. Gillian could not offer the police much beyond his assumptions of why Matt went to Wales and gave them the briefest of summaries about Matt and his background. He related the tale Matt shared with him of being from a laboratory in the states seeking information on diabetic patients and how he mentioned the sister of one such person, a Lauren Champion of Wales. The police were grateful for the information on the young man and promptly relayed it back to Matt's doctors, who in turn, told Elizabeth what they learned.

Upon learning who Matt was, Elizabeth was ready to give him the information he had waited so long to hear, but she held off just a little longer. The doctors thought her decision odd but assumed she knew him since she visited him every day. Now that she finally knew the identity of this young man, she needed to make a call to the States and talk to Ben to find out what the connection was to Kate.

Considering Lauren's murder, it was just too coincidental he had come from the Royal Arms looking for Lauren, and she wanted Ben's advice to proceed. Walking into Matt's room for a visit, she knew she would eventually tell him what she had learned, but before she did, she wanted to know more about him. Elizabeth was surprised to see him just awakening even though the sun was fully up, and noted it was a beautiful day outside.

"Well hello sleepyhead, glad to see you have decided to join us for the day." Elizabeth greeted her friend. Carrying a small bunch of field flowers, she plopped them into an empty glass and filled it with water from his bedside table.

"You sure are quiet today," she added, glancing over her shoulder where she finally noted the pallor of his face. Grey, completely ashen, Matt looked like death had already claimed him.

"I'm sorry, Elizabeth," Matt barely spoke, the feeling from his dream lingered over him like the morning mists so common there.

"Are you alright?" Elizabeth was instantly concerned and was ready to run for a nurse when his hand stopped her flight.

"It was just a bad dream," he mumbled. "I'll be fine in a minute. It was so real, though, I was in danger, and my heart was going to explode. I'll be fine," he said again, reassuring the worried Elizabeth as she continued to fuss over him.

"Was this your same dream again?" she inquired. "Like you've been having?"

"No, no," Matt said, "not at all the same. This was different. I couldn't breathe, and it was so hot. I knew I was going to die, but the worst part was I don't think I was alone. I'm sure there was someone with me, someone I cared about, but now I don't know, I just don't know. It was dark, confining … and horrible. It was so real. Thank God it was only a dream."

For Elizabeth, it was difficult to console this perplexing young man, a friend dropped into her life by strange circumstances. Matt accepted her in his life more readily than he accepted everything else that happened to him daily. With no background to gauge the present, the passing of time was marked by the rounds of the nurses, doctors, and therapists, his meals arrived as scheduled, and this lovely woman visited him as she would. He had no say, no agenda, and no plans. The days came and went, and he floated along with them. He knew this woman was important to him, but determining the reason was beyond his ability to divine, and any kind of deep thought made his head throb even more.

Elizabeth told him of the accident; told him how the motorcyclists struck him and how he ended up where he was. In spite of the questions from the police, from the doctors and hospital staff, and Elizabeth, he couldn't remember where he was coming from or where he was headed. Witnesses described the events that day, and everyone remarked how surprised they were when he just stepped off the curb, without so much as a glance, right into the oncoming biker's path.

She thought several times during the days of his confinement in the hospital, and again now as he sat on the edge of the bed holding his head between his hands and trembling, how awful this all must be for him. He deserved to know who he was. She hadn't talked to Ben for several days, but she was positive he would be in touch with her by the evening. Elizabeth did not doubt that as soon as they discussed the situation, Ben would give her permission to share what she learned with Matt.

Even if she couldn't give him his name and identity yet, perhaps she could share some good news with him. The rehab center doctors decided there was little more they could do for his recovery and suggested Matt would make better progress if he went home. But now knowing where his home was, Elizabeth wasn't so sure it was a good idea to send him back to the States alone in his condition. In spite of his mood swings, she genuinely liked this pensive young man. The mother in Elizabeth trusted him implicitly, and convinced as she was that he was no danger, she wanted to ask him to accompany her to Gwelfor Cottage, her late sister-in-law's place by the sea. There could be no better place to recuperate than on the bluffs of Wales, and once there, she and Franny could make him whole again.

"I don't know what to say, Elizabeth. I can't wait to get out of here that's true, but I don't want to be any additional burden to you. You've been so kind and like an anchor for me throughout this whole thing. You don't even know me."

"Well if you come back to the cottage with me we'll have plenty of time to talk about anything you want. You can't stay here forever … and until you know where home is, where else are you going to go?" Her smile was kind and trusting, and her blue eyes crinkled up when she smiled.

Matt felt he had known her for years and wanted badly to accept her offer, but another problem occurred to him. He owned no clothes of his own since his were cut from him after the accident and the only things that remained in good condition were his shoes. "What will I have to wear once I'm out of these charming hospital gowns?"

"I can pick up a couple of pairs of trousers and a sweater in town. The mackintosh you were wearing when they brought you in will be fine after a good scrubbing, and there are some heavy work shirts at the cottage that will fit you well enough." Elizabeth assured him.

"Alright," Matt finally agreed, a bit relieved to be moving forward, "I will accept your generous offer but only if I can keep a record of all my debts and you will accept payment when all this is figured out."

Chapter Fifteen

Franny kept peering out the door as she paced in the living room like a nervous new father awaiting the birth of his first child. Listening for the crunch of tires on the small pebbles which would announce their arrival at the cottage, she finally saw the car and shuffled off to the kitchen to pour the boiled water over tea leaves. She eagerly prepared a tray with scones, clotted cream, raspberry tarts, and fresh fruit. Laury's spirit had told her that Elizabeth would be bringing home a young man to stay.

Lauren's friend and companion for nearly forty years, Franny was as much a part of the cottage as the very walls which held up the roof. Together for decades, the women shared a unique bond, one it seemed not even death could sever. Laury, as Franny called her, spoke to her often and told her the young man was special and to take good care of him. Not that she needed any prodding, she was delighted to have a guest. It would be nice to have someone else to take care of again besides Beastie, Lauren's small Shih Tzu.

The pain of losing Lauren was still fresh in her breast. Such a hard loss should not have been. Having Elizabeth stay for a spell was comforting, and now, with this young stranger to tend to, she could put the sadness away for a while. *Aye,* she nodded, *the house had been sad for too, too long.*

"Sadness always comes without an invitation, and if you let it stay, you will have a houseguest for life. Happiness, on the other hand, must be sought out, nurtured, and welcomed into your heart." *Hadn't I said that to Laury on many occasions over the passing years? Ahhh, the poor little mite. Such a tragic life, and it coming to such an end, drowning alone, without glory or purpose.*

Lauren Champion lived most of her life in the cottage. It was to be her marital home with her beloved Garwin. Lauren was betrothed to her best friend since childhood. Garwin and Lauren grew up on the bluffs on the short rocky road to Cardigan Bay, never living more than a hundred feet apart. Garwin began pleading for Lauren's hand when they were both about nine or ten years old. He even made a formal declaration of his love and his earnest intentions to her father, Harned. As hard as the patriarch of the family tried, he could not hold his mirth in tight rein. Young Garwin took the laughter in good form but waited another eight years before he asked again. This time Harned Champion gave his blessings most solemnly. They would be married the coming May when Lauren turned eighteen.

Garwin, a fisherman, a son and grandson of fishermen, put his heart and strong back into the sea. Only Lauren was dearer to him than the salt-stained life he loved. At nineteen, he worked as hard as time and weather would allow, and was rewarded with the purchase of his own boat, christened the 'Lauren Lee.' As children, Lauren and her brother Karl played in the crumbling cottage set back a bit from the edge of the bluffs on the lee side of Cardigan Cove. Deserted for many years, it was overgrown with wild roses, seagrasses, and brambles. Decades of weather rotted the door until it fell inward, and the roof collapsed in different places. Salt air and mist invaded the rooms and peeled the ancient flowered paper off the walls and buckled the hand-cut wood-planked floors. Time and weather vied for the right to retake the spot on the rock the cottage claimed for nearly a hundred years. Only the massive fireplace in the kitchen stood undaunted by all that would topple its majesty.

As word of their betrothal spread, neighbors, family, and friends of the young couple donated lumber and nails, shale for the roof, and beams for the ceiling. Housewives tatted lace curtains and hand stitched wedding linens. Hens were plucked of every last feather and lovingly transformed into pillows and cushions. The Cottage was reborn.

Then out beyond the lights of the harbor reflected in the murky water of the Bay, beyond the reef in the Irish Sea that sheltered the crab and herrings, beyond the point where the ruins of Cardigan Castle were just a dot on the horizon, the Lauren Lee and Garwin were lost in a squall. The deadly storm consumed five boats and thirteen seasoned men.

Walking the edge of the bluffs for thirty years, the knowledge she could join him whenever she chose eased Lauren's heart. He was, after all, only a few steps away. She chose instead to live for his memory. She talked to Garwin daily and visited him as often as she could.

At twilight on windy days, she would walk out to the most prominent peak and stand strong and tall, letting the salt spray take her breath away. Arms straight out from her sides, she called upon her beloved to embrace her, to hold her, to make her his own. The wind blew, and she closed her eyes. Swaying ever so gently she left the rocky crest far below her and floated out over the sea, searching the gray waves that rhythmically crashed down upon themselves leaving foamy bubbles floating on the surface. Her eyes became accustomed to the changing swirls of the salty currents. She could see the black mass of herring ebbing and flowing with the tides. Great leatherback sea turtles with flippers barely moving glided in and out among the kelp far below. And Garwin, yes, she could see him clearly, nestled in the bow of his boat, his head gently rocking with the waves. His arm above his head waved back and forth, back and forth, saluting his love as she hovered above him. Silently he pledged his troth, over and over again. She would blow him a kiss and feel his in return.

When her eyes would open, Lauren would drop her arms to her sides. Tired from her flight, she would soundlessly return to the cottage, their cottage, and fall asleep alone again in her wedding bed.

When told of Lauren's death, Franny wrapped herself in one of Lauren's woolen shawls and quietly rocked in one of the big chairs by the fire. "Finally," she crooned to the wind outside, "they can now consummate their love.

Franny shook her wizened old head fussing over Matt on the sofa until Elizabeth chided, "that's enough, Franny, let him be."

The small room in which Matt found himself, was overflowing with dried flowers, bowls of seashells, and bundles of sheaves of wheat like grasses. Old floral prints hung on the walls, and the small glass beads on the lampshade danced each time the door opened and closed.

Matt could have one of the small bedrooms on the upper floor, but until the pain in his head subsided, and he could climb the old stairs, the sofa would have to do. The trip from the rehab center was a long and difficult one over the rocky ground, and Matt's head still reverberated with the pounding it received on the rutted road. He tried not to complain, but Elizabeth noticed his clenched jaws, pallid complexion, and rigid posture and forced herself to drive even slower than the narrow pathways usually dictated. In spite of his obvious discomfort, he eyed his new lodgings with fascination and interest.

Lauren's home was charmingly old. The cottage they approached had been whitewashed hundreds of times, yet the old weathered building still held its own against whatever time and tide could throw at it. Two stories high, it had two nice bedrooms on the second floor with a spindle railing walkway between them open to the rooms below. The narrow set of stairs which ran down the right-side wall, had thick hand-knotted rugs nailed to each tread. On the first floor, there was a parlor on one side and a small dining nook on the other. A short hallway ran back through the center of the house and emptied into the kitchen which took up the entire back side of the structure. More bundles of dried flowers met Matt's gaze, dozens of them filled each of the front rooms. Through the doorway into the kitchen, Matt could see an oversized fireplace, standing squarely in the middle of the far wall commanding veneration with its regal presence. Wood rocking chairs stood on both sides of the fireplace; they too were covered by hand-knotted covers and brightly colored cushions.

What appeared to be a small dog, covered by hair, lay curled in a wicker basket by the hearth. The cottage smelled of herbs and spices, fireplace ashes, and the sea. Although it was cluttered, it was about the homiest place Matt could imagine ever being in.

Something in the house filled Matt's head, and he knew he recognized the scent as soon as the door closed. Flitting through his mind, it would briefly touch an olfactory nerve only to disappear and then alight somewhere else. Without explanation, he knew the scent from some far away time, but annoyingly, he couldn't tell if it brought him pleasure or pain.

"I won't be long," Elizabeth said over her shoulder as she walked down the front step. "I have a couple of errands to do, but I will be back long before dark." She needed to run back to town alone and handed Matt over to Franny's watchful care. Her cell phone was useless out this far, and although she could have used the phone at the cottage since Lauren brought in a line years before, she knew there would be little privacy in such a small space. Her conversation with Ben needed to be candid, and she knew that couldn't happen within Matt's hearing. Elizabeth started the car and was just about to turn out onto the dirt lane when Franny hobbled out to her.

"Oh, and it's sorry I am," Franny wheezed, nearly breathless, "but yer friend, Ben Madison called for ye before ye returned earlier today. I forgot to tell ye when ye came in, what with getting the young man settled and all."

"Thanks, Franny, I'll call him back while I'm in town," Elizabeth reassured her.

"Aye, see that ye do, he said it was most important he speak to ye today," she nodded emphatically, her gray curls bouncing with each word.

Elizabeth watched her limp her way back to the cottage, stepping carefully along the pebbled path. What a dear old woman she was. Lauren had loved Franny like a mother, and when Lauren died, Franny grieved quietly and then redirected her attention to the next Champion family member in her charge.

Slowly picking her way along the dirt road, Elizabeth turned her attention to the remark Franny made about Ben calling. She was surprised he had called much earlier than usual. It would be early in the morning for him in America, and it left her wondering what news would be that important. The town was only a few miles away, but the rains of late had changed the hard-packed dirt to a muddy washboard. "No wonder Matt's head hurt so badly by the time we reached the cottage," she muttered, riding over these ruts again made her own teeth rattle in her head.

Elizabeth headed to a local hotel so she could use one of the public phone boxes in their lobby to call Ben. She would have more privacy and would be more comfortable there than at a roadside box. Placing the call to Ben took less time than she expected, and within moments, Ben's assistant, Nichole, was on the line.

"Hello, Mrs. Champion. I'm glad you called; Ben tried to reach you."

"Good morning Nichole, yes I know and called back as soon as I could. You two are in early today. Is he available now?"

"Yes, he is just finishing up on a call. I'll tell him you're on the line." Within ten seconds, Ben picked up, his voice lacking its usual warmth, and when he spoke to Elizabeth, he was tense and brusque.

"Elizabeth," he jumped in getting right to the gist of the matter, "Have you heard from the girls in the last few days?"

"No, I haven't, but that's not so unusual. We often go several days or even weeks without contact. Why do you ask?"

"I don't wish to alarm you, but the girls have not reported within the last twenty-four hours. They know the rules. I have two agents on their way to Las Vegas to check out the situation. They were on a fairly simple assignment, so I'm not that concerned, but I did want to check with you. Let you know in case you hear from them before I do."

Taken off guard, Elizabeth caught her breath and heard herself respond, "I appreciate your candor." Although the lobby of the hotel was quite warm and cozy, she felt the cold hand of worry wring itself around her body. "What assignment took them to Las Vegas?" she asked, trying to keep her voice from quavering.

"They were searching for the remains of a guy with ties to a project we had in Philadelphia," Ben answered.

"What kind of ties?"

"Well, let's just say without going into a lot of detail on the phone, the group we believe is responsible for Lauren's death has been busy lately, trying to get their hands on some nasty bio-toxic stuff. We think the guy the girls were looking for died holding something in his possession the wrong people could use to make some serious trouble. The department found out where he was and what he had. We aren't convinced anyone else had that Intel yet … but with what happened to Lauren last fall … and now the girls out of touch for longer than usual, I'm erring on the cautious side and sent two of my best guys down there to make sure the Iranian Jihads has nothing to do with them."

Not overly reassured, Elizabeth searched his voice for sounds of worry, trying to keep the concern out of her own.

"Please," she voiced low into her mouthpiece. "You'll let me know as soon as you hear anything, won't you?" Elizabeth sat in silence for a moment, letting her fear subside and trying to reassure herself that her girls were well trained and bright. They knew how to take care of themselves. They had proved it over and over again for nearly nine years. Rarely did she worry excessively about their welfare, but right now she was anything but sanguine about the matter. Maybe it was something in Ben's voice this time that triggered her fright, or maybe it was her mother's instinct. Too many coincidences always felt wrong to her.

"Ben," she said at last, "I was calling you anyway today on another matter. I have something I need to run past you as well concerning the girls, or rather, Kate in particular."

"I'm listening," Ben said, "go on."

"Several weeks ago, a young man was involved in a motorcycle accident over in Aberystwyth. I took it upon myself to become involved in his care. The only reason I'm doing this is because I think he called me Kate. I know that might not make sense to you, I'm not exactly sure how much sense it makes to me … but my gut feeling is to help him, and I have. He's recuperating at the cottage; Franny is with him now. The strange part is I have discovered he came to London looking for me."

"What?" Ben said, "You knew this guy?"

"No, I never saw him before or heard of him either, but I think he knows Kate."

"What's his name?" Ben suspiciously asked.

"Matt Errington." The hair on the back of Ben's neck stood up. One half of his mind immediately started trying to untangle the connections the other half of his brain was spinning.

"Let me get this straight; you have Matt Errington at the cottage?"

"Yes," she answered.

"What does he want with you, and how did he connect you to Kate?" was what Ben asked, but the thought running through his mind was *how and why is he in England at this particular point in time, and why is he looking for Elizabeth?* If he wasn't overly concerned about the girls before, he was heading in that direction now.

"I have no idea what he wanted," Elizabeth responded. "He didn't find me actually, but I believe he spotted me and mistook me for Kate. From what I learned; I think he came to Ceredigion to find Lauren. Since his accident, whether it is fortunate or not, he has no memory of who he is or why he's here. The police traced him back to the Royal Arms in London, and we were able to get his name and some minor info about him from them. Matt supposedly came to London to find me for some diabetic study he was doing in the States; he was told I was dead and probably came here looking for Lauren. I have no idea what it all means, but just before his accident he yelled 'Kate' in my direction, and I've been looking for answers from him ever since.

"I only found out yesterday who he is and where he's from. I know he is anxious about his identity, but I didn't want to share any of that with him until I spoke to you and got your opinion. I think from time to time … he believes he knows me, but since the girls do look like me, I'm sure he is unconsciously remembering Kate."

Ben sat for a moment and let her story wash over him as he tried to find a fit for the puzzle. "You don't have any health problems, do you?" he finally asked.

"No, never … which is what makes this so odd. What did the girls have to do with him? I know they were in Philly last year, were they working with a medical center there?"

"Elizabeth," he started, not sure exactly how much he should say. "First of all, I can't believe you took a stranger back to the cottage with you considering what disturbing things you know go on in the world." He wanted to assure her the man in her care was indeed, not dangerous, but considering the coincidences, he wasn't all that confident that was the truth. "I do know him. Yes, we used him as an asset last year in Philly. But Matt was not the target, he was only the informant, although he was unaware of his role.

"Last summer, one of my best agents, Samir Ali Mansoor, was murdered while he was embedded in a cell in Philadelphia. Matt's name was one of the last things he was able to get out before he died. The only way we could get additional information was to use Kate. We suspected Matt's employer, and a colleague … and we had Kate create a relationship to gather information. We suspected there was a buyer for some deadly toxins Matt was working on, but we weren't sure who the seller was or even if a deal was made. Our contacts in Iran have given us some real cause for alarm. We've been chasing leads for years to a group who sends teams into the States, blends them into the landscape, and uses whatever they learn to find ways to attack their enemies. Meaning us. We hadn't gotten even close to a source … until we learned of Matt."

"Not Matt!" Elizabeth exclaimed, ignoring Ben's disapproving comments. "I don't see him in that role at all."

"No, I have not suspected Matt of being involved before this," Ben answered with a slight hesitation, "but certainly the people close to him, so we used him for intel. Trouble was, he fell in love with Kate … and although I can't for the life of me figure out how he found you … or even about you, it's quite possible he is looking for her. I aborted the job last October, and we did a clean out on the place, and I have to admit I haven't given him much thought since then. We thought he moved on with his life. I know he was offered a big position in Washington. It's more than a bit disconcerting that he is there now with all the alerts on the net, especially with heightened activity in England. Agencies all over the States and Europe are tingling, and so far, nothing has gelled when we try to get a fix on what is going to happen … or when and where. Reports all over the wire are talking about something called 'The Breath of God.' Not at all sure what that is, but the lab Matt worked for has been linked, and we're pretty sure his co-worker is involved. I don't usually miss a connection. I'm pretty certain Matt is clean, but I'm not so sure I want him there with you and Franny just in case I've read him wrong. It's pretty strange he shows up in Great Britain when we suspect something is about to blow there."

"Well he is here in Wales, and I'm sure it's only a matter of time until he starts remembering. To be totally honest, Ben, he doesn't impress me as a potential threat to anyone, not me, not the girls, and certainly not national security. I'd like to give him his name at least, and see what memories it jogs."

"Hmm," Ben replied, "not so sure we want to do that just yet, I'd like to look into this a bit more for a day or two. Are you certain he doesn't know who he is? I know you have a pretty good head for the business … and a good feel for people, but Elizabeth, are you so certain that you'll bet your and Franny's life on it? You don't think it's possible he's playing you?"

"Ben, I know you're cautious, and I probably would be too in your position, but I'm confident he's the real deal. The doctors are convinced, and so am I."

"Well, although I can't see any connection to the girl's current whereabouts and him, once he puts the past together, he's just another loose end flapping around. Let's hold off for now; I'll give you a call tomorrow and will probably have some more information about the girls by then. Since he's over there and has been there for some time, I'm sure he has nothing to do with them, but I'd like to be sure, okay?"

"That's fine, I trust your judgment … which is why I waited for your advice, but as soon as we can, I would like to give him something."

"I understand. I'll talk to you early tomorrow morning. Is there anything else you can tell me about him?"

"No, I only know what the Royal Arms gave the police. He talked to Roger Gillian about searching for me, that's why we know that much, but nothing more. And Ben, please call at any hour about the girls, won't you?"

"Of course, you know I will." As soon as Ben hung up the phone, he asked Nichole to find Agent Jensen. He wasn't completely comfortable with Matt at the cottage with Elizabeth and Franny and wanted to have a man headed in that direction if a buzzer should go off in his head.

Elizabeth stopped at the market and spent the next half hour trying to calm her nagging thoughts before returning to the cottage. Franny's intuition was keen, she would see through her attempt at nonchalance. "Better get my head around this quick," she muttered. As she battled the coincidences which closed in around her, she picked up the makings for dinner.

All the way back to the cottage, Elizabeth fretted about her daughters and what would possibly keep them from reporting in on schedule. Ben didn't have to say he was worried; she could detect it in his voice. And it wasn't her imagination that he became more concerned after she mentioned Matt.

Chapter Sixteen

Franny cooed, and Franny fretted. She patted his back and brought him tea. She couldn't keep her hands off of him. Matt tried hard not to laugh, she only wanted to take care of him he knew, but it was so amusing watching her. Every step she took bounced her long gray curls out from under the little lace cap she wore. *She could have been a stand-in for Aunt Pitty Pat right out of Gone with the Wind*, he thought. Looking every minute of her ninety years, her face had the texture of dried, cracked mud. With a frame bent over with a dowager's hump, she was forced to look sideways even to see where she was going.

"Please, Franny, I do not need anything," Matt kept telling her. "You do not need to wait on me; I can help myself." But his entreaties were useless. She was there to serve and serve she would, whether he liked it or not.

"Mrs. Champion asked me to look upon ye, and ye would have me do otherwise?" she asked him petulantly.

"No," sighed Matt, resigned.

"Ever since my Laury has been gone, I have been too idle, ye needs to get yeself better, and I can help ye."

"Laury? Is she your daughter? Where is she?"

"Na, she was not ma babe, but truer than me own child could be, she was to me. She is buried in the churchyard, but her soul is with her love."

Having absolutely no idea who or what she was talking about, Matt murmured his condolences and made a mental note to ask Elizabeth about her when Franny was out of earshot.

The cottage was warm and dry on the drizzly afternoon, and altogether quite comforting. Matt's head was finally clearing of a horrendous headache that had kept him company since they left the rehab center. Agreeing to stay with Elizabeth felt weird to him, but then his entire life for the past month or so felt entirely weird.

Little nagging things would go through his head, and he wondered if they were bits of his life he was trying to remember or just brain clutter. He remembered nothing of his past, even his name was still a mystery, and it was difficult not to worry there was a family somewhere who may be frantic about him. Being in this place, in Wales, didn't feel right, of that he was certain. He had no idea whether he was there on vacation or business. Either way, he wondered if there wasn't someone looking for him. Surely someone must miss him. The idea no one might ever track him down or even try to, disturbed him deeply.

That was a long and troubling thought that plagued him at night when the others were asleep. During the day he managed to put it out of his mind, but how was it a man of his years had no one who cared about where he was? Was he such a bad person? Was he a loner who spent his life on the road, traveling to odd places like Wales, or maybe that wasn't so odd after all? Maybe he was a frequent visitor. But if that was true, why didn't anyone know him? The questions didn't help his headaches, nor did the nightmares. Strange places and feelings haunted his sleep. Without any way of knowing for sure, he grimly hoped the places weren't real.

The doctors warned him as his memory came back to him, things would seem strange and not to worry too much. But could the troubling scenarios he saw in his dreams be his real world? The feelings the dreams invoked; such intense fear, pain, danger, even remorse. Upon waking in the mornings, it took nearly an hour to clear his head of the night's damage. It wouldn't be so bad if he just knew they were dreams and not his forgotten reality. But the remnants of the night's images floated through his waking hours like driving in and out of a light fog. There one minute, gone the next. Daylight hours faded the clarity of the details, but the feelings they instilled continued to haunt him.

One recurring dream, in particular, left him fearful of closing his eyes. In this dream he was running through a huge airport, he saw people all around him drop to the ground in deliberate slow motion. Their faces contorted in pain and disbelief, they writhed and flopped like fish on the ground when hauled out of the water, until they were still. Holding their baggage and belongings, clutched in frozen fingers, he realized the fish–people wanted his help, but he could do nothing but watch as their eyes pleaded with his. He struggled during the day to find hidden meanings in his painful images but found none.

Perhaps if he shared them with the doctors and Elizabeth, it would help, but he always decided against that course. He was already treated with kid gloves, and the doctors seemed to be looking for signs of dementia or hallucinations. He didn't want to end up in a padded room somewhere in the Land of Oz. No, he knew he must keep his strange reverie to himself and hope either the dreams stopped, or they would work themselves out to a solution.

Elizabeth returned to the cottage and carried in the fresh vegetables she purchased at the market. She was grateful Franny was half asleep in the big faded chair in the parlor, she wouldn't have to try so hard to hide her concern about the conversation with Ben. Tomorrow they would talk, and she would hear how the girls were found safe and sound, with some logical explanation for their absence. In the meantime, she checked on Matt, covered Franny with an old handmade quilt, and busied herself in the kitchen making soup.

"Can I help you?" Matt asked, limping his way into the kitchen and leaning his weight against the heavy wooden planking of the door. "I think I know something about cooking," he added. His leg hurt if he put a lot of pressure on it even though the bone had mostly healed successfully. "I can sit and cut up the vegetables," he offered.

"That would be nice," Elizabeth smiled and handed him a small knife and a pile of washed carrots, "thanks, I could use the company."

"Did you have a good trip to town?" Matt asked, trying to make conversation.

"Umm, yes," was the casual reply, but her mind wandered regretfully back to the call to Ben. "I may have to go out again tomorrow too; I hope you can fend off Franny without me."

"I'm sorry if I'm a problem for you here," Matt remarked, unsure why he suddenly felt uncomfortable. Although Elizabeth reassured him on several occasions he was welcome; he still felt he was imposing on her good nature.

"Listen, you should not feel that way at all, honestly. I am happy you're here. It's always a little too quiet out here on the bluffs. This old house has been sad for so long; it needs visitors."

"Oh, that reminds me," he said, quickly peeking around the corner in the direction of Franny's slumping form, "who is Laury and how did she die? Franny mentioned her, and I felt bad … I didn't know what to say."

"Lauren was my sister-in-law," Elizabeth answered watching him for a reaction. "She lived in this cottage most of her life. It was to be her home with her husband, but he died in a storm on the seas before they could be married."

"Has she been gone for a long time?"

"No, as a matter of fact, she passed only last year, in October to be exact." Nothing, she noted, neither on his face or demeanor; there was no look of recognition, and no twitch of insight lit up his eyes. If he was acting, she decided, he was good at it. She was convinced he remembered nothing about his search for her.

"I'm sorry to hear that, I thought she was Franny's daughter or something."

"No, they weren't related, but Franny was a neighbor of Lauren and Karl's parents, and having no family of her own, she adopted them and then Lauren in turn when they were gone. She has been a part of the family for over seventy years."

"You said Lauren was your sister-in-law. Karl is your husband? Is he away on business, does he live in Wales too?" Elizabeth chose her words carefully, and took the opportunity to haul out a large kettle, fill it with water and light the fire under it before she answered.

"My husband was born here in Wales, but he died many years ago. He was the editor of a newspaper in the States. We never lived here together. This was Lauren's home. I'm not a permanent resident here either, although the cottage now belongs to me, and I visit often, but it will never be my home."

"I'm sorry," Matt felt bad for bringing up the topic, "I just assumed …"

"I know. It's alright. I've lost a few people along the way, and it is painful, but my husband and I had a wonderful life together, and even though I miss him terribly, I don't look back in sadness." Before he could ask the next question she was sure was coming, she offered him the answer, "we have two daughters, they live in the States as well," still watching him for a sign that never came. She wanted to go further, tell him a little about the twins and her concerns, but she would heed Ben's cautious warnings and wait for his response.

During all of her visits in the hospital and the rehab center, their conversations concerned his care and his memory; Matt focused so much of his attention on himself he never bothered to ask about the people around him. For this, he felt ashamed, especially since Elizabeth had been so good to him.

"Elizabeth," he stammered, feeling remorse for his lack of manners toward this caring woman, "I have been so immersed in my misery, I've taken you and your kindness for granted. I apologize for my self-serving introspection for all these weeks. I must have better manners, and you have my promise, somehow, someday, I will repay you for everything you have done for me. I can't stay here forever, but I need your help to go home. I would like to ask you for another favor. Because the police have not discovered anything about me in this country, I would like to find someone to contact in the U.S. I'm sure I'm American, and it's where I feel I belong, but I don't know exactly where to start. There must be a missing person national hotline somewhere. Maybe I can become the face on a milk carton and get some answers," Matt rambled on.

"When you finally find all the answers to your questions, we can worry about repayment," she smiled, "but in the meantime, please relax, I have enjoyed our friendship all these weeks. Your concern for your health and missing memory is understandable. Please do not think badly of yourself. The doctors have told you, and I believe it as well, your memory will return, and you'll find your way home. I may have someone in the States to help, and I promise to see what information I can find for you."

"That would be so great," he flushed; childlike anticipation lit up his face. "This is a horrible existence," he blurted out and then thought better of his comment when he saw the look she shot him.

"Hey, horrible, is it?" she replied, brandishing a wooden spoon in his direction, "You haven't even tried my cooking yet." His embarrassment made Elizabeth laugh but seeing his discomfort, she added gently, "I'm sorry for teasing you, I know what you mean."

The way her eyes crinkled up at the corners when she laughed burned through him in a painful stab. What was it she just said that cut him in two? Silently he filed it away for future review. His headache threatened to start up again and to protect himself from the pain he deliberately changed the subject and joined in her fun.

"Okay, bring on the turnips already, the carrots are done. This place sure has a slow cook, and I'm getting hungry."

Later, alone in his small room, he would examine more closely the cause of the pain his damaged brain wanted him to remember.

Chapter Seventeen

Blind in the dark, Kate felt her way along the edge of her surroundings. She was up against a flat wall, rough, like jagged concrete. Her reach was limited to an arm's length; it hurt too much to move her body. She was dazed, and waking from the stupor was painful. She wanted to close her eyes and go back to sleep. The air was so hot it took great effort to breathe. *Where the hell am I?* It hurt to think. *Where's Lilly?* The image of her sister lying on the ground snapped her to full consciousness. "Lilly," she yelled, and her voice bounced off the dusty walls.

"Here," came the terse reply, "I'm right here. Are you okay?" Lilly felt the dried blood on her head and shuddered.

Her pain forgotten; Kate reached over the ground in the direction of the voice. "Kate, what the hell happened?"

"I don't know, but are you okay?"

"Yeah. Pretty woozy. Got a good wallop on the head, but nothing else hurts."

"Same here."

"Give me your hand," Kate said, trying to feel for Lilly in the dark, running her hands along the walls and swiping through thick filaments of spider webs. A shudder went through her when she felt something move across her hand. As the girl's fingers touched, they realized they were in a fairly small space.

"Can you see anything at all?" Lilly asked. "I can't make out a thing."

"Nope, the little crack of light over your head is the only light there is. If we can stand, maybe that is a door behind you." Both girls crawled onto all fours in an attempt to stand but screamed out at nearly the same time as their injured heads hit the low ceiling.

"Omigod, that hurt," Kate swore. "No wonder it's hard to breathe in such a small space."

"I'm not sure, but I don't think we want to be here much longer," Lilly answered her, gingerly massaging the top of her head. "The air is pretty bad, and if we stay too long, we'll both pass out again."

"Try the wall behind you," Kate offered. "See if there is any give to it. The faint line above your head is an opening."

Lilly dug her feet into the floor and pushed her back against the wall with all her strength. "That's not going to work," she wheezed, "no movement at all." The slow dawning of their predicament hit both of them about the same time.

"Unless I'm mistaken … and God knows I hope I am, we are in a vault in the cemetery." In spite of the heat radiating through the walls from the outside, Kate felt goosebumps go down her spine.

"Uh yeah, I had the same thought," Lilly added. "Now what?"

"Okay, let's not freak out yet, do you have anything on you, your phone, a lighter, a candy bar?" Kate asked her sister.

"Gee, since when, do I smoke, and I thought you were in charge of bringing lunch," her sister replied, trying to match Kate's wit.

"Yeah, well, if I'd known we were going to be boxed up together, I would have asked you what you thought we might need in case an escape was called for." Kate shot back. Even though they had a serious problem, the twins knew panic could be held at bay with humor and neither wanted to acknowledge the seriousness of the situation.

"Okay, check your pockets," Lilly ordered. "I had my phone on me, but I can't feel it now."

"Nope, mine's gone too," Kate replied. "I have no idea how long we've been here; it was getting dark before we were attacked. Judging by the sliver of light, it must be early morning. Ben knew we were searching for Eddy; he won't let it go too long without sending out the Marines on our trail."

"Yeah, but he wasn't sure which cemetery we would be at. We searched nearly a dozen before we found the right one. It could be days before they figure out where we stopped and then figure out where we are." Lilly voiced both their concerns.

"True, but you know Ben, he's a bulldog. He'll find us," Kate assured her twin.

Not wanting to make painful contact with the ceiling again, Kate felt her way up the web covered wall, mentally shaking off any thoughts of which deadly spiders liked dark spaces, and determined the roof was about five feet tall. She couldn't stand, but she might be able to get her face closer to the crack above Lilly's head.

"Move over a little; I want to see what's outside." It was painful to turn her head sideways, and the slit was only a few inches from the ceiling. She was, however, able to distinguish the shape of some barren looking trees around her. "I can see something. Nothing in my line of vision to get us out of here … but at least I think I know where we are. Remember the vaults over by the scrubby woods, behind Eddy's grave; we saw them on our way in?"

"Oh great, they aren't even close to the road." Lilly groaned. "We can yell ourselves silly, and no one is going to hear us."

"Uh, well, yeah that could be a problem." Kate acknowledged. "This wasn't a well-tended end of the cemetery. Probably aren't too many caring friends and family that head out here, I don't remember seeing many flowers, do you?"

"Nope, but the weeds were pretty tall, someone should be coming around sooner or later to cut them, you know. Although that probably won't do us much good, trying to yell over the sound of a tractor."

"Okay, okay, got any better ideas, Miss Optimistic?"

"Yeah, stop talking. We're both using up too much air." Lilly was right, but Kate did notice she could breathe better up near the slit, so they might be okay a while longer if they stayed near the crack and didn't panic.

Dr. Nowak had waited as long as he could for Matt to return from his vacation, and after the four weeks was up and no word from Matt, he knew something was seriously wrong. Matt wouldn't just change his mind and disappear without a damn good explanation. The Washington office wanted a body to fill the position, and without any more options, Jeff regrettably offered the position to Phil. God how he hated seeing the smugness in his eyes. If he didn't know better, he might think Phil had something to do with Matt being a no-show. The guy was a little shit, but he couldn't believe he would be that malicious. While Phil was gleefully packing his personal belongings, Dr. Nowak was on the phone with the police. He wanted to report Matt's absence in the hope they could trace his whereabouts. Since there was no immediate family, he felt it was his responsibility to at least begin a search for the guy.

The police took all the information about Matt, and what little Jeff could offer about Matt's itinerary and plans and ran some preliminary checks. No one matching his name or description came up on the Philly police system. No hospital or police records were found to give them any help. Jeff remembered what Matt said about looking for a new place to live in Washington and suggested the police check around the D.C. area as well. The police promised to link up with other departments and see what could be found. Jeff was concerned, as well as curious. Matt was a good guy, with a few problems sometimes, but he liked him and sincerely wanted to know what happened. When all of their queries through the regular channels came back negative, the police decided to check out his apartment to look for evidence of foul play.

Fred Lafferty was surprised and more than a little shaken when he looked out and saw a police squad car pulling up in front of his apartment. *What the hell do they want now? I ain't done nothing wrong … not lately.* His first thought was to hide and not answer the door but then realized his damn car was right out front in plain view and it would probably look better if he met them head-on, like he wasn't worried about anything.

"Howdy guys," he said, opening the door before they could knock as if he was on his way out and was surprised they were there. "You fellas looking for something?"

"Yeah. Are you Fred Lafferty, the superintendent of this complex?"

"Yep, that's me, what can I do for you?" He hooked his thumbs in his belt loops and tried his best to look innocent.

"We would like to check out number 360. Can you let us in?"

"Uh, no problem if you guys have a good reason and the owner says it's okay." Fred's relief at not being the target of their visit showed all over his face, and the officers picked it up immediately.

"Have you seen the tenant of apartment 360 around lately; a Matt Errington?"

"Nope, can't say I've done any work down that way in the last few days."

"Well how about if you check your records for the past month and see if anything jogs your memory."

Not sure what they were after, Fred was nervous opening the door to his apartment. He walked in ahead of them and quickly scanned the entire room to make sure no sign of his tenant's belongings were present. He wasn't too worried. He was pretty careful not to be stupid and leave evidence around.

"Sure officers, come on in. I'll go get my log book and be with you in a jiffy." The place looked like it had been tornado tossed; and even though the police got bad vibes from the guy, they couldn't tell what they were suspicious of, nor did the mess inside give them any clues.

"Here, I found the last few week's logs and don't see anything done down toward that end of the complex. I have about two-hundred units to tend to, you know. Do it all by myself, too. I'd get around to checking on things more often, but with so much work, well, I just don't have the time."

The officers looked at each other and nodded, "Yeah, okay, let's take a drive over to 360, and you can check it out right now."

"What about the owner's permission," Fred answered, hoping there was something in it for him. "I can't just let you guys in without checking with the guy first."

"Yes, you can, and you will," was the reply. "Just grab your master key, and let's go."

Fred stepped aside after unlocking the door to let the officers go through first. They thought the super's apartment was a mess, but it didn't come close to what lay before them. Matt's apartment had been thoroughly ransacked.

Little was left untouched. The couch was cut up and stuffing strewn around like snow on a January morning. It covered the mess of papers, food, clothes, and some broken furniture. Walking through the room was difficult without stepping on something; the entire floor was covered. Taking his radio out of his pocket, one of the officers called the station to report their discovery. "Yeah, we have a 10-59," he said, "better send the lab guys. No sign of the owner, but whoever did this was looking for something a lot smaller than him."

Within twenty minutes, the apartment Matt called home was crawling with detectives and a forensic team.

It was obvious whoever created the mess did a professional job. They were methodically looking for something in particular. The books were rifled, and ripped covers were in a pile. Cushions and the mattress were shredded, which accounted for the snow effect, and some of the furniture was broken up and drawers stacked on one side of the room. Clothes were turned inside out, and the hems and pockets were ripped out of jackets still hanging in the closet. In the kitchen, there was food all over the floor, and everything except sealed cans had been emptied on the table. One detective noted he was relieved the stench from the kitchen was spoiled food from the freezer and not a rotting corpse. Adding to the sense of chaos were shards of a broken mirror lying on the living room floor. The pieces eerily multiplied the reflection of the people who moved cautiously about the room, fanning and folding them in upon each other, like the chunks of color in a kaleidoscope.

Whether or not the ransackers found what they were searching for would be anyone's guess. As for finding Matt, it would be several hours before the police could sort it all out and several days before they could determine if there was anything useful there which could help them track him.

Chapter Eighteen

Nearly two years before, Marsh Laboratory, Matt's employer, had been awarded a huge government project which Matt, and for a short time, his co-worker Phil, both worked on. Each with a different set of protocols for their research, but both aimed toward one goal. After years of research, a virus had been isolated, which could help find a cure for diseases like muscular dystrophy.

Normally a slowly developing disease, Matt had discovered a way to manipulate the virus to cause full-blown symptoms in mice within minutes of contact. In seconds, nerve tissue damage caused almost instant paralysis of all voluntary muscles. First, the animals would be unable to move or swallow. Heart, lungs, and organ muscles were secondarily affected with the brain stem and brain neurons the last to be attacked. In essence, the victim would slowly suffocate while staying fully lucid and aware they were dying.

The second half of his research was to find a way to stop and reverse the progress. Matt was developing the antidote, but the timing was crucial. If given early enough, the serum may, theoretically, restore the damaged nerves. If it was administered too late, it might not save the victim's vulnerable involuntary system before irreversible damage to internal organs occurred and ultimately, the victim's death.

The purpose of such dangerous research was not to create another deadly disease but to use what they learned to reverse-engineer a cure for current diseases. Determining the cause was always the first step toward developing a solution.

Matt had great success in the last few weeks before he left and felt comfortable his test results were repeatable and would sustain his theories. Although the testing was limited to mice and would have years of trials before any human subjects would be used, Matt was glad he played a role in its development. The belief he was helping people was the part about the job he loved best, and it kept him working late at night long after his colleagues went home.

Years of hard work and a lot of government grant money was poured into this project, and fire or damage to the lab computers could wipe it out in an instant. Over time, Matt transferred his work to microchips and stored them in his lab's safe for protection, along with a sample of the virus.

He gave Dr. Nowak several reports along the way, at least what he finished, and shared with him his optimism about the final stage of the developing serum. Before he left for England, when his trials were finally complete, Matt finished the final report. He was anxious to share his findings with Dr. Nowak and the group in Washington, but Jeff had left for home hours before, and his safe had automatically locked at six o'clock.

Matt intended to return to the lab before he headed to Washington to clean everything up for the next team, but he wasn't overly confident about leaving his work unattended for what could be weeks while he was gone to England. Ever since the suspicious activity with his lab notes, he no longer thought his lab to be a safe place. He transferred the entire research project from his computer to something more portable and shredded every last page of his log books. He could reload and reprint it all later. Since no one was expecting him or his research for another month, he felt the only safe place was to take his work home with him. He completely erased everything off the computer, going over several areas to be certain it was all deleted. He could leave feeling secure his entire project, the research and his potential cure, and all of his back up files would be safe.

Rashid Zand said he would contact him by Friday and Phil knew time was running out. If he couldn't find the rest of Matt's notes by then the whole deal would be blown. Phil copied all of the information he could find from Matt's office weeks before, but he knew there was so much more of the final research results missing, and what he had so far wouldn't be of much use to anyone. He knew it, and so would the Iranians. But he couldn't have known Matt wouldn't be back.

Phil knew Matt was always thorough in his protocols and note keeping. He also knew he would have finished the project and documented every step and procedure. *So, where the hell are the rest of his notes?* He spent several hours in the dark after his co-workers left for the day examining Matt's laboratory computer and came up empty-handed. Nothing, not a single solitary page of notes. *Damn, just like Matt to screw me up again.* There were too many gaps in the data that needed filling before he could pass it on to the Iranians, and he worried what their reaction would be if they thought he was cheating them. *Probably not a group you want to mess with,* Phil decided.

Getting the job in Washington was a plum, he was going to have access to more confidential information Zand and others like him would pay dearly to get. He just needed to finish this deal before he left so they would trust him again. *Trust!* Not that it was Phil's nature to trust anyone or anything himself. Too many things in life got way out of control if you weren't careful and he liked control. Phil was no dummy; he believed what Zand said about having eyes and ears all over. It would be hard for him to securely hide the copies of research documents without fear of their discovery. As a precaution, he sent all of the data he collected so far from Matt, off to his brother, Eddy, for safekeeping. But he still needed to find the rest to make the deal happen, and he needed to find it soon. Zand was not a patient man, and it had been months longer than Phil anticipated.

"What are you thinking about?" Lilly asked her quiet twin. Kate was lost in thought.

"Oh, just worrying about Mom, you know. I hope she doesn't try calling us and get all upset when she can't get in touch. You know how she is; she's so neurotic about us."

"Yeah, but she isn't due back from Wales for another couple weeks, and it's not like she calls every day anyway. It could be a week before she has any idea we are out of touch, and by then we'll be out of here. I worry about her too since Aunt Lauren's death. Mom isn't a trained agent, and she can be so trusting of people. I know Ben has a lot of confidence in her intuition … but we know how evil the world can be."

"I know, I think about that too," Kate added. Neither girl wanted to dwell on the possibility it would be a long time before Ben or his rescue party would find them, and what condition they might be in by then.

"Mom will be fine," Lilly assured her.

Not usually pessimistic, Kate just sighed, "And if we don't get out of here, that would be hard on her."

"Alright, just shove that notion outta here," Lilly practically yelled at her sister, causing her voice to ricochet off the walls. "We don't go that route, and you know it. Let's stick to developing a plan instead of planning our funerals, okay?"

"Fine," Kate answered, "I'm not trying to be maudlin, but I haven't been able to come up with a solution, have you?'

"Not yet, but I'm working on it. I've been thinking about Dad and when we were young. Remember how he always told us he was Superman from the movies, and we believed him. Said Mom made him give up the career when they were married and how we begged him to show us how he could fly."

"Oh Lord," Kate laughed in spite of their situation. "I hadn't remembered that in years. He got us going didn't he, and we tried to convince our friends, but they just thought we were nuts. I miss Dad a lot, and I know Mom does too even though she has a façade of steel, but she lets down her guard from time to time."

"Well I sure wish Superman was here now, he would just push the door open, and we'd be free."

"Good thought, let's hang on to that one for a while. It's so damn hot in here, must be middle of the day by now, maybe we should try to sleep for a while, take turns, save the air. Ben has to be on his way soon."

"Alright," Kate agreed, "and Lilly,"

"Yeah?"

"Thanks for the memory and the laugh. I needed that."

"No problem. You sleep first. I'll keep an eye out our window, just in case someone strolls by. I don't want to miss an opportunity while we take a snooze."

"Good idea, wake me when you start getting sleepy."

"Deal, now shut up, you're using up my air."

He felt hot. Uncomfortably hot. Matt tossed and turned until the heat woke him fully. He threw off the smothering blankets. He couldn't get enough air. The small bedroom closed in on him as he lay awake and wondered why a sensation of panic repeatedly washed over him. He was weaning himself from several different pills the doctors prescribed, and he told himself it was just the change to his system. It was early, probably before six o'clock and he hoped he hadn't made a lot of noise in his sleep again. Elizabeth heard him thrashing around the night before and asked him about his apparent nightmares. He wasn't ready to share his insanity with her yet and hoped he wouldn't ever need to.

Tentatively crawling out of bed, Matt realized how cool the room was and grabbed for one of the heavy woolen shirts Elizabeth gave him and the warm flannel trousers. It wasn't easy to make his way downstairs in the early morning light; the old floors creaked with each step, but he tread carefully to make as little noise as possible. Matt wanted to start breakfast before the women awoke. Both Franny and Elizabeth waited on him, and although he appreciated their concern, he knew it was time to get moving. Hopefully, Elizabeth would be able to link him up with someone in the States and help him get his life back together soon.

The kitchen was cold, and he was glad for the heavy shirt; some type of handspun wool, the fibers were softened by years of wear. Wondering who the original owner was and what was their fate made Matt shiver again in the cold. Several times he turned around to check behind him, having the unmistakable feeling he wasn't alone, but nothing and no one came forth from the shadows. Not even Lauren's small hairball of a dog had made its appearance at such an early hour. His nerves were sorely tested of late, and he assured himself it was just a case of low blood sugar, pills, and anxiety setting off his imagination.

Next to the door leading down to a small stone cellar, Matt found a box of firewood and starter sticks, and it didn't take long before a small fire was going in the ancient hearth. He sat down in one of the old rocking chairs and watched the flames dance their fiery ballet as the heat finally penetrated his clothes and warmed the room. He probably would have continued to sit there watching the fire and enjoying the peace of the moment except his stomach rumbled, and he was rudely reminded of his good intentions.

Matt hauled himself to his feet and took stock of the room and decided coffee was his first objective and was thankful at least one modern gadget was available. A cup of hot, steaming coffee had never tasted so good, and Matt was on his second as he finished his inspection of the cupboards. *Must be eighty years old at least,* he decided as he opened the small icebox which ran on propane. *This belongs in the Smithsonian.*

Digging through its contents, he found eggs, mushrooms, and onions, and was surprised when the taste of an omelet struggled to the surface of his memory. Heavy iron frying pan in one hand and a tub of butter in the other, he stopped in his tracks and wondered out loud, "How can I remember things like the Smithsonian and not even know my name?" *Did I go there? It's somewhere on the east coast I know, not sure where, but why does it sound so familiar?* He could picture different objects like the antique appliances in this room. *Antiques.* What was it about antiques that rang some hidden bell inside? Frozen, he stood mid-thought trying to focus on a vague image that taunted him as it played a childish game of peek-a-boo behind the haze in his mind. A hint of memory there one moment, but gone the next, tantalizing him, frustrating him.

Elizabeth walked in behind him and found him standing in the middle of the room, staring out the window, pan and butter forgotten in his hands.

"Matt, are you alright?" Turning around swiftly, he put too much weight on the newly mended leg and nearly crumpled to the floor when the pain shot up to his thigh.

"Arrghh, guess I shouldn't have done that," he said through clenched teeth.

"No, I suppose not," she agreed, pulling out one of the wooden chairs for him, "here sit down. What are you doing up so early anyway?"

"I wanted to surprise you both and have a nice breakfast waiting for you, but I guess I haven't gotten far yet. But I did have a remarkable thought just now. I think I live on the east coast, maybe somewhere warm too. I'm not sure if it's the pills I'm still on, but I sense I'm used to warm, humid air, at least it feels that way. I remember being near the ocean but not sure exactly where."

Elizabeth smiled and hoped she would have good news from Ben today, and she could give this nice young man something more to remember. "That's great, but why don't you sit for a few minutes and let your leg rest. Franny will have both our heads if we mess up her kitchen. We'll leave her something to fix. I'll get the eggs going before she gets up," she added. "It makes me nervous her bending over the stove as she does. We'll have her make some of her buttery cinnamon toast, believe me, it's wonderful. She will light up like a Christmas tree if you ask her to fix it for you."

Matt couldn't fight the urge he wanted to belong there, even if he knew better. *This,* he thought for about the tenth time in two days, *is what family feels like.* He must have one like it somewhere, and the desire to find his home was becoming more urgent each day.

Elizabeth hurried through her breakfast and left Matt and Franny to clean up the dishes. Worry about the twins kept her from sleeping most of the night, and by morning she was jittery and anxious, ready to head to town to call Ben.

She sped as fast as she dared down the dirt packed road, past the small rocky outcrops, farms, and herds of wooly sheep. Elizabeth summoned her considerable common sense around her. The twins were not invincible; she knew, but they were level-headed. Ben had kept his promise to her, and their father, that he made many years before. He kept the girls out of harm's way. Their assignments were mostly intelligence gathering, and even when she grilled them as only a mother could do; she discovered no rationale to worry about their profession. Normally logic would have convinced Elizabeth it was only her imagination which fueled her speed toward town, but since Lauren had been killed, her apprehension for her children had also kicked into a higher gear.

The lobby of the small hotel was empty, and there was no trouble getting an empty phone box. Counting the hours of the time difference in her head, she knew it would be very early in Washington. She hoped she could reach Ben at his home.

"Ben, thank goodness you're up," she said as she heard his familiar voice on the line. "I'm sorry to be calling so early, and I know I have been worrying needlessly, but please tell me you have found the girls." The pause at the other end of the line made tingles go marching up her spine, and the knot she was trying to ignore in her stomach wrenched itself in a tighter grip.

"I didn't want to call you just yet," Ben began. "Now Elizabeth, I don't want you to read more into this than there is, but I have no conclusive answer for you. Two teams are looking for them, and we should have some news soon. We know where they were headed, and my agents just reported in an hour ago, they found the girl's intended destination. The fact the girls aren't there doesn't naturally imply anything yet."

"Yet," she repeated back at him.

One nice thing about Elizabeth, Ben knew, he didn't have to sugar coat his words. She was level-headed enough to handle the truth, but there was no sense worrying her with the total truth. He already decided to share with her only the details she absolutely needed to hear.

"I've already told you most of it, but several months ago a no-account guy died in Las Vegas, and Kate and Lilly were looking for his grave. We believe he was in possession of some valuable information and hoped the girls could retrieve it without too much effort. The girls should have been able to dig up the information we wanted, excuse the pun, and be back in Washington by Monday. There was some confusion about which cemetery had the body, but we know we have found the correct one. It could have taken us a while to locate the guy, but monitoring the local police reports, we discovered a grave which was vandalized, and by checking records, we knew it was our boy's. Kate and Lilly would have had it exhumed by the cemetery management, and we know that didn't happen, so our guess now is someone beat them to the site, and the girls are following, trying to recover what was taken from the grave. If this is the case, and they didn't call for backup, I'm going to personally have their heads handed to them as soon as I find them."

Elizabeth listened to his words, but more intently to Ben's voice. He was holding back, she could tell, and knew he would only tell her so much. "Okay," she exhaled slowly, "I appreciate the update, but I've already decided I'm going to get a flight out today, and I should be there by tomorrow morning."

"What good do you think you are going to do here?" Ben asked, his voice steely, a rebuttal already in his head. "We have trained field agents out there looking for them, with assistance from all possible government agencies at their disposal."

"Yes, I know, but I can't sit here … thousands of miles across the Atlantic and worry," Elizabeth added. The timbre of her voice convinced Ben, and he knew it was useless to try to discourage her trip.

"Alright," he softened, "but what about your houseguest? Is he up to taking care of himself or at least defending himself from Franny's attention?"

"He'll be alright while I'm gone, but since you brought him up, what are your thoughts on letting him know his identity? Little things are coming back to him, but if he had some facts, it might trigger a lot more."

"I've given it some thought," Ben said, "and I don't wish to subject him to more uncertainty than necessary, but I would like to hold off a little longer. Since you are coming here, we can discuss it further, and I promise we'll go over my reasons in more depth. Then it will be up to you to decide when the time is right when you go back."

Ben conceded the battle about her impromptu trip to Washington much more readily than she anticipated, which told her she was right. He was more concerned about the girls than he would admit. Her call completed, she made flight reservations for later in the day. She wouldn't be leaving for hours, but she needed to get back to the cottage, pack a bag, offer some excuse to Matt and Franny, and make the hundred-mile drive to Cardiff Airport to catch a connecting flight out of Birmingham.

Matt's reaction to her upcoming trip was instantaneous, "I'll go with you," he beamed, ready to go. "It doesn't matter where I land; I won't be any trouble for you. You can leave me to my own means. I'll figure out where I'm going when I get there. I will head straight to the nearest police department and throw myself on their mercy. If you pay my fare, I'll get it back to you I promise, and everything else I owe you too." Matt was giddy, the thought of going to the States invigorated him, and he practically babbled in his excitement. He knew he would figure out where he belonged if he could just get over there. Her excuse of an unexpected business matter necessitating a brief return to the States was accepted readily by both Matt and Franny. But his enthusiasm was shot down immediately as he caught sight of Elizabeth's face.

"I am so sorry," she said, sitting down next to him on the sofa, her hand on his arm. "I would love to have you go with me, and I agree being over there would help you find yourself faster, but you have no passport, no identification. We couldn't even get you a ticket out of here without some I.D. Even if we could get you out of Wales, all U.S. airport security is extremely tight, and you wouldn't be allowed to enter the States. Perhaps if we had more time, we could obtain letters or documentation from the police or the doctors, but that could take days, maybe weeks. Even then, I don't know if it would be accepted on the U.S. side."

The letdown was physically painful. Matt felt his chest constrict as he recognized the truth of what she said.

"But" she tried to brighten the moment, "I will do whatever I can while I am there to find a resource for you. I am going to see an old friend of mine, and he will help me, I'm certain. Although we are happy to have you with us here, and you are welcome as long as you wish or need to stay, I understand how frustrating this must be for you. You have handled this whole ordeal remarkably well, and I promise to do whatever I can to help you get home."

Elizabeth's sincerity touched a raw nerve in Matt, and he looked away from her. Now and then something about the way she looked grabbed at his heart and he wanted to hold her, touch her, and caress her face with his hands. When she sat close to him like now, his emotions boiled over, and the confusion was like torture. She was near twice his age, but he had a disturbing urge to blurt out he loved her, knowing that wasn't quite right. He was so close, why couldn't he grasp what it meant? What was it about her that made him feel happy, sad, relieved, and lost, all at the same time?

He pulled his arm away from her hand and sat looking at the floor. The headache, which was a constant companion throbbed a little harder behind his left ear. It frequently whispered to him, "take care, don't think so hard, be content in the moment, or I will take control."

"You're right, I wasn't thinking," he admitted, swallowing his disappointment. "What time does your flight leave?"

"Four-fifteen, but it is quite a drive to the airport on these old roads, I don't have much time to prepare. Franny, could you make a list of anything you think you will need for a few days and I will make a quick trip to the market before I go."

Franny was up and hobbling to the kitchen in a blink, her mind going a mile a minute. *I will have him all to myself, I will. Ahh, the delicacies I will fix for a healthy appetite like his. Yes, I will take very good care of this young man. Old Franny will make him happy he stayed behind.*

Chapter Nineteen

"It's been at least forty-eight hours," Kate spoke in the darkness. "At least two full days since we woke up, trapped in this hot, airless tomb." Besides the thirst and hunger which plagued them, their doubts about being rescued caused them discomfort.

"I know, I figured about the same," Lilly responded. "I don't know about you, but it gets harder to stay optimistic as each hour passes."

"Well, we know Ben will have launched a search party by now." Kate offered. "He knew who we were after, and the agency only needs to follow the same trail we took. Certainly, by the time they discover Eddy's grave, they would know we were in trouble, right?"

"Right," Lilly answered.

"And," Kate continued. "We've hashed this over for two days now. What's the first thing Ben would have decided when he heard we hadn't called in to report? We know he would have searched the cemeteries until he found the same one we did. Granted, it took us several tries to find the right one, but Ben would pull out all the stops, and he has considerable resources on his side. It's been nearly seventy-two hours since we last called in. Ben would have acted days ago. There is, however, the nagging thought he wouldn't assume we are still within the cemetery grounds. Or there is the possibility our attackers drove our car miles away and abandoned it, to throw off the trail."

"I'm trying to stay more optimistic about that," Lilly said. "Especially since they didn't kill us. Maybe they were just grave robbers who wanted us out of the way. They may have been amateurs and left a sloppy trail."

"I'm not so sure about that. I suspect because they left us here, entombed in the hot Nevada desert, they are not only experts but well trained in cruelty."

Kate had no memory from her time with Matt of Eddy or his Bible. Neither was ever mentioned, so she guessed Matt did not know of Eddy. But CIA intelligence had tied Phil to a jihad faction working in Philadelphia searching for information on a weapon. Ben suspected the same jihad group was responsible for their Aunt Lauren's death. The CIA didn't know what was in Eddy's Bible, but Kate was beginning to believe the jihads did. Kate feared the Bible contained the sought-after recipe for mass death. And if it did, their attackers were certainly capable of taking great pleasure knowing the girls would die slowly without any hope of rescue. And that plan seemed to be taking shape in the hot, airless tomb.

They were quickly dehydrating in the Nevada heat. Even though it was spring, the outside temperature was probably past ninety. They wouldn't last much longer without water. The crack at the top allowed them to get more air, and when either girl felt faint or light-headed, they would pull themselves up, tilt their head sideways and breathe deeply through the narrow slit. No more than an inch in height, it allowed them to survive. Unfortunately, as the air in the tomb grew heavier with carbon dioxide, the necessity for trips to the ceiling became more frequent, and sleep became a danger.

"Come on, Kate," Lilly ordered her sister, "get up here, you've been sitting there too long."

"No, I can't … I'm so tired," came the reply. "My head hurts just to move."

"So does mine," Lilly insisted. Lilly's hands were cut and raw, as were Kate's, as she tried to hoist her sister to an upright position. Both girls had followed the rough, jagged walls within the tomb with their fingers, trying to discern any cracks or openings they may have missed. The slit above the door, their only source of air, at least kept them alive. The box was less than five feet high and not more than eight or nine feet square. There were no coffins in the vault as the space was empty. "Well, eventually someone will find us," Lilly quipped. "This vault will be needed by its owner and won't they be surprised to find us squatters here when they open the door."

"Oh yeah, too bad we'll miss the fun. But," Kate added, "the good news is, I can cross estate planning off my To-Do list." Her humor was returning. "And I for one am glad if I have to go, at least I know you won't be rifling my closet and stealing all my CD's when I'm gone."

"What do you mean rifle your closet?" Lilly retorted in mock anger. "Who stole some of my best shirts and my favorite little black dress before your assignment in Philadelphia?"

"I didn't steal your clothes," Kate answered in kind, "besides you never wore them anyway. I only borrowed a few things, and you got them back no worse for wear. And who are you to talk, when we were kids, who took all of my old Nancy Drew books Dad gave me. You knew how I loved them. Every time you went through them, you turned the covers in, and they were never put back where they belonged."

"That's because you are such a fussy nitpicker, they don't have to be in alphabetical order, you know." Both girls had to laugh at themselves. Their old arguments strengthened the bond between them. It eased the tension but made both of them scramble back up to get more air.

Just the mention of Philadelphia and the memory of the Matt Errington assignment hurt Kate. It was months since she left him behind, and although it was her job, she cared for him more than she could admit to anyone. The Philadelphia assignment was the only one in her nine years on the job she regretted. It should never have ended as it did. Matt was the greatest guy she ever met, and she knew he loved her. Remembering the way he held her touched her soul. Memories of their time together made her smile in the dark—thoughts she couldn't share, even with Lilly.

It was a good time in her life, in spite of it being an arranged relationship and the fact she had been using him for work. Not since she was a little girl in her father's lap did she feel so loved and treasured as she did with Matt. A single tear slid down her cheek, and she let it fall, not bothering to wipe it away. It was too late now she knew, to regret that terribly important bit of unfinished business in her life, he probably moved on and forgot her, but how she wished she could go back to his little apartment, pick up where they left off and not have to explain her deception to him.

Chapter Twenty

Piecing through the fragments of someone's life to determine what may be missing is difficult, especially when you don't know the owner of the pieces. The police sifted and sorted Matt's apartment based on what they believed should be there. What may be clues to his disappearance could be right there next to his dirty laundry for all they knew. Nothing stood out and screamed at them, or gave them any indication who had ransacked the place or why, or what they may have been looking for.

"Pretty boring existence," one officer noted, "not a Playboy in the place."

Matt Errington appeared, to those who analyzed his belongings, to be a straightforward guy, who led a simple life. But people who fit that description don't usually piss someone off enough to have their home taken apart, and then disappear for no apparent reason.

It didn't add up, and the police detective in charge of the case decided he wanted more information from Dr. Nowak.

Eager to learn what happened to Matt, Dr. Nowak was glad the Detective called. "I've been waiting to hear what you found. Any sign of Matt?"

"Nothing conclusive yet. There was little to go on, so we checked Matt's apartment. Found it pretty torn apart. Other than the obvious damage, there was nothing out of the ordinary. No sign of personal violence, no indication he was harmed. You reported he was leaving on vacation. His shaving things and toiletries are gone. Empty hangers in the closet. His apartment was probably ransacked in his absence. Can't tell if anything was stolen, but a computer and TV were there, and some cash in a drawer. Hard to know what else a guy like that owned. Did you know where he was headed?" the detective asked Dr. Nowak.

"No. He did say at some point he wanted to find a place to live in Washington. He was under a lot of pressure. He'd had some personal health problems, didn't tell me much, but I know he took a long time to decide to move to Washington and the new position the company offered him."

Detective George Jorgenson nodded, "Not much to go on. We have no idea where he was headed or if he got back. He could be staying with someone leaving us empty-handed. Without a destination we're at a dead-end, we don't have the manpower to search. He could have gone anywhere in so many weeks. The only thing we have to go on is the guy never returned to work when he said he would, and his place was thoroughly demolished. It looks like someone deliberately tore the place apart, but we have no apparent motive."

Dr. Nowak recognized there was no more anyone could do, but asked the detective to keep him informed anyway.

"I will let you know if we find anything, and just to be certain we haven't missed something here, I am putting a bulletin out on him throughout the different state agencies, it might generate some information we can use."

Detective Don Orliss couldn't believe his eyes. Scanning a police report, the name Matt Errington grabbed his attention. *Missing. Those dummies over in the Fairfield Department. The guy's not missing; he went to England.* Glancing at his calendar, the detective counted the weeks since he remembered speaking to Matt about his trip. Four, almost five weeks since then. *Guess the guy decided to stay there. Must have found what he was looking for, but he should have let someone know.* He'd grab a fresh cup of coffee and give Fairfield a call.

He was even more surprised when he reached Detective Jorgenson and heard about Matt's apartment. Filling in some of the details about Matt, he agreed to fax a copy of their department's report to Jorgenson. He had to admit the whole thing was strange. First, the guy was looking for a non-existent missing girlfriend, and now he had failed to turn up as well. It was obvious something was going on with the guy, and perhaps there was more to it than Matt's apartment being trashed.

Once again, he thought back to their doubts about Matt's mental state, although he declined to share that bit of info with Detective Jorgenson. There was no need to go in that direction yet. He wanted to talk to Brian York first before he said any more about Matt. The Fairfield Department might read between the lines of the report he was sending them, even though he finished his report for the file without adding his opinion that Matt's girlfriend was all in his head.

If the Fairfield cops came to the similar conclusion that Matt was a lonely-heart, it was their case after all and their call, but they might drop the investigation, and Detective Orliss wasn't sure that was a good idea. He liked Matt. If the guy truly disappeared, and it somehow involved a mysterious girlfriend, Don wanted them to do whatever they could to find him, and he wanted to help.

Sergeant Brian York called his cousin Jeremy and was relieved to hear Matt had arrived and had been deposited at his hotel. Jeremy told Brian he half expected Matt to take him up on his offer to tour London, but never heard from him again so there was little he could report about the guy.

"Thanks anyway," Brian told him, "at least we know he stayed at the Royal Arms. We'll get in touch with the manager there and see what else we can find out. It's a good lead; it will help a lot."

Chapter Twenty-One

"I hears ye at night ye know."

"What?" Matt barely heard the whisper from the drooped gray head. "What did you say, Franny, I'm sorry I couldn't hear you?"

"I hears ye when ye cries for ye lassie, ahh and a mournful sound it is too." Matt was standing in the doorway, watching the sea terns swoop and dive off the bluffs. Far below the craggy walls, the Irish Sea roared as it crashed thunderous waves upon the bulk of rock protecting the western side of Great Britain.

"I don't know what you mean," Matt hesitated, unsure if he wanted to start a conversation about his nights.

"Ye cries, and ye moans and calls out for a lassie. I hears ye, and it breaks me heart, ye are in sich a painful state."

Matt's bad dreams haunted him he knew, but he didn't realize he was vocal or let any part of them escape his lips.

"What exactly do I say?" he asked, half afraid of the answer.

"Ye say, 'Kate, oh Kate, have I lost ye?' Then the moaning and thrashing starts. I can hear ye through the walls, it's a sad keening, and I ache for ye." Completely unsure of what to say, Matt turned back to the door and tried the name over in his mind. *Kate? Kate?* It sounded right, like it fit in his mouth. He liked the way the name made him feel.

"I don't know who Kate is," he finally answered. "I don't even remember my own name yet."

"Aye, I know," she nodded, "but I do." Shocked by her answer, Matt spun around again and stared at the bowed back once more.

"What do you know of me," Matt asked, "please, Franny is there something you can tell me?"

Franny raised her frizzled head, and her cloudy grey eyes bore into his. "I can tell ye, but ye will not believe me."

"Yes, I will, I have no reason to doubt anything you say, please tell me what you can."

Concern for this young man was strong in her heart, but a warning was needed here. Laury urged her to be cautious. She could not hide the truth from him any more than she could hide the horror she saw all about him, the horror she knew he would cause. Each time she looked at his face, she had to look away, the vision too strong. She wanted to show Elizabeth, but Elizabeth wouldn't see it, she never could. Not like Laury. Her Laury had the sight. Together they saw a world only a few others shared.

Franny's voice started low but rose in timbre, and she grew agitated. "There will be scores of people, dropping like the fish flies when their time is gone, dropping with their eyes bulging out of their heads. Staring they will be at ye, and ye will only watch them struggle. Ye will walk among them and hold out ye hands over them. Young and old, men and wimin, they will gurgle and choke. Ye made them sick; ye will cause them to die."

A horrible, sick feeling washed over Matt as he listened to her weird premonition, so similar to his recurring nightmare. Franny sat as if in a trance, waving her gnarled fingers in the air, reading him and the future like the pages of a book. *Did I say all this in the night? Are my nightmares being described out loud for the women to hear?*

"Franny, how do you know this, what have I said to make you say these things?" Franny slept on a small bed directly beneath his bedroom. If she had heard him, then Elizabeth must have as well. She crooked her head to the side and sat with her mouth slightly ajar, a little glint of spittle sat at the corner of her lips and threatened to spill down her chin.

"Laury told me to heed ye, and I hears the voices in ye mind, I listen, and I hear them. Ye cannot stop them; they will come as they will. It is not a thing to be undone. But ye must remember and bring the secret, or they will all die."

Reeling from her words, Matt believed, without knowing why, that she spoke the truth. "You said you know my name, Franny, what is my name?"

Her head dropped so low he thought it would hit her knees. In a voice so low as to be barely audible, "Death," she whispered. "Your name is death."

The punch of Franny's words hit Matt squarely; the blow knocked him to the floor. Franny had labeled him "death." His body physically recoiled from the impact of her words, but his mind subconsciously assessed them to be true. Instinctively he knew in his past life he handled death, manipulated, and controlled it. Somehow, someway, he felt it all the way to his core, something about his past told him he was an instrument which could cause great pain and suffering. His nightmares hinted at this knowledge, but his waking mind refused to follow the thread to enlightenment. The conflict within shot him through with lightning bolts of pain as his eyes beseeched Franny for a retraction. Slumped in her chair, eyes closed, her body was rigid while her head danced up and down, up and down, from right to left and back, reminding Matt of a bobblehead doll.

A pounding in his ears matched the crashing waves out on the bluffs, and a mist swirled the room making the air heavy. Franny's eerie words opened a portal from his nightmares to the room in which they sat, and malevolent electricity jumped the gap from one to another, enveloping them, running through them and setting his hair on end. The pounding became louder, and he could feel the vibration of it on the floor beneath him. A voice from beyond the door, deep and demanding rudely shocked them both from the murky reverie, but it saved him as it did from a decline into an abyss.

Matt lurched to his feet, his vision dimming as the blood drained instantly from his head, blacking out his sight. He felt his way to the door with his hands to keep from falling. Unsure of what just happened, and still reeling from the oppressiveness of the event, he looked back with narrowed sight at Franny who made no sound, her head lolled sideways so her eyes could follow him.

Two men stood side by side, filling the doorway as Matt yanked open the old heavy boards. Quizzical looks on their faces told Matt he must appear as deranged as he was feeling. "Matt Errington?" The taller of the two barked.

Suspended in silence, seconds ticked passed.

The pounding in his head grew. His face pale, no sign of recognition lit his eyes as his vision returned. Matt made no answer but looked from one man to the other, then back again. He shot a quick look back at Franny, half expecting her to challenge the name and substitute it with her grim tag for him. When she remained silent, he turned back to the strangers who once again demanded, "You *are* Matt Errington, aren't you?"

"I … I'm not sure," he began, his voice distant in his ears. "I, uh, was in an accident and have no real memory of anything."

"We know about your accident, and we've just come from the hospital where you were treated, but we assumed your memory would have returned by now, it has been several weeks, hasn't it?"

"Well, yes, but more importantly, you called me Matt, so you know who I am?" The mist from the outside poured in to swirl with the dark vapors inside the cottage, and the two entities battled for possession.

"May we come in Madame?" the shorter man addressed Franny. She nodded permission and the closing door crisply cleaved the tail of the entering fog.

"I am Ted Mannion, and this is my partner Averil Brindly, we are from Interpol."

Confusion flashed across Matt's face erasing the hopeful look which had eased his features only a second before. "I thought you said you were from the hospital," Matt stammered, looking again from one to the other.

"No, the hospital gave us your location; we just arrived from London this afternoon. Why didn't the hospital tell you of your identity? They knew who you were-"

"What? What are you talking about, I'm not even sure that is my name, and even if it is, why would the doctors keep it from Elizabeth … or from me?" Matt's confusion picked up steam and spun him around once again to seek confirmation of his words from Franny's eyes. Her face toward the floor gave him no sanction.

"Elizabeth? You mean Mrs. Champion?" Ted Mannion asked.

"Yes, Elizabeth Champion, she is letting me stay here in her cottage. She has been in touch with the doctors after my accident and while I recuperated. She is a friend and has opened her life and her home to me. Why would she … or they hold back my information?"

"I can't say, Mr. Errington, but I can assure you, that *is* your name. We have a copy of your passport photo and additional information about you in the car, let me run back and get the folder." Averil Brindly opened the door and seemed to almost flee the ominous feeling of the small cottage. He noticed as soon as they entered how something acrid assailed his sense of smell and burned his eyes. Thinking it was smoke from a fireplace, he scanned the room, but it gave him no hint of the bad aura's origin. Ever since he was a young man, Averil was sensitive to feelings and sensations around him others did not detect. The cottage had a definite bad feeling to it, and he found it difficult to stay within the walls and maintain his composure, so he welcomed the excuse to bolt back outside.

Catching his breath, he retrieved the documents from the car and slowly made his way back to the door. With a hand on the doorknob, he chastised himself to get a grip on his senses. Entering a second time, he found the atmosphere a bit less overwhelming and let out his pent-up breath. His partner stood rooted to the same spot. Matt had collapsed to a chair.

With the information thrown at him, Matt found it difficult to think. Truth, knowledge, doubt, betrayal. Thoughts and emotions flooded through him and caused his legs to buckle.

"Please tell me everything you know about me; I want to know, I *need* to know. Who am I?"

Averil opened the folder and took out a passport photo. The picture was grainy and of poor quality, probably a faxed copy. The photo appeared to have been taken several years prior: a man's face—younger, heavier and less anxious, but it was Matt's face staring back at him. The revelation should have been uplifting, but it had no such accompanying impact. Matt stared at the photo as if for the first time, no hint of memory, no emotion stirred to remind him of his life. Inked words filled the page of the report, but meant nothing beyond the telling: Matt Errington, 360 Alstead, Philadelphia. Age thirty-four.

Philadelphia. He had felt he was from the east coast. Other than confirmation, the information gave him no relief, just more questions. "I guess I am Matt Errington," he said finally, his eyes never left the page before him. "I am sure Elizabeth was never told any of this or she would have told me. She would have no reason to keep it from me. Would she?" he said, finally looking up at the visitors.

"Don't know about that," Ted nodded, "but the doctors knew, which makes me think she did as well. In any case, Matt, we need you to come with us back to London, there are some things I would think you want to clear up, and we have a lot of questions for you."

"What kind of questions? Go ahead, ask me anything, right here and now. I'll tell you what I can, but just because I have my name doesn't mean I have any clue about my life yet."

"No," Averil nearly snapped at him, eager to put distance between them and the cottage. "We are here to escort you back to London, and we need to get going now to catch the last flight back. Get your coat and shoes."

This latest development, in a very strange day, kept Matt frozen in his seat. Unable to rationalize the fragments of data bouncing from brain cell to brain cell, Matt could not get his thoughts to coalesce. He heard the man's instructions but could not make his body respond. Franny's bony hand on his arm broke the spell.

"Ye need to go," she whispered. "Ye will remember, and they will not die." The visitors could not catch her words, but they saw the instant effect on Matt. He bolted out of the chair as if launched by catapult. Whatever she knew, he must follow. Truth was in her words, dark and thick, and menacing, but salvation was also there. If he was to escape the macabre premonition her words and his nightmares evoked, he must heed it.

Chapter Twenty-Two

Elizabeth sat in Ben Madison's office staring at the calmly folded hands in her lap, totally belying the turmoil seething within. "How could this have happened Ben?" she spoke through barely moving lips. "I trusted you to protect the girls, how could they just disappear?"

"Now, Elizabeth, I know you are worried, but don't lose hope." Ben was sitting on the edge of his desk but moved into the chair at Elizabeth's side, trying to give her as much comfort as he could with his presence.

"They will be found! I know it." Ben nearly whispered. "I have always kept my promise to you and Karl; the girls would not be involved in dangerous situations if at all possible. The leads they were following are not like TV drama espionage, where everyone is a super spy and has to shoot their way out of trouble hour by hour. If anything, the only complaints I ever got from the girls is how boring it all is. The spy business is so much more attractive in the movies."

In spite of her concerns, Elizabeth laughed. They had told her themselves, how unbelievably boring the spy business could be. "I know you have done what you can, Ben, but what's the answer, where are they? Have you rechecked all of the cemeteries in the area?"

"Yes, we have. We don't know for sure, but it seems they were close to finding the target when something happened. My theory is they got to the last cemetery too late and discovered the Iranian's already dug up the body and took the Bible with them. The girls probably would have followed and tried to get it back. Which way they went is harder to say. We have no way of knowing where anyone went from there. Our Intel unit picked up some chatter suggesting a package, probably the Bible, was to be on a plane heading to Belize late the day the girls went missing. We have checked our sources from Las Vegas to the island, and no sign of the twins can be found anywhere. If they were following it, they did a bang-up job of staying undercover."

"Yes, but what if they weren't following it? What if something happened to them in the cemetery?"

"There was no sign of a struggle, no sign of their car, or anything to give us that kind of scenario. We didn't rule it out. However, nothing has panned out in the area."

Elizabeth continued to sit with her head down, trying to control her fears. "I admit I am worried. I keep thinking if they were injured and hauled out into the desert somewhere, out there in the heat, it could be days before we found them and by then it may be too late. They wouldn't have water or shelter at night," she shivered as the reality of what her loss would be overcame her. "Ben, please find them quickly."

"We're trying Elizabeth; you know we will do everything possible."

Elizabeth stood up; her hands automatically smoothed the front of her jacket; she should leave Ben to do his work. She would head back to the hotel and wait. A fleeting thought struck her. "Ben, you said Matt Errington was in love with Kate, right?"

"Yes, I think he was, but months ago. But he is over in Wales with you and Franny; he couldn't have anything to do with the girls being missing."

"I know, but remember the time you were at the cottage, after Lauren's death, how weird you said it felt to you. You said the cottage had an eerie, mystical feel to it. A 'presence' you called it."

"Where is this going, Elizabeth?" Ben asked, shaking his head at her ramblings.

"Matt has been having nightmares for the past few nights, I heard him a couple of times mumbling about heat and fear, and he even mentioned he was suffocating once. What if the cottage is having some kind of effect on him as well? Tuning him into the girl's … or more precisely, into Kate's location somehow. Isn't it worth at least checking?"

"I don't hold a lot of stock in the paranormal realm Elizabeth, and I'm not about to go off half-cocked chasing a nightmare, wasting valuable time and resources on a whim. If you were to tell all of this to Matt, for clarification's sake, how are you going to explain

Kate and his relationship? He doesn't remember his name, his life … or her. I'm not so sure it's even a good idea to tell him what has been going on. You will need to have quite a conversation with him, and you don't know if he will believe any of it or how he will relate it to his nightmares."

"I know you have reservations about him Ben, but my instincts tell me he is just as solid as he appears. Learning more about him, I'm convinced his motive for going to Wales was to find me to help him find Kate. He still loves her, and I believe somehow his love transcends space and time and may give us the lead to find her and Lilly. I can't and won't wait for a better time to have an enlightening discussion with him if it means we can find the girls sooner. He deserves to know who he is and who Kate is, and there is just a chance he can help."

"Alright Elizabeth, you do what you think is best for the girls, and if he can give you something more tangible to go on, we will check it out to the most minute detail. Okay?" Ben would have done anything to give her the reassurance she so desperately sought but chasing leads from a head injury patient was about as good a shot as letting Franny read his tea leaves for him again. The whole idea was stretching faith a bit far, in his opinion.

"I'll call him as soon as I get back to the hotel," Elizabeth promised, "and I'll let you know exactly what he tells me."

"Of course, I promise to check out any substantial leads he may have. But please, try not to give him more information than the situation deserves." Elizabeth nodded. Ben watched her walk out of his office; her shoulders squared to the world. *Always in control,* he thought. Elizabeth was a special person, and he would do anything in the world to keep her respect and make her smile again. After his divorce years before, Ben believed his job would be enough to keep him company, but that resolve was truly tested every time he saw Elizabeth.

Matt was moving slowly, not so much because of the injured leg, but because he couldn't feel his feet at all. His body was still reeling from the latest twist of events. His name was Matt Errington, and he was being questioned by Interpol, and he had something to do with a lot of people dying. *What a way to get my*

memory back, he thought as he headed toward the small upstairs room to gather what little possessions he had. He didn't know if he should take the clothes Elizabeth lent to him or even how long he would be gone. *Do I need to pack anything at all? How far is the trip to London?* The thought occurred to him he didn't want to go with the officers, even though his need to find his place in the world was a great incentive. Something was wrong with the whole thing. Maybe it was Franny's dire prediction or his nightmares, but the little cottage was about the closest thing to a home he knew, and like leaving a sanctuary, the thought alarmed him to his core.

He wanted to turn around, head back downstairs to tell them he wasn't up to the trip, but he was stopped short by the black framed mirror over the washstand in his room. A face, his face, stared back at him with a different look than just a few hours ago. It wasn't the beard growing in thick and curly, or the eyes still bloodshot from lack of sleep the night before. The face was different because it had a name. He had a name. An identity. He belonged somewhere else, and the only way to get the answers he needed to go home was to face the unknown in London.

"All I need is a jumper, a mackintosh and a taste for warm beer," he mumbled to himself. Surprised such a strange list of items should flash through his mind, he wondered about it but did not take the time to analyze what it meant. *Mental note, find out if I like warm beer.*

Franny's voice on the phone was clear as a bell in spite of the distance from Elizabeth's hotel. Franny didn't like telephones and never would have used one except Lauren insisted on having one in the cottage for their safety, since they were so isolated out on the bluffs. Elizabeth noted immediately Franny sounded tired and asked her if she was well.

"I am well enough, don't ye go worrying about me, tis been an eventful day, it has."

"Well, you take care of yourself, and I want to hear how things are going there Franny, but before I do, please let me speak to our guest for a few minutes. It's important."

"I would do that thing, but ye cannot," Franny answered haltingly.

"Why, is he asleep?"

"Our guest has left us with two fancy dressed gentlemen from London. They knew his name and where he was from. Told him he must go with them to London to talk to them, to answer many questions. I told him to go … to remember why he was among us. He must remember."

Fear crept into Elizabeth's voice while it raced through her entire body. "What are you saying, Franny, who did he go with and why? When did this happen?"

Franny was tired; she wanted to lie down and ease her old rheumy pains. "If ye want to talk to the young man, the gentlemen were taking him to Swansea. They wanted to catch the last flight going to London tonight. I would think ye kin ask him yeself all ye wish to know if ye will make a call there."

The plane wouldn't leave for another half hour, and Matt found himself anxiously staring out of the window trying to catch a glimpse of the world beyond Swansea. His nerves were badly frazzled, and he could barely sit still as he was forced to sit between the two agents in front of the telly. Standing on the precipice of getting his life back was making his head hurt again. If he kept his mind loose and didn't concentrate on anything, he could head off the pain threatening to bulge out of his eyes. *What a great life I'm in for,* he briefly decided. *When I try to use my head, it explodes like fireworks.* The agents told him little and would not or could not divulge the reason to necessitate his trip to London. *Somehow Franny knew I needed to go, so here I am. Mental note: Pick up something nice for her and Elizabeth when I finally get wherever it is I'm going since I'm assuming I'm never coming back here again.*

As she rocked in the old bent chair by the fireplace with the dog on her lap, Franny slowly stirred her tea and watched the leaves swirl around the bottom. "Our young man is beginning the end of his journey, Beastie. I hope he truly has a good heart, but I fear he will not be much help to his young love. And aye, tis a sad affair for the babes, and them being sich nice young lasses too. But, I'm just an old womin, what is it you would have me do? I kinna help them." Tilting her old head sideways, the frizzled grey hair dusted the rim of her cup. As she watched, the companion chair by her side kept pace with hers, back and forth, pushed by unseen feet upon the worn braided rug at its base. "Ahh," Franny murmured at length, reassured by some inner resolution, "that is good Laury, let them be heard."

Chapter Twenty-Three

"Enid, it's not in this direction … I'm telling you, there were more of those scraggly trees around. I don't know why I let you drag me out here in this heat to search for some old coot's grave."

"Oh, you don't know everything, Mava, it was nearly twenty years ago, and don't you think maybe they cut some of the trees down by now? I remember the road running alongside the fence just like it is here. We have been all over the damn cemetery in the last half hour, and I'll bet you ten dollars this is the spot."

"Yeah, you would bet on anything wouldn't you? That's what got us in the cheap-ass joint we're in now, isn't it? You bet, but you don't win."

"Now Mava you know that's not my fault. The cards just haven't been lucky lately. My luck will turn around soon, you wait and see. And besides, if you hadn't picked up that skuzzy little weasel Barry, we'd have more than enough money to find a better place to stay."

"Humph, you didn't think he was a weasel when he was coming on to you, did you? Just because he chose me instead of you, you're just jealous he ended up taking me back to the motel that night."

"You're such an idiot Mava, the creep had you from the get-go, you practically threw your body at him, and he didn't have to work hard. But you didn't have to let him have all of our money too."

"Well, how was I supposed to know he would find my purse under the … oh geez! Did you hear that?"

"What? Did I hear what?"

"That noise, like a whining. Come on, let's get outta here; this place is giving me the willies."

"You're just changing the subject because you know I'm right and you can't stand to lose an argument."

"I'm not kidding Enid; I heard something."

"Well, it's not a ghost, silly. Everyone knows ghosts don't go around spooking people in the daytime, and it's only a little past six o'clock, not exactly haunting time now is it? It's probably the trees rubbing together. I'm surprised with your bad ears you can hear anything at all, you certainly never hear me."

"Shut up Enid; it was your bright idea to come looking up old flames today. You never had much use for your husband when he was alive. Why bother looking for his grave now?"

"Mava, I told you to get going earlier today, if you weren't so damn lazy we would have been here before the office closed and looked up the grave number. But no, you needed to have your beauty sleep, hell; you'd have to sleep for a month to get rid of your uglies. And Richard wasn't such a bad husband, and you know it. He let you stay with us whenever your current boyfriend threw you out. I just had an urge to visit him today, can't say why, kinda strange the way the idea popped into my head and all, but since we were in town anyway ..."

"See there it is again." Mava interrupted her companion, and both women simultaneously looked toward the scrub line of dying trees as the source for the low moaning. With barely a whisper of wind, it was doubtful the sound was emanating from that direction.

"What the hell was it?"

"Nothing, it was nothing! Since we've already spent so much time looking anyway, let's just find Richard and get outta here."

"Fine," Mava sputtered, "If it's so important to you to visit his rotting bones, but I don't want to spend one extra second in this place, it's just too damn creepy."

Why is Mom fighting with Laverne? They always get along so well. It was a strange argument, and Lilly was surprised to hear her mother swear. *She was always such a lady. Probably the heat is getting to them too,* she thought. *Such terrible heat. Why is it so uncomfortable ... and why doesn't someone turn on the air conditioning? What time is it anyway? It must be close to dinnertime, my stomach hurts, and Papa is probably home by now.* She wondered what terrific dessert Laverne had made for them. *Her girls,* Laverne always called the twins. This was always funny to Lilly since Laverne was only a young woman herself. When the twins were five, Laverne came to live with their family to help out with the housework and give Elizabeth a break from chasing after two highly charged imps. *So, what are they fighting about,* Lilly wondered again. *Maybe I should go break it up. If Papa heard them, he would be upset not knowing which side to take. Papa!* The memory of her dad jerked Lilly from the daze.

Voices, she heard voices. But they weren't her mother and Laverne; she wasn't a young girl at home. She was trapped in a stone room with her sister. And they were dying.

"Kate! Kate!" she reached as far as her arm would go trying to feel for her sister's body. "I hear voices outside!" With no response from Kate, Lilly tried to bolster what little strength she had left to reach the crack in the wall far above her head.

"Help," she rasped through parched lips and throat. But the words drifted back to her, lifeless. *Where are my shoes, I took them off somewhere in the dark, they have wooden heels, maybe I can tap an SOS if I can just find them quickly.* The voices were starting to fade. Either the arguers were finished with their debate, or they were moving away.

Tap, tap, tap, tap. The energy she exerted was about all she had left, but was it enough to get the women's attention?

Tap, tap. Her hand dropped from the weight of the effort.

"Did you hear that, Enid?"

"What? That tapping? Yeah, probably a woodpecker, I'm sure the trees are full of birds."

"Well, maybe, but that didn't sound like no woodpecker to me."

"Oh, shut up Mava, you are always so melodramatic like you're some expert on what a woodpecker sounds like."

"Help, please help us!" Kate roused to the tapping noise her sister made and crawled her way up the wall to add her feeble voice to the plea.

Mava's head spun around in the direction of the row of crumbling vaults as shivers went up her spine. "Enid, that was a voice … and there is nowhere else for it to come from except one of those little brick houses over there."

Enid was as white as a ghost herself and was taking small steps backward away from the source. She heard the same sound and could barely find her voice.

"Mava," Enid pleaded, shaking from head to toe, "get over here away from it. Whatever it is … it's no concern of ours."

"What are you talking about you ninny, ghosts don't cry for help, do they? There is someone in there. We can at least find out what's going on." Tentatively Mava crept forward toward the vault and called out in a low, unsteady voice. "Hello, who are you?"

Kate nearly fainted again, but the surge of adrenalin pushed her face back up to the crack. "Help us, please help us. We're trapped."

Within ten minutes of their call to 911, Mava and Enid stood on the sidelines, beaming with the pride of heroics, as two emergency vehicles stood at the ready for the twin's emergence from their tomb. A fire truck was called to help open the heavy stone door with thick metal bolts holding it closed, and in a matter of minutes, the dying girls were gingerly brought out. Dehydration and the desert heat nearly claimed two victims.

Right on the heels of the emergency team's response was a car with Ben's staff, screeching to a stop in front of the vault. Alerted by the State Department of the search for the girls, the local police immediately informed the field agents that someone had been found.

Minutes after the rescuers brought the girls out, Elizabeth was notified. When the girls were stabilized they would be flown back to Washington, and Ben would send a car to pick her up and she could start to breathe again.

As if from an act in a faraway play, Franny saw the scene unfold before her closed eyes, and her bobblehead danced up and down slowly. "Aiee" she gleefully clapped her rheumy hands together. "Thank ye my Laury, for settin' the lassies aright! Ye're brother will be grateful, he will, for savin' his babes."

Chapter Twenty-Four

"Alright Matt, let's go over this again, shall we. What is your relationship with Kaleehad Khourmy?"

Holding his head in his hands, Matt was so tired of the questions. *Who the hell is this Khourmy character, and why does Interpol think I know him?*

"I have told you over and over; I don't know anyone by that name. And even if I do, it is probably still frozen in my head. I barely recognize my own identity, let alone other people." The agents took Matt to a small room in an Interpol office in the lower end of London. It was dimly lit and rivaled sleazy interrogation rooms he had seen on TV. "I'm not certain about anything yet. Why don't you tell me what's going on and maybe I can get a better grasp of things. I'm trying to help you, but all of this is like mud to me."

The agents shot quick looks at each other and nodded toward the door. Once outside, they both lit a cigarette taking a moment to form their opinions.

"I don't know about you, but I believe the guy," Special Agent Brent Baggins said slowly, the smoke curling above his head.

"Yeah, well maybe he's telling the truth, and maybe he isn't, I'm not sure yet," his partner Special Agent Diabeque nodded. "Just how much can we give him to whet the pump?"

"I'm not sure, but I'll check with the inspector and see what she wants us to do. All we know is the Intel division said his name has bounced all over the internet about the possible attack here in London. He's involved somehow, so he's not going anywhere soon. Unless the home office wants us to let him go to track his movements. Still, I can't figure how an American geek like him is involved with a terror group like Khourmy's thugs. Just doesn't fit the profile."

"Can't say, but I know home is sweating bullets about this latest warning. Pretty sure something big is coming, and they don't have a clue what it is. They want us to follow every lead, especially him."

Agent Baggins shrugged his curly brown head toward the room in which Matt sat. "Intel doesn't have much to go on, and they think this guy has something."

"Yeah, I hope they are right, but if you ask me, we'd be better off spending our time taking the guy to the pub, maybe a few pints would loosen him up. He's wrapped up tighter than your queen's private laundry. Know what I mean?"

"Here now, don't go poking fun at the Mum. She's not to blame for letting terrorists into the Isles. Them blokes in Parliament need a few lessons in counter-espionage. If they'd loosen those purse strings a bit, we'd have a better network for catching the crud in our fair land before they can get a foothold and run amok all over England and Europe. You're just jealous anyway; you don't have any royalty where you're from."

"Nope, you're right, we don't have royalty, but we're not supporting some gem-studded free-loaders by our tax dollars either."

"Hey, watch your mouth, our royals earn their keep, and we're proud to be a part of their heritage. Your country's been overrun with dictators and the economy is in the loo, who are you to talk about what's right or wrong." The argument was an old one between the two agents and was picking up steam once again. If not overheard by Inspector Dare, it would probably have continued as in the past, long after their day's duty ended and wound up with them at the pub battling it out with their fellow drinkers.

Tricia Dare heard the rising voices and stuck her head out of her office. "Any progress with the guy in the holding room?" she asked pointedly.

"Naw, we're just taking a break to figure out the next move," Agent Baggins answered her. "How much info does the home office want us to give him?" he asked quickly, trying to smooth over the pissed look on the Inspector's face.

"Tell him only what you have to, but get him to talk, and do it now, gentlemen! Your politics can wait." Her tone was crisp, and there was no missing her ire.

Both agents quickly snuffed out their cigarettes and headed back in to work on Matt. "You want to be the good cop this time, or can I?" Baggins asked his partner.

"Naw, you always blow the role, let me do it."

The name on the caller ID on his phone threw Phil for a moment. Jan Gabor didn't ring any bells. *Better let it go to voicemail,* he thought. As he played the message back, the sound of a woman's voice pricked a distant memory. "Hi Phil, this is your cousin Janet from Nevada. I had some trouble finding you, so my news is a bit late. Please give me a call as soon as you can. It's important … about your brother Eddy." She left her number and hung up with a "toodles."

New name, he thought. *She must have gotten married again. How many was it, four or five husbands?* Phil was curious about her message, but after giving it some thought, he figured his lazy, worthless brother was probably in debt to his cousin, and if he called her back, she was going to try and put the squeeze on him to bail Eddy out. *No way, thank you. Let the little shit wiggle out of a mess on his own for a change. All of his life, Mom babied Eddy until the day she died. Always saving his ass. Maybe if she had paid as much attention to me as she did Eddy, she would have seen which was the better son and put the asshole in a home and forgotten him. But nooo, it was always "Eddy this and Eddy that, and Phil, be nice to your brother, he has difficulties." Yeah, he has difficulties alright, he's a damn screwed up little shit,* Phil thought again, and he wasn't about to waste his hard-earned money trying to help him.

After all, he was already doing more than enough for the little shit. After he got his money from Zand, he would give Eddy a few bucks to keep him happy for a while.

It was two days later when he received a second message from Jan.

"Phil, I haven't heard from you, and I hate to break the news to you like this about Eddy, but there's been an accident. It's important you call me."

"God damn little rodent, I can't believe he went and got himself drowned," Phil ranted to the ceiling. "What a piss-ant." No sentimental emotion softened Phil's outburst. After learning of his brother's death, Phil was surprised but not shocked to learn what had befallen his only sibling. "Stupid asshole, what the hell was he thinking by trying to break into a casino. I told him to stay out of trouble; I had a deal in the works, and I would have shared it with him, but no, the jackass went and got himself killed."

When the initial impact of his brother's death faded, a brick hit Phil in the back of the head. *THE BIBLE!!! What happened to the fucking book and the computer chip? Oh hell, don't I have enough problems?* Now he'd have to fly out there to dig around in Eddy's junk and find the damn book.

Couldn't life just once give me a break? "Stupid jerk," Phil continued his tirade. "I give you something of great importance to hold for me, and you fuck it up as usual. If you weren't dead already, I'd wring your neck myself," Phil threatened the now decaying Eddy.

Chapter Twenty-Five

The reunion was emotional. Elizabeth had her girls back. It was several minutes before they settled down and complete sentences could be spoken. The tearful scene caught Ben like a punch to the gut. Not many things in his life ever affected him as much as this reunion. Three separate people clung to each other, but each knew they belonged to one another's soul. Ben ached to move, to join the group hug and be a part of the energy in front of him but found himself frozen. *Why hadn't he realized it before now?* He yearned for love and belonging. He wanted to be a part of a family, their family to be precise, to be a part of their private circle. This was not the time he knew, but one day soon, he would try to share his feelings with Elizabeth. There was no question he would have to go slow, but he hoped she could grow to feel for him what he finally admitted to himself he felt about her and her girls. He loved them all deeply and probably had for many years.

Smiling, Ben quietly backed out of the room to give them time to be alone together. Life sure was mysterious; he practically whistled as he headed down the long hospital hall. One day he was content to spend his life committed to his career with his waning years spent listening to his favorite operas and watching the sun go down alone. The next, he was hoping to begin a new chapter with a new family. "Damn," Ben said to himself, "life sure is crazy, but it can be good."

"Matt lets go over this one more time," Agent Baggins slammed his hand down on the table, and the overhead tube-lights flickered in response to the release of energy. We know you are involved with a group of terrorists working out of London. Your name has popped up in conversations ricocheting all across Europe. We have picked up Intel planting you right in the midst of a terrorist attack, and we haven't got time to play guessing games with you. It sure is mighty coincidental you happen to be in the Isles when we're under attack and you just conveniently forgot it all. Talk to us, or you will never see your sweet little home across the pond again. What's the plan, and where is it going down?"

They went over, and over the same topic for hours, Matt had no idea what was going on or if he did have anything to do with it. While the façade he hoped he was maintaining would belie their accusations, deep inside his reeling mind, Matt's greatest fear was in spite of what he believed to be true about himself, there was the possibility he was involved in some kind of terrorist activity and would spend the rest of his life in a London prison. What other explanation could there be for him even being in England?

Agent Diabeque sat across from Matt and held his hand up to stop the attack from his partner. "Take it easy, Baggins. Can't you see the guy is trying to help us? Look, Matt," his palms up in a pleading gesture. "Interpol has known for some time something is in the planning stages, and all reports point to London as a target. There is chatter all over the Internet, and all agents watching known terrorist cells have reported a dramatic increase in activity in the last few days. Something big is brewing. It has been mentioned hundreds, and possibly thousands of people could be involved. Do you know anything that can help us?"

The memory of Franny's dire prediction and his unexplained nightmares kept playing over and over behind his eyes. *Tell them! Tell them*, his mind screamed until he thought they could hear the words themselves. *Yes, but if I do,* he reasoned to himself, *and I am involved in something terrible, I could spend my life in prison … and if I'm innocent how can I defend myself and prove to them I don't remember anything.* Outwardly Matt just stared at the table, unable to answer their questions or his own.

Slowly he made a decision and started to speak, his words mesmerizing the two agents. "I had a dream," he started in a low voice. "A nightmare really. Hundreds of people were stricken by something terrible. They were dropping to the ground and appeared to be in convulsions of some sort. I walked among them untouched by whatever evil knocked them down. They tried to plead for help, but no words came out, just their faces strained with the effort, and their bodies writhed in silence. I think it was in an airport … it was a huge place, I couldn't see the end of the room, and it seemed to go on forever."

"Heathrow!" both agents declared at once. "When is this going to happen?" Baggins asked slamming both hands on the table this time.

"I don't know. Honestly, I don't. It was a dream, that's all I can tell you. I don't even know what I am doing there or why I would have such a horrible nightmare. I am telling you everything I can. If it helps you save people, use it, but it's all I know." Matt was getting hysterical with the pressure from inside his head and from the agents without. He threw his life on their mercy and hoped what he relayed to them would appease the evil humors in his mind, and he would be released from the pain crushing his skull.

"Okay, calm down. You say it was a dream. Why do you think you would have such a dream?" Agent Diabeque asked, motioning to Agent Baggins to hand him Matt's file.

"Nothing, I have nothing more to give you," Matt answered truthfully, the voices finally silenced in his head. The agent leafed through the reports. "We know you're associated with a lab of some kind in the States. You're a kind of scientist, right? Your name has been linked with some really bad people. Are you providing terrorists with biological warfare? Is that what you make? Are you working on a bio attack?"

"No, of course not," Matt shouted. "I can't answer all those questions, but I know that's not me. I just know it."

"Okay, Matt, talk to us about your work. How is it involved with the people in your dream; is it a bomb, a biological agent, a poison, viruses, or what? Talk to us Matt, people's lives depend on it."

Agent Diabeque stepped out of the interrogation room to brief Inspector Dare on the small bit of information they gained. If they were right, and Heathrow was the target it would have to be closed and inspected from top to bottom for bombs or biological agents; though God knows how it could be accomplished in such a mammoth facility was beyond his knowledge. He was thankful it wasn't his problem as he knocked on the inspector's door.

Inspector Dare listened intently as the agent relayed what they learned. She wasn't, however, as convinced as her agents, the guy's dream was a true premonition to be followed blindly, nor should they close down the largest and busiest airport in the world. The magnitude of such an undertaking made her head spin. Interpol would be the laughing stock of Europe if they went ahead with such a huge endeavor, on the sole basis of a dream, and it fizzled out.

More than anything else, the inspector wanted to play this right. Not only was her entire career at stake, but if her beloved London was in jeopardy, the thought of anyone hurting its people was not acceptable. It was not going to happen on her watch if she could help it. But close down Heathrow? What if they were wrong and in error, they aimed a huge portion of their resources toward protecting the airport? Taking the focus off of other possible targets that would be left vulnerable. London was a large city with hundreds of sites bustling with activity. Heathrow, it was true, was busy and could easily have thousands of people passing through it in a day, but was that enough for terrorists to choose it as a target for their evil? In her long career in police work, the inspector had followed her gut on most occasions, and it usually worked out right. But she needed a lot more to go on than a nightmare and a hunch. Pacing within the confines of her small, cluttered office with its stacks of files and folders, she efficiently used her years of experience to come to a decision.

"We must be extremely certain before we notify the Secret Service, London Police, or airport security that we have something more substantial than a dream," the inspector said. "And, I don't want word of this to leak to the local US Fed's office. Even if he is American, they'll muck up the waters. Just because this guy works in a lab isn't enough to assume he has any role in a terrorist attack. Put out a notice, however, to increase surveillance of all international and domestic chatter targeting airports and Heathrow, laboratories, biological agents, etc. Got that?"

Agent Diabeque nodded.

"Anything else from him?" the inspector asked.

"I honestly believe he is telling us what he remembers. He has no idea of what is going down. The hard part is trying to determine if his dream is merely a memory of something he doesn't want to remember, or an overactive imagination where he wants to play a superhero."

"Well we can't play psychiatrists all day, can we? Get with HSS and tap into every source you can." The inspector jabbed her thumb toward the telephone on her desk, "and find out all you can about this guy, not just where he works, but what he does there. What does he work on? Get it all. Something tells me you may be on the right track, but if what you say about him is correct, we're not going to get much more from him without more forceful encouragement. Get going and let me know what you find out. Time is of the essence, gentlemen. Tell Baggins I want to see him. Maybe we should put the guy in the back room and turn off the lights. If given a chance, he might have another enlightening dream for us."

For the first time in days, Matt felt relief. He had shared the dark images in his head with no idea where it would take him, and was yet to be determined, but at least for the moment, he felt good about the decision. Left alone in the small interrogation room, Matt mulled over the facts he had been given about his life and who he was. *A scientist? Doing research?* Well, that certainly surprised him, but, yeah, he could picture himself in a lab. Small bits of mental flotsam were floating before his mind's eye. People, places, a small card and tinkling, sparkling glass. Like jigsaw puzzle pieces behind a thin sheer veil, they wove in and out, not staying long enough for identification of where they belonged in the picture, tantalizing him with a hint of the truth. It's all in there. He knew it was. His world, his reality was still there in his head. But how much time was needed to get it out? Matt was ready to remember. He was on the brink. Good or evil, scientist or terrorist, he was ready to know it all.

"Bring it on," he said to himself, "bring it on."

Chapter Twenty-Six

Rashid Zand was hungry, and the waitress was nowhere in sight. *Lazy American bitch.* Angry at being kept waiting, Zand tried to control the turbulence inside himself. Allah was testing him again, he knew. He could hear Allah's voice in his head. "Patience, my son. Your time for glory is coming. They will all know you." Zand lowered his head, listening to the words of his master. *Yes, they will soon know me.* His lip curled up slightly in a half smile. Soon his name would be respected throughout the world. They would know of his deeds and his honor to Allah. If he could just complete his assignment soon and be gone from this stinking hell on earth.

New York was teeming with humanity. People jostled him and pushed him around. *No manners, no respect.* He lived in this horrible country for years, and each day the stink of filthy Americans clung to him like fleas on a dog. *Stupid people like Phil Forester, they are all stupid and greedy. These people, in this city, they should be the ones to die*, he thought, as the thousands in 2001. Thousands more should perish … but Allah had his ways, and it was not his place to question his leaders or their plans. He almost wished he would be able to dance and celebrate when their newspapers spread the word of his deeds, *and these stupid infidels mourned and wailed.*

The young waitress arrived at his table and saw only a boyishly good-looking young man. He was not dressed in the typical attire of a sloppy college student. She thought him neat and clean-cut. Impressed he was not wearing jeans in shreds or a t-shirt emblazoned with cartoons or politics, she pushed a loose strand of hair back behind her ear and gave him her prettiest smile.

"Are you ready to order, sir?" she chirped.

"Ah, yes, if I may have your special," he deliberately smiled a brilliant smile at her. "It is prepared fresh today, is it not?"

"Yep, that's what makes it the special," she giggled the reply.

"Stupid bitch," Zand said under his breath as she walked away in her tight black pants and gauze shirt, jiggling her back end for his benefit. *They are all so easy to fool.* He would have his women soon. They would throw themselves upon him and anoint his body with precious oils. Not American trash like this one, but the beautiful, chaste women of his home. They would honor him and call him their beloved. It would be as Allah promised. His time for glory was near, he had waited so long for this day to come, and he was impatient.

He couldn't help but smile at the memory of his special day. The day he had found his salvation. So many months had gone by already, it seemed like ages. This was the culmination of years of restraint and sacrifice. All his intense training taught him to use caution, but that day, the need to boast of his success was stronger as he met with his brothers and told them of his meeting with Phil Forester.

He had paused dramatically in the doorway of the small row house they shared, in a poor area of Philadelphia, and inspected the dimly lit room. Five men sat in silence as his probing gaze rested briefly on each man. Their faces were closed with practiced calm, but the eyes spoke, and he knew some lied. He had smiled at them. His white teeth flashed across his dark face, and with a wave of his arms, he invited them close.

"Come, embrace me, my brothers," he said to them. "I have found what I need to punish the ignorant for their lack of faith and blasphemous tongues. Soon I will know great glory." One by one, his brothers approached with kisses and praise.

"We prayed for such good news." Abel Farhat, Rashid's closest friend, clung to Rashid's arm. "I envy you, my brother. I, too, have spent nearly all of my allotted three years of this mission seeking redemption and glory with no success, but you will be in the arms of Allah."

"Thank you, my friend," Rashid answered, "but as many of our brothers have done, we came to this diseased country to seek our one true purpose. The Master has generously provided the money and identities we need. We have only to use them wisely. This is truly a land of opportunity for us. For a long time, I was unsure how this would happen for me. But just as I did, you must open your ears to the possibilities around you. As the Master has taught us, if you listen, you will learn."

The room grew silent once more as elated voices died to catch Rashid's words. "In our homeland, men do not speak their minds. Fear silences their voices and knowledge is passed from one to another in secret, if at all. But here, in this land, freedom of speech is sacred, is it not? Men talk of all things to anyone with ears, which is exactly why our leader wisely chose jobs in places where we would have access to a wide range of voices. At first, I was offended, serving these dogs in menial positions. But soon, I understood his wisdom. In the hotels, gyms, restaurants, and bars, people are at ease. Arrogance, my dear brothers, will be their undoing. Foolishly they fear nothing. To learn a man's secrets, you only have to wait. Just listen. These Americans do not understand the purpose of silence. I listened and heard an unhappy voice, of which there are many. As I listened, the idea of using their own medical research against them came to me, and with the grace of Allah, I will silence many of their voices."

"Your news is wonderful indeed," Samir Ali Mansoor, the newest member of the group added, as he came up behind Rashid and patted him on the back. "Tell us, Rashid," Samir asked, "What is the name of the man you met with, the scientist, is it he who will create the toxin for you?"

Rashid had taken a moment to answer. "He is not the one. The man I met is merely a vehicle to obtain the substance and the information. He will help me because he is a greedy man. He has no morals or soul. Like filth on the bottom of my shoe, I will scrape him off when I am finished. But for now, we will play the game."

"If he is not the maker, how will he get what you want? Can he be trusted not to speak of this to the authorities?" Samir asked.

"He will not. I have promised him much for his silence and participation. As for the substance, he will borrow the research of his co-worker, a biochemist. Someone called Errington."

"Was it difficult to convince the man to give you what you asked?" Samir pursued.

"Not at all. He was not chosen randomly. Like a book, each man can be read if we take the time. Many weeks went by before I knew he was the one. Many in this land are dissatisfied, but not many hold something of such great value as he. As I listened, I learned this one's weaknesses. His deepest concern was the money he expects when the deed is accomplished. He does not comprehend the significance of his contribution to our cause. He is a needy little toad who wants to believe there is an easy way out of his misery. A delusion I was happy to support."

"Has our Master decided on a date or a target yet? Is it here, in this land or some other?" Samir asked.

Rashid's eyes narrowed, and he cast a questioning eye toward his friend Abel's direction but curtly answered Samir. "You know he will not make such information known until all is in place. Why do you ask so many questions Samir? You who have left the Master's side only a few months ago, have you forgotten his teachings so soon? It is not our place to question the Master, or our need to know his will. How is it you forget so often so many of his words?"

"My apologies Rashid. I speak out of my excitement for your news. Of course, I remember our Master's teachings," Samir's gaze dropped to the floor as he backed into the small kitchen to retrieve a platter of meat. He knew he could wait no longer for more details. He needed to send Ben a brief warning immediately.

"We are all truly excited for you Rashid." Abel interrupted. "Please sit, dear Brother. In anticipation of your victory, we have prepared a celebration." He waved toward the table which was laden with traditional delicacies: Chelo rice and lamb, pomegranate soup, a large bowl of prunes and apricots. "Let us eat and rejoice and give thanks to Allah. We want to hear what occurred between you and the scientist," Abel continued. "Such an ideal place you chose to meet. The Rumpass Room."

"Yes. It was noisy, but our voices were not easily overheard or recorded." Behind Samir's bent head, Rashid and Abel locked eyes in a meaningful look. "I followed one of our Master's most primary directives; avoid detection and not betray ourselves or our purposes. Also, in such a setting when a man is easily distracted, he asks fewer questions. I was not surprised the little man only wished to know about the money and if he could have the seat closest to the stage."

Rashid and Abel took their seats at the table on either side of Samir. A long thin knife sat on Rashid's lap, hidden beneath the cloth.

Out loud, he prayed. "Today, we give thanks to Allah for his many blessings, and we rededicate our lives to destroying his enemies. The Master teaches us it is better to lose a possible friend than to be betrayed by a possible enemy." At such a prayer, Samir's instincts jerked his head up, but before he could move to protect himself or the rest of the group could raise their heads, Rashid swung the knife and drove it deep into Samir's back.

Abel caught Samir's head as it pitched backward and neatly sliced his throat from ear to ear. "Allah be praised," he said, wiping the blood from his hands.

As the gasps of the others faded, the celebration continued without pause after Samir's murder. Rashid was empowered by the act. He had ferreted out an unproven but possible threat and dealt with him accordingly. Rashid hated traitors. Even those who he used to further his plans. *Like Phil Forester. Truly a weasel of a man. No morals, no conscience. Only greed.* How it had thrilled Rashid to crush Phil's plans as well, with one phone call. Another memory to make him smile.

"You asshole!" Phil had shouted into the phone. "You can't just cut me out of this deal. I've spent months gathering the documents you want, at great personal risk, I may add. If I'm caught, I could get the death penalty for treason, or at least spend the rest of my life in prison." Phil raged, his anger exploding. "You son-of-a-bitch, we had a deal. What about my money? I didn't risk everything for nothing."

Rashid could hear Phil punch the wall in frustration. Rashid savored the moment.

Yes, little man, you may do penance for your deeds, or even die, while I will be showered with praise for mine. There was a sweet taste to his words when he responded, "There will be no money for you." He had deliberately refused contact with Phil for over two weeks, although Phil had repeatedly called. When Zand finally answered, he could barely hold back his pleasure when he told him he was no longer needed for the project.

Phil had exploded in frustration. "How can you just cut me out, you need the data I have. You told me how important this stuff is to your people. Having the ability to drop people in their tracks was going to give you bargaining power against Iraq and your other squirrelly neighbors in the East. What happened to all your plans for retaliation for the crap they did to your family?"

The tirade widened the smile on Rashid's face. It had been such sweet pleasure to crush the selfish little man. "We no longer need your help, because we have everything we want already," Rashid told him.

"What? What are you talking about?" Phil blurted. "You have what? I haven't given you anything yet."

"No, but your brother did. You gave us a sample of the virus months ago and the notes you hid in the book, were most efficient and concise. The instructions for the deadly mist were easy to follow. Our scientists have already produced sufficient quantities to serve our purposes. And, who but Allah knows who our enemy truly is?"

Phil's heart was pounding, and his breathing came out in rasps. "You killed Eddy? You camel-fucking Arab. What did you do to him?"

"We did nothing to your brother," Zand answered, smugly ignoring the insult. "His greed, like your own, decided his fate. We merely learned where he and his treasured book were buried and borrowed it." Laughing, Zand thoroughly enjoyed Phil's inability to grasp what was happening.

"How did you know about the Bible? I told no one." Phil sputtered in anger.

"I told you before, we have eyes everywhere, and Allah is most generous," Zand snickered. "He tells us what we need to know to punish our enemies."

"But you don't have it all. What you found wasn't complete. You have only half the project." Brushing the issue of his brother aside, Phil heartened at the thought they still needed him to deliver Matt's finished work. He was convinced if he hadn't found the rest of Matt's notes, they hadn't either. There would be no antidote, only mass murder.

Ahh, yes, Rashid could smell the fear through the cell phone in his hand. He could hear the thoughts inside the infidel's head. He reveled as the power pulsed through his veins. The little dog understood what his greedy actions had wrought.

"We will find the rest of the information I am certain of it, just as we found the microchips you tried to hide with your brother. Allah is our guiding light. He knows all and reveals it to us to be victorious. But, if the rest of it comes too late to save our enemies, well, alas, their fate too, is in Allah's hands."

It was early morning, and a hazy light wormed its way through the holes in the brittle, tattered window shade, caramel colored with age. It was difficult to sit up. The ancient, Naugahyde couch, upon which Matt napped, was several feet too short for him to comfortably stretch out, but sleep overcame him anyway. The stiff, cracked surface of the armrest chafed his face and neck, leaving marks along his cheekbone. Rising to his feet, Matt stretched and inspected the small room. It was used as a storeroom as evidenced by the stacks of boxes against two walls, but now served as his jail cell pending a formal charge related to terrorist activity, he was under Interpol arrest. It was painfully obvious he would not be leaving anytime soon. The agents made that clear to him after their extended interrogation.

Although he could not give them much information, they believed him to be a threat to national security. Brief as it was, it was the first good sleep he had in weeks, devoid of his usual nightmares. With the coming of daylight, the idea seemed almost laughable to Matt. *Me a spy? Or worse yet, a terrorist?* He was completely refreshed, in spite of the punishing bed. Without a logical reason, the weight of the world felt lifted from his shoulders. The deep sickening ache in his gut which plagued him for days was gone.

Almost giddy with relief, the change also brought a new resolve. He felt so much better than he had in weeks, more energy, less pain, better attitude, whatever the cause, he was eager to get on with his life. If he had a role in some diabolical scenario, he wanted to jump in and sort it out. But after he got something to eat.

A young man with a gun on his hip, who introduced himself as Officer Davis, unlocked the door and brought Matt a muffin and a cup of black coffee.

It's a start, he thought and offered the kid a smile.

Surprised by his friendliness, the officer was visibly taken aback. Not many people in this guy's situation were as amenable after spending time on the couch. "Want to use the loo?"

"Thanks, I would appreciate that."

"Someone will be in shortly to talk to you." Officer Davis accompanied Matt down a short hall to a dank, windowless washroom. "Sorry about the accommodations here."

"It's okay. I know you guys are under a lot of pressure about some terrorist doings. I will do whatever I can to help."

The young agent-in-training relocked the door when Matt returned to the room and went back to his workstation to prepare reports for the day ahead. He didn't think Matt was so bad. He might be only a rookie, but his instincts told him they should be working with this guy, not against him.

"There's not much more I can add about the whole incident," Kate said. She sat on the couch in Ben's office. "When I headed in the direction of our car, I saw a middle-eastern group, slowly driving through the cemetery as if they were visiting a grave. The car was light tan, older model, kind of beat up; I think it was a Ford. Broken taillight, dents on the rear quarter panel. There were two men; one was older, maybe early fifties, thin-faced, clean shaven, salty hair, and one much younger, around twenty, twenty-two, heavier, with a dark beard and mustache. A woman was in the backseat. Didn't see much of her as she was in a grey burqa, but I got the impression she was a rather large woman, maybe in her forties. The men smiled at me; the woman nodded.

"After I retrieved some things from the trunk, I turned and saw Lilly on the ground with one of the men behind her. There was only a slight noise behind me before I was clobbered. I was barely conscious as they carried me over the ground, but the bag over my head was loose. I could see names on the gravestones; some had pictures. Nothing more until I woke up hours later in the vault."

Kate's recollection mimicked Lilly's and gave Ben little information.

The twins and Elizabeth were trying to piece together the events of the prior week. As soon as it could be worked into the conversation, Ben brought up the subject of Matt's research and how it was tied to the trail of Eddy's lost Bible. Questions still haunted him about Matt's subsequent trip to England, especially the timing which was suspicious to be sure, and he outlined for the women what he was doing to get Matt back to the States for the CIA to handle. Not an easy task he admitted, considering Interpol wasn't cooperating and in no hurry to surrender the man they believed could save them from imminent danger.

Elizabeth jumped in with what had occurred in Wales and brought them all up to date with Matt's accident, his lost memory, and long recovery. She finished with Franny's limited account of how Matt was whisked back to London by government agents. If not for that bit of news, they would have no idea what had befallen Matt, or enable Ben and the CIA to extract him from Interpol. There was a great deal of concern, considering the enormity of the situation; Matt would be tortured if he failed to give up what he knew. Whether he honestly remembered any of it or not.

Kate was speechless when she heard what had happened to Matt in the last few months. She sat, staring out of the large window behind Ben, her emotions on overload. "But, why was he over there?" she wanted to know. "What was he doing in London of all places? It's not like him to go traipsing all over Europe. How would he have been able to find Mom or decide to go to Wales?"

"That's what we all want to know." The truth of the matter was still a mystery to Ben, and Elizabeth as well; and with Matt's memory still eluding him, their questions were not likely to be answered even after he returned to the States. No one noticed or thought it strange that only Lilly sat quietly, not offering much to the animated discussion.

Ben was more focused on the girl's abduction itself and how it connected to the terrorists and their operation. The group of Iranians was going to be hard to identify from such scanty information, but the individuals themselves were not important in the larger scheme of things. Like Lauren's killer, they would be found eventually.

A more pressing matter was the excitement all over the airwaves which talked of "God's Breath" and the hideous threat it held. It was linked with the gambler's grave and Matt Errington's lab in the States. Once the chain was formed from Eddy to Phil to

Matt, the CIA's focus was to bring Matt Errington back home immediately and find out exactly what he knew.

Ben and his superiors were fairly confident Matt had no role in a terrorist plot, they believed Phil was the seller. But they knew from Kate's assignment, Matt was working on the development of a potentially lethal agent, which could be the 'Breath of God' as it was referred to in the intelligence reports. If Matt's notes were in the hands of terrorists, which after the loss of the Bible they must assume they were by now, an all-out press must be made to acquire a duplicate "recipe" for the mixture and get Matt's help to produce the anti-serum he had finalized. Ben's report to his superiors caused a flash storm of communication around the world. Her Majesty's Secret Service, Interpol, and every friendly foreign intelligence agency throughout Europe were put on the alert for activity signaling the start of an attack that might give them Intel as to the targeted area.

Ben had to fight through the highest government channels of both countries to get Matt returned to the U.S. as soon as possible. That's how Agent Baggins started his day. A copy of Matt's passport photo and American I.D. stared back from his desk. An order arrived from Washington. Matt must be granted clearance to leave the country and be on his way home immediately.

The whole affair had the markings of a national emergency in Britain, HSS and Interpol weren't happy about turning over a key part of the play to the CIA. As he headed down the hall to Inspector Dare's office, he could hear the shouting through the closed door. Baggins knew he wasn't the only one with such an opinion. There was going to be a full-scale war over the handling and control of the guy. They had possession, and it didn't sound like they were going to give him up easily. The inspector already had permission from her superiors 'to do whatever it takes' to get the information they wanted. If need be, extreme force would be used to strongly encourage him to cooperate with the agency. It was not often torture was used, but this was, after all, a potentially catastrophic situation and if his memory didn't come back on its own, they were fully prepared to help him remember.

Chapter Twenty-Seven

What a perfect opportunity he had before him. A disheveled apartment just ripe for the plundering. Fred Lafferty took his time making his way to Matt's apartment as he checked out the empty street. The police caution tape was still in place, crisscrossing the entrance, and it gently puffed outward as he closed the door. Things were stacked or thrown toward one side of the room. Government agents and police had gone through each piece looking for something of great importance Fred decided, but whether or not they found what they were looking for was none of his concern. There were other prizes to be discovered in the mess lying around. Bills and bank statements gave up valuable personal information on a guy who had been missing for months. No sense leaving good money in a bank account when Freddie could put it to use. Even the small appliances could be pawned and would bring him a few bucks.

By the time the owner got back, if he ever got back, Fred would be free and clear of any evidence, and the missing items would just look like part of the vandal's work. He knew the cops wouldn't bother to take inventory. Yep, ole' Fred never missed a thing. He was building a treasure pile by the front door and was slowly working his way through the rest of the belongings in the bedroom when he was startled to hear the outer door open and shut quickly.

"Shit," he swore under his breath. Maybe it was another cop or some relative, or even the owner himself. It didn't matter anyway, he was trapped where he was and would be discovered if someone walked into the back room. Too much stuff cluttered the floor to be able to quietly reach the closet and hide, and the only window was visible from the front room. He froze where he stood. He pulled out the small gun he kept in his waistband, prepared to be confronted by whoever just entered the apartment.

Phil had little trouble opening the apartment door this time. Not like the last time when he broke into Matt's home. On his last visit, the tip of Phil's pick broke off in the lock. But this time he tumbled the lock easily and stepped over the police tape.

In what was once a neat apartment, the scene that met his gaze was alarming. Someone beat him to the punch and probably found Matt's work. "Damn Zand and his stinking camel jockey friends," he muttered. The entire apartment was thoroughly, and from the looks of it, professionally ransacked. Phil was now more worried than ever the Iranian's could eliminate him from the deal. Phil went to Matt's apartment, intent to go through his things one more time. If he could find the rest of Matt's notes and put together another tempting package to buy himself back in again, he would beat the Iranians at their own game.

Now that he knew the world was full of buyers, he would reach out to some other groups who would want what he had to sell, and if he could find Matt's notes for the antidote as well, he could sell it to the highest bidders to protect themselves from the nuts in Iran. *There was more than one way to skin those fucking Arabs*, he thought. *Cut me out will they; I'll give their enemies the same weapon and let the whole damn middle-east duke it out. See how Iran likes getting screwed. Won't that make an interesting front page news picture?* The image of thousands or even millions of people dying made Phil smile.

Phil was faced with the dilemma of where to start. The entire apartment was littered with pieces of Matt's life. Phil had gone through most of it before when Matt's apartment was neat and tidy, but he had looked for files or manuscripts, lab books, or pages of reports. This time he had a much smaller target in mind. He put all the data on microdots. He knew Matt could have done the same thing. It would be much harder to find them now with the place in shambles, but there was plenty of time, and he would examine each inch of the place until he found what he was looking for. He conjured up two images again; the first was his favorite of him spending his golden years basking in the sun overlooking his vineyard in the hilly fields of southern France, and the newer one of hordes of dark, swarthy-skinned people gasping their last breaths. "Ahh, here's to the good life," he chuckled. He took off his jacket, threw it on the floor, and prepared to start his search.

"Damn," Fred swore under his breath. Whoever came in was surely taking their sweet time about leaving. He didn't dare move and give away his presence, but he was getting a leg cramp standing in one place for so long. He couldn't quite decide what to do, wait a while longer and hope the intruder left, or sneak to the edge of the bedroom door and bully his way out with the gun. The decision was made for him when his cell phone went off, clearly blasting *Layla,* his favorite tune.

"Damn," he whispered again, not sure if the sound carried into the next room. All was quiet beyond the bedroom door, but now he felt he must either hide or force the confrontation. He inched his way slowly, careful not to step on any pieces of broken furniture. The cracked dresser mirror propped against the wall caught his reflection. He turned his head slightly to get a better look. He was a picture of deadly stealth, gun in hand; a true predator, dangerous. If the girls could see him now, with his head back, flexed muscles, power crouching. He loved the look, even if it didn't last long.

So absorbed with his image, he didn't see the lamp come crashing around the door to hit him squarely in the face, driving his nose into his brain. The impact made him squeeze the trigger.

Phil's body hit the floor only seconds after Fred's did. The two men lay a few feet apart on opposite sides of the doorway. As their lives drained away, their greedy blood mingled into one giant pool.

Chapter Twenty-Eight

For his flight back over the Atlantic, Matt was almost as wide-eyed with excitement as was the young girl seated directly in front of him, who kept peeking over the top of the seat. He didn't remember flying before, so it was as if it was his first time too.

"Hi, my name is Mary Kathryn," she said to him as soon as he and the accompanying agents sat down. Putting her small hand out to shake his. "What's your name?"

Hampered by the hand-cuffs he wore, discreetly hidden by his jacket, Matt could only smile and nod at the heart-shaped face beaming at him.

"Well, I am told, I'm Matt Errington."

"That's a funny answer," she replied, cocking her head sideways giving its mop of dark curls a shake. "No one has to tell me my name, I always know it. Since I was little," she added. "If you have trouble remembering, you can pin your name onto your shirt like the teachers did when I was in pre-school."

Matt couldn't help but laugh at the wisdom of the pint-sized imp staring at him, clad in too small jeans and a cheap, thin sweater. "Well, Mary Kathryn, I was in a bad accident, and I got hit on the head, and I haven't been able to remember much since it happened. It's called amnesia. It made me even forget my name and where I lived. But there were people in London who found out who I was and told me what I needed to know to get home. So now that's where I am going. Where are you going?" he asked, trying to deflect the conversation from himself.

"I'm going to live with my aunt and uncle in a place called Brooklyn," she answered, with a definite tremor in her voice and a pained look on her small dimpled face. "Do you know where that is?"

"Yes, it's not too far from where I live in Pennsylvania."

"So, we can be friends, and you can come and visit me?" The child beamed with delight. The agent seated next to Matt scowled at her. She stuck out her tongue.

"Um, well it's not that close, and besides you will be so busy going to school and meeting new people, you won't have time for an old man like me."

"No, I suppose not," she agreed, eyeing the surly agent again, and giving her mop another sad shake. She folded her arms defensively across her chest. "I probably won't have time for anything fun anymore."

"Why do you say that? School is fun, and making new friends will be a little scary at first, but you will see, the kids in Brooklyn will be just like the friends you left in London. You are from London, aren't you?"

"No. I didn't live in London, and I didn't have many friends either. My mom and I lived in Bristol. She's dead. So I have to go to Brooklyn to live with her sister, Aunt Edith."

"I'm so sorry. What happened to her?"

"She put some pills in a bottle and mixed it up with something and got sick and died," Mary Kathryn replied as matter-of-factly as if she was discussing the weather. "She told me she hated me and couldn't stand the sight of me anymore." No tears or clouds of emotion scudded over her face. She was just stating the facts. But before he could think of anything more to say by way of solace, she changed the subject and her previous excitement of flying returned. "I'm glad I get to sit by the window when we go over the water. My teacher said it would be huge and not to be afraid to look down. I've never seen so much water."

"For what it is worth, I don't remember flying over the water before either, so I can't wait to see it too."

How strange that is, he thought as he half listened to the flight attendant perform her pre-flight ritual. "In case the cabin loses pressure …" he gave her routine the most minimal attention.

"Mr. Matt," said the small voice in front of him, "did you hear what the lady said?"

"No, I'm sorry, I wasn't paying attention. Why? What did she say?"

"She said the plane would land in New York, not Brooklyn. Am I on the right plane?" Matt smiled at the concern in her voice.

"Yes, honey, you are," he said, trying to relieve her fears as she crawled up the seat again. He couldn't help wondering about this fragile creature and how she would fare in a rough place like Brooklyn. She seemed tough on the outside but so young. In her shoes, he probably would have been scared to death. Even as the idea went through his mind, he admitted he wasn't at all sure he wasn't scared about what waited for him on the other side of the ocean.

Glad he had something to take his mind off the other end of the journey he was content to play the role of the girl's traveling companion. The elderly gentleman next to her was already asleep, so she aimed all her pent-up excitement in Matt's direction. *What a poor little thing,* he thought, *to be so alone in the world.* But, upon closer introspection, wasn't he just as alone? Going back to the States was exciting for him too, but a bit terrifying as well. He wanted to get on with his life, but he knew from the way he was treated when he left Interpol, he wasn't going to be a completely free man for a while. It was a definite relief to be out of Interpol's hands, even if he was still in their possession, so to speak, glancing over at his two suited companions. Before he was released, the questioning had taken a harder line, and the agents had lost any disguise at amiability. The tone of the interviewers had drastically changed for the worse in the last couple hours, and without being told, he had the distinct impression they were not happy about putting him on a plane out of England. They were terrified of something big, and they strongly suspected he was a part of whatever it was. And, more to his concern, they seemed prepared to learn one way or another what his connection was, regardless of whether he knew it or not.

One minute, there were angry fingers pointed in his face and barely disguised threats hurled at him about what would happen if he continued to refuse to help them, then all of a sudden the door was opened, and he was ushered to a car and headed to the plane. No explanations were made. All of which made him wonder who, or what, he should thank for his deliverance, for there was no doubt, he had been saved from something worse.

Mary Kathryn grew silent, and he realized she was asleep. He wondered at her future and his own. For the first time in days, he was able to spend some quiet time inside his head and to reflect on what he had narrowly escaped at the hands of Interpol. *How did I get into such a mess? Who the hell am I anyway?* Yes, he had a name now, but nothing in his limited memory or the little he had been told about his life, gave him a clue as to how or why he was in such a terrible position. The only information they would give him was his destination—Washington, by way of New York as it was the soonest flight out of Britain—and there would be someone to pick him up as soon as they landed.

He asked to be allowed to collect his belongings from wherever they were in London, but the request was ignored, and he was given a promise his things would be forwarded to him later. Nor was he allowed to contact Elizabeth and Franny. He particularly felt bad about not being able to tell them where he was or say goodbye and thank them. He had expected to be granted the customary one phone call.

It was past two o'clock in the morning when the plane touched down at Kennedy Airport in New York. Mary Kathryn slept for most of the trip and needed to be roused as they approached their destination. "Did you have a good nap, sleepy head?" Matt asked as her head popped up again above the seat.

"Not so good. I was dreaming I was home with my mom and Billy. They were fighting again, and he broke my toys. Billy got mad if I left things on the floor. I didn't mean to, but he came home early, and I didn't have time to put them all away. He yelled at my mom and made her cry. That happened a lot."

Matt wished he could pluck her out of her seat and hold the tiny body in a tight hug. What a lot of crap she had in her short life; she couldn't be more than five.

"How old are you Mary Kathryn?" She seemed so small and frail.

"I'm nearly seven," she told him with a certain amount of pride in her voice.

"Well the plane is getting ready to land, and I'm sure your aunt and uncle will be happy to see you." He tried to put more excitement into his voice than he was feeling for her at the moment.

"Yes, maybe they will, but I know my cousin Rachael won't be so happy to see me. I'm sure she doesn't like me coming to live with them. My mom always told me she was a princess, pretty and smart and everyone loves her and gives her nice presents, but now

I guess she will have to share her things with me. She's older than me too. She's twelve."

"Well, I think you are pretty and smart, too," Matt reassured her. "You two may become the best of friends." Even though he wondered at his own words, he hoped things would turn out better for her.

"Really? You think I'm pretty?" The hopeful look on her face tore at his heart.

"Yes, positively beautiful," he honestly told her. "If I have a daughter waiting for me, I hope she is as lovely as you."

Suspected of terrorism as he was, Matt was treated like any other prisoner, political or otherwise, and kept on the plane until all other passengers had disembarked. He watched the attendant take Mary Kathryn by the hand and escort her to the cockpit for a short tour. Delighted at the VIP treatment, she smiled at Matt as he exited the plane sandwiched between the two stone-faced Interpol agents.

As the ramp opened into the reception area of JFK International Airport, Matt turned his attention to the two men in dark glasses walking directly toward him.

"Will you come with us." It was not a question. It was obvious the two agents from the CIA cared little what his thoughts might be and were no friendlier than his Interpol escorts and were in no mood for chatting.

Under any other circumstances, he may have felt like a celebrity with his security detail as they by-passed the customs ritual. Heads turned curiously as they skirted around long lines of travelers. Two sets of suits now escorted Matt through the airport.

On a backward glance, Matt saw a young couple about his age, sweep Mary Kathryn up in their arms and shower her with kisses. A young girl at their side was aglow with delight at meeting her new sister. Mary Kathryn, with a huge smile on her face, turned to look for Matt in the crowd. As she spotted him, she gave him a final happy wave. His parting thought for her as he watched her head off to a new life, was that hopefully, she was going to find a loving home and a normal childhood. Heaven only knew what his homecoming would be, but he was fairly certain it wasn't going to be as sweet.

The CIA suits parted company with the Interpol agents, who reluctantly released their charge. Matt was loaded onto a private jet and given a seat in the rear of the plane, in front of the agents. Another man unlocked his handcuffs and handed him a cup of coffee and an egg and biscuit sandwich. Not a single word was spoken.

Sitting in Ben's office in Washington, Elizabeth and Ben went over the same topic for several minutes and neither wanted to concede their position. Elizabeth wanted to try one more time to sway his opinion of Matt. "But I still don't understand why you can't just tell him everything. Matt is a wonderful man, and no matter what you think of his employer or colleagues, I am certain he would do everything he can to help us. I think you are wrong about keeping Kate out of the picture. He will find out about her somehow, and maybe getting them back together is a good thing. She can help him heal."

"No! I'm not completely opposed to telling him most of the story, he already knows who he is and where he's from, but bringing Kate into the picture is not going to happen, and now you have the girls back, there is no need. She is my agent, and I have no doubt she would be professional, but first of all, she is still in a fragile state. I want her completely recovered before she resumes active duty. Secondly, he is the key to a potentially lethal product, and I want him focused on diverting a possible tragedy, not wasting his time and energy rekindling his love life."

"That's not what I meant," Elizabeth shook her head at him. "He may relate to her, connect with her, it may bring him back to reality and help you find the missing notes for the antidote."

"Maybe it will and maybe it won't, but we will get what we need to stop the shit heads, excuse me Elizabeth, from killing an enormous amount of people without using Kate. You have no idea what it took to get him over here in one piece. Every agency in Europe wanted him. I was seriously afraid if we didn't get him back here soon, he would have been tortured to death. Not everyone believes he hasn't regained at least some semblance of his memory. I have to admit it sure is convenient for him to just blank out his role in an international crisis."

"But he doesn't even know about the crisis, does he?" she argued. "How would he know about anything going on? He's been in Wales with me and out of touch with the world for several weeks. There's no way he could have any part of a plot, directly or indirectly."

"I am sure of one thing, Elizabeth; our friends in London told him a lot, probably a lot more than they should have and a whole lot more than he needed to know. Of course, with the threat of being involved in some horrible terrorist attack hanging over his head, and the thought of spending the rest of his life in a British prison, he's not going to remember anything he doesn't have to or want to. He's got you and the staff of the Welsh hospital ready to testify he has no memory. If he does have anything to hide, he certainly has no reason to 'suddenly remember everything,' does he? Let me handle Matt; I've even had to fight off my superiors over him. I'll find out what he knows, and then we'll talk about giving him all his information back. I'm sorry, Elizabeth. I don't mean to be harsh, but it is my job, and it's my call."

"I know you have to do your job, but take it easy on the guy please," she begged Ben. "You can't know him the same way I do."

"He'll be fine in my care," Ben assured her. "You go back to the girls. Take them home to Michigan for a rest. I'll be in touch." Ben watched her walk out of his office and felt torn between doing his job and wanting to promise her what she wanted to hear. "Sorry, Elizabeth," he said quietly after she closed the door behind her. He hoped, unlike his wife, who had resented every nuance of his career; Elizabeth would be more tolerant and understanding. Duty came first.

"Please come in Mr. Errington, how good of you to join us." Ben's warm smile never touched his eyes and belied the circumstances of their meeting. The irony was not lost on Matt.

"Like I had a choice," Matt wanted to reply but held his tongue.

"I'm Ben Madison, and this is my colleague Gino Genetti. Please have a seat. I know it's early in the morning, have you had anything to eat, or would you like some coffee?" Ben motioned toward a chair up close to his massive desk where he wanted Matt to land.

"Yeah, great. I only had a bite to eat on the plane, and I would like some coffee, black."

Ben pulled up the second chair for Gino and walked around to his own worn black leather chair. "Marcy, be a doll," he spoke into the phone on his desk, "and bring us some coffee on your way in, will you? I don't normally ask ladies for such services," he winked a conspiratorial wink at the men, "you know how touchy people get over being asked to do menial duties, but Marcy is a rare find. She won't mind at all."

A minute later, the door opened, and the most, muscularly built, manly looking, black woman, Matt had ever seen walked through it. Given the need, Matt was quite certain she could do laps around the room, carrying him as easily as she balanced the scuffed wooden tray, which she set down none too gently on the desk. Walking around to where Ben was sitting, she poked her finger up close to his nose.

"Now Ben Madison, you and I know I would do practically anything for you, but don't push your luck so early in the morning." She good-naturedly laughed and slapped him on the back, nearly knocking him out of the chair. "It's a good thing you got company, or I might have had a few comments on your request."

"Yes, I'm sure you would have, Marcy, and colorful they would have been too," Ben shot back at her with a smile matching hers.

Matt had the strangest feeling the stage was being set, and the actors were all doing their bit for his sake. Maybe they were trying to make him feel at ease; help him regroup from the past forty-eight hours. It could just be his imagination, after all, he had been through a lot since he left the cottage, but his senses told him they were nervous about him too, and just like Interpol, they wanted something important from him. It surprised him, however, when Marcy pulled forward another chair and sat down right next to him. He didn't expect her to stay in the room.

"Hi," Marcy said to him, extending her hand as Mary Kathryn had on the plane. "I'm Dr. Marcy Owens, and I'll be your psychiatrist for the day."

Chapter Twenty-Nine

"I'm sorry, Mr. Zand, but the flight has been delayed coming out of Boston, due to the severe weather. If you have a seat with the other guests, we will notify you when it arrives."

"I don't want to take a seat. I have already waited nearly six hours, and I want to know what time you expect the plane to get here. I have important business and must be in England by early tomorrow."

"Mr. Zand, all of our guests would like the same answer, but we are waiting for the weather to clear. There is nothing we can do to speed things up. Please have a seat." The attendant walked away from the desk before he could argue any further.

Rashid's plans had been made cautiously, allowing for unforeseen delays, but this was too much. *First, it's my passport;* there was something wrong with it; he was told by the security guard who made him wait while they verified his information. *It's insufferable. I know they target me because I'm middle-eastern. Their rudeness caused me to miss my scheduled flight. Now, this flight is delayed by the storms along the east coast. Is there no end to the insults from this hostile country? How I wish I could make them all pay for the disgraceful way they have treated me.* It would give him great joy to smash them all. *But Allah is wise. He will not let these insults go forever without retribution.*

Remembering this made Rashid Zand feel better. He prayed for patience. But patience was one thing, and timing was another. He knew his contact in London would be concerned when he did not arrive as planned. Would they go ahead without him? He knew it was dangerous to call his brothers.

Many times, he had been wisely instructed by Khourmy to refrain from anything but the most urgent communication to not draw attention to themselves or their upcoming events. They must be told, however, that he had been delayed and to wait for his arrival in London. He had waited and prayed so long for this time of glory to come. Allah was counting on him, and he could not disappoint Him. He could not miss Allah's punishment of the infidels because of stupid airline people getting in his way. It was *his* plan. *His* work led them to this moment. He found the scientist willing to sell human lives for a handful of gold. He had been the instrument that created the 'Breath of God.' It was to be *his* moment of glory. It was insufferable. He would get to London if he had to walk across the ocean. Allah be praised.

Earlier in the morning, a CIA agent working in the airport placed a call to his boss, Ben Madison. "Yes, sir. I inserted the transmitting strip into the fold of his passport. It was a perfect job if I must say so. He'll never notice it."

"I hope not, a lot is riding on us tracking him all the way to London and beyond, and if we are right about his cell being the group planning an attack, we might get lucky and stop them in their tracks. I'm always amazed at the new technology you guys come up with, you know. That strip couldn't be any bigger than a sliver."

"Yeah, that's why I wanted to go into the tech side of the agency business. It sure makes my job more fun." Agent Williams laughed. "Always some new toy to play with."

"Thanks, Glen, good job." Within minutes Ben was giving his intelligence department the GPS coordinates for the satellite to lock onto Zand. The bird was loaded. The bird dog was ready to hunt.

"Well, Matt, are you getting used to your name yet?" Ben was working hard to break the ice and make Matt feel more comfortable before the real questioning began.

"I guess so, although I can't say anything feels normal yet. Being back on this side of the ocean seems right, but since I haven't been allowed to go home, I don't have a complete answer for you."

"Yeah, well, Matt I don't want to sound like an alarmist, but you were headed for some pretty uncomfortable days if we had not used considerable clout to get you sprung and back here in one piece. I'm not going to pull any punches with you, you have gotten yourself into a pretty mess, and whether you remember it or not, might not have saved your hide over there. It seems the Brits, Interpol and most of the agencies in Europe are convinced you are hiding a duplicitous role in a rather nasty bit of business with the Iranians behind a curtain of amnesia."

"Well, I'm not. At least I am pretty damn sure I'm not. I know that's not my personality at all!" Matt jumped to his feet, red-faced at the mere insinuation of his involvement.

"Hey, not so fast." Ben patted the air in an appeasing manner. "We didn't say we share their opinion, but the intelligence we have captured indicates the target is in Britain, not the good old U. S. of A. Maybe if we had the bulls-eye on us, Homeland Security would be up my behind, and we would be taking a different tack too. We do believe you don't remember the whole affair. But, more to the point, we know you work at a laboratory and were the principal investigator with some toxic agents … which we're pretty sure the head of a terrorist cell, an Iranian named Kaleehad Khourmy, has gotten his hands on. Your work is impressive, I must say. You tweaked a viral component to create instant paralysis, and eventual death if not treated immediately with an antidote … which you also created. The bad guys are calling it 'Breath of God,' and we're well aware of its potency. Unfortunately, we also think it has been duplicated already. Our scientists are working on it as well with the partial data you left with your boss at Marsh. They are desperately trying to formulate an antidote, which we also believe you already finished. Several government labs have been working on this … just in case it's needed. However, since we have managed to save your butt from torture, we know you are more than eager to return the favor and help us in any way you can. Isn't that right, Matt?" Ben nodded in Matt's direction but didn't pause long enough for an answer.

"We need you to retrieve your final reports and data from whatever secure place you put it." The air in the room became uncomfortable and crackled with unstated urgency.

Vestiges of his nightmares and Franny's dire predictions swam before his eyes. Franny called him death, a title of which he had no memory to either comprehend its precision or deny its validity. But there was some truth in Ben's words, as there were in Franny's. His doubts played havoc with his deepest insecurities. *I'm responsible.*

Something I created is going to harm and possibly kill a lot of people. He couldn't remember it, and he did not know how to stop it.

"Where do you think I should start?" Matt wasn't sure what he could do, but without a doubt, he had better give them something.

Ben was up and motioned for Gino to give him a large red folder. From it, Ben handed Matt a new driver's license and passport.

"Since these were never found … I thought you might need replacements. I was able to pull a few strings to get them for you quickly," Ben said, noting Matt's surprised look. "Kind of a welcome home gift. Okay, let's go. Are you ready?" Ben asked, opening up Matt's file. He urged Matt to move closer. "This is your life, Matt Errington."

"How do you know so much about me?" Matt asked at one point in the lesson, totally impressed with the depth of the details Ben unfolded before him.

"We were able to piece together a great deal of your life from your employer, and easily traceable records." Considering the power Ben wielded through various government departments, Matt never doubted the answer, and Ben was spared from naming Kate as the real source of information.

Opening the door to his apartment seemed like entering a foreign land. He had no memory of what would be inside. Matt felt his stomach roll over, and his guts turned to water. For hours Ben went over the details of Matt's life with him; from his birth to his mother's death, from his childhood to a stellar career at Marsh Laboratories. Feelings, more than memory, engulfed him. Throughout the history lesson on who he was, Matt sat silent and still, only occasionally asking a question when some detail of Ben's story caused him pain for which he had no explanation. His questions were unemotional and centered mostly on the loss of his mother. He had a hard time getting past that part of his life. Everything else Ben painted could be true or false, it all meant little, but learning he caused his own mother's death, shook him to the core.

The door to his apartment swung open, and Matt was face to face with his past. A past that only hinted at a real life. The room was neat, sparsely decorated but looked like furnishings Matt would choose. *Simple, functional, no, clinical would be a better word.* The word struck him, and without a better explanation for it, he tucked it away for future exploration.

Agent Jim Jensen, assigned to Matt by Ben, followed closely on his heels and closed the door behind them. "Well, Matt, does it look like home?"

"I don't know, I guess so. It doesn't feel right, but your Ben Madison's friend, Dr. Owens, says being here will speed up the process. I sure hope so; this is getting old, you know?"

Agent Jensen nodded. "I guess it must feel weird," he agreed.

"I can't believe I was so neat. Even with limited knowledge of who I am." For the first time in days, Matt laughed at himself. "Dr. Owens didn't have me pegged right. She called me unpretentious and casual. I would loosely translate that to slob. But this place is clean as a whistle and almost antiseptically clean."

The quiet shadow behind him nodded in agreement. "Uh, yeah, I guess so. And, pretty boring," he added with a grin. "Of course, it was put back together by agency staff, you know, a lot of your things were destroyed, and the agency replaced them with as close to duplicates as possible."

Matt absently nodded, inspecting his home. "Yeah, that's what I have been told. But I would have thought I would at least recognize something here as mine." Matt slowly toured the rooms. He ran his fingers over the edge of each piece of furniture and across the back of the couch. *My stuff. Or mostly, my stuff. It's my home anyway. My life. Well almost.* He belonged here. But nothing reached out to him. He felt no oneness with the rooms. No blink of the mind's eye followed by a hint of a memory. Nothing felt right. That was the problem he knew instinctively. *Nothing feels right.*

"Are you sure this is my place?" he turned to the agent. "I don't know what it is, but this isn't me."

Agent Jensen nodded, "yeah, it's your place all right. Give it some time. Anyway, Mr. Madison wants you to look closely at what's here, try and feel your way back to the days before you took off for Europe. Try to piece your actions together. Maybe we can figure out where you put your notes."

"Right! That's the game plan, I know. Hard to do when I don't even feel like I belong here, you know? Why is everyone so sure I hid my work here anyway? After all, I worked in a lab. If I had notes, wouldn't I have left them there? Someplace safe."

"Our point precisely, Matt. We aren't sure where you left anything. Your boss, Dr. Nowak, went over your lab with a fine-tooth comb. He swore you finished the project before you left; he spoke so highly of your dedication; he was convinced you wouldn't have left it undone. But, if you did, you cleaned out your work, and our guess is you took it home. What you did with it is anyone's guess."

"Ben thinks I was protecting it from someone there. Couldn't that person have taken it just as well as me? What if I did finish the research, lock it up, and leave? Who's to say someone else didn't get to it and make it look like I cleaned out my computer files?"

Matt wasn't convinced with Ben's story of his past and his potential role in the whole mess unfolding across the ocean. And, he still had no logical reason for going to Great Britain. Ben contrived to blend reality with a simpler suggestion of why Matt was in England, leaving out Kate and the search for her mother. The trip was suggested to be a spur of the moment vacation to relieve a stressed mind.

Dr. Owen helped Matt 'remember' through the power of hypnosis, his need to get away from the potentially deadly substance he created. With his job pressing on him and the upcoming move to a more responsible position, it could easily explain a sudden flight out of the country, right? She cited similar experiences of WWII researchers who worked on the atom bomb. They too refused to acknowledge the devastation they wrought even as they celebrated their success, and many of them suffered for the rest of their lives for their roles in the Manhattan Project. Dr. Owen assured Matt finding the antidote would help clear his deeply submerged guilt and free his memory.

Chapter Thirty

"Ben, I'm forever grateful to you for my daughters. And, it's not my place to tell you how to do your job, but I've said it before, you aren't being fair to Matt, nor are you using all of the tools available to you."

"Now, Elizabeth, you know we have been over this a dozen times or so." Ben was in the middle of a meeting when Elizabeth called. Just hearing she was on the phone put a little extra spark in his walk as he made his way down the hall to his office where he could speak to her privately. His staff was pretty astute, and if he lost his composure for even a second, a smile or a look could give him away, and he would never hear the end of it. It would not be appropriate for his underlings even to guess he had a soft spot in him, and if they suspected he cared about two of his agent's mother, oh shit, what a ruckus that would cause. *Elizabeth.* He liked saying her name and tried to fit it into the conversation whenever he could.

"Elizabeth, I can't just waltz Kate over to Matt's place and lay that whole thing on him. We're pretty convinced he is more than just a little messed up right now. Adding Kate to his welcome home party would not offer any further advantage I can see."

"But you don't know him as I do," she insisted. "If he is in love with her, even if he doesn't remember it, having her back might trigger whatever spark he needs to become whole again. You want him to find his missing work, don't you? Kate may be the spark to help him."

"Or it might be the biggest shock of his life and send him deeper into the abyss he's in," Ben countered. "How do you think he will feel about her when he finds out she was a plant in his life? Or learn their whole relationship was set up? Where is he going to run, mentally or emotionally or physically, this time, when he learns who she is? Think about it, Elizabeth … we, the government

… Kate and I … and a team of people have used him. We caused him a great deal of pain. How is he going to feel when he hears the truth?"

"Ben, if I didn't know you better, I would think your main concern is the end game." Even Ben had to laugh.

"I'm afraid you have me there. I must, and I will do whatever it takes to get the antidote, and it needs to be done pretty quickly. We know Khourmy's cell is active, and timing is critical. I will use every tactic I have to get Matt's head back together, but right now; it doesn't include Kate."

Elizabeth sighed. "Alright, I gave it my best shot. Lilly and I think you're wrong but—"

"Oh, so you've got Lilly against me as well," Ben smiled as he thought of his girls. "I guess I'll have to have a serious discussion with her. Even though it won't change a thing, just what does Kate think about reconnecting with Matt?"

"Oh, she doesn't know I've even mentioned it to you."

"What? Don't you think she has as much right to a voice on this topic as you seem to think Matt has?"

"Yes, of course, she does, but given the circumstances, I know she would want to help in any way she could if she gets the green light from you." Elizabeth didn't want to share with Ben, what Lilly confided about Kate's feelings for Matt. Knowing Ben's penchant for professionalism, Elizabeth feared he would reprimand Kate for something, not her fault. Elizabeth knew all too well how emotions directed your life, with your permission or not. If Kate did fall in love with Matt, as Lilly seemed to think was the case, it might be rocky for them at first, but Elizabeth had faith in the two young people and hoped with time they could sort it out.

It didn't take being her identical twin for Lilly to see how Kate cared for Matt, yes, even loved him and the safe, normal world she wanted so badly. But she knew her sister well enough to know her loyalty to the government, her work, and Ben took precedence over her happiness, and she would follow orders and leave him behind. Lilly had no doubts her sister would be happy with Matt, and she secretly had hoped Kate would have rejected the order to leave months before and would stay in Philadelphia with him. But, when Ben said, "Wipe it clean," Kate followed orders. She would have left nothing for Matt to trace. She was methodical.

As they packed up the proof of Kate's existence from the apartment, Lilly had already decided to change fate. She knew she was breaking protocol and could be punished for her actions, but there was only a little more than a year left of their commitment to Ben and their service to the U.S. Government. They would be free to build normal lives soon. Somehow, she must leave Matt enough clues to find her sister, but not involve Kate in the plot.

Lilly knew Matt had shopped at the antique store before and passed it on his way to and from work. Kate's glass vases were too lovely to be forever buried in a government warehouse, and for some reason, it didn't sound like Kate intended to take them with her. Lilly tucked them into a small satchel she carried. One of them was chipped, and the sharp edge sliced her finger as she slid it into the bag. Without drawing attention, she couldn't stop to clean up the drops of blood that splattered to the floor. A few days later she gave the vases to the antique dealer. They were unique and looked stunning in the window of the shop, just like she suggested to the owner they would. Eventually, Matt would see them. It was just a matter of time.

If Matt was indeed half as smart as Lilly thought he was, and if he loved Kate like she believed he did, he would find her. Lilly, determined to help him, left several clues behind. Matt's long days in the lab gave Lilly the opportunity she needed to slip back into his apartment and plant a book of Kate's in a place he would find it. She knew Kate wouldn't break the rules, even to follow her own heart. The book should have been enough to send Matt searching.

Although in hindsight, she had no idea he would run all the way to England to follow the postcard. She only meant it to be the impetus to send him looking. She thought he would search locally since the stamp inside the back cover was a downtown bookstore and should have aimed him toward a local quest. When she heard about his trans-Atlantic journey, she realized she was right about his love for Kate, and just how far he would go to find her.

However, in a debriefing session with Ben, Kate mentioned Matt's job offer from the Washington laboratory. If he accepted it, he would be leaving soon. Lilly realized a broken-hearted Matt may go, unaware the missing Kate loved him too.

She would have to take further action to ensure her sister's happiness. The envelope instructing Matt to go to Washington, in script nearly identical to her sister's, was the clinching detail. Matt would realize Kate cared for him. It was easy to pose as a man, trail him to his destination, and slip the paper to Matt before he knew what happened. The fog, a bonus, helped her quickly disappear into the night.

Ben's orders were specific. Agent Jim Jensen was not to leave Matt alone for a minute. Spend whatever time it took but find those notes. Matt knew about the events which took place in his home. His apartment was ransacked. Twice. First by the Iranians, then by the CIA. Some of his furniture was smashed and his belongings scattered like garbage over every inch of the floor. Two people, he couldn't remember killed each other, leaving a huge bloodstain it took experts days to remove.

With the help of pictures Kate took of Matt's home before she moved in, Ben's agents put the place back together as best they could. The agency was able to reassemble his home with nearly identical furnishings. Every piece of broken furniture or belonging of Matt's, too badly damaged to be repaired, was replaced. The scraps were wrapped and secured in a government warehouse, just in case, they were identified as holding the missing notes.

"I don't know what I expected," Matt said. "I had hoped something would trigger at least a glimmer of who I was, or I mean who I am. But so far, all I get is a recurring message, like a neon light flashing in my face."

"And what's that?" the agent asked hoping it would add some insight to the day.

"It's not right! It doesn't feel right. That's all I can tell you for sure. I don't know what 'it' is supposed to be, but 'its' not here."

Several hours in the apartment weren't productive. Matt went through the rooms twice. Several things in his home had been replaced or restored and what was left of his personal belongings were back in the drawers and cupboards. No clue jumped out at him about where the hidden data was. Pressure from Ben Madison and his agents and the increasing feeling of impending doom weighed on him, and although it would have been his highest priority if left to himself, there was no time to give a great deal of effort to recapturing his life.

"How about a trip uptown?" Jim asked, grimacing over the cup of instant coffee in his hand. They were sitting in the kitchen at the end of the fruitless day. "We can follow the path you probably took on your way home from work each day. Maybe something will hit you." Nodding in agreement, Matt grabbed the jacket off the back of the chair, and they headed toward the door, but stepping outside, they were surprised to find Dr. Owen just getting out of her car. The trip downtown would have to wait.

Matt's memory was as cloudy as it had been since the day he woke up in Wales. Learning who he was and the details of his life only added to his frustration. With relief, Matt accepted Marcy's suggestion to allow her to relax him back into a hypnotic state. If Matt could find a narrow thread with her help, maybe he could find his way back.

"Flying, I'm flying," he told her. "It's so pretty and blue."

"Where are you flying Matt, are you in a plane? Are you taking a trip?" Marcy's voice rose and dipped as if she were a bird in flight. "Where are you going, Matt?"

"No, I am the plane. I can see to the horizon. Oh, it's so still and quiet. Franny is here too. Franny is afraid of me. She is very old; I'm afraid I won't see her again."

"Matt, I want you to open your eyes now," Marcy spoke in a bare whisper. "You will stay deeply asleep, but you will be able to see when you open your eyes." Matt's eyes popped open as if loaded with springs. "Matt, can you tell me what you see?"

"I see you."

"And where are we?"

Slowly Matt's head rose from the couch, and he swiveled it as far as he could to look around the room. "This is my apartment," Matt confirmed in a slow, dreamlike voice. "This is my home."

"That's right, Matt, this is your home. You have lived here for several years. Do you recognize your things?" Matt hesitated, then nodded.

"Yes."

"That's good. Is everything the way it should be in your apartment?" Again, Matt slowly swiveled his head, seemingly taking in the room's details before him. When no answer came forth, Dr. Owen asked him again. "Is everything okay, Matt?"

"No. I don't like it like this." A sob nearly broke his voice, and a violent shudder went through him. "It's all wrong. Where are her things? Where is Kate?"

"Kate? Why do you want to know where Kate is? Are you expecting her to be here?"

"Yes, she's late, and I can't find her. Something happened to her, and I've looked everywhere for her."

Dr. Owen was clearly startled by the vehemence of Matt's answer and tried to redirect his subconscious back to the job at hand.

"We will look for Kate later, please calm yourself, Matt. I want you to relax, relax. Lie back down and close your eyes once more." Matt's eyes clamped shut, and his head dropped like a stone onto the pillow. "Where are you now, Matt?"

"There are people on the floor. There are some children here too. I don't want to look at them. I can't walk without seeing them."

"All right, don't be afraid. I want you to look up Matt, look away from the people. Can you do that?"

"Yes."

"Okay, is that better?"

"Yes."

"Good. Will you take me to your lab now? Please tell me about your work. Can you do that?"

"Yes. I make death."

"Who told you that?"

"Franny."

"Did you know Franny said you could also help people?"

"Franny said that?"

"Yes. She wants you to help us to save people. Can you help us do that?"

"I don't know. What do I have to do?"

"Remember, Matt. Remember. You finished an important project. You created a serum to save people. Do you remember the project and the serum Matt?"

"Yes."

"Fine, good. Can you tell me what you did with the notes about your serum?"

"Yes."

"Wonderful Matt, it will make Franny happy if you can tell me where your notes are. What did you do with them, Matt?"

"I destroyed them." The tension affected Dr. Owen, who was not prepared for the answer he gave. She nearly sprang from the chair she was sitting in across from Matt.

"Why would you destroy them?" she asked, trying to keep her voice level. Matt didn't move or make any attempt to answer her. A strange look came over his face. She asked him again.

"Matt, you spent years developing an important serum, one which had the potential to save lives if it was needed. You are a dedicated scientist. When you were finished with your research, what did you do with all of the notes?" Matt's face turned almost hostile, and Dr. Owen thought he might fly from the couch at any moment.

"Don't you understand what I did," he shouted at her. "I'm to blame for people suffering, dying. Me, I killed them."

"No," she said, in as calm a voice as possible. "You help people Matt. You are not responsible for the evil people do to others. Your work is good. You are good. When you finished your research, you knew it was good. You wanted to protect it. You put it someplace safe, didn't you? Can you remember where that safe place is?" A calmer Matt peered into his mind. *A safe place,* he thought in his dreamlike state, *a safe place?*

Pieces of places and things swam past his mind's eye. A woman called to him, and the man next to her stood quietly pointing at the stars. Yes, he was safe, but the mist swirled, and there was blood. Blood on his hands, blood on the road. Bodies sprawled on the ground dried up and crinkled like fallen leaves before they blew away and the particles turned to thousands of twinkling colored lights that sparkled in the air like fireworks. And then he saw her. He knew the taste and the smell of her. Oh, so beautiful she was. Curled up like a cat on his couch. Enticing him to kiss her. Her lips were wet and inviting, but as he bent to kiss her, the image started to change. Her hair turned gray and tangled. A bony finger pointed in his direction and a voice sadder than anything he had ever heard before called to him. 'Remember,' it said.

"No, come back," he pleaded, don't leave me again; spinning around in the rain, he spied his love. "I love you," he called out. But, the woman of his dreams gently glided through a door and disappeared. Silent tears rolled down his cheeks. "Come back," he pleaded again in a near whisper.

"Where are you, Matt?" Dr. Owen gently asked him.

"I'm lost," he answered. "I've always been lost."

"How's it going Marcy," Ben asked as she plopped into one of the overstuffed chairs in his office.

"Not so good, I'm afraid. There is a massive wall Matt can't get beyond. Stops us every time I try regressive therapy. For some compelling reason, he doesn't want to remember." Ben's brow furrowed.

"I thought you could get past those kinds of obstacles. We don't have the luxury of slow therapy here, you know. Our reports indicate a catastrophe is imminent." Ben was tired, and it showed in his patience. Or lack thereof.

"I know," Marcy nodded, I know what's at stake, but there is only so much these techniques will uncover. If he is blocking his memory, it will take time to break down the wall. I've given you other options before; there are drugs that will work better. And some shock treatments are possible, but there are no guarantees any one method will be better than another. And, there is always the possibility of further damaging his memory."

Ben stood before the large window in his office, hands thrust deep in his pockets, eyes squinting in the low afternoon sun. "Do what you have to do, Marcy, but we must find that antidote. I don't have much confidence our guys can duplicate his work any time soon. It was his baby, and it took him nearly a year. Just get me the information. I'm depending on you, Marcy."

Chapter Thirty-One

Heathrow security was on full alert for days, and the strain was affecting each of their employees. With such a huge and diverse population streaming through their gates each day, the constant stress of watching for signs of covert activities rubbed the guard's senses raw. No one wanted a crisis on their watch, but the constant search for minuscule clues caused a contradictory effect. Eyes grew tired, and suspicious details were increasingly overlooked.

Khourmy knew this and flagrantly took advantage of the lapse of attention. His people were ready. The venomous poison had been painstakingly duplicated in sufficient quantity to bring the infidels to their knees. He would have his day, and Allah would be pleased.

It was only seven-fifteen in the morning and the airport already hummed with thousands of travelers, each preoccupied with their journey. Families herded together corralling youngsters; some showing the obvious fatigue at a trip's end or others full of anticipation just beginning their holiday. There were hundreds of soldiers recently arrived from a base in Spain; they were sleeping in chairs, reading or calling loved ones during the brief layover in London. An announcement was repeated about a young boy, eight-year-old Sammy Campbell, who could not be found. The child had become separated from his parents, and all visitors were asked to report any sightings of lone children to the nearest concierge desk. Loudspeakers blared with flight information, and various service announcements played every ten minutes. Vendors hawked maps, sandwiches, fruit drinks, coffee, and magazines.

Three of his best men were already in place. They arrived in London by train the night before. Trusted men. Khourmy wanted only his most loyal people for this great endeavor. There must be no mistakes. Their last supper together was simple and humbling. Samid Alhammah, Rashid Kopranah, and El Ganah Mal Bennin were good friends. They grew up together in the streets of Pardis, Iran each vying for leadership of their neighborhood band. Khourmy had taken control early in his youth. He knew the pain each of his warriors carried within their hearts. He worked their pain. By the time he was seventeen, Khourmy was in control of several hundred soldiers for Allah who had come together from cities all over Iran and the middle-east. His plan was simple in its development, but promised maximum results, he chose four or five of his most dedicated soldiers for a chance at martyrdom.

He promised passage to glory for Rashid Zand as well and mourned the fact it could not be. Rashid deserved this moment. He fulfilled his three-year mission in America to find a suitable weapon to serve Allah. If not for Rashid, they would never have developed the 'Breath of God' at all. But bad luck delayed his arrival in London. The plans they labored over for years were near at hand. He could not wait for Zand; there would be another day for his destiny to be fulfilled. Today the strike against the infidels must be completed. All was ready for them to grab their place in history. Standing at the railing overlooking the lower concourse, Khourmy smiled and prayed to Allah to blind his enemies to what was to come.

After Dr. Owen's impromptu visit, Matt needed to get out of the apartment. He felt invaded. "How can anyone ever get used to having someone traipsing around inside their head like that?" he asked Agent Jensen. "Hey, still want to take a break and get something to eat?"

"Absolutely." Agent Jensen nodded his head toward the door. "I don't know about you, but I'm nearly starved." Matt would have made a flip comment about the condition of the agent standing in front of him having a way to go before starvation but thought better of the dig since he liked Jim. *No sense needling the guy.*

Grabbing his jacket again, Matt rubbed his eyes. "What the hell are we doing here anyway? This is useless. We don't even know what we are looking for … and for all we do know, the data could be long gone. Since this place was taken apart a couple of times, I don't think we have a ghost of a chance finding this proverbial needle in the haystack."

Jim nodded but kept his opinions to himself. He had worked for Ben Madison for eleven years and had a great deal of respect for the man. Ben believed there was a chance they would find the missing data in this guy's apartment, or it would give Matt a clue to where it was, even after the vandals tore it all up and CIA inspected every square inch themselves.

Something was bothering his charge, but Jim couldn't put his finger on what it was. It was probably strange to be home where nothing looked familiar and with no memory of your life. "Where's a good place to eat around here?" Jim asked, startled when Matt just stared back at him with a blank look. "I'm sorry." Jim laughed. "Guess you're the wrong person to ask, huh? Well, we can head toward town and find something along the way."

"Hey, let me drive?" Matt was anxious to get behind the wheel of a car since arriving back in the country and now back in his territory; he needed to take charge of his life by whatever small measures he could.

Unsure if it was a wise decision and probably against some agency rule, Jim thought for a moment then hesitantly threw Matt the keys. Maybe something as normal as driving on familiar roads might spark a memory. Ben told Jim to use his discretion and do whatever it takes, well this might help, Jim decided.

As Matt pulled away from his apartment complex, he tried to keep his mind blank. He had driven those roads every day for more than three years; maybe his subconscious would take the place of his memory, which was being seriously obstinate in its recovery.

A hazy sun was nearing the horizon as they made their way along the back roads scanning the side streets for a restaurant. A curious prickling sensation was working its way down Matt's backbone as he swiveled his head back and forth in his search for a restaurant. Just out of reach of cognitive thought, a hint of memory tantalized him. Squinting against the glare, Matt pulled the visor down and was surprised when a CD fell in his lap.

"What you got there?" Jim asked. "What is it?"

"Based on the cover, it's a Christmas album. Nothing special. Looks like a homemade mixture of old tunes. I suppose it's mine."

"Probably," Jim added, "but let me see it." Matt tossed the disc to Jim, surprised at his interest. "The department wants to know of anything unusual," he nodded at the silver disc in his hands. "It could mean something."

"Yeah, it could also mean someone else drove my car while I was gone."

"Why, who else would have access to it?"

"How should I know?" Matt said, half laughingly. "I didn't even know it was my car until you told me."

"Oh, yeah, right! But I'm sure Ben will want to check it out," he said, dropping the CD in his pocket.

Not as sure about the importance of the piece of plastic, Matt just shook his head. "Well if some guy broke into my car, although there is no evidence of any such act, and took a spin around the block in it, and even if you found out whom, what could it possibly tell you about me your department hasn't already learned?"

"Well, for starters, maybe why you have a no-name Christmas CD in your visor and were too cheap to spring for someone more famous …"

"Oh, like Nat King Cole or Bing Crosby doing White Christmas you mean," Matt interrupted, laughing at the turn of the conversation. Matt found he liked Jim. Of all the agents he met in the past couple of days, Jim was the most normal, down to earth guy yet.

"Yeah, like them." Jim retorted. "And, by the way, how is it you can remember those guys but not your own name?" Jim threw back, making a strange face. "That's weird, you know."

"No kidding." Matt laughed again. "Things like that freak me out all the time. The worst part is this selective memory thing. It's playing frigging games with my head. I think I start to remember something and it slips away like mist. I can't—" Matt slammed on the brakes, making Jim wonder at the wisdom of letting him drive, and motioned to a small restaurant across the road. "Hey, that place looks good! How about it?"

"Looks clean anyway," Jim added. "Yeah, fine with me, don't know what else we're going to find around here."

Matt saw a parking spot a few doors down and maneuvered the car into the tight space like a pro.

"Pretty good job," Jim noted, impressed.

"Hmm, I don't know what that says about me," Matt laughed, "but it's good to know that whatever else I've done in my life, I can park a damn car." Both men were hungry and headed down the street into the lowering sun. Shielding his eyes with his hand, Jim was ten paces ahead of Matt before he realized his companion was no longer at his side. As he spun around, he saw Matt staring at an old, dilapidated building on his left, apparently hypnotized by something in the window. Mouth open, his arms limp at his side, Matt stood glued to the spot; frozen in time and space.

"What? What's wrong, Matt?" Jim hurried back to Matt's side, aware something was up, and dinner was going to have to wait, again.

"I don't know exactly," Matt answered as if speaking from a distance. "I need to go in here."

"Now?" Jim asked. "It's probably closed." Jim wasn't up to wild goose chases on an empty stomach, but the look on Matt's face made him forget his urge to eat. "Right, let's check and see if it's open, maybe someone is still here even if it's not." Matt was already heading toward the door when it opened right before he reached for the knob.

"Sorry, fellas, I'm closed for the day."

"Uh, sir," Matt stammered, "I am not sure why, but I know it's important I go into your store, right now, while the sun is shining through your window. Please, sir, it is important. I mean it's urgent. I just know I have to do it now." Matt was practically babbling, and even Jim looked at him in surprise.

Saucy Abernathy just stared and scratched his head. "Why?" he said. "You can come back tomorrow."

"No," Matt shouted. "I have to go in now."

"Hey now, listen here young man, this is my store, and I say when it's closed or not. You want to start trouble with me, I'll scream for the police, they're usually eating right next door at that little restaurant. See there is even a cop car out in front now. Better not do anything stupid. Now get on with you, and I don't think I even want you coming back tomorrow. Go find someplace else to freak out." Saucy put one foot in the door to go back inside and get away from the wacko on the sidewalk, when the older guy braced a large hand against the door, pulled out a badge and flipped it in his face.

"CIA, sir. We would like to take a closer look at your store right now." Jim advised in a quiet but unmistakable voice.

"What's going on here?" Saucy was not going to be intimidated by a suit with a fancy badge, "I've got lots of cop friends around here. I haven't done anything wrong. You can't push me around."

"No sir, we're not trying to push anyone, but we would appreciate a few minutes of your time. My friend here has lost his memory in a bad accident, and for some reason, he is attracted to your fine store. Now I'm sure you don't mind helping the guy out a little. Huh! What would it hurt if we just looked around for a couple of minutes? Whaddya think?" Jim knew there was no time to get a subpoena the way Matt was acting and was grateful he had won the match. Saucy grudgingly stepped aside to let his visitors in.

"Two minutes, that's all I'm gonna give you. You want any more you can go get a warrant if you can."

"Thank you, sir, we appreciate your time." Jim's eyes were on Matt, who seemed to be lost in some other place. He floated through the door. Seeing Matt's puzzling behavior sent shivers down Jim's spine. Something was happening right in front of him, and he wasn't sure if it was going to be good or bad.

"Where did you get those colored glasses? Those little vases." Matt was practically sobbing as he shoved aside furniture and junk, antique hat stands, and old washtubs, anything that got in his way. Matt neither heard nor realized the damage he was causing as he single-mindedly reached for the vases high above his head on the shelf which ran across the window.

"Stop that, you son-of-a-bitch. Look what you're doing to my shop!" Saucy leaped forward in an attempt to grab Matt's arm but was spun away by Jim's huge hand.

"Let him go. I'll compensate you for whatever happens but let him go."

"You're damn right you will. He's making a goddamn mess of my store, and you got the balls to tell me to let him just keep on doing it."

"That's right." Jim calmly stared down the agitated owner; all the while hoping Matt was on to something good, or Jim's ass would be in the hopper tomorrow with Ben.

Matt saw her hair, golden, shining in the sun as he watched it curl around her face. So sweet, she was smiling that special smile at him. Her eyes crinkled up at the corners. "Look what I found today!" she told him. Pulling a small bag out from behind her back, she held her treasure out for his inspection. A miniature vase winked with the lights behind it. She was so pleased she lit up the room. And he loved her. He reached the shelf and fingered the shape of the vase. The feel of it caused him to shiver all over. Cool and smooth. He saw her smile again. Blood pounded in his ears. Music played, and they danced. Matt swung her around, and the tinkling of her laughter filled his soul. Mindless bliss washed over him, and his knees buckled. The glass trinket hit the floor and shattered into a million shards of light.

"Matt! Are you alright? Matt, look at me. Can you focus?" Jim was concerned and not at all sure what was happening. He probably should have called for backup when the whole scene started getting weird.

"She's gone. I couldn't find her. I tried, and everyone thought I was crazy, but she's real. These vases were hers. I remember them. I remember her."

It was a forlorn picture Jim and Saucy shared of Matt sitting on the floor holding his head in one hand and trying to scoop up sliver size pieces of his memory with the other. His vision reeled as his past swirled around him and clung to his senses. Kate, in his arms, Kate dancing, Kate dangling a bare leg out of the shower. The parts involving Kate were clear, but everything else was like swimming through murky shadows. The past came at him with the roar of a freight train, racking his body with waves of nausea and leaving his chest heaving as his memory returned. There was no stopping the flood once it began, and his mind field cleared. He knew who he was. He remembered his life, and there wasn't much in it he'd welcome back.

Jim was immediately on the phone to Ben's office, and within ten minutes, Matt was bundled off to a twenty-four-hour Emergency Clinic, and two more of Ben's agents arrived. His hands were embedded with slivers of glass.

"Matt, congratulations, you're back!" The Ben who strode in the door twenty minutes later was a strikingly different man than Matt met days before. This Ben was calm and smiling, genuinely pleased at the turn of events. "So Matt, where did you put your notes for safe keeping?"

Without any further hesitation or need to consider his response, Matt blurted out, "Ask Jim. He has it. The Christmas CD is in his hands. I remember making the CD before I left for Europe. The notes you want are on it." Ben spun around. The smile was gone.

"You better be sure. We're not playing any more games with you."

"What do you mean games? That's what I remember. If you think I'm wrong, go check it out." Matt was angry at Ben's attack, and something snapped in him. "I have given you everything I can, and I'm sure you'll find what you are looking for on that damn CD." Without batting an eye, Ben walked out motioning for Agent Jensen to follow, letting the door close behind them. Within seconds, the two new agents filled the spot Ben vacated.

"Mr. Madison wants you to accompany us to his office as soon as possible," one of the guys informed him.

"Get your coat," the other agent added.

A young doctor with a tray in his hands heard their remarks as he joined the group, "Uh sorry, guys, I've got to sew up his hand before he goes anywhere. There are some nasty cuts in need of attention, possibly some shards of glass still in there. You guys can watch if you want or wait in the hall until I'm done."

One agent looked to the other who shrugged at his companion.

"I don't mind the blood. I'll wait if you want to get a coffee."

"I'll be back in fifteen minutes, make sure he's ready," the departing agent shot at the young doctor.

"Sounds like a plan. I'll have him good as new." As the door closed, the resident smiled a slow lopsided grin. "Sorry to interrupt, but it seemed to me like you could use some help," he said in a low voice gently turning Matt's hand over to check the wounds. "Those two sounded a little heavy-handed," he added, nodding his head at the lone agent now leaning against the far wall.

"Thanks, I guess. It's been a difficult day."

"No problem, how's the hand feeling?"

"Funny thing about my hand, I'm not sure how this happened, and I can't even feel anything. It's pretty numb. Guess I've got too much crap to think about to worry about a few cuts."

"Well let me take a look at it anyway, you're bleeding pretty bad. While I do, you can go ahead if you want and tell me what's going on. I'm a good listener." He hadn't intended to say much, but almost without hesitation, Matt poured out most of his life in a torrent of remembered words, and once started, he was helpless to stop the flood. He never felt a single stroke of the doctor's needle, just sat there staring at the neat stitches as each one pulled the flaps of skin closed.

"Wow, what a story." The young intern, Dr. Joe, examined his handiwork and cleaned the blood away from the wounds; pleased it was one of his better jobs. He bandaged Matt's hand before he spoke again. "You've had a rough go of it, are you sure you can go with them now? I can get an order for you to stay here for observation if you want to collect yourself."

"No, thanks, I'm okay. Don't know why I dumped all that crap on you, guess my head was so full of all my new, or my old, memories, it just exploded, and you got the full load. More than anyone else I want to finish this garbage and get my life back."

"Well, that's good because your escorts are ready to go." The returning agent was seen through the window of the treatment room, heading in Matt's direction.

Ben's office discovered the CD held what Matt told them it would, and it was on its way to the lab for analysis and to start the serum production. For the first time in days, Ben took a deep breath and let it out slowly.

Chapter Thirty-Two

Heathrow Airport, suspected as it was to be the target for whatever attack was to come, was relieved of as many flights as possible, which still left it nearly bursting at the seams with hordes of scurrying travelers. Loudspeakers announced incoming and departing flights over the cacophony reverberating within the vast enclosure.

Two small children fell first. They dropped to the floor at their mother's side, causing her to stop and reprimand them for their misbehavior. The laugh on her face froze as her muscles and bones no longer held her up, and she too hit the floor. As she fell, her eyes brimmed with tears as she helplessly watched her thrashing children. All around her pockets of unearthly quiet mushroomed, spreading from one cluster of people to another. Whole families dropped simultaneously onto the cold, ages-worn floor.

The small band of martyrs watched London unravel from various positions around the arena. Khourmy thrilled to the macabre show, euphoric as the actors fell on cue. Just as they knew it would happen when they opened small containers of the toxin and let it drift downward with the movement of the air currents within the terminal, his brothers watched death play tag with the infidels before them. Their prayers to Allah would touch his ears this day. They would be blessed with unbelievable glory. This day was their duty, their right, and their destiny.

Khourmy spied his best friend Samid Alhamad on the ground floor below him, with his arms outstretched, blessing the crowds with the small vial. Khourmy envied Samid. His friend would be in paradise today, but alas, he could not claim his eternal reward as well, there was still much to do. "Allah be praised. We come to you and join your resplendency," Samid was praying. "You have vanquished our enemies. Your glory is forever. Death to all who would defy your name. Allah be—" His lips froze mid-sentence as he fell with the multitude around him, frozen in semi-death, his eyes staring straight ahead, but seeing only his ascent to the heavens. Khourmy slowly turned and headed for the exits. Allah was wonderful, indeed.

"It's only been thirty-eight hours since we found the notes," Ben yelled into the phone. "There have been five labs producing the serum for nearly two days, but they can't expect us to produce vats of the stuff on such short notice." With little sleep, Ben was pushing his people to push others to beat the attacker's timeline.

Already two shipments of the antidote jetted across the world in a race against time. Word of the horrendous occurrence in Heathrow had only come in four hours before. Thousands of travelers lay in near death conditions, with their vital organs barely functioning enough to keep them alive.

Teams of medical personnel in Hazmat suits descended upon the stricken hoards within minutes of the assault, but until the serum was available, there was little they could do to save a single life. As they moved from one dying person to another trying to make them more comfortable, only the squishing sounds of rubber-soled shoes broke the unearthly silence, totally unnerving the rescuers down to their toes.

Judging by Matt's experiments, those affected by the plague would slowly die within hours without the antidote. British intelligence estimated nearly six-thousand people were dropped by the lethal product, and the dying would begin in less than two hours. Military jets were on the way as fast as technology could fly. The race to the finish would be a close one.

Quick to accept the glory for the deed, several radio stations in Tehran proclaimed Khourmy's loyal cell responsible for the attack. They claimed credit for a vastly exaggerated number of people dying in the huge English airport. Celebrations broke out all over the territory as thousands of people spread the word they were dancing while thousands of their enemies lay dying. Gunshots rang out over the Iranian cities.

"Almost eight-hundred people so far." Ben was poring over the reports coming in by the half-hour. "How many more will be lost before the antidote gets there?"

"It's tragic," Abe Curly, Ben's boss was on the speakerphone. "At least the number is slowing. Hopefully, thousands will make it.

It's too soon for anyone to guess what the recovery rate will be for the ones that do survive. Good job, Ben, on the progress so far, and for finding the serum. But we know the threat hasn't been neutralized yet."

"Yeah, we're aware we've only solved part of the problem," Ben agreed. "The 'Breath' is still out there. Even though we now have a way to save people, it can still happen somewhere else, and we may not be on top of the site like we were at Heathrow, before it's too late."

"The shit-heads keep popping up like mushrooms all over the world." Abe lamented. "We squash them in one spot, and they stick their ugly heads out of the ground somewhere else to cause more grief."

"I know sir, we're all frustrated playing games with the assholes, but we do our best to stay ahead of them. At least we win one occasionally," Ben pointed out.

"I'm not sure if I'd call losing hundreds of people winning a round," Abe chided, "but I do know what you mean. Well, I'm headed to Washington for a briefing with the President, keep me up to date."

Ben's mind was already miles away as he disconnected the call. There was nothing more he could do for the poor souls at Heathrow, and other security matters already demanded his attention.

Now that the crisis was out of his hands, on a less serious note he thought of Elizabeth and the twins who would be heading home soon to Grand Rapids. Ben smiled, knowing her as he was growing to do; she would visit him before she left Washington to plead her case for reuniting Kate and Matt. Only partially did Ben admit to himself the reason he kept refusing Elizabeth was to keep her in close contact with him. *But the main reason*, he argued in his head, *is Kate's duty. I can't afford to lose a good agent just because of a silly love affair. There are more important things at stake in the world than a lost boyfriend.*

Ben hadn't voiced his idea to the twins yet, but he was already planning on having them re-commit to the agency when their contract was up next year, and adding a love interest would hamper his efforts at recruitment. The girls were young; there were plenty of years ahead of them for romance. Another five or ten-year contract was doable, at least from his point of view. They just hit their stride. "Nope," he said out loud to the walls, Matt would just have to find someone else to help him heal. Kate was an agent of the U.S. Government, a damn good one too. Not a nursemaid for some guy in need of TLC.

Heading down the hall to the conference room, a nagging thought played at the back of his mind. *How did Matt recover his memory in the antique store? What was the trigger?* Agent Jensen hadn't known for sure according to his report, but it was a question, and Ben wanted an answer. He didn't have time to dwell on the issue right now, but he would make certain he got to the bottom of it soon. Maybe at the same time, he would finally discover what sent Matt flying across the world in search of Kate's mother, to begin with. "Yep, another mystery," he smiled at the warm feeling thinking about Elizabeth always gave him. *I'll have to investigate this thoroughly.*

Chapter Thirty-Three

"You did what?" Kate was staring at her sister as if she had just sprouted a second head. "Are you out of your mind? What would make you do such a thing? I'm a big girl, you know. If I wanted to leave a trail behind me, I could have done it myself. You had no right to do such a thing!" Kate was sitting quietly looking out the window of the plane on their way back to Michigan, her mind a million miles away when the conversation between Lilly and their mother broke through to her.

"Now, Kate," Elizabeth hushed her. "Lilly only meant something good for you. She understood how much you felt for Matt."

"That didn't give her any right to break the rules or take my life in her hands. I can't believe you are sticking up for her. Did you plan this together?"

"No, you idiot, Mom didn't have anything to do with this," Lilly shot back, "at least not at first, but she's okay with what I did now. Aren't you, Mom?" Without waiting for a reply, Lilly went on, "I left a few clues for Matt. Mom didn't know about it until I told her everything after she couldn't figure out how Matt had found his way to England. That's all."

"That's all? That's *all?*" Kate was bright red from anger. "Do you know what happened to that poor man because of you? He could have been killed. He has lost his memory, his job, and his future because of what you did. It was only an accident Mom got involved in his care. What would have happened if she wasn't there to take care of him? He might still be lying in some antiquated hospital with no identity, no money, and no nothing. And all you can say is 'that's all!'"

Miffed her sister was missing the point of her heroism, Lilly was beginning to see red herself. "Listen, dummy, he wouldn't have been run over by a motorcycle if he hadn't seen Mom to begin with, and he wouldn't have been in Wales if it hadn't been for the murder of Aunt Lauren. I didn't cause his amnesia, nor did it change his life for the worse. He wasn't going to be happy without you anyway, so missing a few months of time finding you, is not the big deal you seem to be making it."

Kate was seething inside from the deception, but beneath the anger, a tiny spark of joy was trying to get her attention. *Matt was looking for me. He loves me.* It didn't exonerate Lilly, and she would never admit it to anyone, ever, but Kate felt the spark growing and the prospect, no matter how remote, of being back in Matt's arms again, made her feel warm all over. As quickly as the flame grew, she stomped it down. *How can I ever explain all that happened to him? How can I explain myself to him?* A single tear formed at the corner of her eye. Staring out the window so her mother and Lilly couldn't see, Kate deliberately squashed the hope inside her again. Matt could never be told the truth. He would hate her. It was better he never saw her again, never know how she betrayed him than to have him look at her and turn away. The tear fell, and she let it drop in her lap.

"Matt, please come in and sit down. So good of you to come back." Ben waved to the familiar chair by his desk.

"Your agents never give me much choice," Matt added sarcastically.

"Yeah, hmmm, well, anyway, I wanted to personally thank you for your contribution to the Heathrow efforts. A rather nasty bit of business over there, you know. Don't know how many more lives would have been lost if you hadn't been able to produce the notes when you did."

Matt refused the seat and continued to stand, just looking at Ben as he spoke. With arms crossed belligerently across his chest, Matt gave way to the months of frustration bottled up inside of him. "I have done all that you asked; I have given you what you wanted. Why am I here?" Matt demanded to know.

"Matt, there is more we have to talk about."

"Like what? I don't know anything else about your spy business. I barely remember who I am. But I'll tell you this, I have just gotten a taste of my life, and I would like to get back to it. I don't belong here in your world. I would appreciate if you would stop dragging me here, there, and all over the place. I understand the pressure you had to find the antidote and why it was important to make me remember, but it will haunt me until the day I die. I was responsible for the deaths of those poor people, and I swear to you and everyone else, I had nothing but good intentions when I worked on that research project. My lab … and your government, I may add, wanted that specific work done. It was supposed to be used for good in spite of how it turned out. I don't know how the whole damn thing went wrong … or how it got into the wrong hands to be used so brutally on innocent people. I've asked your agents to explain it, but all I get are the blank stares they are so good at. At this point, I'm still damn curious about the whole thing, but I doubt you're going to give me any more answers than they did. So, I'd just like to say I'm glad I could give you what you needed to fix it, but I'm done now. Let me go home and get on with my life. There are things I have to get back to."

Ben's face grew solemn as he rode out Matt's tirade.

"I know Matt, I … we here in the CIA believe what you say to be true. International terrorism is not your battle to fight, even though it could be argued it does indeed belong to the entire country, but be that as it may, you deserve to get back to your life. However, because of your relationship to the *product* created at Marsh Labs you have a responsibility, a duty, in fact, to spend a bit more time being briefed on all that has transpired since you last shut the light off in your lab, so you may shed whatever further knowledge you have on the catastrophe."

"Further knowledge, such as?" Matt demanded in a little less irate tone. "You know a whole lot more than I do about every detail of my life."

Ben took his time responding; he had to make a decision before he spoke again. "Alright, Matt, what do you want to know?"

Doubtful he was going to get the truth; Matt was ready to stay defensive. But something in Ben's tone and body language lessened the static in the air. Hesitant at first, not exactly sure what he would get, he tentatively asked, "I would like to know about everything. What happened to my work? How did it get around the world?" Before long, without realizing how it happened, he was sitting in the previously offered and declined chair. Matt and Ben were about to have their first real discussion, and neither one of them knew how it would change their lives.

Matt sat in silence while Ben finished his tale. No shock registered when he learned about Phil's betrayal of his work to the Iranian terrorists, nor did he doubt for a second Phil was capable of such treachery. But it was hard to swallow that Phil was killed in Matt's apartment, and by the superintendent of all people. He always thought Fred was squirrely, but he was surprised he could commit murder.

Theft was probably Fred's motive, although they would never know for sure. After the sound of the gunshot that took Phil's life, the neighbors called the police, and the bodies were found. Fred's apartment was inspected and turned up a stash he was growing for years. He amassed quite a collection of odds and ends picked up from his tenant's homes. When the items were returned to their rightful owners, some were grateful, some cursed the thief, and others felt violated by a man they trusted in their homes and around their families. No one missed him.

Several hours after they began their discussion, Ben walked Matt to the door of his office and instructed an agent to take Matt home. Ben told Matt what he could about the events which led up to the mass murder in England. He tied all the loose ends up and neatly presented them to Matt to sort out in his own time. Ben explained the brother in Las Vegas and the microchip in the Bible, he told Matt about Phil breaking into his apartment, and the destruction of his things as the Iranians took the place apart looking for the lost data. The only piece he left out was Kate and the government's surveillance of Matt and his apartment. Matt remembered Kate on his own in the antique shop, but there was no way of tying Kate to the CIA, and if Ben had anything to say about it, and he did, Matt may never find out that piece of the story.

Opening the door of his apartment, Matt was surprised how easily the lock turned. In a flash, the memory of his former frustration with the door returned. *Hmm, well the dead maintenance guy did something right before he got himself wasted,* Matt thought to himself. It was an eerie feeling going home alone.

No agent to dog his footsteps, no feeling his every move was open to inspection. It was the first time in many weeks his life was his own again. He wasn't sure what it meant for his future, but at least he was free to figure it out himself. Back on home territory, with nothing and no one to stand in his way, he was free to think about her. His Kate. The golden dream at the end of the path he took to find her. All the pain and suffering of the past months would have been whisked away with no more substance than a cobweb if he found her in the process. He remembered her all right, and he remembered why he went to England. Although his memory was still pretty foggy about the events leading up to the accident in Wales, he was slowly putting all the pieces together about what happened after.

He would sort it out. His scientific mind wanted to analyze everything that happened. There were so many pieces to the puzzle, Phil, and the Iranians, Elizabeth supposedly drowned in London and then nursing him back to health in Wales with Franny at the cottage. *Are they tied together? Can they be, or is it all a coincidence?* The reason he had been attracted to Elizabeth in the road was obvious; Kate was a ringer for her mother. B*ut why did the Royal Arms deliberately concoct a story substituting Elizabeth's death for Lauren's?* In spite of the mystery, he marveled that it was Kate's mother who nursed him back to health. That was something he hadn't thought to ask Ben about, but Ben seemed to be pretty foggy himself about what happened to Matt while he was in England, or so he said.

Matt reflected as he sat on the new couch staring at a blank wall, *it was Interpol's men who tracked me down to El*izabeth's cottage hadn't they, so …, Matt mused, how did they do that? Ben hasn't been telling me everything he knows, after all. First thing in the morning he was going to call Ben and ask more questions. What he needed now was a hot shower, and then a good night's sleep.

Tomorrow I need to get in touch with Dr. Nowak and see about my job. Matt had no idea how he was going to explain the whole affair to him, but he needed his job, and that was the best place to start. *Maybe Marsh would understand how stress drove me to leave the country. I don't owe them an explanation for my time off. But I know they won't be happy why I didn't return on time.*

But after all, it wasn't my fault what happened to my notes. It should earn me some points I followed my instinct not to leave everything behind in the laboratory. Shouldn't it? Phil is to blame for what happened. Him and his greed. There was always something wrong about him; now I know what it was. Poor Dr. Nowak, he's going to get a lot of heat for hiring Phil.

Matt continued his mental defense; *I did save thousands of lives with the serum, yeah, yeah, even if it was also my work that caused the tragedy in the first place, well that's what they paid me to do.* It would take some doing, but Matt was ready for the battle to reclaim his place in the lab. No doubt the position in Washington was already filled, but that was okay as well. He enjoyed working with Dr. Nowak. He would give it his best shot and be happy just to get his old job back.

Then there was Kate. She was the last thing on his mind before sleep claimed him. He knew he would find her now and have the chance to ask her what went wrong between them. All he needed was to contact Elizabeth, and she would help him. Considering all that happened, it was a stroke of luck in the end. The link to Kate was right there in front of him the whole time he was in Wales. How astounding it was to know where to start. Matt was smiling as he drifted off. He slept well. His reunion with Kate was only a phone call away.

Matt's call to Dr. Nowak was anything but fruitful. He couldn't get past the secretary and was only able to leave his number. *What the hell is going on there?* The woman was evasive and kept repeating the same line; 'someone would be in touch with him.' *What the hell does that even mean? Is my career blown?* He couldn't believe Dr. Nowak would blow him off like that. He should at least give him a chance to explain. But it didn't look like it was going to happen easily.

Unfortunately, Dr. Nowak was no longer with Marsh Labs. He was given an early retirement after the fiasco with Phil and the theft of Matt's work. Not that they suspected he was involved with the plot to supply the 'Breath of God' to Iran, but it did happen under his watch, and he should have picked up on Phil's character flaws long before the damage was done. Dr. Nowak had given Phil, albeit reluctantly, a recommendation to take the post in Washington after Matt disappeared. He superiors wondered what kind of a supervisor he was to miss assessing Phil more accurately? Not to mention he had falsified the reason for Matt's delay in reporting to Washington.

The new man in Dr. Nowak's job was briefed on the incident in England and Marsh's involvement. He would be extremely cautious about whom he hired in the future. He recognized the name Matt Errington when told who was on the line. Matt had disappeared without a trace for months, with no explanation. It wasn't hard to figure out what he wanted, but he would take his time and do some research of his own before he would take Matt's call.

Chapter Thirty-Four

"Those sure are beautiful, what are they?" Kate asked her mom.

"They're delphiniums. Your dad loved those deep blue ones." It was a rare occasion when the twins were able to visit Elizabeth at her home in Michigan. Elizabeth's gardens were in full bloom, and she spent as much time as she could in her favorite place.

"Mom, Ben called. He would like you to call him back when you have a moment. Nothing urgent," Lilly called from the door.

"Okay, thanks, honey. I'll be right there," Elizabeth responded with a lilt to her voice. Kate's trained ear picked up the subtlety in the response and cast her mom a suspicious glance.

"Wow, you seem particularly glad to hear from him," Kate teased.

Elizabeth blushed. "What do you mean; we always enjoy Ben's visits. He did say he had business up this way. I know he is still concerned about your health since Las Vegas."

"That may be," Kate continued in the same teasing voice, "but you used to be annoyed when he would call here."

"Yes, I supposed I did at times," Elizabeth stared pensively at her flower beds, "but his calls usually meant you girls would be going away somewhere and that always made me worry. I can't explain the difference now, but ever since we almost lost you in that dreadful tomb, I seem to have lost some of that fear. I saw how much he cares for you girls and I have more faith now he will protect you." She turned to Kate with a wistful smile on her face.

"Mom, you know we can take care of ourselves; you don't have to worry about us."

"Yeah, right, I'm sure getting out of that cement house was all of your doing, wasn't it? We owe a lot to the women who heard your cry for help. It was a pure stroke of luck they were there that day."

"I don't believe that much in luck, Mom. I have more faith Dad was watching out for us. He always said he would."

"I know if he could, he would," Elizabeth agreed. "Ben does the same thing I think, he spends more time with you two than with any of the other agents he handles," Elizabeth said as she handed cut flowers to Kate.

"Oh, we're back to talking about Ben again," Kate chuckled, watching her mother closely for any telltale signs of affection.

"Oh, Kate," her mom laughed, "stop that. You know we all care for Ben. Now help me bring all of these flowers inside before they wilt. I'll go call him back."

"You run ahead, Mom, I'll get your flowers. You don't want to keep him waiting." Kate was laughing, and so was Elizabeth. "Hmm," Kate said out loud, "Elizabeth Madison, has a nice ring to it, doesn't it, Mom?" If Elizabeth heard her, she paid no attention, but her step quickened as she headed for the house.

It took tremendous effort, but Kate finally forgave her mom and Lilly for intruding in her life. She also gave them strict orders not to interfere again. If she was going to have a normal life, it must happen, well, normally, not contrived or set up. Not that Matt looking for her made anything contrived, actually, but, oh, well, how could she explain to them, the whole relationship was set up from the get-go. It wasn't straightforward or honest. How could she expect to have a normal life with someone like Matt when their time together was a lie?

Kate spent her nights alone, hashing over and over her feelings for Matt. She tried to put him out of her mind, let him go as she had other assets in the past, but she hadn't succeeded. He was different. There was so much good in him, so contrary to the type of people her world revolved around. He loved her deeply, she knew that, and a weird pain ran through her each time she pictured his face or saw couples in a crowd that reminded her of their time together.

True he cared for her in the past, but she also knew that being the type of person he was, he would never be able to get past the deception she and her job pulled on him. It was decidedly better just to 'let sleeping dogs lie' and put Matt and their feelings for each other behind her. It was probably the kindest thing she could do for him and maybe even for herself. As painful as it was considering her feelings for him, she was, after all, a professional. It was just one more door she needed to close.

During the weeks that followed the tragedy at Heathrow, a combined team of British Secret Service, some of Ben's agents, members of SO15 British Counter Terrorism Command and SO18 Aviation Security Forces, worked tirelessly to find the terrorists responsible for the attack in London.

With the help of the GPS strip the CIA planted in Rashid Zand's passport, members of the cell were found to be hiding in a small stone structure in a remote village near Kabul, Afghanistan. In the ramshackle house Rashid Zand, Kaleehad Khourmy and thirteen of their newest recruits for martyrdom, rode the lingering wave of success of Heathrow as they hungrily plotted their next target.

"But why can't we make a strike on the Americans?" Zand argued for the hundredth time. "Because of them, I missed the greatest day of my life." His hatred of the U.S. and its people was well known among his friends and the cell leaders. "I have seen them, and I know their ignorance. I have lived among them. They are like the fleas on a dog and are easily fooled," he pleaded. "We could strike their schools and their homes. If we wipe out the ignorant families that breed more infidels and kill more of the children, there will be less of them to grow up to wage war on us." Khourmy smiled at his friend and patted the air to calm the rising tide of anger.

"I know Rashid, we all feel the same about the infidel cities of the West, but it is not our choice. That right belongs to Allah. He chooses who should live and die. Allah be praised," he invoked the group.

"Allah the Almighty be praised," the others responded on cue.

"The American's will pay, I promise you my friend, but here, sit with me. Let me tell you what I heard today in the—"

"Brothers, listen!" A young member of the group, who was sitting in the open window, jumped back into the room screaming the alarm.

The whistling sound of the approaching missile fired from an overhead drone could be heard above their terrified cries as each man registered the fact they were about to die.

The warning gave the men little time to escape even if fifteen grown men could have squeezed through the tiny door at the same time. The men pushed and clawed trying to get out crushing those in the front as those in the rear pushed ever harder. Khourmy and Zand trapped with the others; were blown to pieces, their screams of terror matching those of their companions. Their prayers to Allah, if they remembered to say them, had failed to reach him in time. It is doubtful their last thoughts were of the glories and the seventy-two virgins awaiting them.

Watching by satellite as the hovel was leveled with the cell leaders inside, the recognizance team exploded in a rush of held breath and adrenalin. The moment had a small taste of sweet revenge for the atrocities of Heathrow.

Chapter Thirty-Five

With the CIA out of his hair, Matt could now dedicate himself to finding Kate. Realizing he was right back where he was before, the only source was her mother, Elizabeth. He wasn't sure where to start looking for her and doubted she was still in Wales. Nor did he have the funds to go jetting off around the world again even if he could. His savings account had been nearly drained since he left for England and the bills were piled high on the old antique desk, ironically one of the few pieces of furniture which had escaped destruction. He needed a job right away, but that would come. At the moment, his priority was to find Kate.

Somewhere in his belongings sent over from the Royal Arms, he found the business card Jeremy York gave him on his arrival in London. Maybe Jeremy could lend a hand again. England was several hours ahead, and Matt determined when Jeremy would be in his office.

Jeremy answered on the first ring and after learning it was Matt calling, boomed his promise of assistance through the phone. "Absolutely, my friend, I would be more than happy to do whatever I can to help you find this woman. I was surprised when I never heard from you months ago, my cousin even asked about you. We both hoped you had reached your objective and went on with your life. I can do some research and find the cottage phone number in Wales if it's listed, if not, I may need my cousin back in the States to lend a hand through his connections. Either way, we'll get you the number you need. Talk to you soon."

As he hung up the phone, Matt felt the first wave of relief since arriving home. He melted his long frame into the chair. At least something good might happen soon. Whatever her reasons were for leaving him, they didn't matter anymore. He only wanted proof she was real, tell her his feelings and then let her go. If that was still what she wanted, he was prepared, even after all that happened in her pursuit, he would let her go. He swore it to himself.

The phone rang and rang, but no one answered. Jeremy had come through for him, and within minutes of his call, Matt was on the phone trying to reach Elizabeth or Franny at the cottage in Wales. Days went by without any success. Neither one of them were staying there now. That worried Matt, particularly about Franny. She was so old and frail. What if something bad happened to her? He would never know. He would feel terrible, after all she did for him, and he wasn't able to help her. So much had occurred since he was pulled away from the cottage that day.

Even before he realized who Elizabeth was, as soon as he reached the States, he asked Ben to contact her and let her know he was home and okay. Ben said he would, but Matt didn't know if the message was delivered or not. But now, knowing Elizabeth was Kate's mother, Matt was driven to make contact with her himself. It was his quest for her that put him in harm's way, thus landing him in her hands after all. What a weird coincidence, he often thought. What a story that would make to anyone who would care enough to listen. It made all the sense in the world looking back over the prior months' events, to remember her kindness and how warm she was to him. It was obvious why he was so attached to her and why he came to care a great deal for the woman who replaced his subconscious Kate.

If I can just reach her, I know she will be surprised how fate threw us together, and how our lives crossed. Matt had no doubt Elizabeth would help him reach Kate. Of that, he was certain. But other than the Welsh cottage, he had no idea where to start.

Saucy Abernathy stood in the doorway of his *House of Antiques and Oddities* staring at the young man on the step. "You're damn right I remember you. You nearly tore my entire store apart. This is my livelihood; does that mean anything to you? No!" he stopped to spit on the ground at Matt's feet. "I'm just an old man. You kids got no respect for anyone but yourselves. Don't come around here again. I've got enough problems paying my bills without you breaking half my merchandise." Saucy was headed back inside when Matt's pleading voice stopped him mid-step.

"Please, sir, I am truly sorry for what I did. I can't explain exactly what happened, but I will repay you for whatever damage I did to your shop. I came by for the glass vases you had in your window. I want to buy them and pay you for whatever else you feel I owe."

Saucy wasn't sure his tirade had run its course yet, but he felt his anger giving way with the sincerity of the young man's apology, and the mention of more money. Hell, he'd already been paid enough by the other guy in the suit on the night of the rampage. Saucy tossed it over in his mind before answering. He didn't think the CIA would find out if he charged the guy again, but he didn't want any trouble with the government. Better to lose a few bucks than open up a hornet's nest.

"I don't have those little trinkets anymore," he spit again, making Matt jump back a foot. "Gave them to the guy you were with. Go take it up with the government." It pleased him immensely to see the downcast look on the guy's face. Serves him right if he is disappointed. If Saucy couldn't keep them pretty little doo-bobs, then this little shit shouldn't have them either. Didn't matter much anyhow. The government took them, and that was that.

"Why the hell would Agent Jensen take all of Kate's vases out of the shop?" Matt wondered aloud, climbing back in the car. *That doesn't make sense. Certainly, they have no meaning to the investigation. The government has the data they wanted from me; it has nothing to do with glass vases or Kate. Why would they take them?* He needed to find a way to contact Jim and get an answer to that question. *Good Lord another mystery to solve.* It was getting harder to move his life forward when everything kept getting stuck in the past. He was mired down in questions and no one to help him find answers. 'One step forward and three back,' his boss used to say. He was no closer to finding Kate or putting his life back together than he was last spring. Life had a nasty way of going around in circles. He was back where he was before, only worse off, no Kate, no job, no money, and still no answers.

"Hello! Elizabeth, it's so good to finally hear your voice. I've been trying to get in touch with you. I kept calling hoping you would answer, not knowing how else to reach you."

"Matt, is that you? We've been so curious about what happened to you. It's been so long since you disappeared from the cottage. What happened? Did you get your memory back? Are you back home and well?"

"It's a long story, Elizabeth … and yes, I have most of my memory back, and yes I'm home, but things aren't too well yet. But, like I said, it's a long story. You said 'we,' is Franny okay? I was worried when I couldn't reach either of you that something happened to her. You don't have an answering machine at the cottage, and I didn't know anyone else to call over there to check on you ladies."

"I'm sorry you were worried, but we had no way to get in touch with you either." She lied, but there was no way she could tell him the truth. "So many things have happened, but things have calmed down. Franny suffered a small stroke and was in the same hospital you were in, but she's doing better and doesn't seem to have any serious lasting effects, which is remarkable for her age. I got back here yesterday to hire someone to stay with her. I'm only here for a week, so I'm glad you caught me today. You said things aren't too well, what's the matter, Matt? Are you okay?"

He didn't want to just blurt out the reason for his call. In his head, he had long conversations with her in which he explained all the coincidental details that brought them together. He imagined Elizabeth would be thrilled to learn of his relationship with Kate, and would eagerly set up a reunion. But now on the phone with Kate's mother, his confidence wavered. *What if she doesn't approve of me for Kate? What if she tells me Kate is with someone else?* There were so many 'what-ifs' again. The conversation faltered, and for the first time with her, he was at a loss for words. "I'm sorry I don't mean to worry you. I have some things to straighten out in my life." Matt took his time and tried to choose his words carefully. "Finding myself and my identity was a remarkable event. The whole story is astonishing, and I'm sure you will be amazed when I tell you what happened."

Elizabeth held her breath, trying to prepare a response for what he was about to tell her.

Refusing to give in to his nervousness, Matt went on. "You found me Elizabeth, which is uncanny because I went to Wales to find your sister-in-law, Lauren. It seems quite a coincidence because, in London, I was told you were dead, and Lauren was my goal in Wales."

There was silence on the line for a moment, then Elizabeth asked, "Why were you looking for me in London, Matt?" even though she knew the answer.

With the line he had waited months to say, he went on, "You were my lead to your daughter, Kate." There, he dropped the bomb. His head was spinning, and he thought he would pass out with the suspense while waiting for her to respond.

"I see," was all she could say at first. Then she added, "How do you know Kate? Why would you come all the way to England to find her or me? I don't understand the connection."

"No, I don't suppose you would until you hear my story. Do you have the time to listen? I hate to do this long distance."

"I have time, Matt, please go on."

Without further invitation, Matt poured his life out to her and how events led up to his loss of Kate and everything he endured since she left him. Although he never said the words, his pain and loss, his love and his loneliness were all there for Elizabeth to hear between the lines.

Her heart broke for him and for the love her daughter gave up in the name of duty. She was faced with a real dilemma. She had given Kate her word she would not interfere again in her life, and she knew Ben would be displeased if she gave Kate up to Matt. She knew her instincts about Matt were right, but that didn't give her the right to follow them. Searching for a way to answer him without breaking her word to Kate, Elizabeth grasped upon the only solution she could.

"Matt, that is an incredible story … and more than anything I would be happy to help you." Matt's heart soared. "However," she tried to put a smile in her voice knowing his hopes would be dashed. "I know my daughter well, Matt. If she left you as you say she did, she must have had her reasons. I can't answer the big question you want to know, why she left. Only she can tell you that. But I have learned a great deal about you and what a fine young man you are. I would never wish to interfere in my daughter's life, but I will tell you what I can do. I will take your number and pass it on to her. If she wants to get in touch with you, she will. That's the best I can offer Matt."

The roller coaster ride was over. He was up, down, and up again, only to stop right back at the starting gate. "But …" he started to argue then changed his mind. *What good will it do? Kate already has my number*, he wanted to say, *she lived with me, remember?* It was he who didn't have hers. Elizabeth was not a stupid woman, she got the facts, and he knew that. This was her way of closing the door to him. Perhaps Kate already told her about him and why she left. He put Elizabeth in the middle by his call and made her uncomfortable with his request. He wanted to let her off the hook as best he could.

"That's a great idea," he said, with as much enthusiasm as he could muster. "I wouldn't want to intrude in her life. I'm sure if she is interested, she will call me back. I appreciate you passing on my message to her. Please let me know when you are back in the States. I'm trying to get my job back so I can start paying you back for everything you did for me. It was great to talk to you again. Give Franny a big hug for me."

Elizabeth sighed, hearing the pain in his voice so poorly disguised. But it was all she could offer. "Well, good Matt, give me your number, and I'll make sure Kate gets it. You take care of yourself. I'll tell Franny you called."

Sinking deeper into the couch, Matt let the last of his energy seep away. *The one thread I had to Kate was Elizabeth.* As it had been all along, it was Kate's game, his only path was to follow. *Right back to where I was before. Everything is in her hands as it always is. I never had any control at all, and I probably screwed it up more by my call to Elizabeth. Maybe I could have worked on Elizabeth differently.* He would have liked to have more time to open the conversation slowly, to lay all of the pieces out for her, to have pleaded his case in person, not thousands of miles away. *I probably should have waited until I could see her when she returns to the States. But it probably wouldn't matter anyway.* Judging by the tone of Elizabeth's voice as she tried to let him down easy, Matt was sure now Kate left him because she didn't love him, she wasn't happy with him, and everyone seemed to know it but him. *I should just let it go. Let her go.*

Chapter Thirty-Six

"She doesn't want to see you."

The words rang in his ears, and even though they made sense, he couldn't understand their meaning. Kate was standing in his door and saying, "She." Matt's senses were failing him. He was in a sound sleep when he heard a light tapping on his door. He was certainly dreaming or having one of his nightmares. He dreamt of her so often it was not much of a surprise when he opened his door to find her standing there. But how goofy was this, she was calling herself, "she." Hallucinations were part of his past, and he understood them for what they were. He was confused, however, why this was happening now. He had been well lately, and this one seemed particularly real. He must be having a relapse from the accident. "Better go get a pill and go back to bed," Matt said out loud to himself as he started to close the door.

"Matt! What are you doing? Aren't you going to let me in?"

This hallucination was more real than most.

"No, you aren't Kate."

"Well, you are completely right about that. I'm Lilly. May I come in?"

Matt thought his heart would explode; it was pounding so hard. Staring at the figure in front of him and not knowing for sure if she was real or not, he was afraid to speak for fear she would disappear.

"I'm Kate's sister, as if you couldn't figure that out. Her twin." Lilly smiled. She was concerned about his lack of color. Matt blanched white as a ghost.

Fearing he would keel over at any moment, she put her hand out to steady him and lightly touched his arm. Her touch sent Matt jumping backward as if burned.

"You are real," he stammered, holding onto the wall behind him for support. "I'm not imagining you this time."

"No, Matt, you're not. I'm sorry if I startled you. But after all you have been through, I needed to come. You deserve some peace of mind." She nodded for him to sit, and he dropped onto the couch beside her, never taking his eyes off the apparition before him.

"Please," he said, looking into blue eyes identical to Kate's. "What the hell is going on? I need to know about Kate."

"I will try to tell you everything, Matt, even though you may not like what you hear, but I'll tell you what I can." Lilly knew the risk she was taking going to Matt's and breaking her word to Kate. But she also knew she didn't have a choice. Even if Kate had no feelings for the man, he didn't deserve to be left in limbo any longer, and especially considering what he had gone through, he at least deserved the truth. Well at least as much of truth as she could give him. Elizabeth and Lilly decided the kindest thing they could do for him was to make him stop wanting her. Stop looking for her. Tell him how she deceived him. That should do the trick. He would be heartbroken, but he would heal.

They sat facing each other on the couch, but Matt's mind was miles away as Lilly poured out the truth about Kate and the CIA. And her confession. "I'm the one that left the book here after her assignment was over, the book and the postcard. And it was me, not Kate, who gave the glass vases to the antique store." Lilly felt terrible for the pain she was inflicting; Matt's face reflected it all. "I realize now it was wrong, but I hoped you would follow the leads to find my sister. I'm truly sorry for interfering and the way it turned out for you in England."

When she finished, Matt sat as if in a trance; it was hard to speak, his voice was deep and constricted. "Our meeting was arranged? I was set up?"

Lilly nodded.

"She never cared for me at all, did she? It was just a job. She lied to me from the first time I met her." The honest man in Matt balked at what he was hearing. *How could she have done this to me? She played me for such a fool. How she must have laughed at my simple ways and boring life. I knew it was too good to be true, someone like Kate caring for me.* Heartbroken wasn't the right word. He was traumatized beyond words. But the truth had the desired effect. He no longer wanted anything to do with Kate. Before

Lilly walked out of his home, he made that quite clear. His dreams and his Kate were gone, there was nothing left. His life was a complete shambles.

The pain of finding out about Kate and her duplicity left Matt devoid of all feeling. As he stumbled through his days, Matt was merely a shadow of himself. He nearly lost everything he had worked for; his career, his home, his memory, and his future, all for Kate, and she only used him for her job. Matt was desolate and deliberately shut her out of his mind.

After a careful review of the circumstances surrounding his disappearance and with more than a little pressure from the CIA, thanks to Ben, Marsh Laboratories offered Matt a job back in the labs. He was to report back to work in one week. The advanced position he hoped for in Washington was gone, but at least he would have his work again to take up his days, fill his head, and pay some bills. Matt knew it wouldn't be easy to get back to the daily routine, and he needed to clear his head and his heart of the muck that swirled around inside him. But to do that, Matt needed to escape his apartment and its memories. Seven days alone with the thoughts of Kate's deception haunting him and nothing to do but replay the events of his life over and over again would have torn him apart. He needed a temporary respite from his life.

He loaded up his car with just a few belongings and headed down to the Carolina's, back to the place of his childhood and the days of safety with his mother and Mickey. It was the only place that now held happy memories for him. Back in his home town, the pain he buried for so many years after his mother's death wrapped around him in a stranglehold and for a brief time, he doubted the wisdom of the visit. Gradually he made his long-delayed peace with the world and his past. He visited his mother's grave next to Mickey's and shed the buckets of tears that had never come before. He ranted at the sky at the unfairness of life, and he made resolutions about how wise he would be in the future. He probably sounded like the madman he had been, but when he was spent, he knew he would heal.

For the first time in decades, he made peace with who he was. Somewhere during the long drive home, he knew regardless of how it happened or how he had been deceived; Kate had been good for him. She offered him a way out of his loneliness, and he realized, at last, he would be okay, and he could go on with or without her. Being angry was not the answer. Forgetting was hard, but forgiveness was not. He made peace with all he knew about Kate. He had tried to forget her, tried to exorcise her from the deepest darkest reaches of his mind, but after all, he loved her still, and all he wanted out of life was for her to know that, and then he would let go. And he knew exactly how to find her this time. He would make Ben Madison give him the answers he wanted, and this time, there would be no more lies.

Never in her entire life had Lilly seen Kate so mad. *I guess I did it by going to see Matt, but if Kate didn't care how devastated he was, someone needed to take pity on the poor guy. Sure, he was hurt, but at least he knew the truth and could make his judgment call on where to go from there. He needed to be told so he would stop chasing ghosts and throwing his life away.*

Kate was angry, but she would get over it. She was sensible and logical. Eventually, she would see what Lilly did was the right thing for the guy. *Besides, Kate said she never wanted to see him again anyway, so let him heal and get on with it. I've done them all a favor. Kate will realize it when she stops being such a control freak.* In the meantime, Lilly intended to steer clear of her twin and the thunderstorm crackling in the air around her.

Lilly couldn't know how Kate ached inside. Not just for Lilly's irresponsible act of telling Matt all about her, but for how hurt Matt must be by the misuse of his trust. He knew how she had played him, deceived him, and he would suspect everything she ever said or did was a lie. She knew the truth would hurt him more than anything else, even the confusion of her disappearance. It had been hard on her as well to leave him in such a way, knowing the pain it would cause. But this truth, the whole truth might be more than he could bear. He was such an honest man. He would never understand her world of role-playing and deception.

I do care for him, deeply, love him even. But he'll never believe that now. Even if given a chance to see him again, he would never want me back. She was furious at Lilly, in spite of the fact she understood why she went to see Matt. *Yes, I want him to forget me, it's for his own good, but no, I don't want him to be so hurt by my lies and the truth about our relationship, and yes it was logical what Lilly did, but why does it hurt so much hearing he is done with me, once and for all. He never wants to hear my name again, and now he doesn't ever want to see me either.* It was Kate's turn to be devastated. Pain cut through her as only the loss of love can do.

"Ben, Matt Errington is here to see you," Nichole announced Ben's visitor.

Meeting him at the door, Ben beamed a sincere smile and said, "Come in, Matt, good to see you looking so well. I was delighted to hear you were coming in today. Surprised though, I thought you would be busy with your new job and all. You must be happy to be back in your own home." Ben slapped Matt on the back as if they were longtime friends and motioned to the usual leather chair.

Matt remained standing and barely shook the proffered hand. "I'm not here for a social call or to chit chat about my life," Matt declared in a friendly but firm voice. "I have some questions I would like answered, and I can't think of a better person than you, Mr. Ben Madison, CIA agent, and savior of the free world."

The smile never left Ben's face, but his eyes went steely cold. "Well, you can conduct your business standing up or sitting down, makes no difference to me," as he walked around and took his seat facing Matt. "I thought we went over everything, Matt, but just what questions would you like answered?"

Without hesitation, Matt calmly sat down on the edge of the chair and leaned forward to bridge the distance between the two men. "Who is Kate Champion and why did you think you could just pop her into my life and then out again, without so much as a 'thank you, sir, for your cooperation.'" Matt was trying to maintain his composure, but the irritation he was feeling sitting back in Ben's office was growing by the minute. "I'm a citizen of the United States, and I feel used and abused by Ben Madison and his people, which of course includes Kate. I feel I'm entitled to some answers. My privacy was invaded. I was lied to, you tapped my home, and while I was gone, you tore it apart. I want to know why. With what justification was that done? I have rights." Matt was getting angrier by the minute. He'd been set up and used. "Didn't you guys need a search warrant to do that? Didn't you have to have justification?"

Ben sat through the outburst and waited for Matt to run out of steam which he did eventually, while, as usual, Ben sat there smugly quiet. "Fine, Mr. Errington, since we are being formal here, did you come here looking for an apology, an explanation, and a promise we won't do it again. Well, I'm sorry to break the news to you. We didn't need a warrant, you invited Kate in, and the suspected threats to national security and your relationship with Phil justified everything we did.

"Did you have a right to be told? No, you didn't. It was a need to know basis, and you didn't need to know. We deal with shitheads like Khourmy and Rashid Zand all the time, every day. We went over all of that the last time you were here.

"We don't know where they are going to strike, but strike they will if we don't keep on the alert. And they will use every tool at their disposal to wreak the most havoc … tools like your research project. Yes, we know it was meant for good, but you can see how the bad guys turned it around and used it to kill for the pleasure of killing.

"I don't owe you an explanation or an apology, but I will tell you this. We determined you are an honest man. But you were working with some potentially dangerous stuff. You were never suspected of working with the Iranians, but we had no other way to evaluate Phil or even Dr. Nowak. We couldn't get close to either of them, but we knew Zand was making connections with one of them. He murdered one of my best men when he was suspected, and I had to get information another way, so I sent Kate in to learn more. We don't always know the target, but we get pretty damn close to the source. If we have to borrow some of your privacy to stop attacks on our shores, we do that. I'm sorry if it bugs your ass, but that's the way it goes." The smile faded rapidly from Ben's face, and there was no longer any hint of pleasantry.

"Who the hell do you think you are, demanding justice? Did you think the poor souls who died in Heathrow got justice? Or the thousands who died in 9/11? What makes you think there is any such thing as justice? We, the people of this government, people like Kate and thousands of others like her, put their lives on the line every day to keep your butt safe. They stop hundreds of other attacks you'll never hear about. Hell, we think it's fair what we do. It's the only way we have of leveling out the playing field. So, before you start whining again about a little intrusion in your life, stop and think about all that."

Matt's anger was fading, and he knew Ben was right, to a point. He hadn't intended to crash into Ben's office and start punching away, it just happened, and he couldn't stop the anger that spilled over. Everything was so wrong in his life, and he wanted an explanation from someone as to why.

"Look, Matt," Ben started more calmly, "you played a huge role in preventing a much larger tragedy. We are grateful for that. As a citizen, you are entitled to your privacy by all means, but you have to try and understand the nature of terrorism today and how invasive it is in our society. They aren't like you and me; they aren't like anyone you have ever known in your life. They don't care about your justice, your privacy … or your life. We must do what we can within the limits of the law to stop them. And sometimes we have to bend the laws when we know it's the only way to save lives. You got caught up in something which went horribly wrong. But you also were the only one to turn it all around again. That should give you some comfort."

Matt stared at the ivy pattern in the carpet at his feet and saw how life twisted just like the intricate vine, weaving people, with all their complexities together as it snaked through time.

"What about Kate?" Ben neatly avoided answering the question about Kate. "I still want to know who she is and how much was real between us and how much was staged."

"I can't answer that for sure, Matt. But I can tell you this, Kate was given an assignment, and you were the asset. She is a thorough and well-trained agent. She will do whatever it takes to get the information she is after. That's all I can tell you. What happened between the two of you was her job. Nothing more."

Stabbing pain went through the heart Matt thought couldn't be hurt again. He even surprised himself when he blurted out, "I'll believe that when she is allowed to tell me to my face, not through a messenger, not through you or anyone else, face to face. Can we do that?"

Ben thought it outrageously presumptive to force the issue like this and was on the verge of telling Matt just that when he remembered Elizabeth's face and her entreaty that Matt be allowed to see Kate. He softened.

"If and only if, Kate is agreeable to a meeting, I will set it up, and if her answer is no, you will just have to live with that. It is a once only deal. Are we agreed? You will get your answer from Kate and go home."

"Yes. That will be enough." It was a win, sort of. He was finally going to see her, if she agreed, of course. He knew he wouldn't be able to breathe until he got an answer.

It was so unlike Ben. Kate sat, staring at the phone in her hands as if mesmerized. She'd never heard him sound so unsure. Ben was not a person to beat around the bush or mince words. So, it was no wonder she was taken aback by his hemming and hawing on the phone. She only called in to ask his advice on her latest assignment, but mid-conversation she could tell he was not focused on what she was saying. Something was on his mind, and she hoped it didn't have anything to do with Lilly's meddling. Then she got the email.

The message from Ben was short, but the six words shook her down to her marrow. "Do you want to see Matt?" *Crap, what the hell is this all about?* Kate didn't know how it came about, and she wasn't sure what Ben was doing, but the answer was not all that simple.

All of her career she followed Ben unquestionably with no hesitation for personal choices. She did everything to be a good agent, to make Ben and her parents proud of her. Kate longed for a normal life, not that she hadn't been proud of her job and the small contributions she and Lilly made to their country, but lots of agents had families, and she knew her job wasn't enough anymore. But she also knew Ben Madison well. When they closed a file, they closed the file. This was not like him at all. *What could he possibly be thinking?* Opening up a door with a past asset was a dangerous business. And, for all her training, experience and bravado, Kate was terrified to face Matt again. *Lilly must be behind it,* Kate was sure of that, and she must have used a tremendous amount of influence to make Ben flip on his rules.

She felt squeezed and so empty. The longing to see Matt, to be with him, to have a normal life with him, played war with her heart, especially knowing how repulsed he must have been when he learned the truth. Matt valued truth and trust. Just the opposite of what she gave him. As much as she wished things were different, the reality was what it was; it was best for them both to not look back.

Chapter Thirty-Seven

Resting his head against the cold window, Matt could feel the pulse of the rain as it beat against the glass. It reminded him somehow of a song he once heard but couldn't quite catch the tune. Like a lot of things, he thought, it was buried under months of amnesia and was only just beginning to swim to the surface.

Opening his eyes, he strained to see beyond the blinding stream of water cascading down even though there wasn't much to see; the street was deserted due to the weather. No one in his right mind would be out tonight. Some of the guys from work wanted him to meet up with them for dinner and a couple of beers to renew old relationships, that sort of thing, but he couldn't seem to make his body move in that direction. Besides, he knew part of their invitation was based on curiosity. They wanted the whole scoop about his absence, and he had no intention of adding to the rumors that rolled throughout the labs. He was hungry, but the thought of making small talk over a Coney Dog with a bunch of guys with little more on their minds than sports, cars, or sex, just wasn't enough to make him brave the storm.

Work was alright. It was different since his return. The change wasn't with his co-workers, he knew that. It was him. He had changed. Oh, sure he could get lost in his lab work as he always did, unraveling the mysteries of science still got him out of bed in the morning, but his heart was no longer so idealistic. He saw the world differently now. As he did a million times before, he wondered how something which was intended to do so much good could have caused something so tragic. It wasn't the research he so painstakingly conducted or the serum which could help cure a terrible disease; it was people. People who hated everything they didn't have, hated what they didn't understand or didn't want someone else to have.

The Iranians taught him a lot. Ben forced him to see a lot more. A different reality from a different perspective. He could no longer hide in his lab from the ugliness or see the world with his limited, myopic view. The whole experience broadened him and opened his eyes to the world, but in the process what he believed to be the truth, believed to be just, got tarnished and went bad.

His was a short role in the world of espionage, but long enough to shred the veil of ignorance he hadn't even known he wore. He didn't like what he found, but he couldn't go back to his apathy. Ben was right. There was a lot Matt didn't know about international politics or how money and hatred teamed up to cause terror. But Ben was jaded, pessimistic. His reality was how ugly life could be. That was his job, to watch for and be prepared for evil wherever it was to be found.

Matt knew there had to be more. Certainly, there was an equal amount of good in people around the world to counter the evil in the likes of Khourmy and Phil. People like Elizabeth, and yes, even Kate. She wasn't a bad person. She too only did her job. It still rankled that he was used and was such a dupe in the process, but the pain was growing duller. He didn't hold it against her anymore.

As the rain blew sideways and the wind howled in its pursuit, it occurred to him he hadn't thought of Kate all day. *Now that was progress of a sort*, he figured. *Maybe forgetting her wouldn't be impossible, after all.* He didn't believe it, but there was no other choice anyway since the message he received from Ben was the same that Lilly delivered. She rejected him once again. He might as well let go of Kate. Let go of the pain.

"I found them!" Kate yelled over her shoulder to her twin, who was pawing through the closet, checking each item with a pat and a squeeze.

"Thank God, we didn't have many more places to look," Lilly threw back. "Where were they?"

"I must have dropped them in the basement when I took down the laundry. It's funny I didn't hear so many keys hit the floor, but there they were."

"Well you've been in such a funk for the past few weeks, it's no wonder you lost your keys again. That's the second time this week, last week it was your phone, the week before that it was your laptop, and you drove off twice with your latte on the roof of the car. Everyone has been wondering where you're at. You don't pick up your messages for days, your reports were late to Ben last week, and basically, you just don't look too well. You need this vacation, Kate."

"Don't start on that again, I have told you a gazillion times, I'm fine, I'm tired, but it's nothing more than that. As for my reports, I saw Ben, and he's fine with my work. And I'm not mad anymore. I know you did what you thought was right, even if we will always disagree on that point, but let's just drop the subject, okay? Anyway, thanks for helping me look."

"You're welcome, but when did you see Ben. I thought he was out of the country this week?"

Immediately regretting her comment, Kate answered, "He was. I met with him last Friday while you were in Atlanta." Kate wished she hadn't mentioned her meeting with Ben. It was a strained and difficult discussion, and she didn't want to explain it to Lilly, but now the cat was out and knowing Lilly, it wasn't going to go back into the sack quietly.

"Sooo, what was the meeting about?" Lilly pushed the topic, doing exactly what Kate hoped she wouldn't.

"Nothing much! We needed to go over some details about my next assignment in Houston when we get back from Wales."

They might fool other people, but twins could rarely fool each other. Lilly wasn't buying the story, but as to what was wrong with her sister's comment, Lily couldn't nail it down. It didn't vary from protocol all that much, after all, it was perfectly normal to be meeting with Ben about an assignment, but some little niggling bell was going off, and she knew, for some reason, Kate didn't want to discuss the real topic of her and Ben's meeting. *It's not like Kate at all to shut me out like that*, Lilly thought, *but then Kate hasn't been Kate for some time now.* Yep, this vacation was exactly what Kate needed to let down the shield she put up around herself, and what Lilly needed to pry the truth out of her sister.

Thousands of miles across the Atlantic, Elizabeth smiled as she walked along the grey, wave-washed bluffs. It was going to be wonderful to have the girls spend time with her and Franny. It was a great suggestion, and she was thrilled when Ben said they could take time off. She always enjoyed her time in Wales, particularly when the nights were cool and the days were clear. It would be good for the girls to come over, and now that Franny was back at the cottage, she would love the company. Elizabeth constantly worried about her being so isolated and alone out on the bluffs. Still weak from the stroke, and Franny's hearing was getting worse, it was a miracle she hadn't caught her head on fire over the stove yet. Maybe this time, Franny would agree to go back to the States to live with her. They repeatedly tried to convince her life in the U. S. was not as brutal as the Welsh press liked to report, faster paced to be sure, but with her health deteriorating, she couldn't continue to stay out on the coast by herself. *She would just have to adjust for her own good.*

As much as she hated to admit it, Elizabeth was more than a little disappointed Ben wasn't going to make the trip with them. He talked about the possibility of heading over to Wales to join them for a brief vacation but changed his plans without much explanation at all. It was a new feeling, to be so excited about Ben being part of the family trip. It felt natural for him to join them and yet a bit scintillating at the same time. Elizabeth wasn't naive. She knew what the feeling was. Although she'd known him for years, it was hard to say when her feelings started to change. She realized she was becoming attracted to Ben. What set it off she hadn't a clue; she was just surprised she didn't see it sooner. Elizabeth liked the feeling. *It's time*, she thought.

As the fog slowly lifted, Elizabeth walked amongst the craggy rocks, marveling as they regained their shape out of the mist like objects being viewed through a camera as it became focused. Color returned to the boulders as the last wisps of cloud kissed each one in turn then disappeared, their shapes were worn down by wind, water, and time. The horizon appeared, framing the world.

Another set of eyes also watched the transformation. Old, cloudy, and watery. "Aye," Franny spoke quietly, "the babes will be here soon, Laury. It's been many a day since I could wrap me arms around them young lasses. I have missed them turribly. Tis a shame it is then, Elizabeth's new love will not be acoming too. But, maybe that's for the best. They being so new to the feelin', their time will come, it will."

Franny, head tilted to the side, stood as best she could by the small kitchen window with its thick dimpled glass, leaning for support against the cottage's old stone sink. She watched Elizabeth stroll the bluffs as the sun rose over the sea. "These old walls are much too quiet these days, with just me and Elizabeth left," she spoke to her friend. "We been too much alone agin," Her body, bent and misshapen, moved with the speed of age, each day a test of her endurance. She knew Lauren watched her in helpless silence. But she knew the words the younger wanted to say.

"Aye, what is it ye want with me now, girl? I'm too old to be playin the guessin games with ye. Our young man? Aye, he is gone away to his own life, and with nary a backward glance at the likes of us, he did. Sich a pity, it was, him being so in love with our Kate and him forgetting who she was. Elizabeth says he is a broken lad now since his remembering has returned, but our Kate won't give 'im her heart back. He stopped the turrible thing only he could do, but no happiness did it bring him without his love. What's that ye say? Our Kate loves him too. Aye, I knows that, me girl. But what kin we do? She owns her own heart she does, and we 'ave no right to mess wie that. Aaahh, ye may be right, if our young man was to plead his case, maybe love might take its caurse. Oh, me Laury, you are a wicked one. Wise, but wicked. If we kin git him near her, it could be done. I promise ye, my darlin, I'll think on the idea."

Chapter Thirty-Eight

"May I come in?" The look on Matt's face when he opened the door must have given Ben second thoughts on the wisdom of his mission.

"I guess so … yeah, of course." Trying to hide the shocked look, Matt stepped aside to usher in the last person he ever expected to see appear out of the storm, standing at his front door.

"We have some things to discuss," Ben started. "Do you think I could borrow a towel? I'm drenched head to toe." Frozen to the spot, Matt barely registered the request then slowly headed to the bathroom to fetch a towel.

When he returned, he found Ben stripped of half his clothes. His raincoat was neatly hung by the door on the hook, and his suit coat was draped over a chair. The pelting rain nearly soaked him through, and as he stood shoeless on the entrance rug, the water dripped from his pants and formed a small puddle at his feet. "Sorry about the mess, I'll make sure it is taken care of," Ben apologized, but Matt put up a hand.

"It's just water." Still shaken with Ben's appearance, Matt just held out the towel in awkward silence.

"I suppose you're wondering why I'm here, but if you can wait a few minutes … I'd like to dry off a little, so I can sit without ruining your furniture."

"I guess," Matt answered, not at all understanding the circumstances of the visit, or why he was feeling so uncomfortable in his own home, but he tried to achieve some control of the situation.

"Do you want something, a cup of coffee, or a beer?"

"Sounds good, whichever you have that won't be too much trouble. Coffee might help get rid of the cold in my old bones, but I could use a beer as well. Haven't seen such a heavy downpour in years, caught me totally off guard. I parked my car nearly a block away, not too many empty spots in the lot."

Matt realized Ben was rattling on as he toweled himself off, probably in an attempt to minimize Matt's confusion and fill up the silence, which was quite unlike the Ben he knew, but then what did he know of Mr. Ben Madison, CIA. Doing odd things might be a huge part of his nature. He certainly couldn't even begin to figure out a guy like Ben.

As he handed a soggy towel back to Matt, a more composed Ben took the proffered beer and said, "Good, now let's talk."

"Contrary to what you may think, I don't make a habit of involving myself in other people's lives. I'm sure you have a pretty good understanding of who I am." Ben settled himself firmly on the couch in such a way he gave the impression he wasn't moving any time soon. Caught by the irony of the remark, Matt wondered if Ben could even read minds now.

"Oh, yeah, I'm sure I do," Matt almost laughed at himself for voicing the expected, but untruthful answer. Nothing that ever transpired between them before prepared Matt for the lightning bolt Ben was about to throw at him this time.

"Well, then I'm going to surprise us both about why I'm here. Maybe it's old age, or maybe it's something I won't ever understand, but I want to help you get Kate back."

Speechless with disbelief, Matt sat on the edge of the chair, his mouth opened but no words formed. It seemed to him Ben was enjoying Matt's discomfort.

He was almost self-righteous about the bomb he had just dropped in Matt's lap. Ben threw his arms possessively across the back of the couch and looked extremely pleased.

Matt's first inclination was to put every ounce of muscle into a flying punch to that smug face before him. "You want to help me?" Matt quizzically mimicked the older man.

"Yes, that's right. I don't suppose you have any peanuts or chips to go with the beer, do you? I didn't have time to stop for dinner."

"Is this a joke?" A dam, burst in Matt's head. "You come into my home as if we are some kind of friends, expecting to be entertained, then run a knife through my guts again. I'm a simple man, Mr. Madison; I don't play the mind games you seem to enjoy. I have given everything I have to give to the government. You don't own my personal life too. Just leave me be. Can you do that? Just walk out of here and forget I exist. I don't know what you're playing at this time, but you aren't going to do it with my life. And, no, I don't have any peanuts. Go find your laughs somewhere else."

Matt was steaming. Months of pent-up frustration, hostility, and pain exploded. Running his hands through his hair, he was surprised his head wasn't pounding from his volatile outburst. Instead, for the first time in months, he felt totally in control of his mind, of his life, and the thought gave him new resolve.

"I loved Kate, you know that I would have gone to any length, done anything to prove to her how I felt, and let her know how much I wanted her in my life forever, but we both know, you told me yourself, how she feels. I was a job to her; I can live with that, I'll have to, I have no other choice. I'm sure as you said the last time we talked; she cared about me too, just not enough. There are no more hoops for me to go through, no more plans or schemes to work any magic and make things change. Our relationship was what it was; there is nothing more. It's my pain we are talking about here, not your decision for whatever warped reason you may have you want to change things. I'm done, done, done. Finish your beer if you want, but please leave. I won't give you the satisfaction of causing me any more grief."

Ben sat through the lecture as he usually did, with a placid face devoid of any hint of emotion. *A real poker face,* Matt thought to himself, *even amid this tirade.*

"Well! Maybe I deserved that, and maybe I didn't," Ben retorted, "but before you kick me out, if I were you, I'd at least listen to the game plan. You know, you have some issues that could use some work."

"Issues!" Matt exploded again. "You think I have issues? Well, hell *yes*, I have issues. With you, with the government, with the whole fucking world at this moment. Didn't you hear anything I just said? Go and take your game plan with you. I'm not—"

Ben stood and seemed ready to go, waving his hand in the air and cutting Matt off mid-sentence. "Okay, okay, I'm leaving. But you don't want me to do that, you know."

"How the hell do you know what I want?" Matt pounded his fist on the arm of the chair, ready to continue venting his rage.

"I know you still want Kate. That's all I need to know about you," Ben said as gently as he could. "I love her too, Matt, as the daughter I never had. Maybe I tried to keep her away from you for selfish reasons. No, it's not what you think," Ben added, "I'm not a pervert. I have known Kate and Lilly and their mother for a long time. They are the closest thing I have to a family. I would never do anything to harm any of them. I truly believed I was doing what was right for all of you, yes for you too, Matt. I thought I was protecting Kate, and you would find someone with a more suitable lifestyle for you. Her work demands she keep a level head, stay objective in the field, she has to be able to leave her assignments behind at the end of a job. What would happen if she got involved with every asset? It would be difficult for her to continue—"

"Yeah," Matt interrupted, "that would be terrible for you wouldn't it. You might lose a good agent. You mean none of your other agents have lives? Don't they have families who care about them? They don't go home at the end of the day and say, gee honey, what's for dinner, I'm a starved secret agent? You can't control the whole damn world, Mr. Madison; I blame you for Kate's decision not to see me. You taught her duty was more important than her happiness. If you really loved her, you would have wanted her to be happy, and yes, I could have made her happy. But you never let her decide for herself. You dictated, and she followed. *Issues*, Mr. Madison, yes, I have a whole heap of issues. But, the only one that mattered to me was Kate, and you think she is a game piece and you can move her around a board at will."

"No, Matt! You're wrong, and that's what I have been trying to tell you. You're wrong. I admit I helped her reach her decision, but I'm here to try to undo it if that is what she wants. If we work together, we can get you two back together. That's what you want, isn't it, Matt? You want her, don't you? If you tell me honestly, you don't, and you want me to leave it alone, leave it the way it is now, I will Matt. But think carefully before you answer. I will honor whatever you say." Ben stood poised in the doorway with his hand on the knob, ready to do Matt's bidding.

Confusion and pain ran up and down his body in waves. It was all Matt could do to remain standing. *The last thing I want to do is break down in front of Ben Madison, but what if what he's saying is true. What if Ben could or would get us together?* Matt had been down this road so many times before, hoping and praying for the one person who held his life by a thread. *And, if she sticks to her earlier decision and says no? Again? Can I stand the rejection one more time? Why should I put myself through that again? Haven't I been hurt enough already?*

"What makes you think you can just change her mind? You talked her out of a future with me, what can you possibly say that will undo that?" Matt demanded.

"You're going to have to trust me on this one," Ben said.

"Trust you?"

"Yeah, I'm asking you to do just that."

"I don't know what I want right now. Yes, maybe I do still want Kate, but loving her has been one hell of a painful ride, and I'm not sure I can go through with another round of that."

"Matt, we've not always gotten along, and I admit my personality can be rather abrasive. Okay, controlling. But I do believe we can achieve what you want with Kate if you give me a chance to prove it to you. I'm going now, and I'll understand if you hate my guts, and I never hear from you again, but if you want my help, call me at this number," he handed Matt a plain white card with a single phone number on it. "That's my private number; I don't give it to many people. Let me know what you decide. I'll help you or leave you alone. You have my word; it's not a game." Then he was gone, swallowed up by the downpour as his shape disappeared completely in a torrent of gray.

Sleep was not going to be easy, and he tossed and turned for hours, unable to shut down the mental turmoil. *Why can't anything in life be easy? Why do I have to pay a price for every bit of happiness? More than life itself, I wish I could erase all the time between us, just go to sleep and wake up to find Kate smiling at me.* His stepfather once told him not to wish for a life without problems. That, he had said, would be a life without purpose. Well, his life certainly was fraught with purpose then. There was too damn much purpose from his point of view.

It was hours before sleep finally dulled his senses and gave his tortured mind some peace. But it was short lived. Matt awoke shivering. The whole room was blurry and cold and shrouded in mist. The fog had an odd odor to it, salty but with a heady fragrance of flowers as well. It clung to the inside of his nose, and he couldn't hide from it beneath the blanket. He reached for the lamp beside his bed, flooding the room with light.

The fog rolled and swirled as it gently bounced off the walls of his room. "Alright," he spoke to the fog, "I'm having a nightmare, and if it's not a nightmare then I'm hallucinating again, but I've never experienced anything this weird." His clothes felt real, the bed felt real, but where in hell had the fog come from? Even the strongest of medications never conjured anything like this before. His feet on the cold floor told him he wasn't dreaming. He was awake. Somehow the fog had crept in from the rain-drenched world outside. It was bizarre, but as he walked around the apartment, Matt noticed the fog was only in his bedroom. The other rooms of his home were fine.

Matt returned to the bedroom only to discover the fog was gone. It disappeared as quickly as it came. *Damn, am I hallucinating again? So, every time I get stressed, I'm going to see things.* The bed he found was perfectly dry. No floral scent remained, and no fog. Just the miserable feeling his mind would never be his to control. For the first time in months, Matt pulled a bottle of pills out of the drawer and popped two in his mouth.

"Hey, Doc thanks for taking my call. I'm a little scared about something I'd like to discuss; do you have any time open this morning?" Matt could barely wait until seven o'clock to give his doctor a call, he knew it was early, but given the circumstances, he hoped he would be forgiven.

"Alright Matt," Doc Richards said, "go on over to the office, I'll meet you there in twenty minutes."

"Thanks. I wouldn't bother you this early if it weren't important."

After a brief physical, Matt checked out fine, and the two men sat in the doctor's private office watching the coffee pot begin to drip. "So, tell me what else is happening Matt, what other symptoms are you having?"

"Nothing. I've been feeling good, at least physically, this hit me like a ton of bricks. I never saw it coming. Am I having a relapse or something?"

"You said physically, but how have you been mentally? Is something bothering you? Since you came back from Europe, you've regained most of your memory and jumped back into work. Maybe it's been too much of a strain, too much too soon. That might be all that's happening."

"I'm tired, I know, but that shouldn't create fog in my bedroom, and no, for the tenth time, I wasn't dreaming. I know what I saw."

"Well, I'm no psychiatrist, but in my professional opinion, all I can tell you is in cases like this, the mind is usually trying to tell you something. Do you have any idea what that might be?"

Chapter Thirty-Nine

The plane dipped as it started its descent, circling Birmingham International Airport. Swinging around to make his approach toward the East, the pilot turned the craft into the morning sun. The light danced along the wing and reflected at his window, temporarily obstructing his view of the ground below. Matt hadn't paid much attention the last time as he flew over the marshes and heathers of the British Isles and the beauty of the patchwork quilt below him held his rapt attention. Wisps of gauzy clouds flitted over the ground. Farms with their meandering rock fences framed the picture which was dotted with patches of moving white forms he knew to be sheep. Rough, craggy outcroppings of boulders shone a wet gray in the morning sun. The storms they flew through during the night were all behind them, and the plane approached the runway with a fluid motion and a promise of a beautiful day before him.

Matt was glad he decided to fly directly to Birmingham rather than going through Heathrow again. He wasn't sure if he could handle the emotions and memories which were sure to be waiting in London. Someday he would go back there. He needed to close the tragedy behind him, but not yet, he had too many raw nerves about his role in the London massacre. Besides, in spite of Ben's assurances that his name had been cleared of any suspicious or malicious charges throughout Europe; and neither Scotland Yard nor Interpol, nor any other international agency would be after his hide when he landed on their soil, he was still nervous about going through London. Birmingham was much closer to Aberystwyth and Kate anyway.

After many sleepless nights and repeated coaxing from Ben, Matt finally decided to go. The decision left him asking himself over and over what the hell he was doing, again. The answer always came back to the same thing. He wanted Kate. He needed Kate.

And finally, he knew where she would be. No messenger between them, no waiting for the rejection to come by phone. He would face her and tell her how he felt. *Let the chips fall where they may*, he thought. He could not, and would not, live the rest of his life without this attempt to recapture the one woman he knew was his destiny. If only he could be hers as well.

So be it. The deed was done, and here he was, landing in Great Britain for a second time on the trail of the woman he loved. Ben told him he would find her and Lilly along with their mother at the cottage with Franny. It might be an awkward moment with so many others around, but Matt would get beyond that. He couldn't keep chasing her, and with her job, no one but Ben and the CIA could find her if she didn't want to be found. This was his only chance, and he would have to deal with the circumstances as they were. Not that he thought Elizabeth or Lilly would interfere with his attempt to win Kate back, he believed they were both firmly on his side.

Franny was another story. After his last eerie encounter with Franny, and whatever force surrounded her, he wasn't at all sure she would want him connected to one of the twins; and not have some other terrible prediction about his destiny in store for him. He truly liked Franny, but he had a healthy respect for her 'abilities' whatever they were or however they worked and adding her to the reunion with Kate left him a little uneasy.

But something else urged him on—an omen of sorts. He was given a clean bill of health, at least physically, by Doc Richards, so the nightmare of fog must be something stirring in his brain. Maybe it was the hint of sea air and the scent of lavender delivered by an unseen hand that inflamed his memory and brought forth such a yearning for Kate he could think of nothing else but her. He knew somehow, his vision was linked to Kate. Not that she caused it, but he couldn't shake the feeling once again he'd been delivered a message, and he must heed the opportunity or regret the decision for the rest of his life.

Ben was finally able to convince him the only way to get Kate back was to force a reunion of sorts. Even after a lengthy conversation the morning following the night's ghostly fog sighting, Matt wasn't at all sure it was such a good idea, and his stomach churned with his doubts. Ben shared with Matt some of his conversations with

Kate where she entrusted him with her feelings and fears about Matt. The real shocker to Matt was, first of all, Ben owned a soft side, and secondly, he would divulge their conversation, which Matt was certain Kate had not intended to have repeated. What Matt couldn't get his arms around was why Ben was doing this to help him.

His suspicions rang every bell and whistle in his head, but after three days and nights of trying, he couldn't find an ulterior motive and began to take Ben's actions at face value. His scientific mind analyzed the situation, and although he mistrusted it on several levels, his heart wanted to believe everything Ben said, even his prediction Kate would welcome the confrontation, maybe not initially, but eventually. It was that phrase which terrified Matt the most.

All the way over the Atlantic, Matt scribbled notes in an attempt to find the right words to say to Kate. Everything hung on the first few minutes of their meeting. If he screwed it up, he might never have another chance to win her back. One shot, he knew, was all he was going to get—*one shot.*

No one knew he decided to go, except his boss. He asked for a couple of days off, and although the new head of the department was curious, he said nothing and approved the request. Matt thought better of calling Ben and giving him a heads up. It would be better if he went unannounced. If mid-trip he changed his mind, no one would be the wiser and he wouldn't feel like an idiot or have to explain anything to anyone. The plane touched down with barely a bump, and he was back in England and headed toward his fate on the Welsh coast.

"On me old bones, our young man is coming," Franny crooned to herself as she rocked Beastie in the big chair by the fireplace and cozied up to a hot cup of tea. "Ye did it, Laury; ye brought him back. Aye, the lasses and their mum will be here soon. Better brew up some more tea as well. It's gonna be a long and verra interestin day, it is."

Peals of laughter bubbled out the windows of the little car as it bounced and jiggled over the road to the bluffs. The twins always loved the ride out to the cottage and never minded the ruts cut by car tires or cartwheels or the stones that rose out of the ground after each rain; cobble-stoning the surface and making their teeth rattle. Elizabeth laughed as well. Welsh roads had a way of humbling everyone who ventured forth across the countryside.

"No way you can maintain any dignity or try to look proper," Kate laughed, as her head flipped and flopped back and forth with the dips and thrusts of the bumpy road. The twenty-minute ride turned into an hour because of the condition of the road surface, but the women were in no hurry and enjoyed the country smell of sheep and manure which mingled with the odor of new cut hay and wildflowers, all tied together with the salt spray from the sea in the distance.

"Franny! We're here!" The door swung open, and two young blond heads tumbled into the cottage amid more laughter. "It's so good to see you again," Kate said, hugging Franny tightly. "We were so worried about you after your stroke, but we should have known nothing would keep you down for long."

Franny struggled to keep her balance while being crushed between the girls. "Aye, an glad I am to 'ave me babes back again," she said, grinning her near-toothless grin. "I've missed ye too. Never was one to live all alone ye know, an the house needs some happiness agin, it does."

Elizabeth lagged bringing in a small bag of groceries. "Okay, now you've both smothered her, why don't you go get your bags from the car, and we'll take Franny into town for dinner."

"Ow and that's not necessary," Franny said, finally breaking free of the young women.

"Now Franny, I scolded you not to fix anything while I was gone. You aren't supposed to make so much work for yourself." Elizabeth had ordered her to sit still, but Franny wasn't one to listen to anyone telling her what or what not to do.

"Oh, aye, I've tea in the pot, fresh bread in the oven and kippers. Opened some of me best peaches too. We can go to town on da morrow if ye want."

"Franny, you are impossible," Lilly laughed. "See Mom; I told you she wouldn't listen to you."

"Yes, I know, but I should never have let you know when the girls were arriving." Elizabeth admonished Franny. "Then you wouldn't make such a fuss," she added, shaking her finger in Franny's direction.

"Aye, but I would be knowin it anyway." Franny impishly grinned. "Laury keeps no secrets from me." As much as Elizabeth and the girls wanted to laugh at Franny's belief in some mystical connection to Lauren, there were too many occasions throughout their lives, where her knowledge and how she came to it, could not be explained in any conventional way. "Aye, Laury tells me things and the wind shares it's knowin."

"Alright Franny, we believe you," said Kate slipping her arm around Franny's middle. "Let's go slice up that bread of yours, I could smell it all the way out by the road, and I'm starved."

Franny turned, and in spite of her bent and misshapen body, neatly escaped Kate's encircling arm and hobbled back to firmly close the door to the cottage. A sly smile turned up the corners of her mouth as she bent her head sideways to look off down the road the women just traveled. "Aye, me laddie, we could no have ye come a callin, and us not be here to see the deed through. Just keep a comin and don't be afeared of what is to come, old Franny is here to help ye."

"Who are you talking to?" Lilly called back to Franny, wondering at her delay in joining them in the kitchen.

"Just the wind, me lassie, just the wind."

"I can't remember when I've tasted anything so good, Franny, you outdid yourself," Elizabeth said as she and the twins cleared away the dishes and tidied up the old kitchen. Franny moved back to her rocking chair by the fire. She was the only one not surprised by the knock at the front door. Without turning her head, she said to Elizabeth, "probably one of the neighbors who wants to come and gie ye their hellos. Why don't ye see who it be?"

"I'd be happy to, you just sit there and rest," Elizabeth said laughing, handing her dishtowel to Kate. "You girls keep an eye on her and don't let her do anything while I'm gone. We know she can't be trusted." Still laughing, Elizabeth reached the knob, but from years of habit, she looked through the lace curtain before opening the door. The laughter was frozen on her face as she swung the door wide. "How … why … oh my God, Matt, what are you doing here?" she asked, staring incredulously at the tall man before her.

"Just when did you find out my name?" Matt blurted out without thinking. Seeing Elizabeth's reaction, he felt terrible for the remark. "I'm sorry Elizabeth, I shouldn't have said that. That wasn't how I wanted to greet you."

A guilty blush stole over her face as she realized what he was talking about. "Oh no, Matt please, you don't owe me any apologies, but you don't know the whole story and … well, at any rate, I wanted so badly to tell you everything I found out, but I'm sure you know the reasons, but I am so sorry about keeping it away from you. Not that giving you your identity would have helped much to give you back your life, but I hope you do understand what was going on at the time."

Elizabeth's rambling apology gave Matt a few minutes to catch his breath and take a quick look inside the door.

The scents of heather and lavender hit him as he took in the sight and smells of the familiar cottage. His face was flushed, and his breathing was labored, albeit not from the walk up the drive, but the adrenaline fed by the fear of rejection, as it coursed through his veins. Trying hard to control his breathing, he willed his heart to slow down and hoped he didn't look as stressed as he was feeling.

"Can I start over?" he said, holding out his hand to Elizabeth. "I've been practicing all the way from Pennsylvania."

Elizabeth took one step forward and threw her arms around his neck in a tight hug.

"Please start over," she cried, regaining her composure, "It is truly wonderful to see you. How are you? Your leg has healed, and oh, my Lord, I was so impressed with what you did in London, I want to hear more about it, even after your call we have so much to catch up—"

The look on his face stopped her mid-sentence. Over her shoulder, Matt watched Kate move into the room and take in the scene at the door, the blood draining from her face. Elizabeth looked between the two of them and wondered if she should say something or just stand there in silence. In the end, her dilemma resolved itself, as neither Matt nor Kate remembered she was even in the room and saw only each other.

"I'm sorry if I've given you a shock," his words were directed toward Elizabeth but meant for Kate. "I didn't want to do that," Matt started, "but I was passing by and saw the lights on …" He tried an attempt at humor to lighten the moment.

Kate was struggling to regain her voice, and her hand went to her throat as if she were choking. She tried again, but nothing came out except a high-pitched squeak.

"Well, don't ye just stand there in the doorway letting them fly things in, come in me lad and close the door." Franny came up behind Kate, giving her a little nudge into the room.

"Now Elizabeth, me thinks ye should be helpin me wie the dishes, I should no' be working so hard, said so yeself."

"Right you are Franny, I'm on my way," she said, quickly making her way past the paralyzed young people. Matt slowly pushed the door closed behind him and took his time turning around to delay the confrontation. He had picked a small bouquet of wildflowers on his way from town and stood turning them around and around in his hands.

"I remembered how you like fresh flowers," he said, motioning to the colorful bunch. "Drove myself out here," he went on, trying to give her more time. "I didn't think I would need a map, the roads were pretty easy to follow, and I figured I would remember the way. It still feels strange riding on the wrong side of the road, but I'm starting to get the hang of it."

Kate finally composed herself and turned to close the door to the kitchen as well, preferring what she was going to do and say not have a room full of witnesses. "Matt," she said, the silky voice he remembered so well was full of emotion. "I didn't think you would come. I know Ben thought you might, and he said you would, but I didn't think you would show up." Tears started to flow silently down her cheeks even as she tried unsuccessfully to hold them back.

"What?" Matt could hardly control the shaking coursing down his body. Just seeing her again was almost more than he could bear, but hearing her voice and what she was saying, took his breath away. "You wanted me to come here? You knew I might. I was afraid you would be furious because I followed you."

She was shaking her head up and down and sideways at the same time; tears flowed even faster. "Yes, I mean no, of course, I'm not furious, and why should I be? You came to find me, didn't you? Everything you've gone through was because you were looking for me … all this time. In spite of what I did to you, I lied to you, betrayed you … refused to see you. Why would you still come after me?" Matt's eyes never left her face.

"I thought I was prepared to see you again," he said in a near whisper, his confidence buoyed by her remarks. "I had a lot of time to figure out exactly what I wanted to tell you … what I want you to know, but the words are gone. I only know I have never been able to get you out of my head or my heart. I tried to believe you were only my imagination, even during the long months when I agonized about whether you were real or not, and then when I knew the truth … I wanted to leave you and the deception behind, but I couldn't. It was painful, no matter what course I chose. I needed to come, maybe it won't work out between us, there's so much I would like to talk about, but it was important I saw you one more time, assure myself you are real … and tell you how I feel. All I wanted to say was I love you. I never got to say that all those months ago before you left. That's the one thought that never went away through all the torture and doubt; I just knew I loved you. I know I have no right to intrude in your life … if you tell me to go I will, but please understand I needed it to come from you."

It wasn't easy to get the words out, and his courage was flagging. If he hesitated, he might never get another chance; as it was, he was afraid to take his eyes off her face for fear she would disappear into the mists again.

As if waking from a dream Kate tried to move, she wanted to run to him but was frozen to the spot, unable to believe what was happening. She had given Ben permission to contact Matt, but she held little assurance he would be so easily swayed to see her, considering what she had done to him. Seeing his face again brought such mixed emotions. Pain, happiness, doubt, and regret. The memories of their time together flooded her senses and made her ache with the sweetness. The smell of lavender and salt air filled the cottage, and still, they stood facing each other just a few feet apart. Although it felt like hours, it was only seconds before they both moved together. He was pushed, and she was pulled, and they closed the gap between them.

Matt slowly extended his hand to her. "I found you once and lost you … unless your Ben Madison does me in for tampering with government property, I would like to keep you forever." There was nothing more he could say. He poured out his heart, it was the end of the run, he either won or lost, and he could only hold his breath until she spoke.

Kate nodded toward the closed kitchen door. "We have spies in the family, you know. Do you want to go for a walk?"

Matt smiled, relieved the worst part was over, and the earth had not swallowed him or crashed down upon his head. "Haven't you figured out by now," he laughed nervously, "wherever you go, I'll follow?" The heaviness left her heart about the same time Matt felt the pressure in his head release him from its grasp. She put out her hand, and he was quick to grab it before she could change her mind.

"I'll be sure and leave better tracks in the future so you'll have no trouble keeping up with me." She smiled her dazzling smile at him and pulled him through the heavy planked door out into the salt air.

Far below them, the Irish Sea battered the ancient rocks, the foam rising and settling as it had for millennia. As they walked the bluffs, a salty spray mingled with the heady smell of fish and seaweed and penetrated the pores of their skin as the wet wind took their breaths away. Kate wrapped her sweater tighter around her, and Matt saw her shiver. Overhead, grey clouds scudded past, while two seabirds swooped low flitting in and out of the waves as they crashed loudly against the rocky overhangs.

"I only have a year left of my government contract," Kate began, shouting into the wind to be heard, "I don't have any plans beyond that. Maybe I can find something quieter and more stable somewhere in the department. Funny how life changes, I would never have thought it possible, but Ben even indicated he would help me find something sooner so I can have a personal life. We can work on it if you're agreeable to sharing your home with me again."

"Bless that man," Matt shouted back, surprised at how his anger and mistrust evaporated like the sea air. "I am sorry for all the hostility I directed toward him in the past. He's not such a bad guy."

"Don't go forgiving him carte blanch yet," she shouted back, her tone much lighter. "He probably deserved most of what you threw at him."

"Maybe, but I might have been a bit harsh. Losing you wasn't something I handled well, and I guess he took the brunt of my anger and resentment."

Kate stood frozen in her tracks, and her head dropped noticeably. "Matt," she started to say as he came up behind her and wrapped his arms around her, his mouth on the back of her neck. The wind buffeted them as they stood as one, rooted to the bare rock.

"Don't Kate. There's no need to go there. I know all I need to know, and we can leave the past out here on the bluffs to blow away with the wind. I'm sorry for even mentioning my dealings with Ben. Can we go on from here, as if all the bad never happened and begin again?" All the love he buried for so long bubbled to the surface like the crest of waves on the sea beyond them.

Kate turned to face him. "I tried to put you behind me too," she said, "I never wanted to hurt you by letting you know the truth about us …"

"Kate," he pleaded, lifting her chin until their eyes met. "Can you love me? If you have doubts about us, we can take it slow until you are sure about what you want. But, if you say the word, I'll give you my solemn promise right now in front of your family and the world, I will treasure you and our life together forever. I don't need anything more from you than that, no more lies, no more explanations. It has always just been you I wanted, as you are and as you have been. Please, Kate, don't punish yourself … or me either because of what was."

He held her out at arm's length now but refused to let her go further from his grasp as he closely watched the play of emotions which ebbed and flowed across her face as she came to some life-altering decision. Without warning, a huge wave crashed upon the rocks reaching the top of the bluffs where they stood, making the rocks slippery and dangerous. Kate grabbed Matt around the waist as it nearly toppled them both with its cold, wet impact.

"As if I needed a reason to grab hold of you," she answered him, grinning ear to ear. "I'm not letting anything wipe you out of my life again either," she promised him.

Lauren nodded ceremoniously as she rode the receding wave, and Garwin smiled in his eternal sea sleep.

"A wedding, how wonderful!" Ben smiled as he got the news over the phone in his office. "I truly mean that my dear, I am happy for you," he added. "I rather thought something like that might happen." Never one to play coy, he didn't hesitate to admit his role in the plot, when Kate called him to thank him for sending Matt to her in Wales. "I saw it was pointless to try and keep him away from you, so I left it up to your good head to decide what you wanted to do."

"Your decision wouldn't have anything to do with Mom, would it?"

"Your mother has certainly made her feelings known about Matt, that's true," he laughed, "and she did make some persuasive arguments in his favor I'll admit," Ben went on, "but our conversation a couple of weeks ago convinced me you had your head on straight and could handle your job and a personal life. Besides, a long time ago, I promised your parents I would always make decisions on your behalf based on what I felt was in your best interest. I could never take the place of your father, but I did what I thought he would do."

She never felt closer to Ben than she did at that moment. "Thanks, Ben, for always being there for us. Dad would approve."

The nostalgic mood was not good for his reputation. Ben quickly threw in, "I don't suppose your mother is around right now, is she?"

"Nope," Kate answered. "She and Lilly took Franny shopping. But I'll tell her you asked about her, and maybe she can call you back later if she returns early enough."

"No need, I'll try back later. You entertain your young man. By the way, how is Franny? I know your mother has been worried about her health."

"Franny is fine and has reluctantly agreed to return with Mom to Michigan for an extended visit. Don't know if we can keep her there indefinitely, but we'll try. Oh, and Ben … it had better be a very expensive wedding present or everyone in the department will find out what a softie you are."

"I'll not be blackmailed by one of my best agents," he nearly bellowed into the phone in mock anger. Then added almost in a whisper, "but between the two of us, I'm sure Lilly can help me think of something to keep you silent. Oh, yes, and speaking of Lilly, before I forget, Jim Jensen has some little glass things that belong to you. Haven't gotten to the bottom yet of how he has them or why they are so important but do be sure and ask Lilly about them won't you, and don't be too hard on her, she meant well you know."

Kate instantly knew the vases must have been part of the clues Lilly left for Matt and irritation only flickered a second before it was replaced by sincere gratitude. There would be a discussion with Lilly she promised. "Thanks again, Ben. For everything. We'll be in touch soon."

The wedding wouldn't take place until they got back to the States, but who said they couldn't have the honeymoon first, and Wales was a wonderful place for a honeymoon. Lilly and Elizabeth had headed back home with the reluctant Franny in their care, and Matt and Kate would follow in a few days. The waves crashed against the jagged crags below them as the lovers stood their ground against the wind and the spray. Gulls tipped their wings in the young couple's direction in silent salute of their union. Few places on earth would have made them feel so together or would have offered them a new beginning as did the cottage built by love for lovers.

In their watery repose, Garwin and Lauren gave their approval. Their marital home was finally going to be filled with love.

Carol L. Ochadleus

Carol Ochadleus is a published novelist and short story author. A retired, professional development officer with a background in psychology, she lives in the woods near Rochester, Michigan with her husband and their English Shepherd-Gracee.

Sneak Peek of

DEATH

On the

MARKET

CAROL L. OCHADLEUS

ZIMBELL HOUSE
PUBLISHING
UNION LAKE, MICHIGAN

Chapter One

It was a shock for Ben Madison to get a call from his ex-wife, in fact, it was extremely disturbing since Helen had spent the past eighteen years hiding from him and the world. They hadn't spoken in nearly two decades, yet the sound of her voice on his answering machine hurled him back to another place and another life. It could only mean she was in trouble for her to reach out to him after all that time. Her voice shook as she left her message. Helen lived on the streets of Alexandria, Virginia, amongst the homeless, alcoholics, drug abusers, and the mentally ill. When she called a second time, Ben grabbed the phone and took a quick breath before he said, "Hello Helen. How are you?"

He had found her many times, living as she was with her 'family' of street people, under bridges, in parks or various shelters. But he kept his distance. He didn't want to scare her into running deeper underground. Ben knew to what extremes she had gone to hide her identity; even changing her looks to not be recognizable to the various police, health, and social services Ben had tapped over the years to find her. He only wanted to keep her safe; not interfere in her choice of lifestyle. Even if he didn't understand it.

Why, he thought, *today, as I'm about to marry Elizabeth, did she finally contact me?* There was no 'Hello Ben, how are you,' no small talk of any kind. She jumped right into the conversation as if only days had passed since they had last spoken.

"Ben, you have got to find my Frankie. He's been gone for four days, and that's not like him. He is always here. Especially on Mondays when Mannino's Bakery throws out their weekend leftovers. He's never missed a day. I need you to find out what happened to him." Helen's voice rose higher as she spoke.

"Whoa, Helen, calm, down. Breathe. Tell me, who is Frank?" Ben wanted Helen to catch her breath and keep talking.

"Frank is my friend," Helen, answered. "Frankie and I have been together for a long time."

Taking a cue from her impatience, Ben picked up on the thread. "Can you tell me a little about him? Something to help find him?"

Defensive again, Helen hesitated. "Nothing else you need to know except he is my family, my protector. I'll give you a description if that's what you want."

"Okay Helen, I'm not trying to pry into your life, but I need a little more to go on than a name. When was the last time you saw Frank?"

"Friday, it was Friday. Right after those strange men came around again. I told Frankie to stay away from them, but he thought they needed help. He always wants to help people."

"What strange people," Ben asked. "How many, and what did they look like."

"You know--dark skinned. Different looking with weird clothes. There were two or three of them this time. They come around, ya' know. I've heard them talking to some of my friends. I think they are a cult. They offer people a place to stay, free food, and a warm bed. And TV. My friend Iris, that's not her real name Ben," Helen stammered, "Iris said we could get medical and dental care and a free cell phone. I know it's probably a trap, but it makes some people want to go with them."

"Go where? Can you give me a location, an address?"

"They don't give us an address. They tell everyone to meet them at a different spot; always somewhere in the warehouse district. It changes all the time. If we want to join, we are supposed to ring a bell on a certain building, and we get taken to a brand-new life. Our old lives and past are not a problem; they take care of all our needs. I've tried to tell everyone it isn't true. Nothing good will come of listening to them … but some are tired of living here. They want to see what it's all about. They just don't … come back."

It wasn't rocket science what Helen was describing. Ben knew the homeless were preyed upon by a variety of the unscrupulous. Drug dealers and religious cults were only the tip of the problem. For years, workers at the local homeless shelters had reported recruiters luring the poor away with offers of a better life. There was little the workers could do to stop them. He knew most of the residents of the streets balanced precariously on the razor's edge of mental stability. It was a problem aggravated by the hundreds of government programs that had been cut or dissolved, leaving the poor and ill with no net to catch them. Hundreds, possibly thousands of nameless, faceless wanderers spent their lives in humanity's wasteland. No one monitored their path through life.

"I don't normally pay too much attention," Helen nervously went on. "Except this time, it's Frankie, and I want him back. They can't take him away. I need him." Helen was quickly breaking down, and Ben decided to use that fact to his advantage.

"Look, Helen," he said calmly, "tell me where you are so I can send someone to search for Frank. I'll need a description of him and anything you can tell me about the strangers." The pause at the end of the line told him he still wasn't trusted, but her panic about the missing Frank overrode her doubts.

"There is an old restaurant next to the mall on Fifth Street. The Blue Diamond. It's been closed for months. Some of us have been staying in the back. We didn't break in … the door was open. I swear it, Ben. I'm no criminal, and neither is Frank. No one has come around to tell us to leave. There's an alley next to the building. Go in that way. The front doors are boarded up. I'll watch for you, are you coming now?"

"Helen, I don't know if I can make it personally. I, uh had other plans today. I will send someone to talk to you. Is that okay?"

"No! No, I need *you*, Ben. I don't trust those people you work with. They'll try to force me to go with them. You understand me. Please come, Ben. I need you. It has to be just you."

In exactly two hours, Ben was to be at the city hall to marry Elizabeth. She and the girls would be waiting. The judge was waiting, and there was a reception planned at the exclusive Springs Restaurant after the ceremony. How was he going to explain this to Elizabeth? *What a way to start our marriage*, he thought, *with an untimely problem from the old one.* "Can I call you back on this number? Is this phone yours?" he asked her.

"No, it belongs to a friend." There was hesitation. Helen was still wary. It was difficult for her to give up her long battle to stay hidden. Ben could sense her unease and knew she had to be desperate to surrender her location to him.

"Please … just come quick Ben."

Their divorce had been strangely civil. No shouting or name calling. She wanted nothing from him, but her freedom, which he gave reluctantly.

Although he begged to know the reason, he never got a good answer. Ben's career with the CIA had probably been the determining factor in their marital breakdown. Helen could never adjust to his hours or complete dedication to the department. It wasn't that he didn't love Helen. He did. Deeply. The job, unfortunately, was a more demanding spouse. As his career pushed him higher through the ranks of the CIA, he rode the waves created by the nastier side of people, and the evil that stained the world. As a recruit, a once naïve, fledgling-agent had joined the agency with a determination to make a difference. The years and the accumulation of knowledge hardened him. The ugly reality of life, the side seen by only those dedicated to its eradication, had drowned him in an ocean of malevolence. Helen had loved him once. But she couldn't find it in her heart to stay near the man he had become. He knew he had let her down, but neither of them could find a way to fix what was so severely broken. When they went their separate ways, he would have given her the house, their bank account, anything she wanted, but that wasn't her way.

A house in the suburbs was never where she wanted to be. She walked out of their marriage and disappeared. Through his connections, Ben tracked her down. He wanted to make sure she was okay. She never touched the money he put into savings accounts for her. She left the car, her clothes, and her past with him. She, who had known only luxury as a young woman, denied it all for a life of poverty on the streets. The why of it, Ben never knew. He did know she needed counseling, but without her cooperation, it wasn't going to happen. And not even he, Ben Madison, a director of the CIA, could force her. She opted for a life among the invisible.

Ben pulled his car alongside a strip of boarded-up buildings. The block was an obvious local eyesore. Peeling paint covered the exteriors; multi-generations of graffiti in patchwork fashion made a mockery of the once neat storefronts. Garbage rode in swirls as little gusts of wind steered it up and down the curbs and along the narrow streets. Although the Blue Diamond had been closed for months, the building smelled of unwashed bodies and the rancid odor of years of greasy food.

Helen was waiting outside the back door when Ben walked around the corner. She looked nothing like he remembered. Older yes, but something more, she was changed by the damage done from the ravages of the street. Her hair had at least two inches of pure white roots exposed, surrounded by a halo of various shades of darker grey. All twisted in an unruly knot at that back of her head. It gave the impression that she wore a poorly knit hat. Helen's face, once smooth and pink, had the pallor of school paste. It was apparent she hadn't seen the sun or good health for a long time. Her eyes darted up and down the street as Ben walked toward her, obviously still doubtful he had come alone. She looked rounded, well-fed, but Ben realized as he watched her move, the deception was merely several layers of clothes. There wasn't much to her beneath it all.

In a second, he flashed back to the graceful young woman he had met forty years before and how he had loved to watch her enter a room. At five foot seven, she was tall; a woman who seemed to have a purpose to her life. Men admired her; women envied her. On the outside, she exuded beauty and bearing, the epitome of a pampered woman of means. But her eyes were cold, empty, and broken. Ben thought his love could fill those eyes with life and warmth. But he had failed her in their short marriage. He could never get close to the impenetrable inner icy core. As he watched her approach, he found it nearly impossible to find any trace of the same woman he once held in his arms. Hesitant, guarded, she crouched more than walked, bent with the weight of worry, no longer tall and agile, her spirit was gone; she had shriveled into a soulless wraith.

"Thank God you are here, Ben." Bony fingers grabbed the front of his coat as if she feared he would leave back down the alley from whence he had come. "Something is wrong."

With a quick inspection of the interior of the building, Ben spotted at least ten people in their makeshift homes. Cardboard boxes, crates, and rags served as beds. The garbage bags neatly surrounding each space held their worldly belongings and served as walls. Blank faces studied Ben. No fear, or real interest, just wonderment at his presence.

Helen pulled him into a back room and offered him a broken chair of padded red velvet, which tipped slightly to one side. She was probably giving him the best seat in the room, but he didn't care to park on something so unsteady and briefly wondered what things may inhabit the tatty fabric. It was an awkward moment. He didn't wish to be rude.

"I'll stand, Helen, been sitting all day, need to stretch my legs."

Helen nodded, seeming to understand.

"Okay, I'm here now, what can you tell me about Frank and the strangers."

Helen's eyes swept the room as tears formed, ready to flow. "Frankie is my friend; he's my protector. He doesn't have anyone in the world except me. I know he wouldn't leave me alone by choice. We've been together for years. We take care of each other. You understand … Ben."

"Yes, Helen, I suppose I do." He had so many questions. "How long have you been here, in Alexandria? You know I've wanted to talk to you over the years, Helen. Just to see if you were alright. If you needed anything. Why are you so afraid of me?"

"You? Why would you think I was ever afraid of you? No. It was my father and the … government. I know you never knew who he really was. I didn't want you ever to hear the truth. He isn't the man you or anyone else thinks he is."

Small sobs escaped her now. She was having a difficult time holding in her old pain and her new fears. "He wants to have me locked up, put away in a loony bin. I'm not crazy, Ben. Just because I don't want the life you and I had … or what my father thinks I *should* want. I had it remember. I don't need your money, Ben. We do fine all by ourselves. We have freedom." Heavy tears did flow now, plopping off the greasy collar of her oversized coat.

Surprised as he was by her blunder, Ben would take that enlightening conversation home with him to digest it, but at another time. A quick peek at his watch, and he redirected his attention back to the point of his visit. "Do you happen to have any pictures of Frank?"

"No, but Lyon there can draw him," pointing to the sleeping figure on the other side of the room. "Lyon is a really good artist. He'll help."

Roused from sleep, Lyon stared glassy-eyed at Ben. Not sure if the man before him in the expensive suit was real, Lyon put out his hand to touch Ben's leg, thought better of it, shrugged, then rolled over to go back to sleep.

Helen grabbed his shoulders and gently shook him again. "Lyon, wake up, we need your help. I want you to draw Frankie for this man; he can help me find him."

Lyon shook his head as if to clear it, stared for a few seconds at Helen, then pulled a dog-eared notebook out of his bag. Two magic markers, one black, and one red fell to the linoleum. Choosing the black one, he began to draw, finishing a passable portrait of a man in just a few minutes. He took the marker and shaded in the picture, giving the face a blackened appearance.

Ben hid his surprise. The drawing showed a strong nose, receding hairline, firm chin. *Not a bad looking man if the picture was accurate. Perhaps Mediterranean, or even Egyptian descent.*

Helen looked over Lyon's shoulder and shook her head at him. "Draw it, Lyon. Draw the scar."

Lyon nodded then added a long scar that went from the side of Frank's face near the hairline across his nose and down to the side of his cheek. The pirate-like gash brought the face to life. Gave it character. Albeit scary, but character none-the-less.

Ben could only wonder what had caused it.

"That's better," she said, pulling the pad away from Lyon and tearing the sheet out of the book. "Here, Ben take this and please find my Frankie."

There were a million questions he wanted answered. Where had she been all these years? How had she survived? What did she eat or live on? But Ben knew he would have to go slow. Pressing her for answers wasn't going to get them. His interview was over, and she wanted him to leave. Ben reached into his pocket and took out his wallet.

Helen's face froze.

"No Ben, I don't want anything from you, other than to find Frank."

He knew that's what she would say, what she said years before, but he offered her the money anyway.

"Take it, Helen; if you want me to do this thing for you, you have to do something for me. Take it." Perhaps the years had softened her spunk as it bent her frame, she took the proffered bills and shoved them deep in her coat.

"I'll save this for when you find Frankie. He may need something. Now go."

Ben did need to hurry, Elizabeth was waiting, but one last thought occurred to him as he headed to the backdoor. Hoping she would heed his advice. "Don't leave this area," he said, "if I need to find you again, this is where I will look, okay?"

"Okay," she answered, and he believed her. For Frank's sake, she would let herself be found again.

"I'm glad you called me, Helen," Ben told her honestly. "I will do whatever I can to find your friend." For the first time in nearly eighteen years, he saw a shadow of the beguiling smile he had fallen in love with a lifetime before.

"Thanks, Ben," was all she said and closed the heavy metal door behind him.

Death on the Market is set to release in early 2021.

Reader's Guide

1. If this novel became a movie, who would play Matt? Kate?

2. Which character was your favorite? Why?

3. Which events in this book do you believe could happen today?

4. If you could choose another character's perspective to view this story, whose would it be? Why?

5. How realistic were the villains portrayed?

6. Do you think chemical espionage currently happens in America today?

7. What did you like best about the book? Least?

8. What did you think of Matt's reaction to Kate's disappearance?

9. How do you feel about Lily, Kate's twin sister?

10. Do you think the police did enough to investigate Kate's disappearance?

11. When Matt learns that Kate is real, does that help or hurt his recovery?

12. Franny's mystical abilities are present throughout the novel, do you think this 'gift' helps or hinders the story?

13. Would you read another book by this author? Why or why not?

14. Does the cover accurately convey the theme of the novel?

15. What one question regarding the novel would you most like answered by the author?

A Note from the Publisher

Dear Reader,

Thank you for reading Carol L. Ochadleus' novel, *Death & Other Lies.*

We feel the best way to show appreciation for an author is by leaving a review. You may do so on any of the following sites:

www.ZimbellHousePublishing.com
Goodreads.com
or your favorite retailer

Join our mailing list to receive updates on new releases, discounts, bonus content, and other great books from
Carol L. Ochadleus and

Or visit us online to sign up:
http://www.ZimbellHousePublishing.com

CPSIA information can be obtained
at www.ICGtesting.com
Printed in the USA
BVHW091218160222
629130BV00004B/9